CHOP STIX

Don Kesterson

CHOP STIX

CHINESE SPIES AMONG US

Don Kesterson

ISBN-13: 978-0-9984707-7-1 (Amber Publishers Company)
Library of Congress Control Number: 2021923964

http://www.donkesterson.com

Cover design and typesetting - Eric Fritzius

While historical timelines, persons, and events are depicted, the main characters of this work are fictitious. They interact with historical figures as a way to show a view of the depicted historical events.

OTHER BOOKS BY DON KESTERSON

The President's Gold

Gold of the Spirits *

Pawns: Magic Bullet

Pawns: Kings in Check

Ring of Freedom

Pawns: Stalemate

Tarnished Gold

* Also featuring FBI Agent Tom Warren

CHAPTER ONE

Date: December 3, 1963
Location: FBI Headquarters San Francisco

FBI Special Agent Tom Warren's morning routine had been the same every day since starting his new assignment of leading the investigation into Chinese spy operations in the United States. He boarded the cable car near his apartment to the Powell Street Station, then walked the seven blocks to FBI headquarters. The walk allowed him to enjoy the crisp air, the bright sun glistening off the office buildings, and the spirit of living in San Francisco, the beautiful bay city.

Today, the air was a little cooler than normal. The smell of the Pacific Ocean caused him to sigh with satisfaction. As he exhaled, condensation formed a white puff, as a weather front had come in off the Pacific last night. His morning routine included a stop at the newsstand on the corner of Powell Street.

The old Chinese gentleman who ran it spoke to Tom in *Yue* or Cantonese. "Good morning, what may I get for you today?"

Tom would respond in *Putonghua* or Mandarin. "A *San Francisco Chronicle* and a *Los Angeles Times*." Their exchange in the Chinese dialects never failed to bring a smile to the old Chinaman's face as he bowed in deference to Tom's language choice.

On this particular morning, Tom added in the *Yue*, "This morning air is almost blustery today."

The street vendor turned his back to Tom. Today, it took a little longer than usual to hand him the two newspapers.

With the newspapers tucked under his arm, Tom continued his walk down the street to the building that housed FBI headquarters. Since he'd left Washington, DC, just a little more than a week ago, he hadn't had an alcoholic drink. He was hoping he'd feel better, but it hadn't happened yet. Days like this certainly helped.

He arrived at the office building and strode toward the elevator. He noticed a beautiful woman walking ahead of him. He made sure he got on the same elevator as an elegant Asian woman and enjoyed the scent of her perfume until his floor. He acknowledged her as he turned back for a second look before exiting the elevator.

He entered his office and threw the newspapers on the edge of his desk, dropped into his chair, and slumped down for a moment before starting on his unopened mail. His feet ached from wearing new shoes. Review of the morning mail was always an agonizing drag. It made him wonder why he hadn't comfortably retired years ago by tapping into his family business and money. But that didn't motivate him.

The smell of fresh-brewed coffee finally hit him, and he realized he needed a hot cup before going through the stack of new criminal files and interoffice memos. When he got up to get the coffee, he bumped the newspapers, which fell on the floor and scattered everywhere.

Mumbling under his breath, he stooped down and picked up the newspapers. As he tossed them back on his desk, a white envelope fell out of one of the papers, spilling out a picture of a Japanese Geisha—obviously dead—with a chopstick in her mouth. He frowned at the envelope for a brief second, then grabbed it up.

A chopstick fell out of the envelope.

This can't be. He examined the picture and the chopstick closely. And, there it was, burned into the chopstick—*NanJing.*

Dr. Wang! Tom's pulse increased. *Calm down, calm down,* he coached himself. *Wait until you figure out what's going on.* Still, it had to be the work of his old nemesis.

Tom studied the picture of the girl for clues. Swinging abruptly, he grabbed the *Chronicle* and rifled through the paper. There was nothing about the murder of a Japanese woman.

He sprinted to the door, bumping into another agent just coming through from the other side. He grabbed the elevator door and jumped in, repeatedly stabbing the first-floor button until the door finally closed. The elevator stopped to pick up an elderly office worker, then took forever to reach the ground floor. When the door opened, he sprinted out, again bumping into a well-dressed businessman, spilling his coffee. He ran out the front doors and back down the street as fast as he could go, his new dress shoes still reminding him he hadn't taken the time to break them in.

Where the newsstand had been moments ago, there was nothing. It was gone, vanished! It had been there for days—since he'd returned from D.C.— and in less than thirty minutes, it was gone! Desperate, Tom stopped and questioned a man carrying a newspaper on the street. "Where did you get that paper? Here at the newsstand?"

The man huffed, then quickly walked away.

Tom quizzed several more people. Not a soul knew anything or admitted to seeing anything. Maybe no one thought anything about it—packing up a newsstand and moving out. *Come on.*

He slipped over and entered the closest store, grabbed the closest clerk at the register, pointed, and asked. "What happened to that newsstand?"

The clerk shrugged. "I have no idea what you're talking about."

He stepped back outside and glanced up and down the street. Dejected, he repeatedly clenched and unclenched his fists, then slowly started toward his office. Thoughts flooded his mind. Breathing hard, he realized his feet hurt from those damn shoes. The more he thought, the faster he walked. Had he been set up? Who knew he was in town discreetly investigating Chinese spies? The picture and the chopstick pointed to his old rival and Chinese spy handler, Dr. Wang. *If true, he had been played like Chinese fingers on an abacus.*

The old Chinaman knew Tom's routine and, when undoubtedly ordered by Dr. Wang to do so, he passed the envelope. Did this mean Dr. Wang was in San Francisco, in Chinatown? If so, was he still in the city? *Why would he want to tip me off that he's here?* Dr. Wang was too smart to do something so stupid. What message was he sending?

By now, despite the condition of his feet, Tom was almost running again as he re-entered the office building. He hurried to his office and sat down at the desk. He looked closely at the picture and the chopstick. He sat back in his chair. His mind flashed back to the Philippines. The last time he'd seen Dr. Wang, Tom was running for a dock, headed for a boat. His partners Ricky and Sal were killed in a major shoot out, and Tom was injected with LSD laced with Heroin.

Tom blinked hard. He had no desire to relive those memories. He grabbed the *Chronicle* and breezed through it again to make sure he hadn't missed a story. Then he grabbed the phone and called the San Francisco Police Department. "This is FBI Special Agent Thomas Warren. I would like to speak to the Captain of the Detectives."

"Special Agent Warren, this is Captain Adams, how may I help you?"

"There was a murder of a Japanese woman last night. May I speak to the detective assigned to the case?"

"It's Detective Deshi Lee. He's still at the crime scene."

"And where is that?"

"Webster Tower and Terrace Apartments, 1489 Webster Street. *You know,* on the ritzy side of town."

"Thank you." Tom hung up and yelled over to his new partner, Martin Corley, "Get the car, we're on the move!" *That's over in the Japantown District.*

Dr. Wang must be on Tom's turf. Was he overseeing the Chinese spy operations in the United States? But Tom had to get the facts before he approached Hoover. Otherwise, he'd never let him back on Dr. Wang's case.

Tom pulled out the folder he'd been working on. He stuffed the envelope and the chopstick into his current file. With a vigor he hadn't experienced for years, he jogged out of the office and down the hall, where he punched the elevator button. When the elevator opened, the car was loaded with men and women barely yielding enough room to enter. Tom scrunched in.

When he exited the elevator, he jogged toward the waiting car. As soon as he jumped in the car, he told Marty where to go—and to not waste time.

"What's so important about a Japanese woman getting murdered?"

Tom drew a deep breath. "Dr. Wang . . . ." He released his breath. "Dr. Wang is a . . . ."

"Come on, Warren. Who is Dr. Wang?"

"Dr. Wang is a spy handler at the highest level of China's Central Investigation Department, the CID. When I was in the Philippines to help them set up their Bureau of Investigation, Dr. Wang was involved in several murders." Tom swallowed hard from the bitterness in his mouth. "I watched my team die while he got away. If he's here in the States, he's running some big operation. We need to figure it out, and I mean fast!"

Marty drove quietly for a few minutes, drumming the steering wheel to the beat of *My Boyfriend's Back* by The Angels, then spoke in a southern drawl. "I had *heard* about your past, but I wasn't sure what was true and what was myth."

"I'll tell you some time. When it becomes relevant."

Tom went back into deep thought as they drove across town.

Suddenly, he sat forward. "Wait a minute. Wait a minute. This could all be a set up. He must've known I was coming to San Francisco. How?"

As they arrived at the crime scene, the two FBI agents flashed their badges as they entered the ritzy penthouse. SFPD Detective Lee, half-Chinese, half-Caucasian, slight in build, sat in the living room looking over a notepad.

"Where's the body?" Tom asked as he took long steps up to Detective Lee. "I'm FBI Special Agent Thomas Warren. Show me your notes on this murder case."

Lee gave him a puzzled look. "How did the FBI find out about this? We were just called within the last four hours, and I haven't turned in any reports. Why is this even relevant to the FBI?"

Tom clenched his jaw as he told Lee about the newsstand, receiving the photo, and the chopstick.

"You mean the chopstick is significant?" Detective Lee shrugged.

Tom ignored the question. "Did anyone take any Polaroids of the victim?"

Detective Lee pointed at the man with two cameras hanging around his neck.

Tom rushed to him. "Hey, let me see the Polaroids of the vic."

The camera man reached into his trench coat and pulled out a photo.

Tom studied it. "Corley, this is almost identical to my photo."

By then, Detective Lee was straining to stare over his shoulder. "Naturally, I need the photo and the chopstick you were sent, since it's crime scene evidence."

Again, Tom ignored him. "Marty, look around to see what you can learn." Then he turned back to Detective Lee. "If this is what I think it is, this is a matter of national security. I want this crime scene and all the evidence locked down immediately. The FBI will take over this investigation."

Detective Lee huffed. "What the hell are you talking about? This is just the murder of a high-class hooker. This certainly isn't FBI stuff!" He glided across the room to keep up with Tom.

Tom walked around the apartment, which was filled with spectacular Japanese antiques and art pieces. When he arrived at the bedroom, it was obvious this was where the murder had taken place. Blood covered the bed. However, there didn't appear to be any evidence of a struggle.

Warren glanced around the room. "Was she sexually assaulted?" He focused on two items—a Ming vase and what he thought must be an expensive Persian rug.

"We believe so, from our brief observations."

Tom nodded. "I will be down to your office in a couple of hours to pick up all the collected evidence. Meanwhile, do not file any written reports, do not speak to anybody. I will fill you in then." He took a step back, then paused. "Oh, where did you have the body transported? It is also the FBI's." He raised his eyes to meet Lee's. "Now, leave my crime scene and take all of your people with you."

Detective Lee glared at him.

"And, give me your desk phone number," Tom added.

The detective jerked a business card out of his pocket and handed it to him, then yelled, "Everybody out. The FBI is taking over."

Tom walked to the window of the high-rise apartment and looked down on the street below. His mind flashed back to that day in Shanghai when he and his team looked down on the street below and saw Dr. Wang and his henchmen. But there was another man with them that day. The details were fresh in Tom's photographic mind.

Tom scowled and pointed at Marty. "Stand by the door. Make sure no one takes anything else with them."

Once the plush apartment was empty, Tom walked back over to Marty. "Before we go to the SFPD, we better report this to Hoover. You can bet San Fran will be calling the FBI, questioning my authority to run everybody off their crime scene." His eyebrows raised. "I better be right on that call. I know I am. I feel this in my bones—this is not a coincidence."

As he roamed around the apartment, he shouted out to Marty, "We have to get pictures of Dr. Wang to all authorities! We don't want him to get out of the U.S."

Tom walked up and knocked on Special Agent in Charge Gerald Adler's open office door. "We need to call Mr. Hoover, immediately."

Adler raised his arm and checked his cufflink. "Special Agent Warren, may I remind you of who is in charge here? Which isn't you?"

"Sorry, Chief. We could have a national security issue." Tom closed his eyes for a brief second. Then he proceeded to lay out the entire story to his boss.

When Warren completed his explanation, Adler leaned back in his chair. "You call Hoover. As far as I am concerned, it's yours."

Tom picked up Adler's phone and asked the operator to connect him to Director J. Edgar Hoover.

On the drive over to the San Francisco Police Department, Marty asked Tom, "What did Mr. Hoover have to say? What do you think's going on here?"

Tom closed his eyes and thought for a moment. Finally, he replied, "If this is what I think it is, Dr. Wang may be here in Chinatown running something big—and it must be ready to go down. He only handles the top spies. And if he is here, I want to be the one to arrest him—I owe him *big time*." He shook his head. "It just doesn't make sense that he'd let me know he was here. It just doesn't make sense."

Marty stopped for a traffic light. "Besides him being responsible for the death of your team in the Philippines, I need to know more."

The light turned green, and Corley stepped on the gas.

Tom jerked back in the seat and looked out the side window. "Let's see if I'm right, first."

They continued across town to the SFPD precinct and pulled into the back lot into the only available spot.

As they walked in the building, Tom stopped and looked at Marty. "Don't say anything to anybody. Let's get everything we can from them first."

Detective Lee sat at his desk, sipping coffee with the file on his desk.

From Tom's perspective, it sure seemed like a very thin file. He glanced around at the busy room filled with cubicles. "Do you have some place we can talk in private?"

Detective Lee frowned. "Sure. There's a private office over there." He pointed at a side room, stood, and held the file in front of him as he walked.

When they entered the office, Agent Corley closed the door behind them and folded his big arms across his chest.

Lee handed over the file as he sat down at the small table with several uncomfortable steel chairs situated around it.

The chair Tom pulled over had torn vinyl and some of the foam was missing, which he didn't even feel as he sat down hard. Corley remained by the door.

Tom rapidly flipped through the file. "Any more photos or evidence?"

"It is all in the file there. Based on what we think so far, there were several men in the room where the girl was murdered. You asked earlier if she'd been sexually assaulted. The answer is yes, and while she was still alive." He took in a breath. "But here is the funny thing. If she was a hooker, she had no record. She lived there for a number of years, so she'd been very discreet."

"Was there a john book?" Tom put his hand over his mouth.

"No, nothing."

Tom looked over the crime scene photos yet again. He wanted to make sure he had not missed anything, nothing stood out. Lots of blood. No evidence of a struggle. Nothing was out of place in the bedroom except the bed.

"The FBI has already taken possession of the body." Tom stuck the file under his arm.

Detective Lee gave Warren a questioning look, then rolled his shoulders. "Can you tell me what's going on here? Can our department help?"

"I do think you can help, but we have to draw some conclusions first. You may or may not be aware that we have been investigating Red Chinese spies in Chinatown, and this looks like our first breakthrough. That's all I can say right now. As soon as we can, we'll get you some photos of the man we think is behind this." Tom stood up, then almost bumped into Corley as he exited the room, with Corley right on his heels.

After making sure the FBI agents had left, Detective Lee returned to his desk and discretely pulled out a much thicker crime scene file from his desk drawer. He knew what was so special about the chopstick and a murdered Japanese woman. *National Security, you bet. China's National Security.*

Once they were back in the car, Tom rubbed his forehead. "Everything so far seems to fit Dr. Wang's MO. He is a sadist. He travels with a couple of bodyguards who do all his dirty work. He lets them have fun after he does— that's why it will be important to learn if there were multiple sexual assaults. What I can't figure is why he wants me to know that he's here? That's not how the Chinese spy network works."

Corley glanced at Tom. "I just don't know enough, but I agree they usually operate deep behind the scenes. We are always two steps behind the Chinese spies. That's why Hoover sent you here—he thought you might get us some leads."

"Right now, all I got is a chopstick."

When Special Agents Warren and Corley returned to the FBI office, Special Agent in Charge Adler called Tom in and asked to view the file.

Tom shrugged and handed it over.

Adler looked through it, then his face flushed.

"You alright?" Tom asked.

Adler paused, then nodded. "Yeah. Yes, fine. Everything's fine. Just don't understand the significance of the chopstick." He handed back the file and waited for Tom to leave. Once Tom was safely in his office, Adler rubbed his right hand over his heart as he sat down in his chair, spun around away from his desk, and stared out the window.

Kikue Nakamura was dead? He'd visited her regularly for over two years. Just a few days ago he'd felt her skin against his. And now she was dead?

And then another thought hit that took away his breath. Were there records in her apartment of his visits?

His wife could never find out about this. No one could ever find out about this.

CHAPTER TWO

December 3, 1963 - Mid-morning
San Francisco

There was a faint knock on the door. Dr. Wang nodded at Wu, one of his henchmen, to answer it. Wu peered through the peephole. "It's the old Chinaman."

Dr. Wang waved his left hand.

The henchman opened the door.

The hunched-over Chinaman slowly shuffled toward Dr. Wang.

"Hurry up, old man!" Wang scowled.

The Chinaman spoke in Mandarin. "The agent got the envelope."

Dr. Wang gave him a steely-eyed stare, then waved him off. The old man hurriedly limped to the door, which Wu opened for him.

As the old man reached the doorway, Wu pushed him, causing him to fall face first. The henchman slammed the door and locked it.

Once the old Chinaman had left, Dr. Wang looked around at the henchmen in the living room. He got up from his leather high-back chair and paced. After a few minutes, he stepped to the large bay window and spoke softly. "Will all of our agents working on this assignment be ready to leave tonight?"

Both henchmen replied, "Yes," in unison. Then the older one, Chung, said, "Yes, most are gone already. Two will be on boats tonight. When do we leave, Boss?"

Dr. Wang continued to stare out the window for almost a minute. "We have one last little task to do. Go tell the doorman downstairs we want to meet at Golden Gate Bar as soon as he gets off work tonight." Dr. Wang didn't turn around. "Kill the old Chinaman on your way. Dispose of his body where it won't be found."

December 3, 1963 - Evening

Dr. Wang and his two henchmen, Wu and Chung, walked into the bar and sat in the back corner. They waited. After several minutes, Dr. Wang looked around. "If he doesn't show in five minutes, go look for him."

Chung nudged Wu, who looked at Dr. Wang. "Boss, why do you want to reveal yourself to the FBI agent? I thought you just wanted to know his whereabouts so we could avoid him. We've been delayed here too long. We should just pick up our drop and get out of here. Slip into the night, if you will."

Dr. Wang's muscles tightened. Yet, he kept calm, as his henchmen were new and he needed them—at least temporarily. "Years ago, he was an obstacle in me regaining my family's assets. We have a history. That's all you need to know."

He motioned for Wu to come closer. When Wu did, Dr. Wang grabbed him by the throat with one hand in an Aikido chokehold. "Don't ever question my motives again or I will kill you myself. Your job is to protect me and do as

I order." Wang held onto his neck until the man was about to pass out, then let him go.

Finally, just as Dr. Wang was ready to turn his men loose, the Webster doorman slowly walked in. One of Dr. Wang's henchmen motioned for him to join them. The doorman ambled over and sat down.

When the waiter came to the table, each man ordered a drink.

After several drinks and idle conversation between the henchmen and the doorman, Dr. Wang leaned over to the doorman's left ear. "I need to ask you a favor."

The doorman tried to lean away from Dr. Wang and slurred, "What do you want?"

Dr. Wang grabbed the doorman's chair and pulled it closer to him, then got next to his left ear and snarled, "Look at this picture, Mr. Doorman. All you have to do is call me when you see this man. That is all you need to do. Do that, and I will give you a thousand dollars. That's it!"

The doorman looked at the picture of FBI Agent Thomas Warren, then smiled. "Yeah, I can do that."

Dr. Wang stood and slipped behind the doorman, then leaned into his right ear. "One thousand dollars. Here is the number to dial."

The doorman nodded and took the number.

"That's it. You can go," Dr. Wang ordered.

The doorman hurried out of the bar.

Chung looked at Wang. "Do you really believe that Agent Warren will show up at the crime scene again?"

"He will be there." Dr. Wang emptied his drink. "Because I was there."

Next morning – December 4, 1963

FBI Special Agent Tom Warren and Special Agent Corley pulled up in front of the Webster Towers apartment. They were greeted by the doorman with a big smile. "What floor shall I get for you?"

"Penthouse."

As the two men stepped off the elevator, Special Agent Warren walked ahead of Agent Corley, who, despite having longer legs, struggled to keep up with him. Corley unlocked the door with the key they had taken from SFPD and entered the crime scene apartment.

Special Agent Warren handed the SFPD file to his partner. Warren had already memorized every single detail in that file. "Look over that file. There is no mention of any interviews with the doorman. See if you can tell me what we're missing from the SFPD details? I'm looking for a safe or a safety deposit key. No mention of either in the SFPD file. Wouldn't you think a high-end broad would have one or the other or both?"

Corley sat down on the couch as he picked up the file and started rifling through the pages. "For all the people they had crawling over the scene yesterday, there are no interviews—no one talked to the doorman or anyone else."

Tom nodded. "We'll do that on the way out. What else?"

"They didn't identify the race of the deceased. Obviously, you think that is important."

As Tom scanned his way to the bedroom. "The woman lived here for three years. No evidence of a checkbook lying around. Go look in the bathroom. Check the medicine cabinet. Maybe we can get her name and a doctor's name."

Corley opened the medicine cabinet. No prescription bottles. He heard a noise in the living room and stepped out of the bathroom. He found himself face-to-face with a Chinese man wearing an expensive gray suit. Before Marty could shout or pull his gun, he was grabbed from behind and a handkerchief placed over his nose and mouth, preventing him from shouting. The last thing he felt was a stick in the neck.

Hearing the commotion, Warren moved quickly to the adjoining door and peeked into the living room. He saw nothing, but his view of the bedroom was obscured. He drew his .38 handgun, then stepped in and pivoted in that direction—only to come face-to-face with Dr. Wang.

"Special Agent Thomas Payne Warren, I imagine you didn't expect to meet me today?"

"Where's Corley?"

Dr. Wang pointed toward the couch in the corner. One of his henchmen pulled him up from behind the furniture piece, holding a gun to his head. "Your FBI Agent will be fine, just put to sleep for a minute. Now, you will come with me. We have many things to discuss."

Warren continued to point his gun at Dr. Wang. "You're under arrest. Put your hands up."

Dr. Wang replied calmly, "Agent Warren, you will put down your gun. You are out-numbered and out-gunned. You can see the gun being held to Agent Corley's head. Do you want to be responsible for your partner's death? Yet, again?"

"I might be out gunned, but it is you I will shoot first."

Dr. Wang calmly adjusted his suit and stepped toward Warren. "Yes, that is true, but your Agent Corley will die, as will you."

After a couple of seconds, Warren dropped his gun.

Dr. Wang's henchmen slipped a black bag over his head and tied his hands. Dr. Wang quietly said, "Take him to our apartment."

Tom was pushed and shoved down the hallway to the stairwell and was walked down two flights of stairs, then back down the hallway to another apartment. Once inside, Agent Warren believed he was being walked through a room, then he heard linoleum under his feet. *I'm either in a kitchen or bathroom.* He was pushed, hard, onto a wooden chair and tied up. Then his hood was removed. He was in a small kitchen.

Dr. Wang pulled his wooden chair up close to Tom. "I've missed you. I wanted you back in the game, FBI Special Agent Thomas Payne Warren. You see, I'm about to score a great victory, and you and your FBI are about to be handed a crushing defeat. I want to see your face when this happens."

Tom scowled. "This is not a game. What are you talking about?"

"Agent Warren, trust me, I know this is not a game. I was using American terms that you would understand, Mr. Former Big Time Quarterback. Let me finish, please. I understand you lost your memory. I understand that Mr. Hoover has not been willing or able to help you. So I decided I would help you get your memory back. You see, I owe you that, at least."

Tom looked around the room. "How do you plan to do that?"

Dr. Wang walked out of the room, only to return in seconds holding about eighty sheets of paper. "You see, I've made a copy of my notes from our time together in the Philippines and China. Just to bring you and your photographic memory up to speed. Because, as I told you years ago, I want you to come back to China where I can capture you, torture you, and then kill you. Now, you have nothing to worry about. I am not going to kill you today. As I said, I want you to be alive when I score my great victory."

Tom tried not to scowl at the eighty-page manifesto. *At least he still believes I lost my memory. Everyone thinks the LSD laced with heroin destroyed my memory. Hopefully, I can use that to my advantage.*

17

Dr. Wang looked directly into Tom's eyes. "Agent Warren, how many Chinese spies has the FBI arrested?" He paused for a minute, watching Tom.

"How should I know? I have just started on the case here."

Dr. Wang got close to his left ear and whispered, "I will tell you the answer. *None.* "

With a nod from Wang, Chung punched Tom hard in the side of the head.

"Does it surprise you that within a week of your assignment to the FBI here, I knew and arranged for this visit?" Dr. Wang clasped his hands behind his back. "What does that tell you about my network?"

Tom lowered his head.

Dr. Wang opened the refrigerator and took out a pitcher of water, poured himself a glass, and then moved a chair beside Agent Warren, where he sat and then took a drink. "You have seen to it I cannot go back to the Philippines. I cannot retrieve my family's gold and treasures, nor my country's gold. All my associates there were killed or captured. All because of you. Understand, I will get the gold back. It will just be more complicated to do so."

Warren smiled at Dr. Wang. "Not before I arrest or kill you. You'll never get anything back."

Dr. Wang pointed to Chung, who punched Tom hard in the stomach, causing him to slump over for a moment. Then Dr. Wang leaned back over to his right ear. "After I get my great victory, you will want to come after me." He shut his eyes for a few seconds, then continued, "And I welcome that. I know you will come to China to try to capture me. Thus, I will get my final great victory."

Tom turned his head to come within inches of Dr. Wang's face. "Dr. Wang, you have placed too much importance on yourself."

"This book, right here—" Dr. Wang pointed to the book on Tom's lap. "Will give you your memory back. Then Hoover will assign you to come after me, because both of you will want to capture me and bring me in for questioning after my great victory. But it is I who will capture you, torture you, and kill you. And after I have killed you, you see this chopstick—" He pulled out a chopstick and held it in front of Tom. *NanJing* was engraved on it. Then he turned it over, and *FBI Agent Thomas Warren* was burned into the back side. "After you are dead, I will drive it into your ear until it comes out your other ear."

Dr. Wang pointed at Wu.

Wu swung back his gun and struck Tom on the back of his head.

CHAPTER THREE

December 5, 1963

Dr. Wang looked out the window of his hotel and scanned the skyline. He refused to check his watch. He was a disciplined man. However, he was getting impatient. His bodyguards were running late. He had two appointments—the first at the Chinese restaurant and the second making the Mexican freighter. With Warren tied up and out of the way, he believed he'd make both; it was likely that Warren had made it back to work, but he'd likely be too concerned about his partner and trying to piece together what little evidence he had that he wouldn't interfere with Wang picking up his "package."

Within another half-hour, the two bodyguards came into the apartment. Dr. Wang continued to look out the window, intently staring at that bridge. "Did you complete your task?"

"The Chinaman is dead. He went quickly, painlessly. Body is in the harbor, chained to cinder blocks," Chung replied.

Wordlessly, Dr. Wang turned, picked up his briefcase, and walked. Wu opened the door, preceded him, then Chung followed him.

They had to get to Chinatown soon, as their courier from Los Alamos was making a drop to the cook. For security purposes, Dr. Wang designed the network so that only the cook knew the courier's identity. His rules were clear—once the courier made the drop, the cook couldn't hold it longer than one hour before it moved toward China. This drop was so critical, Dr. Wang was handling it himself. He had been working this project for a little more than three years, since that bastard Khrushchev pulled out his Soviet scientists.

Dr. Wang and Kang Sheng, head of the Central Investigation Division or the CID, had worked shoulder-to-shoulder putting together this network, finding just the right people to assist their country complete the project. This was the most important project in the long illustrious history of China, and he was determined not to fail.

Within a few minutes, Wang and his henchmen walked into the Chinese restaurant. The hostess led the men to a table in the back. When it was time to put in the order, Dr. Wang ordered, "Vegetable egg fu-yung with four vegetable egg rolls," as a cue for the cook.

After the meals were served and eaten, the cook, an elderly Chinese woman, came out and walked around to visit with some of the patrons, passing out fortune cookies. When she got to Dr. Wang's table, she handed out fortune cookies, including a special one that was much larger, which she handed to Dr. Wang. No one in the restaurant seemed to pay any attention to the pass—it appeared natural. He put it in his outside dress coat pocket and soon exited.

It was late evening. Dr. Wang assumed the boat coming to pick them up should be sitting at the dock by now, since they were slightly behind schedule.

On the short drive, he looked out the window. A dense fog rolled in from the bay. *This network is in good shape, but I don't trust Lee. He's mentally weak.*

Dr. Wang pulled the fortune cookie out of his pocket and examined it. "There's a Mexican freighter twenty miles out waiting for us," he said quietly to his henchmen. He reached in his other pocket and pulled out a large ring case, inserted the cookie, and then sealed it. Just as they were about to pull into the harbor, he took out the little black book that had been removed from the dead Japanese woman. He looked at it and smiled.

December 7, 1963

Thirty minutes. That's how long it took Tom Warren and his boss Adler to review Warren's preliminary findings in the Chinese Spy investigation with FBI Director J. Edgar Hoover. The director agreed with Warren's assessment of the situation, immediately expanding his case load to include Dr. Wang. Hoover also agreed if Wang was in the United States, something very large was underway, but he emphasized not to overlook the spy network in San Francisco, his original assignment. The director was not too interested in what had happened to either Warren or Corley, even when he learned that Corley was still in the hospital.

Adler put his feet up on his desk and leaned back in the chair. "So, you and Dr. Wang go back a long way?"

Tom jutted his jaw. Adler probably knew most of the case history, and he didn't need to know any more. Adler's eyes darted back and forth between Warren and the file. "You believe this Japanese woman was a high-class hooker, but no one has found her john book?"

Tom bit his lower lip. "Dr. Wang must've taken it—if one even existed. No one in SFPD reported it, and it didn't show up in any of the crime scene photos."

"Our mortician's report showed the Japanese woman was likely assaulted multiple times, but he wrote it was inconclusive since it was believed she was a hooker." Adler bit his lower lip and rubbed his forehead.

Tom grasped his hands behind his back. "Makes sense."

"You expected that?"

Tom ran his hand through his salt and pepper hair. "It's part of Wang's MO."

Adler's covered his mouth and slowly released his breath. "Are you sure you're ready to return to duty so soon?"

"Yeah, I've had worse. Dr. Wang is my only concern. I have to catch him before he gets away. He's the key to this investigation."

Adler sat up at his desk. "And Marty Corley?"

Tom shrugged. "Has the lab been able to determine what was in those syringes Dr. Wang stuck in us?"

Adler folded his hands on his desk. "Not yet. Those blood tests take a little longer to get results."

"Let's get some sketches of Dr. Wang and his henchmen out to all FBI offices. Put out an APB. Who knows where Wang can be by now?" Tom stood up to leave. No new photos existed of the man. "I will go down and get with our sketch artist. We've already lost two days."

Adler's phone rang. Tom let out a deep breath then walked out of Adler's office and stood by his desk.

He slowly picked up everything from the Japanese murder scene and stuffed it in the file. He had memorized every single detail, but it was what wasn't in the file that bothered him. He pulled out his notepad and pen and added to his notes: 1) Dr. Wang said he was working on something big; *He watched me via the newspaper stand for a week, then revealed himself. Why? He must be leaving town. Is he gone already? He'd have no other reason to reveal himself. He doesn't want me to arrest or kill him.* 2) Is the Japanese hooker part of this, or is she just a victim? The SFPD detective said there was no record of any priors. What about the john book? What could possibly be of interest in it to Dr. Wang? Did it have something or someone's name in it that he couldn't let anyone see?; and, 3) Dr. Wang had an apartment or access to an apartment in Webster Towers, where he dragged me. He watched the Japanese woman from that apartment, observed her every move. But whose apartment was it?

Tom put three stars next to number three, then laid down his pen. He made three mental notes—go to the sketch artist, talk to the FBI lab, and go see Marty Corley at the hospital.

Tom walked into the hospital room. Agent Martin Corley sat on the edge of the bed, fully dressed. His black eye and swollen cheeks looked bad, and his left arm was in a sling. They must have really beat the hell out of him. Corley was no little guy. "You going somewhere?"

Marty looked at Warren. "Wherever you take me? I just want out of here. I'm a human pin cushion. The doc is supposed to be around any minute to sign my release. You just saved me cab fare to my home."

Tom flopped down in the chair at the end of his bed. "Who sent a single guy flowers? That's strange."

Corley frowned at Warren. "Sure as hell wasn't my current partner or anyone from the San Francisco Bureau." He chuckled. "No, it was from one of the secretaries at the Atlanta Bureau."

"She's your girl?"

"No, just a Southern bell. She typed up my reports when I was in Atlanta before they sent me out here to chase down John B. Everhart."

The doctor and two nurses walked in. The doctor glanced at Warren, then at Corley. He walked over and picked up the chart hanging beside his bed. He pointed at Warren. "Is he family?"

"He's the reason I'm in here." Corley shook his head. "Throw him out of here, doc."

The doctor scowled. He shined a light in Corley's eyes, took his pulse, and then signed the chart. "Take it easy for a couple of days, then go see your family doctor."

"Do you know what I was shot up with, doc?" Corley asked.

"Your boys grabbed it before we could look at it. You know, that 'national security' thing." He walked out the door.

Tom turned to Marty. "Likeable guy, hey?"

Corley got off the bed and picked up his fedora. "Now, since I have met Dr. Wang, are you going to tell me more? I think you owe me that."

Tom followed him out the door. "How long a drive is it to your place?"

Tom drove Corley to his apartment. "Dr. Wang claimed he came from a substantial family in NanJing. When the Japanese sieged the city in 1938, all his family's treasures and assets were looted. He said the Japanese also raped and killed his mother and sister. He never mentioned anything about his father, but I assume he must've been killed."

Tom stopped at a traffic light. "Our Dr. Wang became one of China's top case officers for the Chinese CID and answered directly to Kang Sheng. He had requested and received the assignment to the Philippines to help the Huks become communist allies to Red China. However, he also was there to find his family's lost valuables. He recovered a few items."

Tom was quiet for a few moments, then spoke softly. "He seeks out Japanese women, then rapes and kills them, leaving a chopstick with *NanJing* engraved in it with the dead body." He stared straight ahead and swallowed hard. "I got him banned from the Philippines forever, but in the process, I lost three of my men."

Tom rubbed his cheekbone. "He only handles high-level top-secret human assets. I've kept track of him over the years, the best I could. He has never dared come to the United States before now. After the Philippines, he rarely left mainland China, except for an adventure into Hong Kong from time to time. I've an MI6 agent there who fills me in on his activities." He shrugged. "That's everything I know."

Corley let out a low whistle. "Does he always travel with bodyguards? Cause we may need more fire power to get him."

"As far as I know. He always dresses in the most expensive gray suits made of the finest material. He never gets dirty—leaves that up to his henchmen."

Both men were quiet for a few minutes. After three more traffic lights, Corley said, "Turn right up here. It's that big apartment building on the left. But one more thing. How did Dr. Wang know you'd been transferred to SF?"

Tom pulled up in front of the apartment. "I have my suspicions that he was tipped off, but I have no way to substantiate it at this time."

Corley shook his head. "If he is conducting such a big operation, it still makes no sense that he'd let you know he was here." He started to get out of the car, then glanced back at Warren. "So, what's next?"

"We have to interview the doormen. See what they might know. The SFPD didn't do that, which seems odd. Someone has to know something about the vic, and who else was going in and out. Plus, we have to try to figure out what apartment they drug me to and who is registered to live there."

Corley nodded. "So you can put the Dr. Wang involvement in its proper prospective?"

Tom bit his lip. "It's personal between the two of us. He has vowed to kill me, and I have vowed to arrest or kill him. But to answer your question—he must've been finishing up his operation in the US when he found out I'd been transferred here. Then, just before he escaped, he pulled me in. Just to tempt me. He said he wanted to show me what he was working on before he killed me. That's the only reason we're still alive."

CHAPTER FOUR

December 9, 1963
Beijing Police – Detective Bureau

Beijing Police Detective Yu Qiangsheng was working on his latest case file when his desk phone buzzed. He picked up the phone.

"Someone is here to see you, detective." The desk sergeant said.

"Send him back," Yu said.

"You should come up here, detective."

Who was making demands of him? After all, he was one of the top police officers. He made the rules. When he arrived out front, Kang Sheng, the head of Central Investigation Division, waited. Yu invited him back to his office.

"Walk with me," Kang commanded.

Yu rubbed his chin. *What this was all about? Why would his pseudo step-father and mentor want to talk with him privately?* They continued along the streets, Kang reminded him of his family ties. "You are destined. Your related to Mao Ze-dong. Mao and Zhou pay attention to things like that. Trust me."

While Yu respectfully listened to Kang's version of his heritage, he didn't need it. His own version and the Chinese version never meshed. This relationship he was speaking of was figurative, years ago, his mother had been in a relationship with Mao, but Mao wasn't his father. Likewise, she had worked in some capacity with Zhou. But he remained silent. *Get to the point.*

Kang talked like they had been held in high esteem by the government, but it had been just the opposite. Yu noticed he left out his blood relationship to Chiang Kai-shek.

As they arrived at a little park area in central Beijing, Kang nodded toward the entrance. They walked over and sat down on a park bench. Kang leaned forward and put his elbows on his knees, folding his hands in front of him. "We want you to come over and work for the CID. We need someone with your skills to take over surveillance of citizens inside the country who are dissidents."

Yu listened intently as Kang spoke. The Communist Party was fickle with who was and wasn't in good standing, and this could create an unknown problem in the future. While it was an honor to be considered, the offer came with a personal conflict. *His father had been one of those "dissidents" that had been watched.*

When Kang finished talking, he stared at Yu.

Yu forced his eyes on his hands. *Don't show any emotion. Don't let him read anything.*

Kang got up from the bench and glanced at Yu. "Don't take long to decide. If you don't want this assignment, I'll move on. But you have the skills to thrive at the CID." He turned and exited the park.

Yu strolled around the park for a while, pondering.

When he finally returned to his desk, he spent the rest of his shift staring at his blank office wall. *If I accept his offer, then I will have to work around all these people who hurt my father.* He closed his eyes for a minute, then asked himself the important question. If his family had been destroyed by these people, how could he consider working with them?

But it was a tremendous career offer. Maybe he could change the culture of the hierarchies and how they treat families of dissidents. Plus, it could be a means to an end.

Special Agent Tom Warren had lost the trail of Dr. Wang. Over the past three days, he had tried to piece clues together by going to Chinatown looking for any possible tip. Also, he had to keep track of SFPD's activities in San Francisco. He didn't believe he was getting the whole story from them, but he couldn't put his finger on why. It was just a feeling. Everything had gone cold. Somehow or another, Dr. Wang had not only slipped away, but no one claimed to know anything.

Corley entered the office, holding his small notebook in the air. "Got the interviews of the doormen here."

Tom waved him over to his desk.

Marty stood in front of his desk and flipped through the small book. "Webster Towers has four doormen. They work three eight-hour shifts, seven days a week, around the clock for a month. Obviously, one is always off for a month. Pretty good gig, hey? Anyway, I was only able to interview three of them so far. None of them saw Dr. Wang or the two henchmen. All of them knew the vic. Said she never spoke, only smiled pleasantly. They didn't seem to notice any routine in her movements."

"So, who didn't you interview?"

"Jared Samuel," Marty said as he flipped over another page. "Tried to call him a couple of times. No answer. He just went off duty."

Tom's desk phone rang. He scooped it up. "Special Agent Tom Warren."

"This is Captain Dawkins, U.S. Coast Guard. We discovered a Chinese body floating in the middle of the bay. We have a memo you are to be notified. We should be at the docks within the hour."

"Thanks. Appreciate it, Captain." Tom hung up the phone. "Marty, let's roll."

The two men headed out the door.

Marty turned into the Naval Yard. He held his badge out the window for the Naval Officer to check.

The officer looked at it and waved them on.

When they stopped at the dock along the waterfront, SFPD Detective Lee and the city coroner stood at the edge as the Coast Guard skiff slowly pulled up to the dock. Tom and Marty joined the two men from the SFPD.

The Coast Guardsmen brought the body up on the dock, and the coroner opened the black bag. The stench was horrible, but Tom immediately knew it was the old Chinaman he'd bought his newspapers from every day. Tom looked at Detective Lee and the coroner. "Take the body in, but I'll have the FBI boys pick him up, ASAP."

Lee frowned at Tom as he put his hand on the coroner's shoulder, then nodded. "Keep us in the loop. We will do the same."

On the drive back to the FBI bureau, Marty gave Tom a quick glance. "You think Dr. Wang had the Chinaman killed to cover his tracks?"

Tom's gaze remained fixated out the side window. "Seems logical. Anybody who knew anything about him is going to turn up dead. Eliminate all non-essential personnel."

"I'm beginning to get an understanding for how Dr. Wang works."

Tom pounded his fist lightly on the side door. "He always seems to be a step ahead of me. I've got to change that."

Tom went back to the bureau to re-read the coroner's report on the murdered Japanese woman and the FBI lab results from their investigation. The woman had been identified as Kikue Nakamura. But too many things didn't add up. Had she been raped just before she was murdered? Too hard to tell. Yet, this was typical for Dr. Wang's MO. There had been no evidence of forced entry at her residence. Again, typical MO. So she must have known he was coming to her suite. The woman was beautiful, but there was no evidence she was a hooker—at least, not without a john book.

Tom looked through his notes. He wrote the name of the un-interviewed doorman, Jared Samuel. The interviews of the other three had turned up nothing. So far, his theory that the doormen where the ones who knew the comings and goings at the apartment complex had turned up a big fat nothing—except the apartment Tom had been dragged into was supposedly empty for the last three months. The previous renter was an American with no conceivable connection to the Chinese. *Sometimes these doormen were like barbers and beauticians with people talking to them, sometimes they were like British Bobbies. Perhaps Samuel was the one who knew things?*

CHAPTER FIVE

Christmas Eve - December 24, 1963
Virginia Coastline

In the darkness of the night, Dr. Wang stood on the aft of the docked Greek freighter. They were anchored about twenty miles offshore. He could barely see the glow of the nearby city on the horizon. He watched the breathtaking night sky, focusing on Orion the Hunter and the two dogs. Red China was the hunter, and the United States and the Soviet Union were the two dogs. Orion was soon to be reckoned with.

The skiff was due to pick him up just before midnight for the trip to shore.

He'd had to change sea-going vessels before entering the Panama Canal, as the Mexican freighter destination was for the Far East. The change had put him way behind schedule to pick up his documents. At the moment, he couldn't complete personal side of his mission to eliminate the two rich Chinese defectors. For now, at least. He was almost a week behind schedule to meet his contact. Their protocol put them on a backup schedule, as no contact was permitted. The drop was too critical to have any audio contact that could be traced in any fashion. He was determined to complete his primary mission at all costs for his country.

He remained on the aft of the freighter in the dark until he saw the approaching skiff flash their flood light three times. He was off to his cabin, "Let's go, our ride is approaching. Move it."

The skiff pulled alongside, Dr. Wang and his henchmen were lowered down by a net on to the fast craft. As soon as he sat down the boat driver pushed the throttle forward and turned the boat on a dime, coming out of the turn pointed toward shore.

As they approached the shore, a fog started forming along the shoreline and the air temperature dropped significantly. The boat pilot pulled back on the throttle, as it appeared he was having a difficult time seeing very far in front of the watercraft. By the time Dr. Wang could see the shoreline, they could not be more than a quarter mile away. The pilot strained as he got up on one knee looking along the shoreline. Dr. Wang asked, "Do you know where we are meeting the car?"

The boat pilot didn't take his eyes off the shoreline. "Yes."

Dr. Wang stewed, he could not afford any more delays. The pilot started flashing his flood light toward the shore. Within a few minutes, there was a couple of lights flashed answering, it was straight ahead. When the driver saw the lights, he throttled back a little more, the wake of the boat caught them from behind pushing them forward. They started slowly cruising toward the last location of the flashing light. The fog got so thick, visibility had dropped to about one hundred feet. When they pulled up to the dock and tied off, again car headlights flashed ahead. Dr. Wang turned to the boat driver then to Wu and pointed. Wu walked up and pulled his knife and slit the boat pilot's neck. Dr. Wang walked toward the waiting car, followed by Chung. Wu remained behind.

The driver of the car got and walked directly toward Dr. Wang, bowed slightly. "My old friend, how are you?"

Dr. Wang cracked half a smile. "I'm well. It's good to meet face to face, how long has it been?"

The car driver said, "1952, right before I went to California."

Dr. Wang looked back and saw Wu siphoned some gas from the gas tank poured it over the boat then set it on fire. Wu started running toward the car, he slid in the front seat.

Both men walked quickly around the car and got in. Dr. Wang looked at the driver. "Jin, Let's go I have no time to waste." No one said a word in the car, as it turned around and pulled away. Before they could get started up the dirt road, there was a loud explosion behind them. Dr. Wang looked back to make sure the whole boat was on fire.

They drove in silence for more than an hour. As they approached Petersburg, Dr. Wang spoke to the driver. "Find a place to pull over and we can get out and talk." They pulled in at an all night café. Dr. Wang touched Wu on the shoulder. "Jin and I will go in first, after five minutes, come in and sit down at another table away from us."

Dr. Wang and Jin Wu-dai got out of the car, entered the café and sat down in the farthest corner. Dr. Wang sat where he could see the old female waitress every time approach the table. She carried over two empty coffee cups and a pot of black coffee. After setting them down and filled them, asked. "You all want something to eat?"

Both men shook their heads, no.

She left.

Jin whispered. "The FBI found the old China man in the San Francisco Bay. Warren IDed him."

Dr. Wang raised his eyebrow. "How is that possible? They threw in his body in the bay weighted down."

Jin leaned forward. "Before I came back here to find a home. I saw the police and FBI report.

Dr. Wang snarled. "I'll deal with that when I get back to China."

Jin sat back up straight and smiled. "I am being transferred to Arlington next year. The CIA wants me to translate stolen documents from Red China." He reached in his jacket pocket, pulled out three passports. "Here you go.

There is a private French plane at Baltimore-Washington Airport, it's from our Greek friend. These passports will get you and your men through any security check should you get stopped. But don't think you will. They will fly you directly to Paris. After picking up your package, you will go to a different airport and switch to a Greek plane but through the same Greek communist. They will take you to Tokyo with a stop in Tehran and Bombay. If you want them to wait for you in Tokyo they will but we believe by then you could be on the FBI or CIA radar. We have assumed that you have arranged for other transportation back to mainland."

Dr. Wang picked up the passports, just as his men walked in and sat down on the opposite end. He did not look up at them. "I wish I had your language skills in Japanese. Too bad I can't take you with me. What do you have for me?"

"Are you kidding me, you are the best at the Japanese language I have ever met. You know dialects going back a thousand years. You will need all of your skills to complete your mission there." Jin pulled out an envelope from inside his jacket and passed it over. "This is a list of all the current deep cover CIA agents in mainland and Hong Kong." Jin laughed then smiled as he continued. "Also, the address of the two dissidents you are looking for."

Dr. Wang didn't open it, he just stuffed it in his gray suit pocket. "I don't have time to take care of the two Chinese traitors." He pulled out a small piece of paper and pushed it toward him. "You have been my best agent. With your new assignment, when you get to the East Coast, I'll make arrangement for you to meet a courier in Toronto four times a year, otherwise, you can mail information to this Hong Kong post office box. This is my last trip to the U.S. With Warren back assigned to Chinese spying I can't take any chances."

Jin smiled. "You should not have taunted him in San Francisco."

Dr. Wang needed Jin, he was doing too good of a job to get sideways with him. "It's my personal problem. I'll handle him in due course." He cracked his back to calm himself down. "I have set up a restaurant in New York through one of the agents who came over from San Francisco. Also, we have an undercover agent running a church in New York." He reached in his pocket, pulled out two business cards and handed them to Jin. "Here are the addresses. If you need to get out of the country fast, get here. They have the where-with-all to get you out through Canada. Lastly, if ever I need to call you directly, I'll use the phrase, 'Is this the airport', your reply shall be, 'No, old number', that will be your code to call, asap."

Jin picked both of them up. "That's all I have. We need to get back on the road. We shouldn't stay anywhere too long."

As the two men walked outside, Dr. Wang said, "One more thing, with respect to Warren. That man got the best of me in the Philippines, I escaped but he destroyed my mission. I can't go back there, still, after fifteen years. Any time, anything comes up with his name, no matter the detail include it in your correspondence to me. Got it?"

"I will."

Dr. Wang nodded at his two men.

His two men moved immediately, one went and grabbed the old waitress while the other entered the kitchen. Dr. Wang flipped the closed sign out, as he walked toward the car. He and Jin sat in the car for a minute. Jin asked, "Are you sure it's the right thing to do, killing those two?"

Dr. Wang's facial expression did not change, as the two men got in the car. "No witnesses. No chances."

In a couple of minutes, the lights went out in the café.

Ten minutes later, the two men came from around back of the business. When they got in the car, Dr. Wang looked at Wu. "How did you get rid of them?"

Wu said, "Drug them in the woods outback and cut them up."

Jin got a scared look on his face, through gritted teeth. "No more killing or they will figure out your path out of here or it will lead to me. We can't have that."

Dr. Wang did not even look at him. "Drive."

Several hours later, Jin pulled into the private side of the large international airport, then parked in an area where there were no lights in the parking lot. He turned around and looked at Dr. Wang. "We are here. I can't be seen."

"We both have missions to accomplish." Dr. Wang looked at Jin before he and his henchmen got out and walked toward the small office building to check in for private flights. When he turned, Jin had already left the parking lot.

When they walked into the building, Dr. Wang nudged Wu. "We are here for this flight." He pointed to the jet sitting on the runway. He slipped into a corner and looked at pictures on the wall so his face was not seen.

The man at the desk asked. "Everybody got passports?"

Each of the men on cue pulled out the passport given to them by Jin and raised them up in the air.

The man at the desk nodded. "Good to go. Have them ready in Paris." Then he checked on the flight and pushed open the window. A brisk wind blew through. He gave a thumbs up toward them. Dr. Wang glanced out and saw the jet engines revving. He went through the door in the direction of the jet before the ground chief could clear them. The ground chief held up his hand to stop. Dr. Wang did as commanded. He couldn't afford a confrontation with somebody who would go nose to nose with him. It would make it too easy to identify him.

Within a couple of seconds, the ladder dropped from the jet and the ground chief waved them forward. Once on board, the jet taxied out. As they pulled to the main runway, the copilot stepped out of the cabin. "Everybody buckled in? We're next in line for takeoff," he said in French.

Nobody in the cabin said a word. The copilot turned around and went back to the cockpit. Within thirty seconds, they were accelerating down the runway.

When their wheels were off the ground, Dr. Wang smiled. He had accomplished his primary mission—there would be no need to ever step foot on U.S. soil again. Plus, he had provoked his rival, the FBI Special Agent. His next goal was to rub his great success in Warren's face.

As the jet climbed toward cruising altitude, he rested his eyes.

Beijing, China
December 26, 1963

Yu Qiangsheng parked his car behind the decrepit structure. He had been followed most of the drive. While he had lost the tail in the last couple of blocks, he was not so naïve to believe they weren't sitting in front of the apartment complex. As Yu opened the back door, he noticed two men sitting in the lobby watching the front door. *Amateurs.* Then he slipped to the back stairway and ascended the multiple floors. The hallway was dimly lit by a single twenty-five-watt bulb at the end.

He walked down the hallway, the wood creaking under his feet with every step, until he arrived at one of the doors and lightly knocked. An elderly lady cracked it open. Upon seeing who had knocked, she flung it open and hugged her son.

Yu hugged his mother, Fan Jin, with great vigor. "I love you, Ma."

She rushed him in and closed the door behind them. "You are taking great risks coming to see me, son."

Yu sat down on the floor at the low dinner table.

His mother shuffled behind and sat opposite him.

"There is something I need to discuss with you—I need your advice."

His mother reached out for his hand, held it, and patted the back of it gently.

Yu drew a deep breath and continued. "Kang came to see me about a month ago."

His mother smiled slightly.

After reading her body language, Yu continued. "He offered me a position at CID. He wants me to get the training to be an agent. What do you think?"

His mother glanced away for a brief moment, then spoke. "After your father's death, Kang promised me he would look after you. So, I would accept his help. Don't you think it offers you more opportunity for growth?"

"Yes, of course. But—wasn't it the government that caused Father's death? How can I—"

His mother let go of his hand, then waved that hand in his face. "Your father, Yu Qiwei, died of a heart attack."

"Ma, I know the real story. The government killed him because his brother was the defense minister in Taiwan. They did it to send a message to his brother. You don't have to shelter me anymore. I know what happened." Yu's face turned bright red.

His mother got up from the table and shuffled over to the small window.

Yu followed her and put his arm around her. "Ma, I have the connections to read the files on father and *you*."

His mother turned and faced him. "You must take this job. It's a good career change. Plus, it's for your own personal protection. You will not be safe if you stay with the police. They will come after you."

Yu frowned. "What are you talking about? Who are *they*? Protect me from what?"

She coughed several times, pulled a handkerchief from her pocket, and shuffled away from him again as she wiped her nose and mouth. She sat back down at the low table and leaned against the wall. "Mao is losing his mind. He is becoming more paranoid than ever before. He will tighten his grip on our people more than anything he has done in the past. If you don't get into the CID and gain power...."

"Ma, what are you not telling me? Please, don't hold back. This is too important. This is a career decision."

She bit her lip. "You know I know Mao better than almost anybody. The man can be delusional and paranoid. We have seen him go crazy and just start killing anybody who disagrees with him." She shrugged. "He must be stopped. But you, you have to make this move."

Yu drew a deep breath. "Ma, don't do anything to get yourself in trouble with the Politburo and Mao."

She smiled slyly. "I'll be fine. Kang will protect me. Just like he is protecting you. Make the move."

Yu got up and looked out the window. The men who were watching him still sat outside. Are they watching me and my mother? *Damn.* He hugged and kissed his mother. "Okay, Ma. I've got to go. Be safe. I'll call Kang when I get home."

December 26, 1963
San Francisco

Tom Warren sat at his desk, chatting with Marty Corley about the lack of response to the APB on Dr. Wang and his two henchmen. Both men agreed he must have left the country and gone back to China. San Francisco had always had connections to communists. During the McCarthy hearings in the 1950s, several Soviet spies and sympathizers lived in the San Francisco area. He guessed the same was true for the Chinese. San Francisco's Chinatown was the most popular in the United States.

There hadn't been any new developments in the murder of Kikue Nakamura. However, they were informed by one of the other doormen at the Webster Towers that Jared Samuel had unexpectedly retired. It seemed odd.

Tom didn't buy into the story he'd been told that Samuel moved back to Nebraska to his parents' farm that had no phone. Warren had sent a request to the FBI office in Kansas City to interview him, but he'd not checked back in yet. None of the three doormen had seen anyone matching the description of Dr. Wang or the henchmen and couldn't identify them from the sketches prepared. Moreover, none of them knew Kikue Nakamura. She'd speak to them when she entered. Never had a man with her. She'd be gone for several days to a week at a time. Never had anybody strange going to her penthouse. Nothing was adding up. What Warren thought would provide a good lead turned into another dead end. The woman lived in the building for three years.

Warren thought about the doormen's interviews. "Marty, we have got to take Ms. Nakamura's picture out into the community and see who knew her. We start in Japantown, and then head over to Chinatown. Maybe we can find someone who will tell us something. Maybe she had an alias. If she were a hooker, maybe she conducted her business elsewhere? Maybe she wanted her home to be her safe haven—but why would she meet Dr. Wang there?" It still bothered him they'd found no safe, no safety deposit key, no passport, no checking account—nothing. Dr. Wang had taken all the answers with him. It seemed impossible to cover up every single detail—but so far, that seemed the case.

Marty rested his chin on his hand with his elbow on his desk. "I'll get the car and bring it around."

As they drove ten blocks across town, Tom stared out the window. He really liked living in San Francisco. It was so much nicer than Washington, DC. Once in Japantown, he told Corley, "Let's hit the high-end jewelry stores and art dealers. It appeared Ms. Nakamura had money, but it seemed like it all was in cash. Very strange."

Corley parked in front of a jewelry store. "You know, she may have bought her art and antiques here, but I bet she bought her jewelry in the downtown district. Real high-end stuff, you know."

As Tom got out of the car, he said, "The more questions we ask about this woman, the more I realize we don't know."

The two men walked up and down the streets of Japantown, several blocks in each direction. Nobody recognized her picture or had any account of her. He wanted to believe no one was lying to him, but the Japanese weren't the most cooperative people with the FBI. Finally, he told Corley they needed to head to Chinatown. There they could expand and start asking questions about Dr. Wang and his two henchmen to try to break into the network.

The two men spent the rest of the day in Chinatown, adding restaurants to their stops. Some people said no to the pictures or sketches before they even looked at them. While those answers did him no good, they did tell him that the Chinese spy network had tentacles that scared some of the older Chinese. In one restaurant, Tom thought the staff was evasive. He figured they'd seen Dr. Wang in the last few weeks, and they knew who he was. One of the waitresses threw a plate of Lo Mein at Tom when he walked through the kitchen, then she ran off. Corley had started after her, but Tom stopped him with a nod to leave it alone.

When they got in the car to return to headquarters, Corley asked. "Why did you stop me from grabbing that waitress and questioning her?"

Tom laughed. "I thought she was cute. She was just showing her frustration. That is one of the restaurants we will keep an eye on."

Corley shook his head. "You stopped me from grabbing her because she was *cute*? *Damn*."

As they drove, Tom chewed his lip. "I've got to break this network. Look, if you had caught that girl and made a scene, we wouldn't win. Maybe because we showed some restraint, we might get something out of it." He knocked on the side windshield with his knuckles. "Perhaps I need to go to some of the universities in the area. When I was just starting in the FBI, they focused on the colleges—lots of communists."

Corley pounded the steering wheel once. "Hey, do you know anybody at CIA? Or, at least, anyone who will talk to you?"

Tom bristled at the idea. His luck with the CIA had varied between bad and worse. "Maybe. Also, I need to go and dig into some old files. There is bound to be some good stuff in old files on Chinatown."

Marty slammed on the brakes at the traffic light. "Let's get Samuel's local address and go check out his place."

"Wouldn't you think that Detective Lee would have done that already?"

"Maybe," Marty replied. "But we might see something they overlooked. I'll call our office and get the address."

Tom and Marty enter Jared Samuel's apartment. It was near Webster Towers, small and simple, but neat.

"You take the bedroom. I'll go to the bathroom and kitchen," Tom commanded.

Within a minute, Tom shouted, "Marty, come here!"

Tom was standing in the bathroom and pointed around the tiny room. "What do you see?"

Marty looked around. He opened the medicine cabinet and looked in the tiny closet. "I don't see any meds or anything else. What?"

"That's it. His shaving stuff is packed up somewhere," Tom mumbled as he put both hands on his hips.

Both men went back to work, now believing Samuel had packed. After searching the room for several more minutes, they met in the living room. Tom was reviewing everything in his head. "Okay, we have to assume he packed because all of his sundries are missing—razor, toothbrush, etc., and no suitcase. Did he leave for his parents' home? Is that where he is?"

CHAPTER SIX

December 27, 1963

Tom sat at his desk, loafing for a moment, reading the *San Francisco Chronicle*, when the mail guy for the FBI stepped into the open offices shouting, "Package for Special Agent Thomas P. Warren."

Tom waved for the package to be brought to his desk. He examined the box—it was sent by his family back in Boston. Surprised to have received anything from his family, he quickly opened it. Inside was the football from his final game as the quarterback at the University of Arizona. He thought with all the moving he'd lost it over the years. Naturally, he remembered being the season MVP and getting the football, but upon accepting his assignment to go to the Philippines, he'd lost track of it. The accompanied letter from his father said they'd found it in their attic.

For the longest time, his father had been upset with his career selection, hoping he'd return and run the family business. They had mended that fence some time ago. Now he was proud of the size and scope of his son's role in the FBI.

Tom flashed the football around the room, striking the Heisman Pose for Marty Corley, who couldn't believe that Tom had never told him about this accomplishment.

As the excitement wore off, he sat back down at his desk, leaned back in his chair, and started tossing the football over his head, then catching it. His mind was focused on his case and Dr. Wang. He needed to come up with a break. Dr. Wang had disappeared, and Tom assumed he'd gone back to China. More importantly, why had he come to the United States, and what he picked up or learned? Or what had he delivered or who had he brought into the country?

Tom had assigned several teams of junior agents to watch a couple of restaurants in Chinatown that he'd had a hunch were somehow tied to Dr. Wang—or were at least part of a Chinese spy network.

Marty hollered from his desk, "Did we ever hear from the Kansas City agent about the doorman, Samuel?"

Tom continued to toss the football in the air. "No, call them. Let's put that part of the story to bed."

As Marty dialed the number and started talking to the Kansas City bureau, Tom got an idea. He slammed the football down on his desk and looked at his watch. *One of those FBI researchers back East is likely still in the office, even though it's late. They can do a little research.* He picked up his desk phone and called the D.C. headquarters. On the other end, the phone was answered, "Federal Bureau of Investigation, Michelle Galloway."

Tom was hoping either Michelle or Stephanie Keeton would answer. "Michelle, Tom Warren."

"Special Agent Warren, how are you? We miss you here."

Tom smiled as he looked around the office to see if anyone was paying attention. *Nobody was.* "I need some information. Can you look something up for me?"

"I guess so. If it won't get me into trouble. What do you need?"

Tom looked around again. Still nobody was looking, and Marty was on the line at his desk. "I need you to look up the location of two men the FBI has been surveilling for years. The first name is T. V. Soong and the second is H. H. Kung. Got it?"

"Got it. Who are they?"

"Get me those addresses, and I'll fill you in."

Marty hung up his phone.

Tom leaned forward. "Thank you." He returned the receiver to the switch hook. "Marty, what did Kansas City say about their interview?"

Marty looked up and raised both hands out from his sides. "The parents said their son never came home. They turned in a missing person's report last week to the local police, but nothing has turned up."

Tom rubbed the back of his neck. "Did anyone call the SFPD to investigate?"

Marty nodded. "Guess who is handling the case for SFPD?"

Tom pounded the desk like a drum roll. "Detective Lee."

"It's good." Marty raised both hands in the air as though Tom had just kicked a field goal.

Tom got up from his desk and paced. "We have really dropped the ball on this ourselves. We've got to be more proactive. Let's go back through Samuel's file."

"Kansas City is sending over all the information they have."

Tom drummed his lips with his fingers. "Marty, we don't let Lee know we have this information. I want to study it first. Then we'll go by and see Lee."

"It's probably too late. The Kansas City office contacted Detective Lee to get information from SFPD."

Tom pondered this for a moment. *Why the hell would they call SFPD and not us? Crazy. We put them on it.*

His desk phone rang. Tom grabbed the receiver. "Special Agent Warren."

"Special Agent Warren, this is Michelle. Got your information. H. H. Kung lives in Locust Valley, New York, and T. V. Soong lives in New York City. Here are their addresses."

Tom spun around, sat down and wrote the addresses. "Both men live in the city area?" He relaxed. "Hey, how is Stephanie doing?"

"She's doing really well, seems really happy." There was a pause, and then Michelle asked, "How did you know the FBI was watching them and that they were in the U.S.?"

Tom crouched over his phone to shield his voice. "Me and my team were the ones who snuck them out of China after their Civil War turned nasty. I knew they both ended up in the U.S., but Hoover had some other agents take over once we got them out of the country. I was involved in a bigger case at that time. Keep all of this to yourself. And no one is to know you got me these addresses. Got it?"

Michelle replied, "You know me. I can keep a secret. Goodbye, Agent Warren."

Tom hung up the phone. "Marty, I got a plan."

Paris, France

After they landed at Le Touquet Côte d'Opale, Dr. Wang pulled a piece of paper from his breast pocket and glanced at it as he and his henchmen took the cold walk toward their car. Once inside the car, Dr. Wang gave Wu the directions to drive.

Sixty minutes later, Wu pulled into the park, as per the directions. Dr. Wang told him to pull into a secluded location along a riverbank, in the dark along the forks in the river, where they couldn't be seen. He looked at his watch. His contact was running late. He was supposed to arrive about the same time they did.

Chung drummed on the steering wheel with his fingers, Wu turned around and looked at Dr. Wang to ask how much longer they were to wait.

Wang leaned up from the backseat and told his men he was willing to wait as long as it took for his contact, code named "Jacques," to show up. The

Communist Party in Paris had been very cooperative working with Mao. Dr. Wang knew they were just triangulating. The French were pissed off at the United States over Vietnam, and while they had also been cooperative with the Soviets, they didn't want to be tied solely to any communist country. Plus, Mao desperately needed their information, and Dr. Wang couldn't go back to China without it.

Everyone sat quietly. Finally, after thirty more minutes, a Peugeot pulled into the secluded park. The man jumped out of the car, briefcase in hand, and started toward the riverbank, then sat down on a park bench. He took off his tam and waved it around twice in the air. With that gesture, Dr. Wang leaned forward and told Chung to flash his headlights twice. As soon as he did, Jacques got up from the bench, leaving the briefcase. He hurried to his car and drove off.

"Go pick up the briefcase," Dr. Wang ordered.

Chung pulled the car down beside the park bench.

Wu jumped out, picked up the briefcase, and handed it in the back window to Dr. Wang, who quickly opened it.

He pulled out several files, quickly flipped through them, and then slammed it shut. He stroked his chin with his left hand. "Let's get to the airport."

As their Greek-registered plane lifted off from the Beaumont-sur-Oise Airport north of Paris, Dr. Wang called his bodyguards to come over and sit near him.

Dr. Wang leaned forward and gave each man a long stare. "You were selected to protect me and be my bodyguards on this mission. I expect you to protect me with your very lives. We are headed to Tokyo. I'm about to complete the mission that Mao and Kang Sheng assigned to me. This will allow us to achieve Mao's greatest goal. Soon we will stand equal with the Soviet Union and the United States."

Both men glanced at each other and nodded.

Dr. Wang continued, "I have one last package to pick up before we go home. It's in Tokyo, where I'm a marked man. If they see me, the Yakuza, as well as the Navy and Army, will attempt to capture or assassinate me. If that happens, then I fail, which means you fail. This means your own deaths. Do you understand the importance of this mission and your jobs?" He grabbed Wu by the shirt. "We must not fail."

Both men replied in unison, "Yes, Dr. Wang."

With that he waved them away, closed his eyes, and went to sleep. They would be in the air for a long while. It was time to rest and meditate.

CHAPTER SEVEN

December 28, 1963
Tokyo

As their plane started its dissent into the Tokyo International Airport, Dr. Wang called his bodyguards back around him. "When we land, go get the car in this parking lot and space." He handed Wu a piece of paper. "Then pull it around to the plane."

Wu nodded.

Dr. Wang pointed at his two bodyguards. "As I said before, it is up to you to protect me. I want to go over my plan. Pay attention and do exactly as I tell you."

Both men glanced at each other before turning back to Dr. Wang.

Dr. Wang pounded the arm of the plane's chair. "I'm going to meet my contact, code name 'Goro.' I've never met him, talked to him, or even seen a picture of him to protect his identity. Likewise, he knows nothing of me. This meeting is to take place in an area known as Daikanyama, one of the top attractions to Tokyo's young wealthy—you know, the 'beautiful people' of Tokyo. We will wait until evening to move out so there should be some parties going on. Goro and I only know where the drop is to be made and the time of the drop. There will be a piece of pink cloth hanging in the third cherry tree on the left when I enter the walkway at Daikanyama. I will go immediately and pick up the package. He is leaving it in a newspaper machine outside the

Souvenir Shop. It will be crowded, but if the Yakuza are following Goro or me, they will not be able to get off a clean shot." He stared at Wu. "You will parallel my walk on my left side."

Wu bowed his head.

Then he focused on Chung. "You will protect me on my right side until the drop is made. If either of you have to shoot, don't worry about killing any innocent Japanese—they will just be collateral damage. As soon as I have my package in hand, we return to the airport. Got it?"

Chung shuffled his feet but nodded.

Dr. Wang continued, "Take that car and park it somewhere between here and there, near Sarugakucho, so we have a car to escape in after the drop. That way, if they are following us into town, they won't recognize the car." He handed them the address of where he wanted the car parked near the entrance to Daikanyama.

Just before dark, Dr. Wang began looking out the small port window with a regularity. When a Japanese taxicab pulled up next to the charter plane, he stood. "Time to go. Know your responsibility."

The three men hustled down the stairway to the ground and slipped into the cab. As usual, Dr. Wang sat in the backseat opposite the driver. As they accelerated away, the driver glanced back, "I'm from the Japanese communist party."

Dr. Wang nodded slightly while still looking out the window. "Take a lot of turns and as many back streets as possible."

The driver tilted his head. "Why?"

Dr. Wang continued to stare out the window. "Just do it."

"Although the winter had been cold, it was warming this evening," the driver said. "There will be some people in the bar area. Your contact will be dressed like a mime. He will be wearing the classic black and white horizontal striped shirt, white slacks, and a black Beret, with white makeup on his face and a yellow scarf. He will be doing his routine all the way around Daikanyama. When he gets to the Souvenir Shop, he will stop and do some kind of a routine near the newspaper machine. He will open the newspaper machine, drop your file, and pick up a newspaper. As he walks away, he will do a magic trick to draw the attention of the crowd. You must move then and grab the file. You will have about thirty seconds to get it, which will be stuck in the back of the machine."

Dr. Wang was convinced they were being followed, and it was likely the Yakuza—perhaps Yoshio's men. He and Yoshio went way back to World War II. Now Yoshio was the head of the biggest Yakuza crime organization. Plus, he had ties to the Japanese royal family from his days in the Golden Lily. Dr. Wang looked out the front window for the first time. "Do you know who the courier is? Does anybody know his identity?"

This time the driver kept his eyes on the fast-moving traffic ahead. "No one knows who he is. We don't even know whether he is male or female, or of what nationality. Everything has been moved with dead drops to protect everyone's identities. Remember, Japan is almost a police state."

Dr. Wang had all the answers he needed. His pathway to get the drop was now clearer. His tail was going to make his assignment more difficult, but he was focused. He believed he'd come up with the best possible plan.

As they approached his getaway car. Dr. Wang glanced at it but didn't say a word. He couldn't even trust this communist cab driver. They stopped at one of the walkways into the Daikanyama area. Dr. Wang commanded his bodyguards to get in position. Once they were out of the car, he leaned up to the driver. "You have done well, comrade."

Dr. Wang got out of the car, straightened his gray suit, and walked into the commercial area of Daikanyama. He turned up his suit collar to keep warm and hide his appearance. As he walked, he kept his head down. He assumed the car tailing them would stop, also, and whoever was in the car behind him would block his path out. As he continued to walk, he saw the pink ribbon on the third tree. A sense of dread came over him. The Yakuza knew his plan and drop. There would be several men waiting for him ahead. He was walking into a trap. He stopped and snarled, slapping his fist into his open palm. *Is it a trap if you know it's a trap? If they know my real identity, they all will want to kill me.*

The crowd was sparse, but there were a few partiers to ensure no one could get directly to him. He was walking on faith that Wu and Chung were in their places and moving with him. Ahead he saw the mime doing a variety of skits and tricks. Eight or nine partiers in the crowd were entertained or irritated. A few people walked by, seemingly annoyed, but the crowd grew to maybe fifteen people gathered around him. They were younger people who had likely been drinking. The situation was the best that could be expected under the circumstances.

The mime continued to move through the crowd. Dr. Wang identified the Souvenir Shop, one store ahead of where he was conducting his act. He unobtrusively slipped into the middle of the crowd, but his focus was finding the newspaper machine. *There it is.* He started moving around to the side of the crowd, observing the mime so he was positioned just right to get to the newspaper dispenser. One more quick glance around. *I feel eyes on me.* He discreetly scanned the crowd. *Three sets of eyes, maybe.*

The mime unpinned the corsage from his shirt, leaned over, and sniffed it. Then he started skipping around the circle of people, doing what Dr. Wang considered completely goofy things as he moved the crowd toward the Souvenir Shop. When the mime moved in front of the Souvenir Shop, he held the flower out again, then bowed to everyone and yanked a handkerchief from his pants pocket. He put the handkerchief over the flower, then quickly pulled it off. The flower had turned into a metal coin. The crowd clapped and cheered. The mime spun around to face the newspaper machine and bowed.

Dr. Wang watched him closely. As he showed the coin again with his right hand, he slyly pulled a very small envelope from his pants with his left hand, so as no one would see it. The mime dropped the coin into the slot and pulled a newspaper. Simultaneously, he slipped in the envelope.

Dr. Wang was intently focused on the newspaper machine. The mime was quick and good, and no one had noticed him slip the envelope into the machine.

Now was the time for the big distraction to gather everyone's attention. As the mime walked away from the newspaper machine, he skipped again around the crowd, which had grown since his last trick. Once completing the circle of the crowd, he held the newspaper up in the air. Dr. Wang expected this was the time to move as everyone was focused on the mime—except the three suspected Yakuza.

The newspaper exploded with a flash-bang, and the mime now held the flower again.

Concurrently, Dr. Wang had retrieved the small envelope and darted away from the area, running as fast as he could. He had a clear jump on the Yakuza hit men. He secured the small envelope in his coat pocket as he was running through the crowd, which was sufficient to keep the Yakuza from getting a clear shot. However, since the Yakuza were between him and his escape route, he was forced to run deeper into the Daikanyama commercial area, which would be out of the line of sight of his henchmen. He bumped into a few men and women as he bounced around. Soon he was far enough ahead that he could duck into one of the commercial establishments. He sprinted until he spotted a poorly lit bar on his right and ducked in.

But where was the backdoor? It wasn't marked.

The three Japanese entered.

Dr. Wang was in deep trouble. He had lost his advantage being in a dark bar without the ability to quickly find any escape. He went to the darkest corner of the bar—another mistake. The men separated and walked through the bar.

As one of the men closed in on him, he became very calm. They wouldn't fire on him in the bar—but knives were another matter.

When the man closest to him was one table away, Dr. Wang jumped up, grabbed the wooden chair opposite him, and struck the man, knocking him to the ground. Because he'd caught him off guard, the Yakuza man dropped his knife. Dr. Wang grabbed it, pounced on the Yakuza, and slit the man's carotid artery in an instant. He sprinted back out the door with the other two Yakuza in pursuit.

Once outside, he started back in the direction of the escape vehicle, hoping his henchmen were nearby. He was running hard. He tried to blend in with the small crowd, hoping no one would notice the spatter of blood on his suit coat and on his hands. He slowed down to a fast walk, still attempting to stay in the middle of a crowd of eight young people. At this point it didn't matter, he was in a life-or-death situation.

As the group of eight entered a restaurant, he heard pursuing footsteps. Dr. Wang wanted to turn and confront the nearest Yakuza, but believed the other couldn't be far behind. His running was maintaining his distance from his pursuers. Within fifty more yards, he saw Wu and his escape vehicle. As he continued to run, two men stepped from around two different cherry trees and pointed guns at him.

Wu stepped out of the car and aimed his gun with a silencer across the roof of the car and shot each of the men in the back.

Dr. Wang sprinted through the dead bodies, as a few patrons scattered out of the way. Then Wu shot the pursuing Yakuza in the stomach and the head. Chung jumped out of the car and opened the door as Dr. Wang slid in. Wu was back behind the steering wheel and Chung dove back in the open door as Wu pressed down hard on the accelerator and sped away.

Dr. Wang knew there was still at least one Yakuza who knew what he looked like and would be in pursuit. Likely, he wouldn't be alone. Wu drove fast for several blocks.

Dr. Wang leaned up from the backseat. "Drive the speed limit to the plane. Don't attract the attention of the police."

He hoped the plane being registered to a Greek owner would prevent it from drawing attention. As Wu drove the car into the airport lot, Dr. Wang commanded Wu. "Stop here."

He stopped the car on the edge of the parking lot for private planes.

"Chung, double time it to the plane." Dr. Wang pointed as he spoke. "Get it ready. Tell the pilot to get clearance and get ready to take off, ASAP."

As soon as Chung was running off toward the plane, Dr. Wang commanded Wu out of the car. "Trail Chung. Look for Yakuza and snipers—specifically in high places. We should have been chased."

Dr. Wang glanced around. Chung had been out of his sight now for more than two minutes—he should be to the plane. Wang slipped behind the steering wheel, started the car, and pulled out of the parking place. His goal was to drive right up to the plane and board. As he slowly drove through the parking lot toward the gate, he saw Wu look up and get fixated on the water tower at the edge of the taxiway. Dr. Wang stopped and leaned down in the seat to see what Wu was looking at. Was there a sniper perched to fire on him? He leaned more to the left. Somebody was up there.

Dr. Wang pushed down on the accelerator a little, while glancing back and forth between Wu and the water tower. The man on the water tower never flinched. It appeared he was looking through a scope on a rifle pointed down at the tarmac, but it was hard to tell from the angle Dr. Wang had.

Stopping for a second, he glanced at Wu, then back to the water tower. *Do I drive to the plane or implement Plan B? Decide now and commit.* He stomped down on the accelerator and drove up to the gateway between the parking lot and the tarmac. The gate was open, and he sped through directly toward the plane. The propellers were turning and black exhaust puffed out of the motors.

Chung stood at the top of the stairway and Wu was running up.

Dr. Wang swung the car to the opposite side of the plane, so that the plane was between the sniper and him. Slamming on the brakes, he came to a screeching stop just feet from the plane but on the opposite side of the stairway. He drew a deep breath and flung open the door. Sirens sounded, coming closer. He sprinted around the nose of the plane, then up the stairway, two steps at a time, shouting, "Let's go, let's go."

Before he could sit down, the plane lurched forward on the tarmac, headed for the taxiway. As it turned onto the main runway, Dr. Wang looked out the window and saw three Japanese police cars pulling through the gate onto the tarmac at a high rate of speed with red lights flashing. He quickly unbuckled his seat belt, slipped to the front of the plane, and stuck his head in the cockpit. "Go, go, go!"

The pilot turned and looked. "I've been ordered to stop."

Dr. Wang stepped up and placed the blood-stained knife to his neck. "Fly or die."

The pilot pushed the two throttles forward and the plane started down the runway. Dr. Wang remained in the cockpit, repeating over and over, "Fly or die." He looked out the window. The three cars were about to pull on the runway in front of them just as the plane lifted off the ground. Two policemen from each car stepped out, leaned on the roof, and took aim at the plane.

The pilot shouted, "We should be okay as long as they don't hit the fuel tank or fuel line."

Dr. Wang looked back just in time to see a flash from the water tower. The sniper was firing at the police cars—the policemen never got off a shot. The sniper must have been from the Japanese Communist party.

Dr. Wang gasped for air. *Apparently he doesn't know my feelings toward the Japanese.*

Once the plane finally leveled off over international waters, he breathed a sigh of relief. His mission was on the verge of being a major success for his country, the Peoples Republic of China.

He called over his two bodyguards. "Where were you when I needed you? I got dirty. It's your job to make sure I don't."

CHAPTER EIGHT

New York City
January 7, 1964

FBI Special Agent Thomas Warren hailed a taxicab outside baggage claim at LaGuardia Airport. His destination was the T.V. Soong residence in upper Manhattan. It had been about fifteen years since he'd seen the man, but he was gracious enough to agree to a meeting at his residence. Tom didn't need to read any of Soong's file—his photographic memory seemed to be as sharp as ever since he'd been put back on the case and his personal pursuit of Dr. Wang. Soong was the Finance Minister of China before their fall to Mao and the communist movement. It was rumored that Soong was one of the wealthiest men in the world.

Tom never liked New York, and this drive reminded him why. While he didn't embrace his Bostonian heritage, the one thing he got out of it was his hatred for New York.

The cab finally pulled in front of the Soong residence. Tom stepped up and rang the doorbell. A servant answered. Tom gave his name.

The servant didn't say a word—he just walked Tom to the den where a frail man sat behind a large cherry desk in an elaborate office with carved wood bookcases. Soong slowly got up from the leatherback office chair and grabbed Tom's extended hand with both of his and shook it slowly with a bow. Then he pointed Tom toward a seat opposite him.

Soong cleared his throat a couple of times. "Special Agent Warren, to what do I owe this pleasure?"

Tom glanced around the office, appreciating the Chinese antiques. "I need some information. I'm in pursuit of Central Investigation Division Agent Dr. Wang." He paused for a reaction. "Do you know the man? Anything about him?"

Soong slumped over in his chair. "I know of the man. Dr. Wang is his code name. Over the years, I've speculated about his true identity, but I've never been able to pinpoint anyone. Kung and I've talked about this, but neither of us could get any further. As to his mission, I'm not sure, but I will tell you what I know. I owe you much for your sacrifice for getting me out of China. But first, I have a question for you. Where did you see Dr. Wang?"

"He was in San Francisco on a mission. I believe he picked up information there, but I lost track of him."

Soong turned his shoulders so that he could stare out the window for a minute. "I will tell you he went to the Washington, DC, area. Since then, he went to France to get more information. Do you know what his mission is?"

Tom rubbed his chin. "No, not exactly. Hoover has not given me much to work on since I've been assigned to the Chinese Communist spy network. There is just not much in the files. All he told me was that no Chinese spies have been arrested—which is why I was assigned to the case. The FBI wasn't getting any information. Since I've started, I've identified a Chinese restaurant in San Francisco. From my research, I know there's one in Los Angeles as well, and I would guess there's one here in New York, but I've yet to confirm my suspicions."

T. V. Soong nodded. "That's why I'm concerned. I believe part of his mission is to kill or capture me and Kung. The Communists have been after us since we escaped China. They want our money and assets—and our blood spilled." He paused for a moment, seeming to collect himself, then he continued. "According to my sources, Dr. Wang was personally selected by Kang Sheng to gather the materials to complete their nuclear program."

Tom's jaw dropped. He knew of their desires, but according to the FBI think-tank guys and the NSA people, they were at least five years away from being a nuclear power. "How do you know these things? I'm supposedly working with the most recent information, and we believe they are years away."

Soong gave a quick, tight smile. "Do you not think we still have sources in China? Please, Special Agent Warren. My information is very up-to-date. My sources are reliable, at the highest levels. I believe Kang has put out a sanction on me."

Tom nodded, understanding his concern. He pushed his business card toward him. "Please call me if you learn anything else."

With his new information in hand, Tom was ready to leave. He asked Mr. Soong to call him a cab.

Soong waved his hand. "My limousine driver will take you to Kung's residence. Remember, that's my sister's place, too."

Tom looked at Soong. "I was never here."

Soong nodded. "We know the FBI watches us periodically. Let me say today was a good day for you."

The drive up to the Kung residence in Locust Valley was beautiful with fall foliage lining the roadway. At Kung's front door, Tom was greeted by a servant. He was shown into a large living room filled with expensive artworks and a fabulous oriental rug, where he was announced to Ai-ling Soong, H.H. Kung's wife and T.V. Soong's oldest sibling. He'd never met her, as she was out of China when he snuck her husband out. After she greeted him and he sat down, the same servant brought tea in a silver set.

She apologized for her husband's delay in joining them, as he was on a business call. Tom and Ai-ling discussed her brother and her father and his Christian mission in China before World War II.

H. H. Kung slowly shuffled into the large living room. The former Minister of Industry and Commerce of Nationalist China had connections all over the world. He was very wealthy, but not as wealthy as his brother-in-law. He sat down opposite Tom without shaking hands. "I apologize for my tardiness. T. V. called while you were on the drive over. I wanted to get some up-to-date information. As T.V. told you, when Dr. Wang left San Francisco, he came to the East Coast—Virginia—and then flew out of Washington, DC, to France. Now, we believe he's gone to Japan."

"How could you possibly know this?" Tom let out a big sigh, then continued. "I can't believe he'd go to Japan. He hates the Japanese. If he steps foot on their soil, he's a marked man."

Ai-ling refilled Tom's teacup.

Kung laughed as he looked at his wife. "You see, Special Agent Warren, after you got me out of China, I went to Paris to take care of business. I stayed there for a while and made many friends there—to whom I'm still connected. Dr. Wang stole French nuclear secrets. Or, shall I say, he was given information on the French nuclear program stolen by the French Communist Party members. I assure you, my sources are good."

Tom started to get up.

Kung folded his hands together as he leaned forward. "Special Agent Warren, I assume you know that Dr. Wang's men killed the old Chinaman you are investigating in San Francisco. I've been told they also killed some people in a night café in Virginia."

Tom sat back down hard. "How do you know this?"

Kung ignored his remarks. "Dr. Wang came to the East Coast for a reason. Out of fear for my wife and my lives, we keep close contact with our community."

Tom pounded his thigh with his left hand.

The news he'd been given by the two men had been informative, but at the same time, devastating. The Nationalist Chinese network knew more about Dr. Wang's operation than he'd learned since he'd been assigned to break it up.

"Thank you for your time and information." Tom stood and bowed to the elderly man. "Would you be kind enough to call me a cab?"

Kung looked at his wife. "Do need to go anywhere, my dear?"

She shook her head.

Kung nodded at Tom. "My driver will take you back to the airport. It's the least I can do."

"Thank you." Tom said as Kung walked him to the front door. He turned and faced his friend. "Can we agree that my visit was off-the-record?"

Kung replied. "Why, of course. It was an assumption Ai-ling and I made from your first phone call. Soong and I know the FBI watch us, but you are different. You and Special Agent Adler hold a special place in our hearts. Our respect for you endures."

Tom bit his lip. "Good. Do you know anything about a Japanese lady by the name of Kikue Nakamura? She was murdered by Dr. Wang in San Francisco."

Kung shook his head. "Never heard of her."

Tom bid his goodbyes and walked to the limousine sitting in the driveway He was surprised that Kung and Soong had worked with Adler when they arrived in the United States. Then he refocused. *Will Hoover let me go to Paris without more information? I must find out exactly what files have been given to Dr. Wang in France.*

It was late night when Tom got off the plane and entered the far end of the main terminal heading for the cab line. His mind was focused on how to talk Hoover into letting him go to Paris. As he slipped into the normal hustle of an international airport, he heard a voice. "Tom, Tom."

He stopped and looked around as several passengers bumped into him. He didn't see anyone on his right. Then he looked to his left. There was an auburn-haired beauty with fair skin. *Could it be?* He looked closer as the woman waved at him again. *Oh, my God, it is. Judith Ray—or Judith Carter. The woman he'd fallen in love with when he was assigned to the Philippines.* He waved, then walked in her direction.

She ran up to him but stopped short. "Tom Warren! I never ever imagined seeing you again."

"Judy Carter. How are you?"

Judy glanced down at the ground for a brief second, then made eye contact again. "It's Judy Ray."

Tom was speechless, fumbling for words. He decided it was best not to go there. "So what are you doing here in San Francisco?"

"I'm coming back from visiting my parents in Oklahoma. I'm actually moving to San Francisco. Job transfer from the insurance company."

Tom was speechless, again. "Well, it's good to see you. What's it been?" He looked up in the air. Then said, "Since May 11, 1947."

Judy smiled at him. "Fantastic memory as ever, Tom. I didn't think you'd remember. But now I recall you have a photographic memory."

Tom wanted to stop and talk, but he was exhausted. "I'll walk with you to the baggage claim. I'm going to the cab line." He took a couple of steps, wondering what to say. "What's a trained nurse doing working for an insurance company?"

Judy ignored his question. "I never married William Carter. After I wrote you that letter, we had a big falling out, and we called off the wedding— temporarily, of course. But our relationship went downhill from there. We ended our relationship after a few months. I was too embarrassed to write you again and tell you what had happened." She seemed to force a shallow laugh. "I figured you had moved on to the next woman in your life."

Tom refused to take the bait. "Things got busy in the Philippines after that, and…." He shrugged.

They walked in silence down the steps to the baggage claim area. They stopped at the bottom of the stairs as Judy looked for the carousel assigned to her baggage.

Tom watched her.

Judy looked back at him. Her green eyes weren't as bright as he'd remembered. "Well, I guess this is goodbye."

Tom smiled. "Good to see you after all these years." He started out the door toward the cab line. He looked back. She was still standing there, looking in his direction. He walked back over. "Give me your address. I'll call you some time. If that's okay."

Judy's eyes grew large. "You mean you aren't married to some beauty queen and living in Boston?"

Tom laughed. "What's your phone number?"

"Let's test your photographic memory." She gave him the number.

Tom smiled and went out the door.

Dr. Wang stepped out of the elevator in the Central Investigation Division. He had a scheduled meeting with Kang Sheng. The heels of his shoes clicked on the floor as he moved toward the corner office on the lower level of the massive building. Dr. Wang knocked on the large wooden door. The muffled voice from the other side said, "Enter." He stepped inside and sat down opposite the head of the CID.

Kang Sheng sat up straight behind his metal desk. "I wanted to meet with you privately before we had our meeting with Zhou En-lai. While you were accomplishing your great mission, many things have happened here in Beijing."

Dr. Wang's expression didn't change.

Kang leaned over and turned on the small lamp on the end of his desk. "My star is falling here, yet again. There are many with long knives to take me out. Many want to change the direction of this division. Both Zhou and Mao are old and ill. When they are gone, so shall we be. The Politburo may find a way to throw me in prison. Or, they may even try to soft kill me." He looked at Dr. Wang and continued. "The success of your mission—our mission—will re-establish me at the ultimate head. Mao and Zhou are proud. But truth be known, I'm old, and this is likely my last big success. I'm spreading our net, if you will. I'm bringing in another agent from the police department to be placed under our wing—Yu Qiangsheng."

Dr. Wang jutted his jaw. "Your stepson? I thought you were on the outs— or, at least, he wanted nothing to do with you and a few others?"

Kang leaned forward in his chair. "All you say is true. Yet, he knows what's best for his career. He has all the tools necessary to be a great spy and a handler. I want you to handle him, train him."

Dr. Wang wiped his mouth with his right hand, then dropped it down hard on his leg. "I have as many foreign agents as I can handle. You are asking much of me. Plus, he is not one of my favorites."

Kang shook his head. "Use him inside China to spy on foreigners then. But he is not ready for his first assignment. The man is talented—we need him. Wang, *Wang*, we are getting old, even you are now in your fifties. We must start to train our own replacements so they know the ways."

Dr. Wang stared at his boss. *I sure as hell am not getting old.* "Okay. As you say, so shall I do."

Kang got up from his desk and started to the door without another word.

Dr. Wang followed him out the door. The two men walked in silence toward their waiting car. There were two military officers waiting outside to drive them to their meeting with Zhou.

Dr. Wang opened the door for Kang. They walked into Zhou's office, who was seated at his desk with two files on either side of the otherwise neat desk. His arms were folded over the pad of paper. Zhou pointed to the two chairs in front of his desk. As soon as they had taken their seats, Zhou looked directly at Dr. Wang. "On your first leg of the mission, you picked up a file from Los Alamos regarding the United States weapons' program." Then he pulled up the file on his left. "Dr. Wang, this is the materials you brought back from France. It was critical information on their nuclear program—missing information our scientists needed." Zhou calmly placed the file back on the table.

Kang looked at Dr. Wang and nodded.

Zhou looked at Kang. "You know how the Japanese think they are superior to us? Well, Dr. Wang—" He picked up the file on the right and waved it. "This file here contains rocket information from the Japanese program. The world has underestimated us."

Kang and Dr. Wang sat up straight in their chairs.

Zhou leaned back, still focused on both men. "Kang Sheng, Dr. Wang, your actions on behalf of the People's Republic has put us on the cusp of becoming a nuclear power. Soon, the United States and the Soviet Union will have to respect us when we step to the negotiating table."

Zhou reached behind his desk and pulled out a bottle of Red Star Erguotou liquor and three crystal glasses. He poured two fingers of clear liquid in each glass. He handed each of them a glass, then stood up with his own held out. When they clicked glasses, they said, "To Chairman Mao," in unison.

After placing their empty glasses back on the desk, Zhou looked directly at Dr. Wang. "Did you get the Japanese spy's black book?"

Dr. Wang smiled a toothy smile. "Of course. Not only do we know who Kikue Nakamura was spying on, but we have the names of the San Francisco dignitaries with whom she was having sex. The list of influential people is significant. Some were definitely our people. Plus, we may be able to blackmail some to gain more valuable information."

Zhou slowly walked back around and sat down at his desk. "Now, Dr. Wang, let's talk about what almost went wrong on your mission." Zhou maintained a laser focus on Dr. Wang and continued, "When you were in San Francisco, you made some decisions which put the mission in jeopardy before completing your first pass. You personally killed the Japanese spy. Why? You could have sanctioned the hit. Then you taunted FBI Special Agent Thomas Warren. Why? You let your emotions interfere with your focus on the mission. If you had failed your mission, you'd be dead right now. Not prison, dead."

Zhou maintained his stare at Dr. Wang for another moment. "Plus, you got sloppy. The people you had killed have been discovered. You couldn't even hide the bodies."

Dr. Wang was boiling inside. He had to restore his family's pride and wealth. But it was best not to respond. "I made a mistake in judgement."

Zhou nodded. "The CIA and the FBI have not been able to do anything to our network, but because of your poor judgement, you could have jeopardized our networks in San Francisco, Los Angeles, and maybe even Ottawa. I'm restricting your movement to mainland China. In time, I may allow you back into Hong Kong to communicate with your spies. But you cannot go into Hong Kong and jeopardize our network. You are not the only one who handles information dropped off in that city."

Zhou shifted his gaze to Kang. "Tighten up your network, Kang Sheng. Take no more risks until we have successfully detonated our nuclear device. Is that understood?"

Before anyone answered, Zhou stood, giving Dr. Wang and Kang the signal that their meeting was over.

Dr. Wang was seething. He'd just pulled off the biggest spy ring coup in the history of his country—and he'd gotten his wings clipped.

CHAPTER NINE

January 14, 1964
Paris

Tom's flight taxied up to the gangway at the Paris airport. FBI Director J. Edgar Hoover repeated attempts to get an appointment with someone with the authority to discuss the theft of nuclear secrets had been stonewalled. Finally, he was able to make arrangements with several diplomats from the Ministry of Europe and Foreign Affairs. Now, two days later, Tom was deplaning to meet with those French diplomats before flying on to Tokyo the very next day. To prepare, he'd taken a crash course in French while Hoover was making the arrangements—although he still hoped to conduct his dinner meeting in English with a just a little French thrown in. Most French diplomats spoke excellent English—it just depended on their attitude, whether or not his dinner partner would admit it. Tom had slept a bit on the flight across the Atlantic, but he spent more time reading a couple of books in French to see how well he comprehended the language. He hoped the diplomat didn't talk too fast if they conversed in French.

Tom anticipated a driver who would meet him at the airport and take him to his hotel near the French government buildings so he could freshen up prior to his meeting with diplomats at the Ministry of Europe and Foreign Affairs. He was an expert in Asia, but he was out of his league in Europe. He stepped into the gate area.

A chauffeur stood holding a sign displaying *Warren*. Tom and the chauffeur exchanged a polite greeting, then the driver pointed him in the direction of baggage claim.

Within a few minutes, Tom was escorted to a side door at the Ministry of Europe and Foreign Affairs. He was hustled into a small conference room and instructed to wait. He sat there so long he almost fell asleep, suffering from boredom and jet-lag. Finally, two Frenchmen walked into the room and closed the door behind them. One of the men carried a special diplomatic case. "Monsieur Warren, we are painfully aware of the problems within our country regarding the French Communist Party assisting other communist countries."

Tom attempted to spin his role and be a diplomat to the best of his ability. "Which is why I'm here. We believe a master spy handler from Red China arranged for the theft of information regarding your country's nuclear program. I'm here to learn what information he was able to acquire and if this information was capable of accelerating their fledgling nuclear program."

The first diplomat continued. "*Oui, oui*, we are painfully aware of this and, shall we say, it is quite embarrassing for us. We certainly don't want this information to be released to the French public. Of course, you understand."

Tom had reasoned all along this was the reason Hoover had difficulty setting up the appointment with the French. They didn't want to have to answer to the French Press. Knowing Hoover, he probably attacked them, showing his superiority in detective work, and the French probably didn't appreciate Hoover's tack—or lack thereof. They already had a frosty relationship with the United States over several other diplomatic issues. So, Tom could only respond, "But of course."

The diplomat pushed the secured case toward Tom. "Here are copies of all the information we believe the Chinese stole. It is encoded so only your scientists at Los Alamos will be able to unlock these files. They will be able to send their report on to Director Hoover."

The diplomat pointed to the other individual in the conference room. "Monsieur Bernard Boursicot will meet you for dinner this evening. Perhaps show you around Paris."

"I need to grab a few hours of sleep. Then I'll be ready for dinner," Tom replied with a big yawn.

With that, the diplomat, who still hadn't given his name, just walked out of the conference room, leaving Boursicot and Warren awkwardly staring at each other.

Tom decided to speak. "Can you arrange a ride for me back to my hotel?" He looked down at his watch and continued. "Then have your driver pick me up at the front in about three hours?"

Boursicot nodded and bid him goodbye.

Tom picked up the diplomatic case, then walked outside the conference room door to find the same chauffeur waiting for him. It had been one of the strangest meetings he'd ever been to. These men made Hoover and the second in command at the FBI, Clyde Tolson, seem downright gregarious.

While Tom waited in the hotel lobby for the chauffeur to pick him up, he pulled out his copy of the *Washington Post*, opened the front page. and began to read. Just then the chauffeur walked in and motioned him to come to the car. He slipped the newspaper under his arm and walked to the car. He refocused on his meeting.

Tom glanced around at the picturesque scenery as they traversed the streets of Paris on his ride to wherever they were headed.

Director Hoover had believed he'd made arrangements for Tom to go and discuss the spying issue with the Ministry of Europe and Foreign affairs, but after maybe the briefest meeting he'd ever been a part of, he was being "wined and dined" in a remote plush restaurant on the edge of Paris. To his surprise, the chauffeur got out and escorted him in to meet Bernard Boursicot yet again.

Tom glanced around the small dining area. The restaurant was dimly lit but elegant. Soft classical French music lowly played in the background. Almost immediately after the introduction, the chauffeur turned and walked out of the restaurant.

As quickly as Tom sat down and explained that French was not one of his strong languages, Boursicot waved for the waiter to come to their table.

The two ate dinner with small talk over the meeting earlier today and some of the finer things of Paris. Tom was able to get a few bits of Boursicot's background—he was a very young man—only twenty years old—and had led an accountant's stereotypically boring life. When Boursicot asked about Tom's background, Tom provided as little information as possible. He couldn't tell if he was trying to get information for the ministry or for himself. Either way, Tom wanted to be vague.

After the waiter took away their dinner dishes, Boursicot leaned toward Tom. "The reason the Ministry wanted me to meet with you privately is because I was just assigned to the Beijing Embassy and I'm due to report soon. I'm fluent in Mandarin, and I will oversee all financial transactions." He pulled his napkin off his lap. "I may be a little more willing to help the United States than most of the French people."

That was a stretch. The French government wouldn't send a twenty-year-old to oversee all financial transactions, but since he was a little boastful, it was a good opening to dig deeper. "So, do you know what the Chinese were able to steal from your nuclear program?"

"They got almost everything. I wasn't supposed to know, but I overheard our lead scientist talking to the minister. He, the minister, was very upset. He repeated over and over to the scientist, 'How could you let this happen?'" Boursicot swirled the white wine in his glass and tipped it up for another drink. "'What happened to our security?' They stopped talking and went into his office. But I stepped closer to the door. The minister asked the scientist who had access to those files if he'd figured out who gave this information away. Then someone came down the hallway. I had to leave, so as not to be discovered."

Tom had learned more from Boursicot at his dinner meeting than he had at the Ministry Office.

As Boursicot finished his wine, he looked up with a slightly raised eyebrow. "Perhaps I can be of some assistance to you in my new capacity at the embassy." Then he smiled as he turned up his empty wine glass.

Tom was pleased with the offer, but as he read his smile, he realized he probably wanted to be paid to spy on the Chinese. Tom didn't have the authority to offer anything—plus, there was something about Boursicot that made him uncomfortable. Tom replied with a smile to keep him in the game. "I will discuss this with Director Hoover—let him know of your willingness to assist us. You will have to discreetly get me your contact information once in Beijing."

The dinner meeting then came to a quick end, which was fine with Tom. He wanted to get to bed and be ready to fly to Japan the next day.

Two days later

FBI Agent Thomas Warren couldn't believe the difference between the Japanese government and the French government. Whereas he felt like he was pulling teeth from the French government to get what they suspected was the information stolen by Dr. Wang, the Japanese government went out of their way to cooperate. Foreign Minister Shiina conducted a proper meeting with all his vice ministers present. They provided Warren with a complete set of files of all rocket propulsion data stolen from their country. He believed it helped that he spoke to them in the most common Japanese dialects, Tokyo-ben. When they asked Warren to provide the name of the Chinese spy ring involved, he had strict orders from FBI Director Hoover not to divulge any information. This put him in a precarious position, as he questioned those orders. He had learned much from them, and now was not able to reciprocate. He was the one sitting there losing face with the Japanese. Tom looked around the table. "Director Hoover has promised me the United States will provide a full detailed report as soon as the scientists at Los Alamos complete their analysis." The one thing Tom did to save what little was left with his dignity was to tell them, "The French believe the spy ring received all of their nuclear weapons program from a member of the French Communist Party. While I'm unaware of the details of what was stolen, I believe what they acquired has clearly accelerated the Chinese nuclear weapons program."

This caused Minister Shiina to exchange glances around the table at all the other vice ministers, then back at Tom. "This is most concerning. The Chinese developing a nuclear weapon puts our country at grave risk."

Tom folded his hands on top of the conference table. "Everybody on the Pacific Rim would be at greater risk."

As he picked up the documents and shuffled them into his briefcase, he decided to take a chance. "I'm investigating a murder back in San Francisco— a Japanese citizen by the name of Kikue Nakamura. Do any of you know where I can get some information on this victim?"

The room turned ice cold. No one changed his expression nor gave any indication he knew anything about her. Tom was a trained interrogator, and sometimes you learned things in people's eyes without them saying a word. They all shook their collective heads, but he could tell her name was familiar. *Did Nakamura have a role in the Japanese government?*

"Nakamura is a common name in Japan," Minister Shiina finally said. "Perhaps if you could get us your file, we might be able to get some public records on her."

Tom felt he had touched on a subject that might be very dicey. "When I return to the States, I'll get permission from Director Hoover to send over a copy of my file. Thank you."

He returned to his hotel room for the evening. No one was taking him to dinner, so he ate at the hotel restaurant, and then returned to his room.

He started reading the "manifesto" Dr. Wang had given him to "help regain memory of their history in the Philippines and China." *Dr. Wang was out of his mind. His own philosophy was a riddle. On one hand, the man was so committed to the communist cause. Yet, on the other hand, he was committed to recapturing his family's treasures. The man was a narcissist bordering on psychotic.* One detail stood out—the reason he hated the Japanese was very clear. Japanese soldiers held his face and made him watch the other soldiers repeatedly rape his older sister and, to a lesser extent, his mother, in their home in NanJing in the siege in 1938. When the soldiers were done, they bayoneted them both in their genitals.

Tom realized he too would want revenge. He had a mother and a sister, and if that were done to them, it would be his goal in life to get the perpetrators. Until they were dead, hate would burn his soul. It now made sense—in a warped sort of way—why he'd let his henchmen take turns after he'd raped Japanese females.

Tom wanted to find members of the World War II Japanese military staff. To understand Dr. Wang better, he must find out about the Rape of NanJing and more about the stolen treasures. He'd been confronted in the Philippines by Japanese Yakuza when they were there recovering gold. Tomorrow, he was going to endeavor to answer more questions before his plane left to fly back to the United States. He looked at his watch. Hoover was in his office. Time to check in.

The next morning, Tom was up early, his sleep cycle messed up from his travels. He was so close to Red China, but he couldn't pursue Dr. Wang. Sitting at the tiny desk in his room, he set goals for his last day in Japan. His first goal was to learn what he could about Dr. Wang's other enemies, the Japanese soldiers. Do some research, find someone in the military who could tell him what really happened in NanJing. Then, second, see if he could learn more about the murdered Japanese woman, Kikue Nakamura. His second goal was the easiest to solve—just go find out where birth records were kept.

At the Hall of Records, he quickly learned that foreigners couldn't access birth records—and neither could many Japanese. In many ways, this was still a closed society, like it had been prior to World War I. Despite being in the deceased's home country, he couldn't gain any solid information.

Tom had one hope on learning about NanJing—Prince Takeda—or General Takeda—was the president of the Japan Olympic Committee. Takeda had answered directly to his cousin, Hirohito. If he went by there, maybe he could make contact. He got in a cab to take him to the headquarters. Upon arriving, he walked up to the security desk. "I'm FBI Special Agent Thomas P. Warren." He reached in his sport coat pocket and held out his FBI badge. "I would like to meet with General Takeda."

The Japanese chief of security studied the badge, then said, "I don't see your name on General Takeda's appointment schedule. What is the matter of your business?"

Tom lied, as he put away his credentials. "I'm working security with the U.S. Olympic team and was told to speak with him and only him."

"You are not part of the security team we have been working with." The man frowned as he closely examined Tom's FBI credentials.

"You are working with one security team. I'm assigned to another area regarding a high priority matter where we just discovered a new threat." Tom took an open stance as he placed his hands on both hips. "Look, the games are several months away. This needs your boss's immediate attention. If you won't cooperate, let me speak to your superiors."

The security officer stared at Tom. "General Takeda is not in the building at the moment. I will call a member of his staff to meet with you."

At first, Tom thought it was a bad idea, but quickly changed his mind and agreed.

The chief of security nodded at another officer at the desk, who picked up the phone and placed a call. When he hung up the phone, he turned to Tom. "Someone from Takeda's office will be right down to get you."

Tom stood as far away from the chief of security as he could. His bluff had worked, and now the less contact he made, the better.

Within a few minutes, a beautiful Japanese woman came down to take him upstairs. "Hello, Special Agent Warren, I'm Hada Miyoko. I'm an assistant to Prince Takeda. Follow me, please."

Tom smiled as he extended his hand, showing his FBI badge.

She read it out loud, "FBI Special Agent Thomas Warren." She turned and walked away.

Then he got in step with the young woman. Neither of them spoke until they arrived at her desk in a large office with many other desks, yet she was the only one there at the moment. She pointed to a chair opposite her and gracefully slipped around to the other side and sat. "So, Special Agent Warren, what may I help you with?"

Tom stared directly at the young Japanese woman. "I'm here to discuss the security of the U.S. Olympic Track and Field team. I was hoping to brief a just-discovered concern that has only in the last few days crossed the FBI's radar."

The young woman sat back straight in her chair and pouted her lips. "Why hasn't a call been placed first?"

"That is why I'm here. Nothing was to be written down and no phone calls. Those were my orders. Do you have a way to contact Mr. Takeda?"

She replied, "No, he was called out of the office several hours ago. I don't know when he is due back."

Tom jutted his jaw. "Okay, I will come back when Takeda returns." He stood, then sat back down. Maybe he could learn more. "So, how did you get this job? It must be fun working on the Olympics."

Miyoko smiled. "My family and the Takeda family go way back. My father served on his staff during World War II."

Tom couldn't believe his luck. "Did he travel with Takeda?"

"Yes, he traveled all over Southeast Asia. It kept him out of the combat side of the war."

Tom leaned forward. "Would your father talk to me about that? I'm fascinated with the history of World War II."

Miyoko drew a deep breath. "My father has always been very secretive about his role in his service with General Takeda."

Tom thought for a moment. "Okay. That's fine. I was just hoping. No problem." He pulled out one of his FBI business cards and wrote his hotel information on the back. "Would you call me a cab and escort me out, please?"

Miyoko smiled, made the call for his transportation, then stood. Tom handed her the card as they walked toward the front entrance.

When he got into the cab, he noticed it was the same cabbie who had taken him to this building. *What are the odds? Same cabbie in the city the size of Tokyo? The Foreign Affairs people must be having me watched. Fine.* Tom said nothing in the cab ride back to the hotel.

After dinner, Tom got up from his table and walked toward the elevator. The clerk at the front desk called out to him. "There is a message here for you, Mr. Warren."

Tom thanked the desk clerk, accepted the note, and walked over to a couch and sat. *It must be from Takeda, since he never called me back today.* He pulled out the note, it read:

> *You are being watched, but I need to meet with you before you leave the country. I'll be out in the hotel parking lot for an hour waiting if you really want to know about my father.*
> *Miyoko*

Tom looked at the time on the note, then at his watch. She should still be there. He stuffed the note back in his coat pocket. *Unfortunately, I can't carry a gun in Japan. Am I walking into a trap?* Within a moment, he was outside in the parking lot looking around. *What am I looking for?* Finally, a hand popped out of a car window and waved. As he moved cautiously in that direction, he checked to make sure it was Miyoko, while continuing to look around to see if he were walking into a trap.

"I'm sorry to meet you this way, but I'm concerned for you—and me."

"I believe you," Tom replied. Miyoko was gorgeous in a classic Japanese way.

Miyoko bit her lip. "I showed Takeda your business card. He shouted at me. He knew who you were and was told by the Foreign Minister to not meet with or talk with you. Then I went home and talked to my dad. He got scared."

Tom rubbed his chin. "Why was he scared?"

Miyoko replied. "What I didn't tell you today—out of fear that our conversation was being recorded—is that anytime they think my dad has talked or is about to talk, he first gets a visit from a government official. Then, within a couple of days, he is visited by a member of the Yakuza. He said the Japanese government doesn't want anyone to learn anything about its operation during World War II. They are 'very convincing' about keeping people from talking, if you get my drift."

79

Tom nodded. He couldn't take his eyes off the woman. Yet, he still wasn't sure he wasn't being set up.

Miyoko sat for a minute. "I hate the Japanese government and the Yakuza and what they have done to my dad. I didn't know anything about you. But after what Takeda said and I saw how scared my father got when I told him what had happened, I wanted to come and talk to you."

Tom thought for a minute. From his days in the Philippines, he knew Kodama Yoshio once was part of the gold burial operation and now was the leader of the biggest Yakuza operation in Japan. It was likely his henchmen assaulting her dad. "Miyoko, thank you for letting me know."

"There is no security issue is there?" she blurted. "You're here for another reason."

Tom shook his head and reached for the car door.

Miyoko grabbed his arm. "I want to help. Please let me help you."

He'd been offered a possible break in his research, but he was putting a young Japanese woman at grave risk. It was tempting, but not responsible. "Again, thank you very much for your offer, but it is unacceptable. It is much too risky for you."

Miyoko still held his arm. She looked into his eyes and pleaded, "At least tell me what you are really doing here."

"Can't. Top secret. This is my main assignment. But I'm trying to learn about what went on at NanJing. I'm trying to find out about General Nakajima Kesago and General Matsui Iwama. The man I'm chasing is a man who wrote about those two generals. Plus, Takeda. Few people in the world know the terrible things that went on in NanJing." Tom had gotten weak. Was it the girl's looks, or could she be trusted? Tom composed himself. "But the last thing you need is the Yakuza watching you. It's just too risky."

Miyoko pushed another piece of paper in his hands. "This is my home address and phone. If you change your mind, call me. I'm doing this to help my father. I think he knows many things that could help you."

What makes her think her father will tell me or her anything? As Tom got out of the car, he glanced back at the beautiful young woman. *Had he just walked away from his first real lead to get into the head of Dr. Wang?*

CHAPTER TEN

Thursday January 23, 1964
FBI Headquarters
San Francisco

Tom leaned back in his chair, tossing his football up in the air then catching it. Hoover had pressed him to crack the Chinese spy network, constantly reminding him that he'd been in San Francisco for three months, yet still no arrests and not even a lead to follow. Hoover agreed to assign more agents to help generate leads, freeing Tom and Marty to focus on Dr. Wang, but so far, it was all for not.

Marty Corley sat at his desk reviewing his file on Chinese restaurants in Chinatown. His desk phone rang, and he picked it up.

Tom's desk phone rang. He grabbed it. "Special Agent Warren."

The voice on the other end said, "Special Agent Warren, Michelle Galloway. I have some not-so-good news for you."

Tom sat up straight in his chair. "Go ahead."

"The Virginia Highway Patrol sent over a file this morning. They had completed an investigation into a double murder at the little café outside of Petersburg, Virginia. It does appear that you were right—the murders were exactly like you said. The two bodies had been cut up and disposed of in the dumpster. They also said there was a boat that was burnt with a body in it. We followed up on your lead that Dr. Wang flew out on a private plane out of Baltimore Washington airport. It was confirmed."

Tom drummed his fingers on his desktop. "No one checked out the APB?"

"No, according to the Maryland Highway Patrolman investigator. They flashed their passports in front of the man on duty real early that morning. He recognized them after the fact."

While Tom was still talking to Michelle, Marty hung up his phone, stood, and yelled, "Got something!"

Tom held one finger up in the air. "Thanks, Galloway. Great work. Tell Hoover to give you a raise."

"Hey, I'm just happy to have a job at this point." Michelle laughed.

Marty stood beside Tom's desk as he finished his phone conversation. "Galloway, you and Keeton, take care of yourselves." Then he hung up the receiver. *How did Dr. Wang get to the airport?*

Marty grabbed Tom's football and mocked the Heisman pose. "You're not going to believe this. I just got a phone call from that girl in Chinatown who threw the dish at you. Remember?"

Tom jumped up, snatched the football from Corley, then ran his fingers through his hair. "Marty, yes. Yes, I remember. Why?" Before Marty could answer, he detailed what he had just learned. "That bastard Dr. Wang left a trail of murders on the East Coast before he flew to France." Tom pointed with the football at Marty. "We have got to crack this network."

"Let's go." Marty threw his hands in the air. "Did you hear me? We have someone who wants to talk."

"I said that someone there knew something about Dr. Wang." Tom raised an eyebrow as he followed Marty out the door.

As they waited for the elevator, Tom asked, "You got a girlfriend out here yet?"

"How could I do that, as busy as we have been? I've been here a year and still haven't unpacked some boxes."

As they drove, they went past the turn off to Chinatown. Tom slapped Marty's arm. "Hey, you missed the turn."

Marty took one hand off the steering wheel. "Are you crazy? Do you really think this girl is going to meet us at the restaurant?"

Tom shrugged, then looked back out the window.

A few minutes later, Marty turned toward downtown San Francisco. They went into the shopping district. Marty pulled up to the intersection, then parked the car in front of a little grocery store. Marty looked at Tom. "I have to give my signal." He exited the car.

Marty went into the store. Within a minute, he walked back out, put a piece of bubble gum in his mouth, chewed, and blew a bubble. He walked a few steps up the street, then back down before returning to the car. Within seconds, a beautiful, slightly built, twenty-something Chinese girl with a San Francisco Giants baseball cap pulled down low over her face came up and tapped on the window of their car. Marty motioned for her to get in the backseat. She opened the back door and slipped in.

"Please drive," she said quietly as she flipped her long, coal black hair away from her face. "I don't want to be seen, if possible."

As Marty put the car in drive and pulled away from the curb, Tom turned around. "You want to talk about Dr. Wang? What's your name?"

In a barely audible voice, she said, "I'm Shou Li Cao. I worked at that restaurant for three months when you came in there. I had just come to America a few weeks before. I was new and didn't know anyone too well. Everyone in there was very quiet about their personal lives up to that point. I was looked upon as an outsider. I was not trusted. But after I threw that dish at you, everything changed. I was more openly accepted."

Tom looked at Marty. "Okay, we are looking for information on Dr. Wang and his spy network. Can you provide us with any information?"

Still in a low voice, she said, "My father was arrested by the Chinese government, and we think he was put in jail. We don't even know why. We tried to find out, but the Communist government wouldn't tell us anything. After that, his brother came to us and told us to get out of the country anyway possible. My mother and I escaped Beijing by going out through Zhangzhou."

Tom nodded. "I'm sorry you went through that, but how does that help us with the spy network?"

Shou looked out the window for almost a full block. "Yes, I can help. There was a man who came into the restaurant for a meal a few days before you and your partner. I didn't know his name until you just mentioned him. It was the only time I ever saw him. I don't know whether or not it was related, but there was an older lady who was a cook there. Shortly after you two came in, she suddenly moved back to China."

Tom frowned at Marty, then glanced back at Shou. "So, how exactly do you plan to help us? If you don't have any information?"

Shou bit her lower lip. "I want to work undercover for you. I'll go into wherever you need me to help. I'll even go back into China."

Tom tapped Marty on the shoulder. "Let's take her back."

Marty let out a big huff of breath, then turned the car around.

She leaned up. "Please, you have been looking for help, and I'm offering? I'll do it. Train me."

Tom glared at her. "It is personal with you, and you are too inexperienced. You are just doing this because of your father." *Great, first, it was a young Japanese woman, now a young Chinese woman trying to help me. Just what I need.*

"I'm smart! I'm not scared, like you." She paused for a second. "Plus, I can go places you couldn't possibly go. I can set things up for you and your partner. Please, let me help you."

Marty pulled in to where they had picked up the woman. Tom turned around and stared at her.

She grabbed the door handle to get out. "You FBI guys are making a huge mistake. You haven't accomplished anything but exposing me to get caught."

Tom raised his left hand. "Wait. Give me your phone number. Let me think about it."

Shou pounded the back of the car seat of the Ford Galaxy. "*No way*. I can't trust you. If it falls into the wrong hands, I'm in, as you Americans say, 'deep shit.' I'll contact you in a couple of days. Now, I've got to get out of here before I'm seen."

After she was out of the car, Marty looked at Tom. "If you don't use her because it's personal to her, you are a hypocrite."

"What do you mean, *hypocrite*?" Tom's nostrils flared.

"It's personal between you and Dr. Wang. So, what if it is about her wanting to do this because of her father? She's right. You have just been offered a big break, and you're walking away." Marty grunted. "We have to do something about this Chinese spy network. This is about National Security."

Tom was back at his desk again, tossing up the football and thinking. Marty's desk phone rang. He picked it up. As he listened, he put his hand over the end and whistled for Tom to come over. Tom laid down the football and walked over. Marty was writing while the receiver was squeezed between his shoulder and his ear. Tom looked at what he was writing. *Son of a Bitch. They found Jared Samuel's body.*

When Marty hung up the phone, he said, "That was Detective Lee. Samuel's body was found down at a very isolated part of the beach that looks out toward San Pedro Rock. Suicide. Bullet to the head, gun still in his hand. Been dead for a couple of weeks."

Tom walked over to the window and looked out. "A couple of weeks. This doesn't make any sense at all. How do they know he'd been there that long?"

Marty replied. "Doesn't make sense to me either... been there that long, no one found him?"

Tom turned around. "Marty, we'll have to wait on the coroner's report. See if we can make heads or tails out of this. See if it ties in."

Marty rubbed his chin. "That area is fairly open. I don't understand how it took so long to find the body."

"Let's see if his suitcase shows up." Tom walked back to his desk and grabbed his football and acted like he was about to make a pass.

Marty just stared at Tom as though in deep thought.

Tom sat down and thought about everything in Samuel's personnel file. *Dr. Wang's henchmen didn't kill the doorman. Did he still sanction the hit? His family was expecting him to come back home in the center of the country and he turns up dead at San Pedro Rock, which is way to the south of San Francisco. This must have been staged. Been in the apartment and everything seemed as though he was leaving. So, would you pack a suitcase then drive south of the city to commit suicide? Or was he murdered?*

Special Agent in Charge Adler stepped out of his office. "Warren and Corley, in my office, immediately!"

Tom looked and Marty as they double-timed it into Adler's office. Tom seated himself across from Gerald Adler. "What's up?"

The boss picked up his phone, then started dialing. "Hoover wants to talk to all of us."

Tom patted Marty on the shoulder. "It will be all right. Don't worry."

Corley scowled at Tom.

Adler said, "Director Hoover. I have Warren and Corley both in my office now, sir." He nodded as he listened. "Yes, sir, I'll put you on speaker." He pushed down the button.

"Adler, I wanted Warren and Corley to hear this. Yesterday, I mailed to your office the full report from the French government about what was stolen from them and the analysis of the scientists at Los Alamos. But this morning, the Japanese Foreign Minister Shiina called to inform me that their sources inside the Japanese Communist Party said the Chinese will be detonating a nuclear bomb very soon." There was a long pause, then Hoover continued. "Warren, you and Corley better pick it up on this spy network, unless you want to be washing cars here at headquarters." The line went dead.

Tom frowned at Adler. "We are working as fast as we can."

Tom looked at his watch. Almost seven p.m. Time to go home. He got up from his desk, picked up his football, and looked at it for a minute. He looked at the tattooed leather—MVP of the University of Arizona football team. *I wonder what Pete Maston is doing?* Pete was his best friend in college. He hadn't thought about him in years. Last time they talked, several years ago, Pete was working in India. He'd been in the University of Arizona International Business School, one of the top two international business programs in the country. Tom smiled. Pete had made his second million the last time they had talked.

As he was reliving old times in his mind, he rubbed his cheek with the back of his hand, then picked up the phone and dialed Judith Ray's phone number. "Hello, Judy, this is Tom. Would you like to go out to dinner sometime?"

"Why, Tom, are you asking me out on a date?"

"Well, call it what you will." Tom wondered the same thing himself. "I thought we should at least catch up with each other."

"Of course, I will let you buy me dinner. How about Friday night? Your choice of restaurants?" Judy replied.

"Pick you up at seven?" Tom was still wondering what he was getting himself into. The woman who had walked away from him over fifteen years ago. Was he starting something all over again? It had been so long since he'd been on a date, he wasn't sure, but he was looking forward to getting dressed up and going out on the town. *Friday and Saturday nights in Tucson with his old friend Pete Maston, their choice of women. Those nights were truly exciting, particularly during the off season. The choice of hot chicks on both arms, he and Pete could tear up the campus bars drinking to all hours. Then the choice of which ones to take home. That was the last time he could remember the dating scene.*

"Did I just hear you call someone for a date? I can't believe my ears! Does she have a girlfriend?" Marty shouted across the operation room.

"Yes, to the date. Can't believe it either. I have no idea about her friends," Tom replied as he held his football.

Beijing

Yu Qiangsheng walked in step with Kang Sheng down the hallway to their meeting. The first day on the job, and he hadn't even sat down. The minute he entered the building, he was met by Kang Sheng, who handed him his security badge and a Czech CZ-52 handgun, one of the finest produced in the Communist Block. After that, Kang waved for him to follow. As they descended the stairwell to the lower level of the Central Intelligence Division, Kang looked at his watch. "I'm throwing you into the middle of this right away. Dr. Wang—which is how you will refer to him—is one of the top spy handlers." Kang walked up to a solid wood door and knocked.

The door opened. On the other side was a man in a fine gray suit, his gray hair pulled behind his head in a ponytail. Without saying a word, the well-dressed man pointed toward two wooden chairs on the opposite side of his desk. Once Kang and Yu were seated, he walked around to the other side and sat down. Kang started the meeting. "Yu, meet Dr. Wang, his code name. He will show you the ropes on your new assignment."

Kang pointed at Yu. "Dr. Wang, this is your new protégé, Yu Qiangsheng. As I've told you, I've known his mother and father since before he was born. I've watched his career as a police officer. He is the best I've ever seen. The man has keen insight. I'm not saying this because I've known his family. We need to train him our way, the way of the old guard."

"Yu Qiangsheng. You will undergo training on surveillance techniques to observe our citizens, document their activities. Then, if they are to be brought in for questioning, you will be taught interrogation techniques that will get the answers you seek. The time you will spend in this tutelage will depend directly on how fast you process and can implement them." Dr. Wang folded his hands on top of his desk. "Also, when you show up to work tomorrow, have short-cropped hair and be clean shaved. Get rid of that damn mustache. You must look intimidating in your new assignment."

Yu nodded. He believed he was already one of the best at interrogation, but he was always willing to learn.

Dr. Wang looked at Kang. "I'm ready to begin, Kang. A CID agent brought in a dissident last night. I was waiting until this morning to start my interrogation. I will take Yu with me, now."

Yu nodded. He followed behind Dr. Wang. At the end of the hallway, two men waited. Dr. Wang nodded at them. One opened the door, while the other man entered the room first. Yu wondered who these men were. There was a single wooden chair in the middle of the room and a frail, elderly Chinese man sat there with his head down. The gray room was dimly lit by a single, low-wattage bulb.

Dr. Wang walked behind the old man, who still didn't look up. He pointed at Yu to stand on the other side, then at the two men to go stand in each corner. He leaned over to the old Chinaman's right ear. "Chairman Mao sent me to talk with you. Your neighbor told us you do not like Chairman Mao. Is this true?"

The old Chinese man raised his head slowly and made eye contact with Yu. "Who are you?"

Dr. Wang grabbed the old man's face and leaned over his left ear. "It matters not who he is. It is I you should be concerned with. I am Dr. Wang."

The old Chinaman's eyes grew large. "I will tell you exactly what happened. Two government men came and took all my crops in the fall, leaving me nothing to barter or eat. Please believe me, all I did was tell my neighbor what happened. Honestly, I didn't say anything bad about Mao."

Yu saw the stress in the old man's eyes. From his expressions and his willingness to talk, it seemed pretty obvious he knew who Dr. Wang was.

Dr. Wang rested his hands on both the old Chinaman's shoulders, then looked at Yu, then to the larger Chinese man. "Chung, remind him of how we treat anyone who speaks ill of Chairman Mao."

Chung walked over to the old man and kicked him hard in the stomach. Yu glanced around at each man in the room.

The old Chinese man's chair rocked back, only to be caught by Dr. Wang. The man spit out some blood. It drooled off his chin and hung in his beard.

Then Dr. Wang nodded at the smaller man. "Wu, remind the man how we treat anyone who speaks ill of Chairman Mao."

Wu walked over, grabbed the man's chin, raised it up with his left hand, then threw a right-handed roundhouse punch as hard as he could to the side of the old man's jaw, knocking him off the chair and onto the ground.

Yu looked down at the old man. Blood slowly ran out of his mouth. He was out cold.

Dr. Wang pointed to Wu. "Take him to the work camp west of the city." Dr. Wang looked at Yu then walked out of the room.

Yu followed him. He'd learned one thing from these interrogation techniques—fear could be very persuasive.

Friday January 24, 1964

The yellow cab pulled up in front of the apartment building. Tom's heart felt as though it would beat out of his chest, and his palms were sweaty. He took a deep breath as he exited the cab. "Wait on me. I'll be back down in a moment."

The cabbie nodded. "You got it, mac."

Tom shook his head as he walked to the front door. He stood at the bottom of the steps and looked up as Judy came down the stairs. He had a flashback to Manila, the day World War II ended, the first time he'd seen her riding on the front of the Jeep with her flowing auburn hair. Then he thought of them on the picnic, telling his partners, Snake and Ricky, to get lost. "Hey, you look great."

"Thanks. Where are we going?" Judy flashed a smile.

As Tom held the door open for her to slip in, he glanced up at the cabbie. "Take us to the Cliff House." Then he looked at Judy. "This is a restaurant with a great view of the Golden Gate Bridge."

They rode through traffic for a few moments. Tom was uncomfortable, not knowing quite what to say.

He didn't have to wait long for Judy to initiate the conversation. "So, you don't own a car?" And before he could answer, she fired off another question. "You never married?"

"No, to the car. I never have done much driving. Where I've been assigned, I haven't needed one. Just a headache with parking and insurance." Tom shook his head. "I guess I've been married to the Bureau all of these years." He shrugged. "It seems I was always given assignments by Hoover that has never allowed me a social life."

They watched out the cab windows, enjoying the city night lights on the balance of the drive to the restaurant.

The cabbie pulled up to the front door and leaned over the front seat. "Here you go, mac. That'll be ten dollars."

Tom tossed him a ten-dollar bill and a couple of ones, then they hustled to the front door of the restaurant, attempting to avoid the chilly wind coming off the bay.

As quickly as they were seated, they were greeted by a waitress arriving at the table to ask for their drink orders, but neither had looked at the wine menu. She replied she'd give them a few more minutes.

Judy opened the wine menu. "What would you like to order?"

"That's one side of me that's different from our old days. Since I moved here from Washington, I've not had a drink. I thought it would be a good time to do a clean break. But you go ahead and order something. I'll just drink water or tea."

"Wow, you went from a hard drinker to nothing at all? Good for you." Judy put on a pair of glasses before she picked up the menu. "I've been wanting to try a good white wine from California since I just moved here. I guess this is my big chance."

When the waitress returned to the table, Judy asked her for a recommendation of a local white wine.

The young lady quickly replied, "I highly recommend Inglenook Cabernet Sauvignon—never had a complaint."

Judy nodded and closed the wine menu.

The waitress smiled. "And you, sir?"

"None for me. I'll just have a water."

The waitress nodded and left.

They both picked up the food menu. "So, you were a nurse in the military and came home to go into the insurance business. Why?"

Judy pulled out a pack of Pall Mall cigarettes, then tapped one out. "When I returned home, I went to work at the local hospital. One day, some rich exec told me I should go to work for him. Naturally, he was hitting on me." She lit her own cigarette with a lighter engraved with a Blue Cross/Blue Shield logo. "Well, they needed people that understood the health care business and, of course, I did."

The waitress brought over her glass of Cabernet Sauvignon, followed by a second waiter bringing out fresh salads to the table. As they ate their salads, Judy seemed to want to tell her history from the last time they'd seen each other in 1947. He sat and listened. Was she nervous, or was she trying to restart their relationship where they'd left off? As she elaborated, Tom's mind flashed to Hada Miyoko. He pushed it out. She was too young.

After they ordered their main course, he took Judy's menu and handed them back to the waitress. Judy ordered a second glass of wine, then asked, "Tom, what are you working on now?"

"Well, like in the 1940s, I'm involved in an international project. I just transferred here in late 1963." Tom couldn't divulge exactly what he was working on.

Once their dinner was over, Judy ordered another glass of the Cabernet wine. "I really like this wine. I believe I've found my new favorite."

Despite Judy talking a little more than Tom cared for, he passed it off as the alcohol. Still, he wanted to spend a little more time with her. "Would you be interested in taking a ride around the city? I'll call for another cab—kinda sight see for a little bit?"

Judy smiled. "Let me run to the lady's room first, and that would be great."

They stood at the front of the restaurant until they heard the two toots of the cab horn outside, and then they moved quickly to get in. Tom leaned forward and gave the cabbie the address of Judy's apartment, then said, "Take us through Chinatown on the way home." Then he leaned back and smiled at Judy. "This is a really neat part of San Francisco. To see it at night is something special." What he didn't say was how frustrating this part of San Francisco had been for him.

They didn't talk much on the drive back to her apartment. Judy seemed fascinated with the hustle and bustle, not to mention the lights of Chinatown. But she did lean over as close to Tom as she could get. Tom didn't resist her. It was nice to have a woman sitting close to him again.

When they reached her apartment, Judy whispered in his ear. "Would you like to come in?"

Tom wanted to, but decided his best course was to resist. He wanted to process everything in his mind. The last thing he wanted was to jump into this relationship. "No, my partner is picking me up early in the morning. We have an appointment outside the city."

With that, Tom opened the car door and told the cabbie to wait. He walked Judy to the front door of her second-floor apartment.

They kissed passionately before she touched his lips. "Please call on me again."

Tom nodded and bounded back down the stairs to the waiting cab.

CHAPTER ELEVEN

Beijing
October 16, 1964

Yu Qiangsheng sat with his mother, Fan Jin, at her small apartment, sipping green tea. He'd been so busy with his training at the Central Intelligence Division he hadn't been able to check on her in a while. As he looked around her simple apartment, he focused on a stack of papers with anti-Mao slogans written on them.

"Mother, what are you up to now?" Yu pointed at the stack.

Fan took a sip of the hot brew. "Nothing you need to know about."

He raised his hands. "Mother, I work for the CID at the highest level. Soon I'm going to be responsible for all subversive activity inside China, and you tell me nothing I need to know about?"

Fan continued to sip her tea. "I just joined an organization, Three Family Village, to counter Mao's repression of the citizenry. At the moment we are trying to work behind the scenes. But at the same time, we are very aware that at any point Mao could turn loose the Red Guard on us."

Her answer caused him to pace around the small apartment. "Mother, you can't do this."

"Please don't tell me what to do. Don't worry about me. I've been involved professionally with Zhou and Kang for a long time. They will protect me. When I was your age, I was a part of Zhou's personal intelligence network. I know how to discreetly do these things." She picked up her cup. "Besides, Mao knows me from your aunt's affair with him years ago."

Yu sat back down. "Mother, I don't trust any of them, and neither should you. Your role in the Chinese inner circle alone should put you on edge. If Mao issues an order, it gets executed. whether you are friend or foe. You should know that better than anybody."

Fan nodded. "This is my point, exactly. This is why our group has formed."

"Mother, I have to go. I have two appointments this morning." Out of fear of disrespecting his mother, he stopped. Point made.

Yu Qiangsheng was seated across from Dr. Wang, hands folded on this lap, awaiting his assignment. Without a word, his new boss pushed a file in his direction.

Yu picked it up. On top was a photograph. Behind it was the man's biography, which he scanned in thirty seconds. "Yes, sir?"

Dr. Wang straightened his necktie. "Our French Communist contact provided this information. Bernard Boursicot has recently arrived in Beijing to work at the French Embassy. He is a very young man, shy, easily influenced. We have been informed he will see many financial transactions. We need to know what he sees."

Yu bit his lower lip. He was supposed to be responsible for Chinese citizens, but it appeared his role was being expanded. It made him proud. He was being trusted. "I see many things here I can work with. In his youth, he enjoyed homosexual relations with boys his age. Plus, he really likes money—perfect for a honeypot trap."

Dr. Wang smiled, flashing his small front teeth. "Get started immediately. Report back to me as soon as you have something. Move expeditiously but cautiously. Make no mistakes. If you need help developing a relationship, I'm the best. Come see me."

Yu tucked the file under his arm and left. As he walked down the hallway, he realized this was his first big test working with Central Intelligence Division. Finding a homosexual in China would be quite difficult. If they were found out, they were either imprisoned or put to death. But money would be easy. Despite how poor the country was, Mao always had money to pay for information. Money and power were generally the things that lured people to spy. Despite Boursicot's low-level position, he'd see invoices and high-level secret documents. Low-level position, low pay. The man liked money. He seemed like the perfect individual to provide important information on enemies.

As soon as Yu had left, Dr. Wang went to Kang Sheng's office. The two men were scheduled for an important meeting with Zhou En-lai. Two men in full dress military uniforms arrived in a government car to escort them to Zhou's.

Zhou greeted both men and had them sit. "I have a formal announcement to make. I have some news I wanted to share with you. Yesterday, at three o'clock in the afternoon, at Lop Nur, our scientists completed project 59-6. They detonated our first nuclear device. It wouldn't have happened so quickly without each of your commitments to Mao. We have joined the nuclear age."

Dr. Wang and Kang glanced at each other and nodded.

Zhou continued, "I, we, tried to get *all* countries to give up their nuclear weapons. I was a part of those diplomatic negotiations. Yet, they tried to make us sign the nuclear proliferation treaty." Zhou, the consummate diplomat, opened his hands palms up. "No longer will we have to be subservient to the imperialists—the Soviet Union or the United States. They must respect us and treat us as equals. Mao will be making a speech to the people later today, but I wanted to brief you first."

Zhou went to the door to the outer office and asked his secretary to come in.

She entered, carrying a camera.

"Please take a picture of the three of us, then get a copy for each of us," Zhou said. "This photograph is for your private file only."

After snapping several shots, she returned to her area.

Dr. Wang smiled—a genuine smile for a change. Somehow, he would get a copy of his victory photo to FBI Special Agent Thomas Payne Warren.

Zhou returned to his desk. "Dr. Wang, your probation period is over. Our country needs you to resume your full duties. You're free to travel. However, do not take any undue risks or make anything personal. We need you completely focused on handling your spies."

Dr. Wang knew better than to gloat around Zhou or let on to any of his thinking. He knew not to cross Zhou, who was Mao's most trusted advisor. Instead, he humbly bowed his head. However, one thing was for sure—Warren was going to get a copy of that picture.

And now that he had full range to move around, it was an opportunity to not only conduct his business affairs, but he could begin his plot to set his trap to capture, torture, and kill FBI Special Agent Thomas Payne Warren.

October 17, 1964
San Francisco

Tom Warren sat in his office staring out the window. He'd been thinking about calling Judy for another date. Perhaps he would, but first he needed to place two phone calls, one to the U.S. Department of State and the other to European Agency Interpol, seeking information on Kikue Nakamura. What started out as the simple murder had failed to yield any background evidence.

All they knew was Dr. Wang murdered her. The woman was veiled in mystery.

Tom was ready to start drawing hypothetical conclusions based on lack of information. He buzzed his boss, Gerald Adler. "Do you have a minute?"

"Sure."

Tom grabbed Marty Corley on his way, and they sat down across from Adler. "Gerald, you and I have been in the bureau for more than twenty years. Have you ever seen a case have no information like the Nakamura murder? She was wealthy but had no bank records. She had art pieces, but no record of purchases at any store." Tom rubbed his chin. "According to immigration, she came into the U.S. in 1961. While no one has recovered her passport, I'm guessing whatever passport she traveled under was set up, which leads me to the conclusion she was a spy. But for who? I think the Japanese. Just by the looks on their faces when I questioned them in Tokyo, their silence meant they knew her. Lots of assumptions. But who was she spying on here in the U.S.?" He paused for a second, then raised both hands. "I want to send our file to the Japanese people—naturally, with Hoover's approval. Let's see what they send us."

Adler closed his eyes with his arms folded over his chest as he listened to Warren's presentation. He straightened and opened his eyes. "Agreed. Let's test them. But the detail that still bothers me the most is her missing John book. But it does seem to be reasonable that if she were a high-class prostitute, she dealt in cash. But if she really was a 'honeypot' spy, too, then there may be more in her John book than just names and dates. That is, no doubt, why Dr. Wang stole it, which makes me jump to the conclusion she spied on the Chinese here. But the problem with that is why are the Japanese interested in China's activity in the U.S.?"

Tom looked at Marty. "Corley and I came to the same conclusions. She wasn't collateral damage—she was part of his mission. But he had planned to kill her all along. If anything, Wang decided to entice me after he found out I had been assigned to San Francisco." Tom paused for a moment. "He couldn't have possibly known in advance I was here, as I had only arrived several weeks before. The Chinaman in the newsstand was an elaborate plan you just couldn't throw together."

Adler squirmed in his chair. "I hadn't thought of that. So you think he was tipped off that you were coming to San Francisco?" He got up, walked to his window, and looked out for a minute. "Are you implying there's a Chinese spy in the FBI?"

Tom lightly punched Marty in the arm. "Maybe in the FBI, maybe not—but someone on the inside of the government is watching this office, maybe watching me. To argue with myself, Dr. Wang could've had someone watching me all the time."

Adler slowly returned to his desk chair. "Hoover wants you to come to Washington to discuss what you have learned in the past year. You can bring that up to him then." He reached in his desk and pulled out a plane ticket. "Here's your flight. You leave Monday."

A ticket to go get reamed out. Tom snatched the ticket from his boss's hand. He needed to go home and make some notes. Once again, work got in the way of calling on Judy.

October 19, 1964

Tom was seated in the outer office of FBI Director J. Edgar Hoover, waiting to be called in. This was the most relaxed he'd ever been going into a meeting with the director.

The secretary told him that Mr. Hoover could see him now.

He got up, straightened his tie, and entered. As usual, J. Edgar Hoover was behind his desk, and the number two man at the FBI, Clyde Tolson, was seated on the left side. Tom spoke before sitting down, "Director, Mr. Tolson."

Each man just looked at him without so much as a word.

Tom sat down and waited for what Hoover was going to yell at him about.

Hoover reached around on the credenza behind his desk, picked up a file, and opened it. "Special Agent Warren, here in my hand is the official announcement from the People's Republic of China." Hoover started reading the speech from Mao about the detonation of their atomic bomb. When Hoover finished reading, he leaned back. "The area of destruction and the size of the blast is very similar to our Little Boy bomb."

Tom remained seated, waiting for a question.

"We must assume that some of the information needed for that project was what Dr. Wang gathered when he came to San Francisco from Los Alamos." Hoover shifted in his chair. "Do you agree with that assumption?"

Tom leaned over on the corner of his chair. "Of course, it makes sense. But, clearly, he went to France and Japan to pick up information on their programs—particularly France, where I believe he got a large amount of information on their atomic bomb."

Hoover looked at Tolson, then back at Tom. "You have been in San Francisco for almost a year. How many Chinese spies have you interrogated or arrested?"

Tom knew this question was the whole reason for this meeting. He was ready. "Director, you know the answer. The Chinese are shuffling couriers in and out of the country at such a rate, shortly after they are on our radar for activity, they are recalled back to China carrying a package." Tom was ready to deliver his own punch. "Director Hoover, I contend that we have a spy watching the San Francisco Bureau. They maybe in the FBI, or they may be in another agency watching us. But the suspects were tipped off we were coming, then left the country."

Hoover got up from his desk. Tolson stared at him. Hoover leaned over his desk. "Special Agent Warren, there are spies all over this country, and you have failed to catch a single one. You haven't even questioned anyone you suspect of being a spy."

Tom went through step by step about his arrival in San Francisco and the Chinaman, then detailed the suspects who'd left the United States just before Tom and Martin Corley could pick them up.

As Tom was finishing the details of his suspicions, Hoover sat back down. For the first time since Tom had been coming to these "face to face" meetings with Hoover, he believed the director was listening to him.

Hoover looked at Tolson, who scowled. "This is an outrageous accusation. Do you have any idea who it could be?"

Tom was prepared for that question too. "No, but think about it. We have found people who spied for the Soviets and who spied for the Germans, but we've never found a spy working for the Chinese government. They are buried deep, and they have been here for a while."

Hoover looked at Tolson, then back to Tom. "Special Agent Warren, perhaps you are correct, perhaps not. Maybe this has been in plain view for a long time, and we have just overlooked it."

Tom bit the inside of his lip. *Don't say anymore. Let everything sink in.*

Hoover leaned on the desk. "Special Agent Warren, I'm going to tell you something in the strictest of confidence. How big is it that the Chinese have a nuclear weapon? President Johnson told me, again, in the strictest of confidence, but considering what you are working on, you should know this, and that is in 1963 President Kennedy contacted the Soviets about the U.S. conducting a preemptive strike on Lop Nor. The Soviets didn't have a problem with Kennedy's proposal."

Tom was stunned.

Hoover paused. as though in deep thought, "Warren, return to duty and keep us abreast of your findings. But understand, I need to get some arrests.

Johnson is really going to put the heat on me with this development. And I am putting the heat on you."

Tom moved swiftly toward the office door. It was the first time he'd felt Hoover appreciated the complexity of the investigation he was conducting.

Tom had to stop by and see Stephanie Keeton and Michelle Galloway. They had been loyal friends and coworkers. Plus, Tom wanted to do some research digging into some old files. He had several subjects to research— Japanese Golden Lily operation burying stolen gold in the Philippines, Chinese spies, and Kikue Nakamura. Honestly, he didn't expect to find anything directly related, but you never know what might turn up. When he walked into their office area, both waved at him. Tom pulled up a chair between their two desks. They asked how he liked living in San Francisco versus Washington DC.

"I love San Francisco."

"Isn't it terrible about Mary Meyer?" Stephanie asked.

Tom looked at her and tilted his head. "What do you mean?"

Stephanie raised and lowered both hands simultaneously. "She was murdered a few days ago."

Tom's jaw dropped as he stared at her. *Hoover didn't say a word to me about it. You would've thought he'd have said something after he'd assigned me to watch her for almost a year to determine if she was having an affair with Kennedy. The altruistic, beautiful Mary Meyer was murdered? Why was she murdered?* "Do they have a suspect?"

Stephanie replied, "They took someone named Crump into custody almost immediately."

Tom didn't say a word but his mind was charged up. Was she killed because of her affair with the President? No. He'd been dead for almost a year. But it was unlikely some random murder.

"When are you heading back to San Francisco?" Michelle asked.

"Maybe tomorrow night." Tom raised both hands palms up. "I want to go through the files to see if I can pick up any old investigations that could help me with my current assignment."

Michelle asked, "Do you need any help?"

Tom nodded. "If you don't have anything to do, of course I'll take your help. Here's what I'm looking for." Tom paused while the two women got ready to write. "Anything related to a woman by the name of Kikue Nakamura, who entered the country in 1961." He didn't want to give them his other two subjects, the first being the Japanese invasion of NanJing in 1938, and the second, a Japanese operation during World War II called the Golden Lily. Then something else came to mind that they might find. "Look for Chinese scientists who came to the United States and then returned to Red China over the last decade." It was a long shot there would be anything in the FBI files on those subjects.

The two girls got up and went with Tom to the file area. Some of the materials were now on microfilm. Tom didn't like it—it was too hard to look at.

After spending almost three hours in the old case files, Tom, Michelle, and Stephanie returned to Michelle and Stephanie's desks. The two women failed to find anything in the FBI files on Ms. Nakamura. Likewise, he'd found nothing on NanJing or the Golden Lily.

Michelle patted Tom on the shoulder. "Don't look so dejected. We did find some information that China had sent individuals into the United States a long time ago who worked for the Communists." She pushed one file forward. "Mr. Qian Xue-sen, who had his security clearance stripped by the FBI in 1950."

Tom quickly thumbed through the file. In 1938, Qian had attended a meeting of the Pasadena Communist Party. His file was filled with scientific achievements. A Cal Tech colleague called him a genius in the area of high-speed aerodynamics and jet propulsion. The U.S. State Department expelled him.

Tom leaned back in the wooden chair. His theory was right. He figured Qian was one of the men working on the Chinese atomic project. He closed his eyes. He suspected there were more cases of top Chinese scientists coming to the U.S. to study and spy, then returned to Red China. He'd have to return and dig them out. As he got up to leave, he smiled at the two women agents. "This was a great find. See ya around."

Tom realized he needed to pull out all the stops to shut down all Chinese spies inside the United States—particularly Dr. Wang's spy network. Based on what he'd just learned, he and his team needed to expand their search to the academic community. They had done so much damage.

I must do something I have resisted up until now. Should I bring in the Japanese young woman Hada Miyoko and Chinese immigrant Shou Li Cao to take down Dr. Wang's spy ring?

CHAPTER TWELVE

Hong Kong
December 1964

"Wu, you are from Hong Kong, take me to the main post office," Dr. Wang commanded.

He and his two henchmen, Chung and Wu, drove into the heart of downtown Hong Kong. This was Dr. Wang's first trip outside of China in almost a year. He had deep concerns that between Interpol, MI6, CIA, and the FBI, he was a wanted man for his role in going around the world stealing intellectual properties so that China now had a nuclear weapon. He believed the authorities, including FBI Special Agent Tom Warren, viewed him as the number one spy handler in the world. To take him down would be a major achievement.

Wu nodded and continued to drive, maneuvering through the heavy traffic.

As Dr. Wang leaned back into his seat so as not to be seen, he nervously fingered his gold cufflinks.

Chung looked into the backseat. "How long are we going to be in Hong Kong, Dr. Wang?"

He didn't respond.

Within a few more minutes, Wu pulled up on the opposite side of the street from the post office. Dr. Wang sat in the car for a minute, looking up and down the street. Finally, he got out and walked straight across. He entered the building and walked up to P. O. Box 88, inserted the key, and pulled out the large package. No return address. Ah, Jin Wu-dai's first package since being transferred to Langley.

As he walked out, he noticed a policeman walking along the street near his car. Dr. Wang pivoted and walked in the opposite direction on the other side of the street, so as not to be seen by the policeman. He crossed the street at the end of the block, then went straight back to the car. Once in, he leaned up to the front seat. "Take me to the airport."

Wu glanced over at Chung, then pulled away from the curb. On the drive to the airport, Dr. Wang placed the large envelope in his briefcase. As the traffic became heavier, Dr. Wang became more and more impatient. The last thing he needed was any of the Hong Kong authorities to identify him.

Beijing

Dr. Wang was ushered into Zhou En-lai's office. He was surprised to see Kang Sheng already seated on the other side of his desk. Something very important must be going down. He sat down and straightened out his gray suit. "You wanted to see me, Comrade Zhou?"

Zhou stood and pointed his finger repeatedly on the table. "Both of you know, at one time, I was in charge of the Party's internal network intelligence. Kang, you know that when you were handling the outside subversives and interference, I was watching those in the party who may be causing problems for Mao."

Kang sat up straight in his chair. "Yes, comrade. Of course, I remember."

Then he looked over at Dr. Wang. "I will say this as diplomatically as possible, but I have something very disturbing to share with you, and I need your help keeping it under wraps."

Kang replied, "Whatever it is, we can be trusted."

"Let's hope so. You are my inner circle." Zhou paused for a second while not taking his eyes off Dr. Wang. "I have it from a very reliable source that Fan Jin, Yu Qiangsheng's mother, has joined the dissident group, Three Family Village."

Kang frowned at Wang, then looked back at Zhou. "That just can't be. She has always been a part of our network, Zhou. How did she get tied up with Deng Tuo, Wu Han and Liao Mosha?"

Zhou was still focused on Dr. Wang. "Wang, I need you to keep Yu so busy he doesn't have time to be around his mother. He has too much potential to get drawn into this malaise. And as you know, Mao's wife will be watching this closely. If we have to deal with Fan, we don't want Yu in the middle."

Dr. Wang nodded. "I will handle him. Do not worry." Yet he couldn't believe this complication was being added onto his plate. *Now, I'm not only teaching but babysitting the new agent I didn't want responsibility for in the first place.*

Kang looked back over to Dr. Wang. "I'll help keep Yu out of this, if you need. As you know, I've always considered him family." He rubbed his chin, then opened his left hand as he spoke to Zhou. "Should I try to get to Fan? I told her I would protect her."

Zhou stood up from his chair and pointed at Kang. "*Stay away from her.* If anybody would reach out to her, it will be me. But she has made this mess for herself. Her husband once made the same choices and paid the price."

Dr. Wang lightly pounded the arm of the chair. They had soft-killed Fan's husband, Yu Qiwei.

"Can you keep them from imprisoning or killing Fan? We need Yu," Kang pleaded.

Dr. Wang spoke up. "Zhou, I'll keep Yu busy. He'll be fine. He is completely committed to Mao and the Party. Complete your internal investigation."

Yu Qiangsheng drove down the bank into the foggy parking lot outside of Beijing. It was just before daylight on a cold, chilly morning. He pulled his car alongside Dr. Wang's, who waved for him to get in. As Yu climbed out of his car, Dr. Wang waved his two henchmen out of the car. As soon as he'd closed the car door, Dr. Wang leaned over toward Yu. "What have you discovered since you have been tailing Bernard Boursicot?"

"He has slowly been building a relationship with a Chinese citizen, Shi Pei Pu," Yu replied.

"You stay on Boursicot and Shi every waking moment. We must get Boursicot to give us documents, since France is the only Western Power accepting us. We must know what the Western World is saying about China," Dr. Wang commanded.

"I've been following Boursicot. He is oblivious," Yu replied. "I've been planning to grab Shi Pei Pu, but he's been avoiding me the past few days. I've a little plan today to take care of that. I will have you an update by tomorrow— or else."

"Stay on them. Period." Dr. Wang leaned back his head and closed his eyes. "Mao and Zhou are counting on you. You are dismissed."

Yu Qiangsheng walked into the backstage of the theater, searching for the actor, Shi Pei Pu. One of the security guards tried to stop him, only to be met with an open hand palm strike to the solar plexus. As the guard lay on the ground in pain, Yu stuck his CID badge in his face. The other security guard cowered away. Yu slipped into the darkness of the backstage and found Shi on stage practicing for an upcoming play.

Shi had been avoiding him for the past couple of days. Yu wanted answers *now*. No more delays. Within ten minutes, the play's director commanded everyone to take a break for a few minutes.

Shi walked back toward the area where makeup was getting touched up. Yu knew he had him. He waited until he was seated in the makeup chair. As soon as the makeup artist had Shi shut his eyes to do his eyeliner, Yu stepped up to the makeup artist. "Go take a break. Shi and I need to have a conversation."

Shi's eyes opened wide. He tried to get up out of his chair.

Yu pushed him hard back into his seat, then grabbed him by the throat as he leaned over into Shi's face. "Have you made contact with the French man I told you? At the moment, I am keeping your secret that you are a homosexual, but if you don't cooperate with me, I'll have a conversation with Kang Sheng. You know what happens to you next, right?" He let go of Shi's throat.

Shi leaned back as far as he could and tried to twist his head out of Yu's space. "Yes, I've seen him a couple of times."

Yu straightened back up, allowing the small man to sit normally in his chair. Yu folded his arms across his chest. "So, what would you have me tell Kang Sheng?"

Shi looked in the mirror and tried to fix his makeup. "I like the man, I do. We are in the beginning of a relationship. He thinks I'm a woman. But I haven't asked for any documents yet."

"Keep seeing him. Earn his confidence." Yu reached down and grabbed Shi's tiny hand that was holding onto the arm of the chair and squeezed it hard. "But I want some documents soon. Do you hear me?"

Shi winced in pain.

Yu released his hand and started to walk away.

He rubbed his hand. "Boursicot has had sex with me several times. One evening, he mentioned some U.S. agent wanted him to get him information on the Chinese."

Yu stopped and looked over his shoulder. "Did he give you a name?"

"No. I didn't ask. Is that important?" Shi asked.

Yu stepped back in his face. "Get me that name."

San Francisco

Special Agent Tom Warren came into the FBI headquarters early to prepare for his conference call with Director Hoover. As he walked over to his desk, there was a large plain white envelope on top. He opened it up and pulled out a large picture. Immediately, his hands started shaking as he held the picture of Dr. Wang, Kang Sheng, and Zhou En-lai toasting. Tom read out loud the Chinese writing at the bottom of the picture. "We are celebrating our great victory, the testing of the nuclear bomb. Just as I told you, Agent Warren."

Tom slammed the picture down, then pushed his chair hard into his desk. This had happened on his watch, and Dr. Wang had done exactly what he'd said—rubbed it in his face. He gritted his teeth and pounded his desk repeatedly. "This is not over." He picked the picture back up and stuffed it in the envelope it had come in. He jerked his desk chair back out and dropped into it. He pounded his fist on the desk again. "How the hell did this picture get on my desk?"

His desk phone rang. He jerked it from the switch hook. "Special Agent Tom Warren."

"Tom, this is Judy. Since you haven't called me since our first, ah, well, in a while… I thought I would call you to see if you want to take me to my company's Christmas party. I just got in, and there was the announcement of it on my desk, and well, I thought of calling you."

Tom started to answer her. He really didn't want to. He stammered for a minute.

Just then, Adler entered the operation room. He gave Tom a quick wave on his way, as he continued on to his corner office.

"Hey, Judy, my boss just called me into his office. Let me call you back."

Adler, Tom, and Marty had a conference call with Hoover scheduled for eight a.m. local time. Within a couple of minutes, Adler charged back out of his office. As he moved across the large room, he said, "I have a meeting with SFPD Chief of Police this morning. It just came up last night. You and Corley use the conference phone in my office to take Hoover's call. You can fill me in afterwards."

Tom and Marty were sitting in their boss's office finishing up a call with Director J. Edgar Hoover. "Warren, this Chinese spy situation is getting out of hand. The CIA just transferred one of their top linguists from the West Coast to Arlington to start interpreting Chinese communications. He is a part of the FBIS. In case you don't know the acronym, it stands for Foreign Broadcast Information Services. Take down this name—Larry Wu-tai Chin. You should make contact with him, see if he will cooperate with your on-going sloppy investigation. But I forgot you don't get along with people at the CIA, so you probably won't use him. He'll probably be the one to break up the Chinese spy ring."

Tom knew Hoover never missed a chance to get in a dig at him. His years of fighting with the CIA had been well documented. He elected to remain silent and just take it. He'd met Larry Wu-tai Chin in Shanghai back in the late 1940s. It *might* be a good idea to contact him.

Hoover paused for a moment, then said, "Warren, listen close to what I'm about to read to you. It is a communique from the French Ministry of Europe and Foreign Affairs." Hoover cleared his throat. "The French say they believe Dr. Paul Yu, company name AD-YU Electronics and Engineering operating out of New Jersey, is spying for the Red Chinese. He is selling electronic equipment to most of the industrialized countries of Western Europe, including France. So, here I am in Washington D.C., giving you a lead. Warren, there you are in the hot bed of the largest Chinese spy network, and you have yet to produce a single arrest."

Warren glanced at Corley. "Director, I'll repeat what I said before. Every single time Corley and I get ready to grab somebody for questioning, somehow they find out and slip out of the country. They know we are coming. Just recently, I got somebody undercover working for me in one of their spy dens, a restaurant in Chinatown."

Hoover cut him off. "Excuses, excuses, and no arrests. To my knowledge, no questioning still. You are failing miserably. I just gave you a lead, now do something about it. Dr. Paul Yu."

Warren looked at Corley as he spoke into the phone. "But he is not in my—"

The phone went dead. Hoover had hung up on him.

Tom looked at Corley. "Let's arrange a meeting with Shou Li Cao. See what she knows of this Chinese spy network." Both men got up and walked out of Adler's office. On their way back over to Tom's desk, his desk phone rang. "Hoover must not be done chewing me out."

Corley laughed. "Yeah, or maybe he's just going to fire you and put you out of your misery."

Tom picked up his phone. "Special Agent Thomas Warren."

The voice with the British accent on the other end of the phone replied, "MI6 Agent Anthony Middleton here."

Tom sat there speechless.

"Hello, Tom. Are you there?"

Tom replied, "You old Limey, how the hell are you? Are you retired?"

"All right. Are you done having fun? I called with something serious. I didn't even know you were still with the FBI. Truth be known, I thought you were dead," Middleton mused. "I called the San Francisco bureau because I'd heard the Chinese spy investigation was run out of this office."

Tom waved for Marty to come over closer to his desk. "Anthony, how are you, my old friend?"

Middleton replied. "I'm well. Still on assignment in Hong Kong. Right-o. I'm calling on two different matters, yes."

Tom put his hand over the receiver. "This is one of my old friends in Hong Kong, working for MI6." He lifted his hand off the receiver. "Go ahead."

"First off, the French just notified us that they believe a Dr. Paul Yu was spying on several Western European countries, including Great Britain. What can you tell me about him? He is running his operation out of your country. All right."

"Hoover just briefed me. I haven't had any time to work on it."

Middleton said, "By the way, your old adversary, Dr. Wang, just went through security here in Hong Kong on his way back to Beijing. We didn't catch him coming in, but he went out on a private jet."

Tom bristled with those words. "So, MI6 has him on a watch list, too?"

"Absolutely, but only recently. You can imagine we have been fighting spies here in Hong Kong." Middleton paused for a few seconds. "Since I've been here for so long, they had me assemble a list dating back to the Chinese Civil War. No records of him until today."

Tom bit his lower lip. "Middleton, I'll get you what I can on Dr. Paul Yu, ASAP. Keep me in your loop on Dr. Wang."

"Cheerio."

Tom put down the phone and looked at Marty. "We definitely need to set up a meeting with Shou. The scope of our investigation into Dr. Paul Yu just got significantly bigger."

Marty stared at Tom for a brief moment. "What did your MI6 friend tell you about Dr. Wang?"

Tom drew a deep breath. "I can't help but believe Dr. Wang has been going in and out of Hong Kong for a long time. It's just with the Chinese detonating their nuclear bomb, everybody is suddenly scrambling to work on Chinese spies."

"You and Middleton go back a long way, huh?"

Tom didn't want to take the time to tell Marty about his past work with Middleton. It brought back too many bad memories. There was Judy, her leaving him behind, then the sexy socialite Izzy Scarborough—and his old team, Love, Snake, and Sal. All of it had ended badly. As did about everything to do with his time in the Philippines and Hong Kong. His mind was going a thousand miles an hour. Santa Romana—or Father Diaz, as he was sometimes called—and that CIA asshole Edward Lansdale. The shot—the shot of LSD laced with heroin. No good memories.

What do I really want to tell Marty? Then he remembered he still had to return Judy's call, but he really didn't want to go to any company Christmas Party. Maybe too much time had passed to rekindle a relationship with her.

Corley tapped him on the shoulder. "Are you going to stare off into space or tell me about Middleton?"

Tom refocused. "Years ago, Middleton and I worked on a very complex laundered bank funds investigation. The Soviets, the CIA, and the Chinese were all involved. He was excellent to work with…." His voice tailed off. "A real by-the-book agent, which sometimes doesn't work when you're chasing spies." He sighed. "Get me that meeting with Shou, and I've got to reach out to someone in Japan who offered to help. I turned her down then, but now I have to pull out all the stops."

The more Tom thought about Miyoko, the less he wanted to call Judy. But he picked up the phone and dialed her number. "Judy, this is Tom."

"I thought you forgot all about me," Judy replied in a sexy voice.

"No, my boss just got me in his office for a while," Tom said, making notes of information he needed to compile to get to Middleton.

"Well, do you want to go to my company's Christmas party?"

"I'm sorry. I'm just not into company Christmas parties. I would be there with a bunch of people I don't know. A wallflower," Tom continued writing.

"Well, Tom, I think you just don't want to see me anymore. Goodbye."

The next thing Tom heard was the dial tone. He let out a big sigh. *I forgot how needy and demanding she was when she didn't get her way.*

December 19, 1964
Beijing

Up until now, Yu Qiangsheng had observed from afar the building relationship of French Diplomat Bernard Boursicot and Chinese citizen Shi Pei Pu. Yu was dressed such that he could easily blend into the crowded guest area, as per the training by both Kang and Dr. Wang. First, he was assigned to keep an eye on Shi. However, his assignment changed at the last minute to observe Boursicot mingle with other foreign diplomats at a British Christmas Party in Beijing. Yu wandered why Shi had received an invitation to this party, especially since he seemed out of place standing off in the corner in his Mao suit. He could only reason it was because he was part of the actors guild. Several French diplomats talked briefly with Shi, then moved on to mingle with their British counterparts.

Yu was to determine if Boursicot could be developed into a good spy with lots of contacts. When Boursicot finally arrived, he was accompanied by a beautiful blond British secretary. Yu was tipped off at the last minute that Boursicot was ordered to attend this party by the number two ranking French diplomat, who had also assigned him the date. When Boursicot and his date arrived, he took her coat and went to get each of them a glass of wine.

Yu watched intently as Boursicot returned with the glass of wine in hand, only to find the secretary on the dance floor by herself. This would be a perfect time for Shi Pei Pu to make a play for Boursicot. After a few frustrating minutes of the French man standing there dumbfounded, Boursicot finally noticed that Shi was in the crowd and made his way toward the Chinese man.

It appeared that Shi turned down his advances. Boursicot walked away, going back toward the British secretary, who was now in the company of several young diplomats. The secretary didn't seem to want anything to do with the Frenchmen. Boursicot stood there for a moment, looking out of place, then slowly walked back over to Shi. Discreetly, Yu watched out of the corner of his eye as Boursicot and Shi walked outside to a private balcony.

With Boursicot and Shi outside, Yu used his time and his location to observe several other Chinese permitted by Mao to attend this function. He focused on one of the Chinese officials speaking with a British diplomat. He made a note to bring this Chinese official in sometime in the next couple of weeks to interrogate him. However, his first priority was to keep a closer eye on Shi to make sure he was doing his job.

After a few more minutes, Yu had about all he could take of the few Chinese attendees talking and mingling with foreigner capitalists showing off their opulence while people in his country could barely sustain themselves. Likewise, the invited Chinese were only looking out for themselves. It was disgusting.

On the way to his car, he glimpsed Shi and Boursicot talking on the balcony.

Yu smiled snidely. His plan was beginning to take shape. Time to push harder.

CHAPTER THIRTEEN

Tokyo
January 1, 1965

Tom checked into his hotel room in downtown Tokyo. This was an unofficial visit to the city. While not thrilled about spending New Year's in a foreign city, he needed to see if the young Japanese girl was still willing to help him. He thought he'd go to the Japanese Olympic Committee headquarters first thing in the morning to try to meet with Prince Takeda Tsuneyoshi. It was a long shot, but it should put him face to face with Hada Miyoko. At dinner, he sat in the corner of the hotel restaurant by himself in hopes of eating privately without anyone watching him the way they had the last time he was here.

The next morning, Tom waited until mid-day, then called for a taxi to take him to the headquarters. It was very cold when he stepped outside the downtown hotel to board the taxi to the Olympic headquarters. The drive was enjoyable. When he arrived, he briskly walked up to the building. Once again, he was expected to check in at the security desk. Tom presented his FBI badge with the same story about having additional security information regarding the United States Track and Field team.

The Head of Security stepped up and snatched Tom's badge from his hand and examined it, then looked back down at the clipboard. "Your name is not on our list of FBI agents working on this project."

Tom tried his same story from the last time. "I'm working from the United States' side. Something has just come to our attention. I was asked by Director Hoover to come and speak directly to General Takeda."

The Head of Security picked up his desk phone and dialed a number. Someone must have picked up, as he said, "Do you know anything about an FBI Special Agent Thomas P. Warren having a meeting with General Takeda?" He nodded several times, then looked at Tom. "Okay. Thank you."

Within a few minutes, Miyoko walked down the long hallway toward him. She approached him directly without any change in her facial expression. "Agent Warren, General Takeda has a full agenda for the afternoon. He asked that you meet with me. If you can advise me of your findings, I shall pass this information on to General Takeda."

"Very well, Miss . . . ?" Tom tilted his head back.

"Special Agent Warren, my name is Hada Miyoko. Follow me to my desk."

He got exactly what he desired—to see Miyoko. They walked to her desk, then both spoke loud enough for fifteen minutes so as not to appear to be whispering, yet low enough to appear to be discussing classified information. Tom watched others in the open office area observing them. Miyoko sat and made some notes on a yellow pad. When they had finished, she stood. "I'll walk you to the front door to see you out. I will see to it that General Takeda gets this information." Tom reached forward and shook her hand, discreetly passing her his hotel and room number.

It was getting late. Tom sat in his room after dinner, hoping beyond hope that Miyoko would at least call. Perhaps the young Japanese girl had changed her mind, realizing the risks she'd be taking. Finally, just as he was reaching to turn off the light for the night, there was a light tap on the door.

He opened it.

Miyoko pushed past him, bumping him out of the way and going into his room. "So, I assume you really came here to accept my offer to work with you?" She sat down on the chair in the corner of the hotel room and crossed her shapely legs.

Tom sat down on the edge of the bed and looked at her. "Well, yes, you're right. I'm desperate for information on the Golden Lily. I believe your father worked for that organization in the Philippines documenting gold and treasure buried there. It's the only way I can capture the Chinese spy, Dr. Wang, and break his network."

Miyoko stared at him. "The night after you left the last time, several members of the Yakuza paid a visit to my father. He believed they were having you followed. Fortunately for me, he had expected it after I discussed our meeting with him. He sent me to his sister, my aunt's home, out of the city so the Yakuza wouldn't seek me out. I told him that Prince Takeda would protect me at work. The Yakuza worked my seventy-five-year-old father over pretty good. I returned to work three days later. *My job* is safe with Takeda, as long as my father keeps quiet. That is part of the deal—Takeda has me at his fingertips should my father ever disclose anything." She lowered her head. "That is the reason for my job security. You, of course, can see the connection. But I'm constantly at risk."

Tom jacked his jaw. "Are you still ready to take the risks of being pursued by the Japanese government or the Yakuza or who knows who?"

Miyoko nodded. "I told you *yes* a year ago. Then after I saw what they did with my father . . . ." She shrugged. "They have also threatened my mother." She squared her shoulders. "Now, what do you need? *Let's* do this."

Tom smiled. "You accept the risks?"

Again, she nodded as she furrowed her brow.

"Here's what I'm looking for. I need to know what gold and treasures were recovered in NanJing. The bonus would be finding out where was it taken. My suspicions are those items were brought here to Japan, which would make it impossible to recover—which is perfect for me." Tom leaned back on the bed, grabbed his left knee with both hands, and rocked for a minute. "There are only three places that you can likely get this information. One is conversations with Takeda. Two is getting your father to talk—to tell you what he did in the war, where he was, what he saw, etc. The other, and this is a long shot, is that something might be in Takeda's home. I seriously doubt he'd have anything at his office at the Olympic headquarters."

"Without getting an invitation to his home, clearly you are suggesting that I break into it." Miyoko closed her eyes. "I don't think I can do that."

"Good, I'm glad you said that. This is a very delicate situation. Time is on our side, and you must not be suspected of anything. You must try to look like the innocent girl you are." Tom smiled, reached over, and patted her hand. "But, sorry to say, that will very likely change."

"How should I communicate with you if I learn anything?"

Tom got up from the bed and grabbed a business card from his coat jacket pocket. He wanted to ask her to look into Kikue Nakamura, but those questions could get her into real trouble. He scribbled down his home address and handed it to her. "Use a different mailbox every time you send information to this address." Then Tom reached in his pocket, pulled out a mailbox key, and handed it to her. "With the assistance of a French diplomat, a French corporation was set up and licensed to do business in Japan. When rent comes due on the box, I will send you the Yen to renew it. You check the box once a week in the evening when no one will see you coming and going."

She looked at the key and the business card, then flashed a big grin as they walked to his room door. Tom went into the hallway first to make sure it was clear, then waved her out. On the way out the door, she stood on her tiptoes and kissed Tom on the cheek, then slipped down the hallway to the stairwell and disappeared.

Tom returned to his room and started packing to return to San Francisco. He was quite smitten with the young Japanese woman.

January 5, 1965
San Francisco

Tom reached over and turned up the heater on the car. This morning was particularly cold with a strong wind coming off the bay. Marty was driving them to a meeting with Shou Li Cao that he had recently arranged. It had been almost exactly a year since he'd met the Chinese girl. He'd avoided the temptation of getting an untrained youngster acting as an informant on the complex, tight Chinese spy network. But so much had changed, Tom needed a break in the case—or he could be fired for failure to perform.

As they drove up Lincoln Boulevard toward the National Cemetery in the Presidio of San Francisco, Tom glanced down at his watch. Just a little after six a.m. "You're unusually quiet. Anything wrong?"

Marty licked his lips. "I gotta come clean with you, Tom. I've been using Shou as a source for my investigations since last year. The day after we met last year, Shou called me. We met that night. She's been providing me information ever since. I meet her once a month. Two months ago, a soldier slowly drove by our car, then came back and stared at us. So we got out of the car and walked to a gravesite to make it look like we had a reason to be there here." Marty chewed his lip. "When I grabbed her hand, she leaned over and kissed me. We've been dating ever since."

Tom raised his left eyebrow, bit his tongue, and turned back toward the side window of the Ford Galaxy. They were on the way to meet Shou—to ask her to do something she was already doing. He didn't know what to say. However, since there hadn't been any breakthroughs, her information hadn't been helpful to their case, as far as he could tell.

They pulled up near the maintenance garage and parked. Tom looked at the beat-up Ford Falcon in front of them. Probably Shou's car. He got out, but fell in behind Marty and Shou as they walked toward a cemetery marker.

Shou carried flowers, which she placed on the headstone.

Marty looked at Shou. "I told Tom about you getting me information." He studied her eyes. "And about us."

Shou kept her eyes on the grave.

"Did you know this soldier?" Tom asked as he looked at the headstone.

Both shook their heads.

Marty jutted his chin. "We decided to honor a different soldier every time we met. Put different flowers on the marker. That way, if one of the soldiers stationed here questioned us, we would have a good story. Especially since U.S. forces liberated China from the Japanese."

Tom nodded. "That's a nice gesture and makes for a good reason." He opened his stance and folded his arms across his chest. "Let's get down to this. Shou, since I know you've been gathering information for a while now, what can you tell us?"

"A courier comes in from Los Alamos every other month. They drop the information to one of the cooks. That's the last time that cook is in the restaurant. Word is, they leave that night and carry the information back to China. The next morning, a new cook is working."

"Have you been able to identify the courier coming in from Los Alamos?" Tom inquired.

"I asked her the same thing," Marty said. "Also, was there a specific day they showed? How did they get the information to the cook?"

Shou slipped her arm through Marty's arm. "No, to both questions. But I believe this is why you haven't been able to break anything in the spy ring."

Tom rubbed his hands together and blew on them, trying to warm up, as a strong blustery gust of wind hit him in the face. "That makes their operation tight. No predictability, and then a cook disappears. So you can't even watch him or her." He turned his back to the wind. "How many cooks are working in the kitchen?"

Shou shrugged. "It varies. At lunch we have four cooks and several prep people, then several more come in at dinner time and a couple go home. It's like a merry-go-round back there."

"Think they're working on the hydrogen bomb?" Marty asked.

"Maybe." Tom shook his head. "They are doing so many advanced things at Los Alamos, they could be getting literally anything. Let's go." He started walking.

When he got to the car, he turned around. Marty and Shou walked arm-in-arm. "Shou, you stay safe," Tom said. "We definitely need your help to figure this out. Thank you." He opened the car door and got in.

Within thirty seconds, Marty slid in behind the steering wheel. "Tom, I'm sorry about all of this. I been kinda looking for somebody to settle down with since I got here. I just—"

Tom raised his hand to interrupt. "Your instincts were right to get her. I'm just disappointed you didn't tell me—and more disappointed to know she hasn't been able to bust this up. But what they are doing is almost impossible to figure out—until they make a mistake or we figure out a pattern." He scratched his chin. "Get me back to the office where I can work on the Dr. Paul Yu case. I have a few more invoices to review before I'm finished with the information sent over by Middleton. We are due to talk sometime today. I'm also calling the IRS today to get as many of his tax returns that I can get my hands on. I have a theory." He had let Marty handle compiling the notes

125

and transactions conducted by Dr. Paul Yu, AD-YU Electronics. His photographic mind began to review the information coming out of Europe assembled by MI-6 Agent Anthony Middleton.

As they drove away, Tom stared out the window. "You know, I'm actually kind of glad you set this operation up with Shou. While the other agents in the office are making progress, we just learned why we can't catch a break chasing Dr. Wang. I'm going to have to reach out to the CIA, as much as I hate to. Remember, Hoover told us they have someone who is translating captured Chinese documents."

"So you know this guy? What was it, ah, Larry Wu-tai Chin?" Marty asked while he flipped on the turn signal to pull into FBI Headquarters.

"Shanghai. Chin was stationed at the U.S. Consulate. The man patched me and my team up after Dr. Wang's boys worked us over pretty good. Seems like a good guy. He transferred over to the CIA sometime in the 1950s. He's an analyst for them now." Tom opened the car door.

"You know, it has been two years, and we have never solved the Kikue Nakamura case."

"She had to be spying on the Chinese—or on us," Marty said.

"How about both?"

"I've thought the same thing, but I still can't figure why the Japanese would spy on the United States."

"I think she may have been spying for the Yakuza," Tom clarified.

"*What? The Yakuza?* Why would they want to spy on the U.S?"

"We need to figure that out. I think the Yakuza hired her, but I bet the Japanese government hired the Yakuza." Tom shrugged, then a slight grin appeared on his face.

Late February 1965
San Francisco

Tom Warren was going over the latest information from Shou. It was a laborious task but there had to be some clues here. The limited data revealed that the courier coming out of Los Alamos was always the same individual but the hand offs were to different Chinese working at the restaurant who would soon be returning to Red China, it had become very frustrating. The courier was very allusive, as thus far unidentifiable. Maybe there is more than one courier. Perhaps one person working inside Los Alamos but different couriers, just like the cooks. Tom theorized that Dr. Wang's new system for the exchange had also added several different Chinese restaurants in Chinatown. Then that intermediary would return to China carrying the information. What had made him come to this conclusion, was the Chinese restaurant where Shou worked was only getting a new cook from mainland China every several months. Additionally, he wasn't positive but believe they had even switched to dead drops.

Hoover had sent Tom a memo last week that Bernard Boursicot had turned out to be a bust for the Bureau. Hoover had approved the use of the low-level French diplomat to feed information on the Chinese to the FBI, but he was going to be resigning at the end of the year, and to date, hadn't provided any information whatsoever.

Tom sat at his desk plotting how to approach Director Hoover about going to Hong Kong on official business for the FBI to try to catch Dr. Wang, but the spy handler's travel pattern was very limited. Of course, Tom had an ulterior motive. If he could get to Hong Kong, it would be easy to get to Japan. He wanted to go have a face-to-face meeting with Hada Miyoko. After taking several deep breaths he picked up his receiver and dial Hoover's office.

The secretary put him on hold for five minutes before Hoover picked up. "Special Agent Warren, you wanted to speak with me?"

"Yes, Director, would you consider assigning me to Hong Kong to get closer to, and be able to arrest, Dr. Wang?"

"Special Agent Warren, I assigned you to San Francisco, the heart of the Chinese spy network to break it up. Thus far, your best lead has come from me," Hoover replied in a low voice.

"Yes, Director. But I believe—"

"You have an assignment in San Francisco! If you aren't interested in completing your assignment—I can replace you."

"No, Director, I want to stay on this assignment." The next thing Tom heard was the dial tone.

May 22, 1965

Dr. Wang bit his lower lip before he knocked on the door of Kang Sheng's office. Kang had called for this urgent face-to-face meeting. After a brief pause, Dr. Wang knocked on his office door.

Kang pulled the door opened, then looked up and down the hall. "Let's go for a walk."

Dr. Wang knew that meant to not say a word, so he nodded.

Once they were on the grounds surrounding the Central Intelligence Division building, Kang finally spoke. "We have a real situation brewing, and I'm afraid to talk on my phone about it—or in my office."

As the two men continued to walk, Dr. Wang's concern grew.

Kang continued to glance around to see who might be watching the two high Chinese officials. Finally, when they were in the most secluded area, Kang said, "As you know, Mao's Cultural Revolution has become increasingly violent. Mao's youth gang, the Red Guard, is running wild in the streets of major cities throughout China."

Dr. Wang wondered what this had to do with him.

Despite no one being around, Kang lowered his voice. "One of my agents working another part of the city reported back to me this morning that the Red Guard grabbed Fan Jin last night. They tortured her and continually beat her. Finally, they put a placard around her neck and made her march around several blocks, berating and still beating her."

Dr. Wang gritted his teeth. "Why did they grab Yu Qiangsheng's mother?"

"While everyone thinks it was General Lin Piao who Mao put in charge of the Red Guard, there is more to it. My agent says the Red Guards discovered she was working with the Three Family Village Group."

"We have said all along that Fan Jin has no business messing with that group," Dr. Wang snapped. "They are out to undermine Mao."

Kang raised his hand. "You haven't heard the worse part." He looked down at the ground as he paused. "All of this was started by Madame Mao. She has always been jealous of Fan because of her relationship with Mao years ago." He shook his head. "A woman's jealousy can run deep."

"This couldn't have come at a worse time." Dr. Wang stuck out his jaw.

"Let me finish. Mao has told the Red Guard to mess up anybody associated with the subversive group. She is under arrest, although I haven't found out which jail she's in. I have my people working on it."

"Yu is going to be a real problem when he finds out." Dr. Wang straightened his gray suit coat. "Let me brief you about something Yu told me just last week. Shi has been having sexual relations with Boursicot, and he's starting to break him down."

Kang rubbed his forehead with his right hand.

"You'll love this. Shi told him he was pregnant with their child." Dr. Wang raised both hands, palms out.

"I know Shi is playing a woman—" Kang spun around and furrowed his brow. "—but how does he intend to pull this off?"

Dr. Wang shrugged as he rubbed his chin with his right hand.

Kang continued. "We must find another assignment for him immediately and get him out of the city before he finds out. I will protect him but he must get out of the city before the Red Guard comes after him...."

Dr. Wang interrupted. "I haven't heard from him. I assume at the moment he knows nothing. What are we going to do, the man has become one of my best agents. What should I tell him when he confronts me about this?"

Kang replied, "We must get Yu out of the country, today. Send him to Hong Kong, take him to Hong Kong. Just get him out of here. I'm not powerful enough to help Fan at the moment. I'll talk to Zhou En-lai—he is the only hope we have. Remember, Fan Jin was once part of Zhou's own spy network. I'll handle this, but you just have to get me the time and keep Yu Qiangsheng out of this." With that Kang waved Dr. Wang off.

Dr. Wang flexed his jaw. He was becoming more powerful than Kang, yet he was being pushed into dealing with Yu on a situation he hadn't created. Now he was asked to "babysit" it. He could handle the situation with Yu temporarily, but the man was going to find out about his mother's imprisonment. Who knew what he would do? The man would be a load to handle—but right now it was imperative to keep him from ending up in jail or dead. *Kang had to handle his part of this delicate situation.*

May 24, 1965

Yu stormed down the steps to Dr. Wang's office. He had to speak to him. A fellow agent had tipped him off that his mother had been embarrassed by the Red Guard then taken into custody and arrested. He was going to get some answers. He feared for his mother's well-being and her very life. He attempted to compose himself before he knocked on the door.

"Enter."

He stepped into the office and stood at Dr. Wang's desk. "My mother has been taken away by the Red Guard. Tell me what you know?"

"You are supposed to be shadowing Shi Pei Pu." Dr. Wang sat up straight at his desk as he pointed toward a chair.

"I'm entitled to some answers first." Yu refused to sit down.

"Her anti-Mao activities have caused her problems. She is in jail. Kang and Zhou are working on getting her out. I'm protecting you from any repercussions but you must adhere to my orders." Dr. Wang's jaw clenched as he spoke.

Yu felt his insides burn and his face flush. He struggled to maintain control.

"I suggest you go follow Shi Pei Pu."

Yu remained at the desk for a second, he glanced at the two bodyguards, then turned and left. He felt helpless.

The sun was just setting as Yu slipped past the main gate of the Forbidden City. He had been told that Shi Pei Pu was going to meet Bernard Boursicot. Yu was in a secluded location as he watched Shi walk into the courtyard beyond the main gate. Shi had advised Yu this had become one of their favorite places to walk. Boursicot waited for him just inside the gate, in a less crowded area where it would be less obvious a foreigner was meeting with a Chinese citizen. This was frowned upon by Mao. Yet, this relationship had been blessed by Zhou En-lai and Kang Sheng, in hopes of yielding critical information from the Western world that would benefit the Red Chinese.

Yu followed the couple along the five marble bridges across the Golden Water Stream. He tried to meditate focusing on the ancient, legendary, emperors who had ruled China in their glory centuries walking this same path along these waters.

He couldn't get his mother's imprisonment off his mind. His stomach churned, bile raised into the back of his throat.

Shi and Boursicot stopped in the shadow of the Forbidden Place. Yu stepped behind a monument. *Was this where a pass of documents was going to take place? The Frenchman had provided nothing to date. It was time for him to produce.* Shi and Boursicot stood and talked for a long time, but there was no pass—at least, not that Yu could see.

Finally, Boursicot left, walking back in the direction from which he'd come, and Shi remained standing there in solitude for several minutes. As soon as Boursicot was out of sight, Yu marched up to Shi. "Did he give you any information?"

"No, he told me he was leaving the French government and going to Brazil." Shi cowered away from Yu.

Yu stepped closer to Shi. "What was all that conversation about?" He grabbed Shi's shoulders. Frustrated by his own government, he wanted to vent on someone or something, but Shi was so small and weak, he refrained. "I want to know, now."

"I told him that the story of Madam Butterfly is also my story."

Yu removed his hands from his shoulders, despite his inner rage he couldn't help but laugh.

"What's so funny?"

Yu just shook his head. "Go on."

"Then I told him that because having boys was so important in China, when I was born, the third child and the third daughter in my family, my grandmother and the midwife got together and decided to raise me as a boy. I told him that I was trusting him with my very life by telling him that story." Shi spoke in a low voice as he looked down at the ground.

Yu commanded. "Did he buy it?"

Shi nodded, keeping his eyes low.

Yu smiled. "Okay, okay good."

"He still believes I'm pregnant with his child." Shi swallowed hard. "Boursicot told me I was his love and his best friend, and my secret was safe."

Yu shook his head. It didn't make sense for a grown man to believe his girlfriend was pretending to be a boy, and was pregnant, and that this wouldn't be a problem in China. How could he be this gullible? At the same time, he was greatly disappointed. The French diplomat they'd had such high hopes on for getting them critical documents was now leaving.

Yu grabbed Shi again. "If you see him again, tell him to get us some documents before he leaves." He shook Shi. *"Do you understand me?"*

Shi nodded.

Yu let go of him, turned, and walked off. *Totally not believing that fantasy he had been told yet somehow just maybe The Frenchman believed that garbage.* His hard work to establish a contact with the French Embassy had failed. This added to his frustration.

CHAPTER FOURTEEN

Late May 1967
San Francisco

Tom walked by the place where the old Chinaman's stand had been. He stopped and paused for a moment, looking up and down before continuing down the street to the FBI office. Still, he couldn't fully process how Dr. Wang had pulled this off without knowing in advance he was coming to San Francisco. No resolution of Kikue Nakamura or Jared Samuel, and no Chinese spy arrests. Their spy network was kicking his ass.

Tom sat down in his office chair, thinking his way through everything that had happened in the last three-plus years. The only impact he was making on the Chinese spy network was that every single time he was about to close in, the suspects were swept back to Red China. But no one had been questioned.

The front door to the office burst opened. Tom lurched from his seat, his hand reaching for his sidearm.

Marty dashed to Tom's desk. "Shou had something to report last night."

"What the hell happened?" Replied Tom, as the skin bunched around his eyes.

"Let me finish." Marty stood close to Tom. "She said just before closing last night, about ten-thirty, a man came into the restaurant. One of the waiters got all excited, you know, the nervous kind. Immediately, the waiter grabbed the man and whisked him into the kitchen. Shou said she was busing a table at the time, when she carried the dishes into the kitchen, the man, the waiter, and one of the cooks were gone, presumably out the back door."

"Did she get a good look at the man? Obviously, she knows what the cook and the waiter look like, knows their names." Tom's breathing accelerated. "Does she know where they live? If so, let's drive to their residences and see if they're around or if there are any clues."

"Yes, she snuck in and got their addresses before she left work. They live together." Marty handed Tom a piece of paper. "Here you go."

"Let's roll."

One hour later, they drove up the street toward the waiter's address on the far side of Chinatown. Two black and whites and another car with a city license were parked in front. Marty slid the Ford Galaxy into an open space, and Tom and Marty slipped out of the car. They walked to the uniformed police officer guarding the front door of the building and flashed their FBI badges. Before Tom slipped into the apartment, he took a quick glance at the doorhandle, lock, and door jam. Nothing appeared to be out of order.

As they stepped into the apartment, Tom and Marty came face to face with Detective Lee.

"What is the FBI doing here?" Detective Lee scowled from across the room.

Tom surveyed the living area as he slowly traversed the small room toward the San Francisco detective. He elected to ignore the question. "What happened here?"

"Nothing out of the ordinary. Just another double murder here in Chinatown. Happens all the time." Detective Lee put both hands on his hips. "This can't have anything at all to do with your Chinese spy ring. These were just a couple of restaurant workers who got into a fight and killed each other."

Tom quickly glanced at Marty, then back to Detective Lee. "How do you know that? Didn't you just get here?" He glanced at the other two detectives on the scene, who nodded.

"This was just a dispute between two Chinese men that turned violent, nothing more," Detective Lee repeated, louder this time.

"Then you shouldn't care if we look around." Tom defiantly stared at Detective Lee until the detective turned away.

"I assume a black and white called this in. How long ago?" Marty asked.

Detective Lee pivoted, stomped back over, and pulled out a small notebook from his breast pocket. "Disturbance reported at two-oh-six this morning, black and white on scene at two-seventeen. It was quiet when they arrived at the scene. They approached with caution and found two dead victims, each with .38 revolvers by their bodies, each with all six rounds fired. Both vics had multiple wounds." He pointed in two different directions at missed shots lodged in the walls. "There are their missed shots."

Marty examined the bullet holes.

Tom glanced at Marty, then took a harder look around the room, watching the three San Francisco detectives combing over the scene.

"We dug the rounds out of the wall and sent them to ballistics with the black and whites." Detective Lee added, then said in a louder voice, "An ambulance crew showed up at about four o'clock to take the bodies to autopsy. We haven't heard from the coroner."

Tom strolled around the bedroom, slowly examining everything. It must be the cook's room. The waiter must have used a cot or a pull-out. Everything seemed to be in place, totally undisturbed. Tom stared at the single bedside table. He reached down and grabbed the handle, using his necktie to keep from leaving fingerprints, and opened the door. There was a brown book with Phone and Address written on it in Chinese. Tom knew exactly what it said. He grabbed the address book and slipped it into his pocket as quickly as possible.

Tom went back into the living room to find Marty, who had pulled out the couch. That was the last thing Tom needed to see—he just wanted to get out of there immediately. He shouted, "Marty, let's go. We will hook up with Detective Lee later if there's any tie into our investigation."

In the hallway, Marty started to question Tom about leaving so fast. Tom just put his finger up to his lips. They walked back to the car. Once in the passenger seat, Tom pulled out the brown book.

Marty smiled. "Why don't you come over this evening when Shou gets off work? We need to have her identify these names."

"Yeah, sure." Tom stared out the side window as Marty drove. "What did you think of the murder scene? There were some real inconsistencies, didn't you think?"

Marty stopped at the red stoplight. "There was no forced entry to the residence and no sign of a struggle in there, either. Plus, there was no evidence the stranger was ever there. Did they have enough time to drop him off and then to home, if they arrived there at two a.m.? That's a long time between when they left the restaurant and the time they got into the fight."

Tom remained silent a little longer. Marty had picked up on all the right clues. He pulled out the brown address book and started leafing through the pages, reading the names. He paused reading. "Let me ask you a question. Does it make sense that two Chinese men with very little money who share a small flat would each own a .38 handgun? To me, they may have owned knives since they were kitchen workers, but guns would be too expensive. Don't you think?" Tom didn't give Marty a chance to reply, as he answered his own question. "What does that mean? Were they given the guns by the spy network?"

"They could have been stolen."

Tom continued to stare out the window. "I want to see the bodies. See where they were shot. The photos should tell where they were standing after they shot each other. Plus, the shots in the wall weren't random."

Marty threw a glance at him. "You must think the scene was staged."

Tom nodded.

Tom and Marty were waiting for Shou to arrive at her apartment. "What time should she be home?" Tom asked as he looked at his watch.

"She ought to be here any moment. She just got promoted to waitress, so she gets in a little later now. Hanging around, counting tips," Marty replied.

About fifteen minutes later, Shou could be heard on the other side, slipping her key in the door. She stepped into the apartment and was surprised to see Tom and Marty sitting at the kitchen table.

Shou walked over and hugged Marty, then glanced at Tom, who just pushed the brown address book toward her across the table "What do you want me to do?"

"Get a piece of paper and write down every name in that book of individuals who don't work at the Chinese restaurant—and, if you can, identify ones that may be family members." Tom tipped his fedora back on his head. "That's where I'm starting my search for the stranger who came into the restaurant last night."

Shou got up and gave Marty a one-armed hug and a kiss on the cheek as she went over by her phone and grabbed a pen out of a coffee cup and a small notepad.

Tom and Marty sat at the opposite end of the table staring at Shou as she slipped through the pages. Occasionally, she'd lean back and close her eyes, mouth the name, then leaned back forward. After thirty minutes, she'd completed her review of the address book. There were three names on the list.

"Perfect. Long shot. But my guess is that one of these three names is that man." Tom grabbed the list and glanced at it, then walked over to the phone to call a cab.

Tom walked into the small living area and sat on the edge of the chair, trying to figure out his strategy for going after the three unknown individuals.

While he wanted to conduct his own investigation without any help, he needed to move fast. *Time to check what CIA analyst Larry Wu-tai Chin knows. Perhaps I can get ahead of this development.*

San Francisco
Next day

Tom picked up the brown address book, went to the first name, and dialed the telephone number from the book. No answer. Second, the same.

Marty strolled into the office as Tom picked up the phone and dialed the last number. Tom put his hand over the receiver and handed him the phone list. "Get someone to research the first two names on this list."

By the third ring, Marty was sitting at Tom's desk. Tom recognized that the individual answered with "hello" in Mandarin. Tom smiled at Marty, then spoke in Cantonese with a perfect accent. The individual kept talking, as though he wasn't talking to an FBI agent. Tom put his hand over the mouthpiece. "Pull around the car. Let's go visit this guy."

After keeping the Chinese man on the phone for another four or five minutes, Tom decided Marty had the car waiting for him. He ended the conversation and bounded out the door.

Marty was sitting in front of the building. Tom popped in and gave him the address in Chinatown.

After forty-five minutes, they turned down the street where the apartment building was located. Tom turned to Marty. "Park here. We're too obvious in our Ford Galaxy. We'll walk the rest of the way."

"Which side of the street?" Marty asked.

Tom snorted. "Right side." He pointed down the street to a small, dilapidated building on the right. "The man lives on the second floor."

As they walked, Marty said, "I bet the San Francisco's coroner's report on the two murder vics will yield nothing out of the ordinary."

"I bet they were killed so as not to divulge any knowledge of the man who came into the restaurant that they likely helped escape." Tom nodded. "If this doesn't pay off, then the three names in the address book were dead ends, but I have a good feeling about this one."

When they got to the front of the building, Tom looked at Marty. "You wait out here. This guy could be crazy enough to jump from the second floor. Remember, we want to question him. We want him alive."

"You're sure you want to go up to the door alone?" Marty asked.

"I got this. I've handled worse." Tom winked at Marty.

"Whatever you say, boss man."

Tom entered the building, quietly climbed the stairs, went down the hall to apartment B, and knocked on the door. "FBI. We want to talk to you."

Tom could hear some movement on the other side of the door. He turned sideways and stepped outside the door frame, as whatever was going to happen next wasn't going to be good.

Then the door cracked open and a faint voice said. "Come in."

Tom put his hand on his gun as he pushed the door open slowly. He still didn't see anyone. He stepped inside the door. No one was in the living area. Weird. He quickly scanned around, looking for whoever had opened the door. Then he heard a toilet flush.

Tom called out again. "I'm FBI Special Agent Thomas Warren. I would just like to talk to you."

Tom pulled his handgun as he crept in the direction of the flushed toilet. He slowly pushed the door open to see an old Chinese man lying on the bed. Tom pointed his gun at him. "Sit up and show me your hands."

The old man just smiled at Tom and replied in Mandarin. "I'll be dead in minutes. Potassium."

Tom sat down on the floor and watched the Chinese man die.

After a few minutes, Marty walked in. He looked at Tom and the dead man. "What happened?"

"He took a Potassium. Before I could get to him. Let's look around, although I heard the toilet flush. I bet he destroyed anything of value." Tom still hadn't looked up. He knew this man was tied to the Chinese spy network, but once again, it yielded nothing.

Marty called out from the kitchen. "Tom, come here."

Tom slowly got up and walked that way. When he walked into the kitchen, Marty held out a metal wastebasket filled with burned papers.

"He must've burnt or flushed everything." Marty sat the wastebasket back down.

"I'm going to get in touch with CIA Larry. See if he has seen anything in the top secret Chinese documents he's translating. We finally have a name of someone who was obviously in the spy ring, despite not getting any information from him. And as Hoover would say, 'No arrests'." Tom sat down at the kitchen table and just hung his head.

Hong Kong
August 14, 1967

Dr. Wang watched Yu Qiangsheng pull into the vacant lot on the southside of Beijing, then park beside his car. He leaned up to the front seat. "Chung, wave for Yu to come get into our car."

Chung rolled down his window and waved the man over.

Yu slipped into the backseat alongside Dr. Wang, who didn't make eye contact.

"Kang Sheng has offered us a delicate mission assignment. I have accepted," Dr. Wang said as he continued to look out the side window. "Our mission is to assure one of our agents who is being expelled makes it home safely. He was working undercover in the Hong Kong police force when he was discovered."

"What role do you want me to serve?" Yu replied.

"Our agent was uncovered by MI6 and the British Special Branch. After they arrested him, they were going to send him to prison, but due to his connections at the highest levels here in China, they decided just to expel him. My sources in Hong Kong say they are very upset with the British government. I do not trust some rogue Hong Kong policeman or an MI6 agent won't try to take him out." Dr. Wang turned around for the first time to make eye contact with Yu. "I cannot be exposed, as I'm already wanted. I want you to escort him out of Hong Kong. Additionally, Kang Sheng, Zhou En-lai, and I believe this would make a perfect time to develop a plan for moving our people in and out of Hong Kong undetected."

Yu remained quiet.

Dr. Wang picked a piece of lint from his gray suit. "I want you to go and ride with the driver to escort him back to China. You will ride in the car with him as his escort. Watch for any potential ambush."

"When do I leave?"

"You need to be in Hong Kong in three days. The British government is supposed to notify us where to pick him up. As of right now, we do not know," Dr. Wang said. "Here is the file on our agent, Zeng Zhaoke."

"I'll be in place mid-day tomorrow," Yu said after looking at the picture.

"That's perfect, as I wanted you in Hong Kong the day before. I want you to study routes to move our agents in and out of there for the future. Start with the airport and the commercial ocean dock. See if you can find other discreet, dependable routes. I want to know all the main arrival points and the best way to get them back into China."

"Yes, Dr. Wang."

"Here is the address of a café in Hong Kong." Dr. Wang pushed a piece of paper with the address. "I'll meet you there on the morning Zeng is to be released, to give you his location."

When Yu was out of his car, Dr. Wang commanded, "Chung drive on." He cracked his neck as he spoke. He desperately wanted to go to Hong Kong himself, but he wanted to go to look for MI6 Agent Anthony Middleton, who he expected would be the lead agent. Middleton was close to FBI Agent Warren. As they drove, he decided to sneak into Hong Kong to pick up his mail. Since he'd assigned Yu to escort their agent back into China, he might try to watch everything from a distance and perhaps get his chance to strike out Middleton.

Dr. Wang's henchmen drove him into the center of town to his mailbox to gather the spy's correspondence. This was a perfect time to pick it up, as he suspected that MI6 agent Middleton and the Hong Kong police force would be focused on Zeng. He didn't even trust his own henchmen to know his mailbox number—his network was too tight for any slip ups. After he grabbed his mail, he quickly returned to the backseat of his car.

Chung turned around. "Where to, boss?"

"Drive down the street until you see a café on the right. Stop there," Dr. Wang commanded as he looked over his mail. There was a package from Jin Wu-dai. He glanced through it quickly—nothing about Warren. However, there was information regarding CIA operatives working inside China. They wouldn't be for long.

When Chung pulled up at the café and parked, Dr. Wang barked, "Wait here. I'll be right back." He briskly walked to the table where Yu Qiangsheng waited.

As soon as he was seated, he said. "Kang Sheng called. Zhou En-lai was advised by someone in the Mayor of Hong Kong's office that Zeng is being held at the Central Service Bureau. We will have agents on the Chinese side of the border. Get there immediately, look around, and make sure everything is clear. I still think there is a chance that either MI6 or the Hong Kong police may try to kill him before we can get him home." Dr. Wang got up and straighten his gray suit. "Get Zeng safely back to China. You have your assignment."

Yu nodded.

Dr. Wang stepped away from the table and quickly paced toward his car.

February 23, 1968
Washington, DC

Tom Warren walked into the FBI headquarters for a meeting with Director J. Edgar Hoover. As he ascended the steps, he thought about the day last September Michelle Galloway had called to tell him that his old friend Stephanie Keeton had supposedly committed suicide in Miami. She was so lovely and outgoing. In another time, Tom might have tried to ask her for a date. He felt remorseful that he hadn't stayed in touch with Michelle. He'd been close to those two girls. He cleared his mind as he approached the door to Hoover's receptionist. He drew a deep breath, then pulled it open. Before he could even sit down, Hoover and assistant director Tolson walked out and met him. "Come on, you're going with us."

Tom spun around and followed like a whipped pup behind his two bosses. "Where to?"

"You'll see soon enough," Tolson retorted.

They got into the director's Suburban and rode over to the U.S. Capitol. Tom was still wondering what was going on as they walked about halfway down the large hallway to a hearing room where Hoover was taken to the front by a sergeant of arms, while Tom and Tolson were shown to seats in the middle of the room behind the large table where Hoover sat.

After the head of the U. S. Congressional House Subcommittee on Appropriations had J. Edgar Hoover sworn in, the FBI Director issued the following opening:

> "The Intelligence activities of Red China have brought about an increase in our responsibilities…and the work can be expected to mount…In this country, Communist Chinese agent(s) have mounted a concerted effort to obtain highly sensitive data for their homeland. This material goes to Red China by various means. For example, two individuals have been forwarding electronic components, which could be used in a multitude of military equipment, to Communist China through an intermediary in Hong Kong."

Tom knew that comment was made for his benefit. He presumed he was referring to Dr. Paul Yu as one of those two individuals, in front of Congress. He sat there thoroughly embarrassed, but Hoover was right—in three years they hadn't been able to pin anything on Dr. Wang's network. Hoover was questioned about the Chinese activities and other issues relating to their spying. The Subcommittee was heavily invested in getting to the bottom of the ever-developing issue and what Hoover and the FBI intended to do about it. They were particularly disturbed when Hoover had to advise them that there had been no arrests of suspected Chinese spies.

By the time the hearing was over, despite his name never being mentioned, Tom was humiliated with the lack of his own performance. Hoover had to field questions from both Democrats and Republicans regarding all foreign spies and the FBI's role in questioning, arresting, and prosecuting. It was often pointed out that by far their effort against the Red Chinese had yielded nothing. Tom knew he had impacted their spy network by making them change their method of operation, but the bottom line was still no arrests.

On the drive back to the FBI Headquarters, it was very quiet. Tom assumed when he got back to headquarters, Hoover and Tolson were going to chew him out and then relieve him of all duties.

But when they got back to the entrance, Hoover snorted, "Warren, come up to my office for a few minutes before you leave."

Tom nodded and followed the top two FBI officials and took his usual seat in their office. He glanced at Tolson and then at Hoover.

Hoover lit a cigar and leaned back in his chair. It was a strange development, as this action caused Tom to relax.

"Now you see why I'm always on you, Warren." Hoover blew out the smoke. "Congressmen have been on me since the Chinese stole many of our secrets to build their first nuclear weapon. Then when they successfully set off their hydrogen bomb, the stakes went higher. We have been educating the Chinese for years—letting their top academics come here and go to our top colleges, and then they return. How many of them are spies? Who knows? How many just came here to learn and take that education home? Again, who knows?"

"Director, I'm doing the best I can. Our office has made a difference. The Chinese have changed their methods of how they conduct their operations." Tom glanced at Tolson, then back to Hoover.

"Warren, I have always ridden you hard." Hoover raised his hand, followed by another puff off his cigar. "I saw the potential in you with your first assignment. You are perfect to run our investigation of the Chinese. I asked you to come to Washington today to show you how much pressure I was under."

Tom was stunned. Hoover had never shown respect before.

"Warren, I don't disagree that you have impacted the Chinese spy network, but our Congress wants to see results—and what we consider results is not what they see." Hoover leaned forward at his desk. "Believe me, the Chinese will eventually make a mistake, and we will catch them. But, keep in mind, as long as we are letting Chinese come into our country and get educated, as we should, they will always be taking something away with them when they go home. It will be that way long after we are gone. Now get back to San Francisco and be ready."

"Yes, sir, Director. And Thank you." Tom got up and left. While he knew he'd been beaten up, he now knew Hoover was under extreme pressure, too.

CHAPTER FIFTEEN

April 30, 1969
Beijing

Yu Qiangsheng was reviewing the new diplomatic assignments at foreign embassies. When he got to the list of new personnel at the French Embassy, there was the name—Bernard Boursicot. Immediately, he summoned several of his subordinates to work the street in front of the French man's residence. He ordered them to follow his every movement from the French Embassy—a tail on the French man at all times. Yu's first priority was to get Shi's relationship restarted with Boursicot, and get Boursicot to start delivering top secret activity relating to the French Embassy.

But this cold evening in Beijing, it was different. As soon as they tipped Yu that Boursicot had gone to Shi Pei Pu's small home, Yu decided to head there immediately.

As he drove toward the edge of Beijing, he laughed out loud. It still struck him funny. Boursicot was returning to the French Embassy, in the new position of archivist. The French had created a fancy name for file clerk. Had Yu not been diligent in his job of daily reviewing all new foreign service diplomats and officials coming into mainland China, he'd have missed his name.

He waited for Boursicot to leave Shi's house—he wasn't ready to introduce himself just yet, although that may have to happen soon if he didn't start to deliver some documents to benefit Red China. Finally, after sitting for more than an hour, Boursicot left. Once he was out of sight, Yu went to the front door and pounded on it so hard the whole residence shook.

The door opened a crack and Shi peeked out.

Yu kicked the door, which smacked off from Shi's face, then stormed in and pointed toward a wooden chair. His actions sent Shi's mother running out of the room toward what he assumed was a bedroom and shut the door.

Shi cowered.

"Listen to me. We both now know Boursicot is back in Beijing."

Shi smiled but didn't say a word. Yu could tell he'd scared him. This was good.

"What did Boursicot bring you, Shi?"

Shi got up but didn't take his eyes off Yu. He picked up a package lying on the couch. "Here is what he brought."

Yu took a long step in Shi's direction and snatched the package from his hand.

"Have you found the child with the European characteristics?" Shi asked. "Boursicot asked to see our child. I told him the child was not here. He wanted to wait, but I told him it was dangerous for him to be here too long. So he left."

Yu opened the brass clasp and pulled out the contents. "I got this child thing handled." Once he'd scanned it, he slipped the pages back into the white envelope. Yu took a step toward Shi. "Anything else?"

Shi sat back down on the wooden chair and nodded. "He mentioned he was to feed Chinese information to FBI Special Agent Thomas Warren."

Yu maintained his steely eyed stare at Shi. "Has he sent any information to this Agent Warren yet?"

Shi shook his head.

Yu turned and went out the door, slamming it hard behind him.

Yu descended the steps toward Dr. Wang's office, and knocked on the door. Every time Yu came to his office or Kang's office, he had to control his temper. Neither man had helped get his mother out of jail. Only her old friend and employer, Zhou En-lai, had made any effort to get her released. But if Yu was to avoid going to jail and stunting his career path—no, make that his life path—he had to calm himself and prepare himself for his time. K'ung Ch'iu—or Confucius—reminds us that patience is a virtue. He must be very patient.

Dr. Wang opened the door and let him in. Before Yu could sit down, he passed the envelope to Wang. "Here is the first sensitive information from Boursicot."

Yu sat down across from Dr. Wang and watched him take out each page and carefully read.

When Dr. Wang was finished, Yu said, "There is more. Boursicot told Shi that the US Agent he was to feed information to is Thomas Warren."

Dr. Wang leaned across the desk. "*What did you say?*"

"Warren, Thomas Warren. Why?" Yu shrugged.

Dr. Wang sat back in his chair and smiled, his teeth looking like corn on a cob. "This opportunity *just can't be*. Nothing this simple has ever been handed to me."

"*What?* Is that important? What's our next step?" Yu knew he had delivered good news, but was puzzled none the less.

"Stay on Shi." Dr. Wang leaned back up on the desk. "No, I want you to go back to Shi, and I want you to get Shi to introduce you to Boursicot. This situation has changed."

"How so?" Yu inquired.

"I want you to take control of this situation, immediately." Dr. Wang commanded. "I will be preparing a package to have Shi pass to Boursicot to send to the United States, to one FBI Agent Thomas Payne Warren."

"Since I'm going to make contact with Boursicot, what name should I give him?" Yu asked.

Dr. Wang shrugged. "Who cares? Make something up. I don't care."

Yu started to get up when Dr. Wang commanded, "We aren't done. I need to confide something to you."

Yu settled back into his seat.

Dr. Wang jutted his chin. "I'm gaining in power here in China." He flashed a brief smile. "I've even been asked to help improve relations between Red China and Japan, if you can believe that. Zhou En-lai, who knows what happened to my mother and sister in NanJing, has asked me to do this."

Yu knew little of Dr. Wang's mysterious past, still not even knowing his real name.

Dr. Wang frowned. "However, I'm very concerned with the actions and orders of Kang Sheng." He paused for a moment. "I know he has always spoken of you like his stepson, but I fear he is overstepping his authority. He is having me, you, and others interrogate our citizens when they return from foreign trips. He has even gone in and taken artworks and antiques from some of our distinguished representatives. I've spoken with Zhou En-lai about this being bad policy. Soon it could lead to more citizens defecting, not, as Kang believes, stopping them from traveling."

Yu gritted his teeth. He had no choice at this point, but his mother had been so mistreated by the State, it was most difficult. Now, these leaders were bidding for their own power. Kang had told him he was responsible for shutting down the Red Guard, when it was clearly Mao who had reined them in after five years of assaulting their own citizens. *Perhaps, it is my time to sit back and let the dragons take each other out, then my path to the top will be easier.*

Dr. Wang got up from his desk. "Only you and one other of my agents know what I'm about to tell you in the strictest of confidence. A certain U.S. General Vernon Walters, an American military attaché in Paris, met with our military attaché regarding a potential meeting between U.S. delegates at the highest level with Chinese delegates at the highest level. The U.S. is wanting to open diplomatic channels between the two countries. We know this because of my other agent. This is moving very fast. As of right now, only Mao, Zhou, myself, the agent in the U.S., and you know of this. Now, you are asking yourself, why am I telling you this?"

Yu blinked his eyes in disbelief.

Dr. Wang continued. "Because you were able to control yourself when your mother went through her misfortune. Zhou and Mao considered it a test of your character. Your mother did wrong. They knew it was hard for you to sit back and take that. But this has put you on the fast track to power in this country. You will be rewarded for being a good soldier for your self-control.

As Yu listened, he realized he must discover who the agent working in the United States was. He could leverage it for the purpose of his own power. It would be good to find out without anyone's knowledge.

As he walked out of the office, he thought about all he'd been told. *I'll tell Boursicot my name is Kang.* This brought a quick smile to his face.

Beijing
April 30, 1969

Yu's street spies tipped him off that Boursicot hopped in a pedicab. Yu had placed another group of informants in front of Shi Pei Pu's dilapidated residence. When Yu got the tip Boursicot had arrived at Shi's residence, he was on the move. Boursicot's position of archivist should allow him to see lots of top-secret documents.

Yu wanted some action. The more he sat by himself, the more time he had to think of his mother still being held in prison. He'd been promised by Zhou En-lai personally that she'd be released soon, but thus far, she hadn't. Yu had aspirations of taking over the CID, with Kang falling under the scrutiny of the Communist Party, but he had to tread lightly. Kang was still his supervisor. But Kang had always promised he'd protect his mother, too, at which he'd failed miserably. However, because of Yu's good works and growth at the CID, Kang was able to lobby Mao and Zhou to keep him out of trouble with the Communist Party. He just had to be patient for his opening. Things inside China were deteriorating fast, and Mao trusted few.

He pulled up out front of Shi Pei Pu's residence, a very small home situated between two other equally small houses. Boursicot had already left. Yu watched the activity inside the small apartment. Just Shi and his mother were home. Yu knocked on the door. When Shi answered, Yu pushed his way in.

Yu pointed at him. "You will be cool toward Boursicot. Keep your distance from him, yet see him. I'm still struggling to find a child who could fit the description."

Shi didn't make eye contact, but nodded.

"Give me time to find someone who has European characteristics so it looks like the child is his. I'll give you the instructions." He got down in Shi's face. "He must be more productive spying for us."

Shi sheepishly replied, "I'll try. I do wish to see him. I do want to be with him. I care for him."

Yu waved his finger then put it to his mouth. "Listen to me. I don't care about any of that. All I care about is that he believes it. We want him to get us information. He is in the perfect place to do so."

Shi started to speak again as Yu got up and walked to the door. Yu took one step toward him. "Shi, not another word. Do as you are told. Do it my way, or else you will be locked up for being homosexual."

Shi nodded.

Yu slammed the door on the way out to give him one more point of intimidation.

CHAPTER SIXTEEN

April 3, 1970
San Francisco

Tom Warren sat at a small conference table with Martin Corley. They were reviewing tax returns from the years 1964 through 1967 for Dr. Paul Yu's company, AD-YU Electronics. The good doctor had grown. His sales now included business and government contractors in Italy, Britain, France, Germany, Japan, Belgium, Austria, India, and South Africa. Tom leaned back. "Marty, this guy started his business in 1954, with only going to junior college, self-financed, and now he's selling electronics and engineering equipment in all these countries."

Marty shrugged. "How can he be a doctor, having only gone to a junior college?"

Tom raised both hands. "Either we're missing information or he's not a doctor. Think about this—someone or some company or some country has to be helping him with investments. It doesn't show up here in these filings."

Marty winced, then continued through the 1964 tax return.

Tom got up and started pacing. "Marty, this is the proof we've been speculating on. We thought that since Red China set off their hydrogen bomb several years ago, they have changed their spying techniques."

Marty rested his chin on this hand as he placed his elbow on the conference table.

"Think about this for a second. They already stole how to make bombs, so now they need everything else. They are spying to steal business, agriculture—you know, things that improve their terrible economy."

"So you don't believe they have anyone in Los Alamos anymore?" Marty chewed on his lower lip.

"No. Not at all. They aren't removing anyone. *They are expanding.* Take Dr. Paul Yu selling electronics and engineering equipment. With equipment properly placed, could they be listening, recording, and/or transmitting information with equipment that's just sitting there? I don't know." Tom gestured before placing his hands on both hips.

Marty nodded. "You know, that makes a lot of sense. They can't afford to make anything. According to the CIA, their economy is in the crapper."

Tom walked over and pointed at the segment of Director Hoover's testimony in front of the Congressional Subcommittee in 1968. Hoover had made Tom frame it and hang it on the wall for a reminder of his failure to question and arrest any Chinese spies. "It's more than them just stealing highly sensitive data." Then he turned back to Marty and repeated himself. *"It's more than just the sensitive data."*

Marty rolled his eyes as Tom went and pointed at that damn testimony.

Tom raised his hand as he continued. "Let me give you a history lesson. After the Chinese civil war, Kang Sheng and Mao had all Tai Li's spies killed. So the Chinese Communists had to rebuild their spy network. With the exception of a few individuals we believe are working for Dr. Wang, they rely on Chinese individuals to bring back bits and pieces of information, which the powers that be assemble in China. Once again, a network hard to break, because these individuals don't see the big picture assembled by a few in China."

"Where did you get that information? Just from your own experience? Because it isn't written anywhere." Marty licked his lips. "Okay, what do we do different?"

Tom rubbed his forehead with his fingers. "I think I need to check back in with CIA Larry again. See what information he has on Dr. Paul Yu." He sighed. "We need a break to have enough to bring in Dr. Yu for questioning. Up until now, he has been pretty smooth. Doesn't make any mistakes. I just can't help but believe he's part of Dr. Wang's network."

May 8, 1970
Beijing

There was an early morning fog, which was just perfect for Yu Qiangsheng. He was driving to see his mother, Fan Jin, who had just been released from prison the day before. She'd told him over and over the night before to stay away, but Yu wasn't going to allow the government he worked for to deter him from seeing her. Before he knocked, he drew a deep breath. He didn't know what to expect. What did five years in prison do to his elderly mother? He was supposed to be a tough guy—and he was—but this was his mother. He jutted his jaw, gritted his teeth, straightened his shoulders, and knocked.

The door creaked open a tiny bit. His mother peeked out. Then she swung the door open.

Yu stepped through and hugged his mother. He couldn't let go. Then he held her out to look at her. Her left shoulder was lower than the right, the skin around her eyes were permanently darkened from the beatings she'd probably endured. When she turned and walked slowly to the stove, she had a distinct limp.

When Fan handed Yu his hot cup of green tea, her right arm was badly scarred from burns and cuts. Yu's lower lip quivered despite his effort to compose himself. "Mother, the government will pay for doing this to you."

Fan touched his hand and then grabbed it. "Son, you must not retaliate. I knew this could happen. But I was determined to show the treachery of Chairman Mao."

"But, Mother, look at what they did to you!"

Fan wiped a tear from the corner of her eye. "Others were treated worse. Many in the Three Family Village movement . . . ." She gulped hard several times before she could finish her thought. "Died in those work camps."

Yu sipped his green tea. "Mother, I'm just happy you made it home."

He knew better than to say more to his Mother, but he'd deal with this in the very near future.

San Francisco

Tom Warren had come into the office early to sit in peaceful silence and think. On his desk was the latest letter from Hada Miyoko. He quickly opened it, only to be disappointed. Once again, it revealed absolutely nothing. Her infrequent conversations with her father had gone nowhere. This letter only frustrated Tom more with his current situation. He felt like he needed to make another trip to Japan to see if he could get Miyoko's father to meet with him. If he could get any information at all on the Japanese occupation of NanJing, he could flush out Dr. Wang and bring down his entire spy network. It would take so little to get under Dr. Wang's skin. He thought if he could explain to her father that Dr. Wang was the individual who had stolen the Japanese secret rocket technology for China, he might get him to talk, but he couldn't put anything in writing. Maybe, just maybe, her father would be patriotic about China having gained the technology from Japan.

Tom went to the window overlooking the street below. *The old Chinaman's newsstand, Kikue Nakamura, Jared Samuel, the double murder, and now the potassium suicide of another old Chinaman. Nothing solved but all related—and it all led back to Dr. Wang.*

Tom felt the presence of someone standing beside him. He glanced up.

His immediate boss, Special Agent in Charge Gerald Adler, stood next to his desk.

"Boss, I've been thinking."

Adler laughed. "That seems pretty obvious. I been standing by you for a good minute."

"Can we talk? I have a theory." Tom rubbed his hand over his face.

"Sure. Come to my office."

Tom sat down opposite his boss. He paused for a minute.

"Well, are you going to take up my time sitting there, or are you going to give me something to think about?"

"The old Chinaman who took the suicide capsule was leader of the San Francisco operation—or the point man for Dr. Wang."

"How do you come to that conclusion? Do you have any evidence?"

"Whoever the assumed courier was, he was smuggled out of the restaurant by those two workers. His identity was revealed, so they had to die."

"But, Tom, your old Chinaman would have been too old to overpower and kill both restaurant workers," Adler countered.

"You're right, but Dr. Wang's network would have to have a point man—someone to handle the communications and make assignments." Tom shrugged. "Looks like they changed the methods of operations again, 'cause everything has gone dark since then."

"Okay, can you explain how Kikue Nakamura and Jared Samuel fit into that picture?"

"Kikue Nakamura was a Japanese spy, but I can't prove it. And Jared Samuel knew too much. He saw Dr. Wang get in the elevator and go to her floor. He had to be eliminated. That's where the network took over, since Dr. Wang was gone by then." Tom arched an eyebrow. "I suspect that may have been the first order of the old Chinese man who committed suicide before I could interrogate him."

"Warren, even if your hypothesis is correct, which I don't think it is, you have zero evidence. We need *evidence*. We have got to stop this spying." Adler scowled. "Hoover needs arrests. Now, get out of here and go to work. Go arrest somebody."

Tom got up and grabbed the doorknob. "Call your buddy Detective Lee. See if he has anything to tie this together."

"Warren, get out of my office. You get me proof. Not Detective Lee."

Tom walked out.

Marty was in, so Tom went to his desk and sat down.

"Why did you have to go and piss off Adler first thing?" Marty leaned back in his chair. "He's going to be nasty to all of us the rest of the day."

Tom ignored the comment. He didn't care what Adler said. He thought his hypothesis was a good one. "Marty, do you have anything more on Dr. Paul Yu?"

"Nothing. I'm just about through his 1968 tax return. I know he's hiding money, but I can't find it. He is moving around too much on such little income. I think we need to get a forensic accountant on his transactions and deposits. Things aren't adding up, but I can't figure it out." Marty leaned back in his chair and clasped his hands behind his head.

"Marty, I'm going to do some traveling. I think I'm going to have a face-to-face with CIA Larry, then I want to go to Hong Kong and see Middleton." Tom had ulterior motives, too. He wanted to go to Japan and try to meet with Miyoko's father. Plus, he could see Miyoko again.

CHAPTER SEVENTEEN

April 26, 1971
San Francisco

Tom was again first in the office, and, as usual, he made the coffee. He liked to get to his desk before everyone else to think and plan his day. During the early morning, the FBI mailman had placed an interoffice memo package on his desk. He looked at it. It was heavier than normal. *Ugh. Bound to be as boring as ever.* He wasn't ready to go through it until he'd downed his first cup. Tom waited until the pot finished brewing, then took his University of Arizona coffee cup over and poured some of the dark brown liquid before returning to his desk.

He undid the clasp, grabbed the contents, and put them on his desk. A bunch of busy work. He picked up his copy of the *San Francisco Chronicle* and started through it. Flipping page by page with his destination the sports section, he paused at a familiar photo on the obituaries page. T. V. Soong. The man he'd helped escape Communist China had passed away, right here in San Francisco. Soong choked on a piece of chicken that had gotten lodged in his throat at a dinner party hosted by the chairman of the Bank of Canton, San Francisco branch. *Damn. I really liked that man. I wonder why he didn't try to contact me when he came here? Maybe because I hadn't maintained contact with him?*

Previously, he'd totally missed the death of H. H. Kung, the other Chinese man he helped escape the Communists—he had to be told about that by Galloway. Now, both men he'd helped more than two decades ago were dead. Both men had attempted to help him with tips on the Chinese Spy Network, including information about Dr. Wang. But he'd failed to follow up with either man. He realized he'd been so focused on establishing his own investigation that he'd overlooked the obvious—men who had inside connections. An opportunity lost. He had to change his approach and start getting results.

One of the old adages of effective spying was that you had to have boots on the ground. At the moment, he only had Shou Li Cao in the Chinatown restaurant and the beautiful Hada Miyoko in Japan. He needed to develop some eyes inside Red China. But who?

June 15, 1971
Beijing

Yu Qiangsheng was advised by Shi that Boursicot was stopping by his home that evening. Once Yu heard that, he decided to be there to meet him. Yu took a People's Liberation Army officer with him. The two men were sitting there when Boursicot showed up. Yu introduced himself, in French. "I'm Kang. This is Zhao."

Boursicot sat down on the small couch beside Shi and began quoting from the teachings of Mao.

As though that would impress me.

Boursicot turned to Yu. "I would like to do what I can to assist the Chinese government."

Yu leaned forward, placing his elbow on his knee, and stroked his chin. "Very well then, we would like to have you continue to bring us documentation from the French Embassy, but we have another request as well. Shi mentioned that a certain FBI agent asked you to gather information for them on the Chinese government. Is that true?"

"Why, yes, as a matter of fact. Let's see. His name was Thomas Warren, but that was over five years ago." Boursicot fidgeted on the couch.

"I want to give you information to send to him. Do you understand that?" *This is just too easy.*

Boursicot let out his breath as he nodded.

"Did you bring a package today?" Yu inquired.

"Why, yes, I did." Boursicot opened his sports coat and pulled out an envelope and offered it to Yu. Then he continued. "I work at one of the most important French Embassies and have total access to the mailroom, where a diplomatic pouch from Paris arrives twice a week. I'm responsible for properly archiving all incoming and outgoing diplomatic wires."

Yu stroked his chin again. "Do you see any military wires or correspondence?"

"No, Kang. Nothing from the military. While I don't have high enough clearance to be able to unseal the diplomatic pouches, in almost all cases, the staff returns everything to me to archive."

His answer was disappointing. Yu had hoped they could gain access to Soviet military information in particular. First, Yu glanced at Zhao, then squinted at Boursicot to intimidate him. "Okay, fine. We are very interested in correspondence regarding the Soviet Union or the U.S. Assistant Secretary of State for East Asian and Pacific Affairs. Got it?"

"Yes, Kang. I understand. Correspondence from Marshall Green comes about every two months." Boursicot swallowed hard. "So please don't expect information there as often as the correspondence between the French and the Soviets."

"Very well. We will allow Shi to continue to see you. And after you deliver your next package, we will permit you to see your son. Is that understood?" Yu commanded.

Boursicot pouted but wouldn't make eye contact.

Yu glanced at Zhao and pointed toward the door. Zhao headed toward the front door. Yu stood and captured Boursicot's eyes. "The next time we meet, I'll have information for you to send to FBI Agent Warren. You need to do that very discreetly. Do you understand?"

Boursicot leaned back on the couch for the first time.

Yu remained standing over Boursicot and Shi for a moment to intimidate them, then went out the door Zhao had opened.

"Are you spying on the Chinese government?" Zhao asked. "Are you a double agent?"

Yu grabbed him by the shirt. "You idiot. Of course not. But I can't let Boursicot know that. It will make him feel important—while setting up the Americans, too."

San Francisco
June 30, 1971

Tom hung up the phone and waved for Marty to come over. As soon as Marty approached, Tom said, "You're not going to believe this. I just hung up from a French man who about six years ago asked me if he could spy on the Chinese for us."

"You pulled me over here to tell me this? Don't distract me when—" Marty shrugged, then lowered his voice. "I'm trying to make heads or tails out of Dr. Paul Yu's finances. Nothing adds up."

Tom ignored Marty's comment and continued, "I turned him over to Hoover because he wanted paid, and I didn't want any part of it. Several years ago, Hoover told me this guy never came through. Now, he just got reassigned to China and has a package for us. He wanted my address."

"What did you do?" Marty inquired.

"Hell, I gave him my address, a post office box, I can't trust anyone with my home address. But I'm going to notify Hoover that the French diplomat contacted me and wants to do this." He ran his fingers through his hair as he leaned back in his chair. "If Hoover agrees to pay him, this could be a real breakthrough for us."

Marty turned back toward his desk.

"One more thing," Tom called. "I had one of the agents at the D.C. bureau put in a request for any Chinese scientists or businessmen living in the U.S. who have requested a travel visa to Red China. We can assign these names out to some of our agents in the office here to investigate."

Marty didn't turn around but raised his right hand as he returned to his desk to continue through the Dr. Yu papers.

Tom was checking off boxes in his new approach to taking down the Chinese Spy network.

CHAPTER EIGHTEEN

May 2, 1972
San Francisco

Tom Warren was fixing his morning coffee at home, listening to the *Today Show*, when a special announcement interrupted the show: J. Edgar Hoover had passed away. The news commentator was short on details, only saying that Hoover had been discovered dead that morning.

Why hadn't anyone called and notified me? Tom sat there, just staring at the television. He didn't hear anything else that was said. He couldn't believe it. The only director he'd ever known was dead. While Hoover had always been hard on Tom, he'd pushed him to become the agent he was.

Within five minutes, his phone rang. He scooped it up.

"Tom, I'm sure you heard the news. Hoover is dead. Damn, I can't believe it."

Tom still was barely able to speak. "Marty, come by and pick me up. Let's get into the office. Let me get my wits about me."

The phone went dead.

Tom and Marty soberly walked into the office. It was a somber place.

Tom tried to be focused. "Get your file on Dr. Paul Yu. I want to review something."

Marty nodded and headed straight for his desk.

165

Tom went directly to his file cabinet to pull his file on the subject. Marty pulled a chair up to his desk with his file.

Tom said, "Pull that Canadian judge's statement on their customs' findings."

Marty pulled out the statement from the judge. "This doesn't make sense. The Canadian judge contended that this was a smuggling conspiracy. The customs officials seized a shipment of AD-YU Electronics—components consigned to Communist China."

Tom waved his hand. "Ignore the legal facts, look it's the Canadian system. We can't do anything about that. I'm focused on the tax returns. In 1967, he moved all sorts of electronic equipment all over the world but the next year he moves his business from New Jersey to Milwaukee then goes bankrupt. Nobody goes broke selling aerospace and military equipment to governments around the world then goes bankrupt. Think about it. Let's get an FBI forensic accountant to go over this, he is hiding money somewhere." He picked up the phone. "I'm going to check in with Larry Wu-tai Chin at CIA to see, if he has any chatter on his whereabouts. The CIA has been feeding him intel coming out of China."

Marty shrugged. "Because of bankruptcy, they have already liquidated his business and we have lost track of him."

Tom picked up his file. "We dropped the ball, we are the ones who put him on the back-burner, only because we couldn't get anything on him. The man didn't make any mistakes, he handled everything neat and clean. Those four years of tax returns you went through didn't have any clues until I thought about the government contracts exposed in the Canadian trial." He pointed at the Canadian judge's page of written remarks. "We have talked about this before. What if his equipment had transmitter or data collecting devices? Or what if he was learning just from talking to clients? If I'm correct, we may have enough to bring him in for questioning. Just because we've lost track of him, I'm betting either MI6 and/or Interpol know his whereabouts. I bet he's still moving around the world doing business—maybe even under another name."

Marty adjusted his necktie. "Okay, I'll pull all this together and get it over to one of the FBI's top accountants."

"Forget the accountant. Take anything you need out of this." Tom pushed his file toward Marty. "We stay on top of this. You and I can at least get started with the Judge's written remarks."

The phone on Marty's desk rang. He scooted over and picked it up. The first words out of his mouth were. "*Oh no.*"

Tom didn't look up, thinking it was someone else calling to discuss the passing of Hoover. But when Marty slammed down the phone, he looked at him. His face was red.

Marty shouted, "Tom! Come on! We got to go now." He sprinted toward the door.

Tom was bewildered by his partner, but sprung from his desk. "What is it?"

Marty flung the door open. "Shou!"

As Tom got to the elevator, Marty was pounding on the down button. "What about Shou?"

"We had a code word if she was in trouble. She used it and hung up the phone."

The elevator door opened. They were the only ones in the car. "She was to say *Golden Gate Bridge* if she was in trouble. She'd sneak out of the restaurant, if she possibly could, and start walking toward the Stockton Street Tunnel at the edge of Chinatown."

Both men jogged to their assigned Ford Galaxy.

Marty started the car, threw it in gear, and sped off. "What do we do about Shou?"

"Quit panicking. You put a procedure in place. We follow it, damn it." Tom knew Marty's feelings for the woman was clouding his thought process. "She should be fine following that plan. Then we see what spooked her."

It took Marty about twenty minutes to get to the edge of Chinatown. He pulled over at the tunnel and parked.

Tom looked at him. "What now?"

Marty drummed his fingers on the steering wheel. "We wait. She should be here in a couple of minutes."

Tom opened the car door. "I can't sit still. I'm going to walk down the street."

Marty leaned out the window. "We don't know that she'll walk down Stockton. If she shows and you're not back, we'll drive back to headquarters."

Tom walked back over to the car and squatted down. "No, go get her mother, and *then* go to headquarters. If they think she's spying, they'll go after her mother."

Marty nodded as Tom straightened back up and started walking.

Tom continued down the street about a block and a half. No sign of Shou. He continued to scan the people walking in the opposite direction. Finally, he saw her bumping through the crowd in his direction. He craned his neck to look over the top of her head to see if anyone was pursuing her. Nothing looked obvious. He stopped and looked briefly in a small shop until Shou walked by him. Tom turned and followed long enough to ask, "Are you being followed?"

She barely nodded.

Tom replied, "Marty is at the rendezvous point. I'll fall back a little and see if I can pick them out. Tell Marty to wait on me."

Shou started walking faster as Tom pivoted off in the direction from which she'd come.

He moved through the large crowd of Chinese and sightseers. No one stood out. Had they walked by him? After a half a block, he turned around, started back moving faster, almost jogging toward the waiting car.

As Tom approached the car, he saw Marty but not Shou. Now he started running. "Where is Shou?"

Marty waved for Tom to get in.

Just then a muffled voice spoke from behind. Tom leaned back and saw her hiding behind their seats. She'd made it. Tom jumped in his seat and slammed the door.

Marty drove off. Finally, Shou sat up and started telling them what had happened. "Yesterday, a new cook showed up. No one seemed to think anything of it. All day, no one said anything. Then, this morning, when we came in to start working on lunch prep, several of the waitresses and cooks started talking that someone from Mainland had sent in this guy to figure out who was messing with their spying network. Naturally, I assumed this guy was sent here by Dr. Wang. Anyway, he'd supposedly brought files with him on everyone who had moved here from China. He started interrogating employees in the back. One of the other waitresses came out pretty beat up. She'd been a friend. She was the one who told me about the files to question employees. Well, they questioned everyone but me before lunch. So I discreetly kept an eye on everyone because they were keeping their eyes on me. The opportunity presented itself while I was at the cash register. The phone rang, and I picked it up for a take-out order. As soon as I hung up, I called Marty, then sprinted out of the restaurant just as four businessmen came in to be seated."

Marty turned around temporarily to look at Shou. "I love you. I'm glad you're okay. That's all that's important at the moment."

Tom glanced over the front seat at Shou. "We're going to go pick up your mother. We need to get you all out of San Francisco into protective custody. As soon as both of you are back at headquarters, Marty and I are going to the restaurant and grab the cook you told us about. Something about this just isn't right. This isn't how the Chinese spy network normally works. This was a hard play—and Dr. Wang isn't that obvious. If it is him, something must have really spooked him."

"Are you sure that is what we should do?" Marty frowned.

"It's not what we should do. It's what we must do," Tom snapped. "This is our chance to make a difference in this effort. It's not a trap if you know it's a trap." He paused for a minute. "Hoover just died. Everyone will expect the FBI to be in disarray. How do we not know this guy was sitting in the United States waiting for something to trigger his move?"

About that time, Marty pulled up in front of the apartment complex where Shou and her mother lived. Marty got out and grabbed her hand and helped her out of the car.

Tom said, "Get her mother out fast. Get what few items they can gather and get them back in the car. I'll stay out here and guard your back."

Marty and Shou ran as fast as they could into the building. Tom watched up and down the street. Nothing seemed out of place. No one seemed to be paying any attention. He continued to look up and down. No evidence of any gunman anywhere. *Perhaps we are still ahead of them. Or maybe no one is pursuing her.*

Tom still felt uneasy. His mind raced off into the what-if's. *The cook had interviewed everybody but Shou, so he already knew. He wanted her to run. Did he want her to run here? Very likely. So this is the first trap and we have walked into it. Someone is here.*

Tom looked at his watch. Shou and Marty had been inside for fifteen minutes. *If they don't come out soon, I guess I'll have to go in and get them.* He got out of the car, looked around, then opened the trunk and pulled out his assigned AR-15. Tom wasn't as good with the assault rifle as his .38 handgun, but he wanted to be prepared. Traffic was pretty heavy going up and down the street. He hated being this obvious, but his situation called for drastic measures.

Just as he slammed the trunk, Marty, Shou and her mother came out of the apartment, each carrying a small bag. Tom scanned around all the buildings again. Still no evidence of anyone watching. *Are we still ahead of the Chinese?*

A car started up the street. Tires squealed as it sped in their direction.

Tom spun around just as several shots rang out. He took aim at the approaching car just as they took aim at him and fired off several bursts. He hit both the driver and passenger. The car swerved back and forth down the street, crashing into two parked cars before stopping. He was pretty proud of his shooting as he turned around.

Shou leaned over her mother. Marty was bending over to support Shou. *That's not good.* But he had to focus on the car and the shooters. He pulled his handgun and pointed it as he carefully moved toward the wrecked car. As he stepped up to the car, he determined both Chinese were dead. He opened the car doors, pulled their wallets, and went through their pockets to get any information.

Sirens sounded in the distance. He ran back to Marty and Shou. "Come on, let's get Shou's mother in the car and get out of here before the police or more Chinese show up."

Marty raised his voice but choked on every other word. *"We can't just scoop Shou's mother up* and then leave the scene. *We've got* to wait for the police."

"We have to get Shou into hiding." He scurried over and grabbed under Shou's mother's shoulders and started pulling her along the grass.

Finally, Marty grabbed her legs.

Tom put her in the backseat with him, then commanded. "Shou, get up front, now." He tossed the AR in the trunk and slammed it.

Marty sprinted around, started the car, slammed it into gear and sped off. The only noise in the car was Shou curled up in a ball, sobbing in the front seat. Within a block, they passed two black and white units going the other way. After a few more blocks, Marty finally whispered under his breath, "Where to, Tom?"

Tom leaned over the front seat. "Back to headquarters. We've got to protect Shou. And we'll get a couple of boys from the FBI morgue to take the proper care of—" he nodded in the direction of Shou's mother's body.

Marty pulled into the back of the FBI building and parked. Tom got out, opened the door for Shou, then looked at Marty. "Take her inside, try to help her. I'll handle the rest."

Tom walked into the office. A few agents were still chatting about who was going to take over for J. Edger Hoover and what was going to happen to Clyde Tolson. Tom glanced around the room, then spotted Marty and Shou sitting in Adler's office. Tom walked in.

Adler pointed at the chair at the edge of his desk. "Special Agent Warren, what exactly do you plan to do now? You've created a big mess with the SFPD. You can imagine Detective Lee has already called, wanting an explanation."

Tom stood just inside the door. "Marty, Shou, let's go. Special Agent Adler, you'll figure this out. Detective Lee is your buddy."

Tom just kept walking. He'd be in trouble for his actions, but at the moment, he trusted nobody and he was suspicious of Detective Lee and was starting to question Adler.

As he walked out the door, Special Agent in Charge Adler stepped into the main area and shouted, *"Special Agent Warren, you better get your ass back in here, if you know what's good for you."*

Tom continued walking at a faster pace. Marty and Shou met him as he held the elevator door open. They trooped directly to the parking lot and walked toward the car. "Everybody, get in."

Marty got behind the steering wheel and Shou crawled in the backseat. Tom looked at him. "Drive to Oakland. We're going to get a couple of hotel rooms, sit, and figure out what's next."

Marty didn't even look at Tom. "What are you going to do about Adler? He's probably going to write you up—if not fire you."

"*Drive.*"

Marty huffed as he turned up the radio on the drive over. No one had anything to say. Tom didn't care for any of the modern music, unlike Marty, so he just try to focus on piecing it all together. He'd grabbed everything off the two Chinese today, but it wasn't much. He could barely handle the disappointment of not being able to get to the Chinese restaurant to confront the cook. But as Scarlet O'Hara said, tomorrow is another day—or something like that.

Marty and Shou got one room, and Tom got the adjoining room. After everyone had gotten cleaned up, they gathered in Tom's room. He had managed to sneak out and get some fast food and beverages for them to share while they discussed the day's events. When Shou sat down on the edge of the bed, her red eyes broke Tom's heart, who was feeling considerable guilt for putting her in that position.

Tom glanced at Marty, then back at her. "Shou, we need to keep you under protective custody until we can confirm the cook has not only left the restaurant, but the country."

Shou raised her hands. "You're wrong." She paused before continuing. "You and Marty are wrong. I've been thinking about this since I ran from the restaurant. I'm moving back to China, and I want to continue to work undercover for you all in China. I want to help you bring down Dr. Wang. The communists have taken away my family."

Marty leaned forward from the chair in the corner of the hotel room. "Honey, we can't let you do that."

Shou turned toward Marty with fire in her eyes. "You have no say in my life. I love you, but you don't know the pain the communists have inflicted in my life. They must pay."

Tom raised his hand. "Listen to me, I have an idea." He looked at both of them. "Shou, rather than going back to mainland, how about going to Hong Kong? You can still go in and out of China, but you'll have a safer base to work from."

Marty lurched at Tom. "Are you nuts? Are you trying to ruin my relationship and put Shou at risk?"

Tom stood up. "Let me finish. I think I can get you a partial assignment there, too. Maybe a couple of weeks a month. It's a lot of travel. We need to improve our research into the Chinese spy ring. Middleton has been working on this as long as I have. You work with Middleton, but we won't tell him about Shou. I can sell the FBI that we need to expand our operation to two fronts. Hong Kong is a hot bed, just like Berlin was for the CIA at the beginning of the Cold War for the Soviets."

Marty sat back down with Tom's explanation. "You think you can sell this?"

"Tomorrow, you and I go to the restaurant, try to find the cook. We sell it that both Shou and her mother were killed in the shooting. We are there to investigate. We even get our buddy Detective Lee to go with us, if he can."

Marty sat back down next to Shou. "What do you think?"

Shou laid her head on Marty's shoulder. "You'd leave the United States to be with me?"

Marty nodded.

Shou looked at him, then at Tom, and then back at Marty. "You're a Southern boy. You will stick out like a sore thumb in Hong Kong. And you won't be able to get grits or black-eyed peas in Hong Kong."

With that comment, everybody laughed.

"Okay, here's the deal. Tomorrow morning, I've got a telephone appointment. I'm going to check in with Larry Wu-tai Chin and see what he might have found on Dr. Paul Yu. Then you and I go to the restaurant. I'll call Lee and get him to go with us tomorrow as part of our joint investigation. Then the next day, we fly to Hong Kong." Tom pointed at Marty. "I'm going back to the office now. Plus, I'll call Middleton and arrange to have you all liaison with him. I'll sell him with our findings on Dr. Paul Yu's tax returns. It's not much, but it's likely MI6 doesn't have access to that information. Then we get Shou to work undercover for us going in and out of China."

Marty got up off the bed with Shou. "Don't you think you need to get Special Agent in Charge Gerald Adler's permission to do all this first?"

Tom flashed a brief smile. "Yes, of course. Look, if he denies us, we still escort Shou to Hong Kong. We can't let her be seen. Just the few agents in the office know that Shou is still alive. I think I can sell him on you spending a couple of weeks out of each month there. I've been thinking about this for a while, but I knew Hoover wouldn't buy it, this is the time to push for this."

Marty nodded as Tom headed out the door. If everything worked out just right, Tom would sneak into Tokyo to see Miyoko, as well.

Beijing

Dr. Wang hustled into the park in the center of Beijing for an urgent meeting but didn't see Kang Shang anywhere. He sat down on the closest bench he could find. About fifteen minutes later, Kang arrived then sat down next to him. "I have several high security matters we need to discuss. First off, how did your portion of the interrogations go with the twenty-seven traitorous Army officers who tried to defect to Hong Kong?"

"Between Yu Qiangsheng and I, we took care of my group. They were all brutally tortured, an example must be made of those traitors." He replied while jutting his jaw. "I'm only awaiting your orders as to which hard labor camp to send them."

"I'll decide that later. Did any of them give up the one who successfully escaped? Where he went?" Kang snarled. "If so, send Yu to bring him back."

Dr. Wang nodded. "No one, yet. I plan on having some more discussions with the weaker ones and was only waiting for your orders. Your idea to use Yu is a good one, as I want him to start getting familiar with Hong Kong."

Kang looked in both directions before he spoke. "I believe that is the last of the traitors who worked with Lin Piao."

"Yu Qiangsheng had a particularly good time, since these men were loyal to Lin Piao, the leader behind the rise of the Red Guard in 1965. He believed he found a couple that dealt with his mother." Smirked Dr. Wang.

Kang rubbed his hands together. "The second matter is very disturbing. We have an information leak in our nuclear program. I haven't been able to pinpoint it, just yet. Let's get your network on this. Check first the scientists going in and out of the United States. I hope we don't have any double agents but if we do, I want them. I'll make them sorry to their dying breath."

Dr. Wang pounded his fist on the bench. "I thought we had been able to plug most of the holes. That leak regarding anything in our nuclear program, is unacceptable. Perhaps Yu Qiangsheng is getting lacks with his interrogations of people returning from the United States."

Kang frowned. "Then you must fix it."

"Yes, Kang. I'll clean it up. You can count on me."

"We must get some false information out to the western world, I'll put some of our scientists on it. I want you to handle the CIA and the FBI. I'll deal with the KGB, GRU and MI6."

"You get with the scientists and get some data, I can get it out in no time." Dr. Wang nodded. He had already established sending false information to FBI

Agent Warren via Boursicot. He wasn't about to tell Kang about his own efforts but it would serve his purpose.

Kang jutted his chin. "What is the latest from Jin Wu-dai?"

"Jin has become an American citizen. Since the CIA transferred him to Arlington, he is responsible for translating highly sensitive information from China. Naturally, the CIA had the FBI give him a lie detector test before putting him in that position, which he passed." Dr. Wang leaned his head back then slyly nodded. "We know everything the CIA is stealing from us almost immediately."

Kang placed both hands on his knees as though he was about to leave. "Anything else?"

"FBI Special Agent Warren has even occasionally reached out to Jin, seeking information. Most recently, Warren has been asking about Dr. Paul Yu." Dr. Wang replied.

"I must assume Jin has kept him away from our agent?" Kang raised his right hand to his chin as though he was processing the situation.

Dr. Wang nodded. "Of course. Jin is good. He is the best. One more thing, three months ago Jin sent me the last list of CIA undercover agents here. We are dealing with them appropriately."

Kang patted Dr. Wang on the knee. "Since you have verified Jin's information, then you are authorized to release another payment to him. Perhaps he can be useful in getting this misinformation out. Think about it."

Dr. Wang folded his hands together. "No, Kang, we can't expose Jin. I'll find another way. Let me say something, this information of our nuclear program getting out to the Brits and Americans are a result of interrogating our own people when they return from overseas. They are going into the finest schools in the world and studying, learning bringing back technology and then we interrogate them. It is wrong."

Kang slowly rose up from the bench and leaned over Dr. Wang. "Do not question my authority. You know the power I weld with my role in the Cultural Revolution. Let that be your last attempt to challenge my policy."

Dr. Wang didn't say a word as Kang turned and walked away. He knew who had the power and it was him, not Kang. Perhaps it was time to demonstrate that to Kang.

May 4, 1972
San Francisco

Tom went into the office early to make a call to Anthony Middleton to discuss his plan of assigning FBI Agent Martin Corley to liaison with his office in Hong Kong about two weeks out of the month. He thought it was the only way to keep his job. He was genuinely concerned about getting fired, which could happen at just about any minute. If Middleton requested Corley, all the while explaining it was Warren's idea and London bought it, it might take some of the heat off him.

On his desk was an interoffice memo from Washington, DC. He opened it. It was from Michelle Galloway. His inquiry had come back from the U.S. Department of State with the list of Chinese professors working at U.S. colleges who had requested visas to go to Red China. This information could enhance his watch list and produce better results. He checked the clock. It was time to call Middleton and sell him on Marty working out of his office.

Tom picked up the phone and dialed the Hong Kong office for MI6. While he waited for Middleton to pick up, he started reviewing the list. One name jumped off the page. Yang Chen Ning, one of the top physicists living in the United States. This was his second visa application to go back to China. Tom pulled a pen from his desk and underlined his name.

Middleton came on the phone. "Tom, good morning to you. I'm sorry to hear about J. Edgar Hoover. But to what do I owe the pleasure?"

Tom leaned back in his chair. "I would like to set up one of my agents to liaison with your office. I asked Hoover to transfer me there, but he turned me down. So, I was thinking about getting my partner moving back and forth, communicating with your office and bringing you information from my office on the Chinese spy ring."

"I think that would work really well and help us track down these spies. I believe I can make that happen in London."

"Let me know as soon as you can." Tom paused for a second. "And if you could come back and say it was your idea or London's, it would help me a lot."

Anthony chuckled. "So you want me to run interference, right?"

This brought a smile to Tom's face. He imagined the smug look on Middleton's face with that request. "You got it. You know me too well. Let me know when you can."

"Don't hang up just yet," Anthony said. "All is not well in Communist China. A couple months ago, a Chinese Army General defected into Hong Kong. He was one of the generals involved with Lin Piao."

"Wow. So everything isn't so hunky dory over there."

"Not at all. MI6 believes there's a lot of strife in Red China. The old guard are passing away and new leaders are rising who may be more friendly to the West as they continue to distance themselves from the Soviet Union."

"Let's start to finish them off, Anthony." Tom reached for the football sitting on the edge of his desk. "Get Corley that assignment."

About that time, Special Agent in Charge Gerald Adler stormed through the office door and pointed at Tom then toward his office.

Tom knew he was about to step into a shit storm, and he didn't have an umbrella. He quickly hung up then hurried behind Adler.

Adler held the door open and let Tom walk past him, then slammed the door so hard, he thought the glass would fall out. Tom had hoped the night would allow Adler to cool off, but it looked like just the opposite had happened.

Adler sat down behind his desk. "What was yesterday all about, Special Agent Thomas Payne Warren? And, before you answer, you better think real good about what you're about to say."

"I wanted to protect Shou, as you know she'd just seen her mother killed and the murderers wanted to kill her too—and maybe Marty and me. I wanted to get us to a safe place. If we stayed here at headquarters too long, we could've walked out to a hail of bullets. So my thoughts were to move quick. And there was no time to debate."

Adler stood up, placing both hands on his desk. His jaw was clinched as he leaned forward. *"That is strike one. I should fire you right now. You better tread lightly around here and remember who is in charge. You can bet if Hoover were still alive, it would've taken one second for me to relay that bullshit story to him, and you would've been gone. Now, get the hell out of my office. Not another word. I'm putting you on a week's leave, unpaid."* Adler's face turned redder still. *"Just get out of my sight, before I change my mind. Get out of my office, get out of this whole office."*

Tom was out of the door in a second. He knew what Adler had said was true.

October 1972
Hong Kong

As usual, Tom was in his office early before anyone else. He had put the coffee on and sat down to review reports from the other agents in the San

Francisco bureau. They were starting to squeeze the right Chinese scientists and academics in the area. It was resulting in some strong leads, but still no arrests. but at least they finally had "people of interest" to watch and question.

Tom reached over and picked up the most recent fax from his partner, Martin Corley, who'd been in Hong Kong for almost a month straight working side by side with MI6 Agent Anthony Middleton. In the fax he'd sent last week, despite working hand in glove with MI6, he still hadn't been able to locate Dr. Paul Yu. Ever since going through Chapter 7 bankruptcy in the United States, the man had just seemed to disappear. He'd even missed his final hearing. Yet, by all records available, he hadn't returned to Communist China.

Tom had followed up with CIA Larry several times over the last month to see if their office had any intel on the man, but he said the CIA had lost him, too. How could this man disappear from MI6, the CIA, and the FBI? Had he stopped doing business? Had he set up a new corporation or new identity?

Tom thought one more try, he picked up his desk phone called for CIA Larry. The voice on the other end said, "Larry Wu-tai Chin's desk."

"Is Larry available?"

"No, he's on vacation. He's out for the remainder of this week."

Tom slowly placed the receiver back down. *This is just my luck. Everybody else in this office is starting to make some progress, yet Marty and I are striking out, left and right.*

CHAPTER NINETEEN

January 1973
Beijing

Yu Qiangsheng continued to check his review mirror as he drove across town. He was certain there was a car with a couple of agents from the Ministry of Public Security following him. *They are amateurs. I'm not even going to try to lose or confront them. They know exactly where I'm headed.* It would be pointless. In the last couple of months that he'd gone to visit his mother, he was always followed. Losing them would be easy, but still there would be the agents outside her apartment building. He knew exactly how to take care of this problem. It would be easy, but the timing was critical.

Yu knocked lightly on the door.

His mother opened the door and glanced up and down the hallway. "You were followed again?"

Yu slipped by her. "Mother, what are you up to? The first few times those agents followed me I thought they were just updating their file on me, but now my intuition tells me something different."

His mother shuffled over to the window and discreetly peeked through the thread-bare curtains. Yu observed her actions. Her suspicions aroused *his suspicions*. She closed the curtains and stepped over to the tiny, dilapidated couch in her living area.

Yu pouted his lips. "Mother, what are you up to? Have you rejoined the resistance?"

"Why, son, what would ever give you that idea?" She smiled.

"Mother, they will put you back in prison, maybe this time for good. All the old guards are flexing their muscles, struggling to hang on to their powers, but they are diminishing, including Zhou En-lai. He had his final day in the sun with arranging that meeting between Chairman Mao and that capitalist Nixon."

Fan licked her lips. "Yes, Yu, the whole world is changing. But not Mao. He's just afraid of losing his power. Soon they all will be dead." She raised her eyes and met his. "If only I can help influence the next generation."

Yu got up and stood over his mother. "You are such an idealist, a revolutionary. But you're correct. The next generation, my generation, must be the ones to institute the change. You need to stay out of trouble. I do not wish to see you get arrested again."

Fan got up from the couch with the help of her son and walked him toward the door. "Yu, look around you." She pointed at her apartment. "If I must die in prison by helping to introduce that change, it will be all worth it. I have nothing to lose here. The reward is too great to miss the opportunity, which I believe is at hand. Besides, we have not started anything. Yet."

Yu kissed his mother's forehead, then left the tiny flat. Her words confirmed the reason for the surveillance by the Ministry of Public Security.

As he drove back across town toward his office at the CID, he was no longer being followed. This was his chance to put his plan into action. He slipped his hand into a pocket of his Zhongshan suit and pulled out a slip of paper. He glanced down at it at the intersection, then slipped it back in his pocket. The address was on the other side of Beijing. He slowly passed the residence, then stepped down on the accelerator and pulled away. He spoke out loud, "Time to go by Shi Pei Pu and pick up the last documents Bernard Boursicot snuck out of the French Embassy."

As he walked toward the door, he saw Shi peeking out the window. Yu went straight up and just opened the front door without knocking. Only Shi's mother was in the living room, but she jumped up and ran out. Yu bellowed at the top of his lungs, "Shi, I want those documents from Boursicot now!"

Shi sheepishly came around the corner with a file in his hand. He held out the file as far as he could to stay from Yu Qiangsheng.

Yu demanded, "When will he be bringing the next drop?"

Shi slumped down on the decrepit couch. "Bernard is being transferred back to Paris within the next few days. I'm so sad. We are so in love. Will the Chinese Communist Party allow me and our son to move there with him?"

"I have no interest in your love or your feelings. Is Boursicot bringing any more documents before he leaves?" Yu pointed his finger in his face.

Shi looked down at the ground and appeared to be on the verge of crying.

Yu shook his head in disgust. He quickly glanced through the file of documents. It was going to be a real loss to not having this material. He stuffed the file under his arm, pivoted, and went out the door.

When he arrived at his office, there was a note attached to his door. He snatched it down as he entered. The note read: *I want to see you in my office before the day is out. Dr. Wang*

By early afternoon, he'd completed his review of his own surveillance reports on foreigners from his teams around the country. He rubbed his chin. It was no coincidence that since Nixon had come to China, getting documents from the United States had been much easier to obtain. Not from the government side, but the private side. He looked down at his watch. Time to go to see Dr. Wang.

Yu knocked on Dr. Wang's office door.

"Enter," came the muffled order.

Yu stepped into the office and laid the documents from the French Embassy on his desk.

Dr. Wang looked at the file for a brief second, then pointed for Yu to sit down. "I'll review these later." He straightened his gray suit. "Something has come up. I have a mission for you."

Yu nodded for him to go on.

"I want you to accompany me to Hong Kong. We are to meet up with one of our spies who is being watched by the FBI and MI6. We must get him safely back into the country."

"When do we leave?"

Dr. Wang looked down at his desk. "In the morning. We will drive across the border before daylight."

"When is our rendezvous set for?"

He got up from his desk and walked toward the door. "Unknown. It will depend on how soon he can get there. He is currently in the traitorous territory of Taiwan." He paused at the door and looked back at Yu. "This is not one of my spies. He got sloppy. Kang wanted me to handle it without the knowledge of his handler. I'm to handle the man, and Kang is going to take care of his handler."

"I'll be here shortly after midnight awaiting your orders." Yu wondered what he wasn't being told. Why was he being included? Up until today, his assignments had been restricted to cases inside China.

When his workday was completed, Yu went to his car and drove to observe the parking lot of the Ministry of Public Security. Now the waiting game. It was time to put an end to the surveillance of him or his mother. He knew where those orders were coming from—the very top. Cut the head off the snake, the body will die.

After about a half hour, Li Zhen, the head of the Public Security, walked out with four bodyguards surrounding him on all sides. Li got in the back of his car, slipped into the middle seat with bodyguards on each side and two in front.

Yu checked his Czech CZ-52 handgun on the seat beside him. He knew right where they were going—he didn't need to follow too close to avoid detection. He parked down the street from Li's residence and watched his security team get him into the house and drive off. *Now, wait for dark to make my move.*

About an hour later, it was time. Yu's intricate plan called for a dark, moonless night. No one was out on the cold street, allowing Yu to move through the drifting snow flurries without detection. He went to the back door of Li's residence. It was locked. Yu quickly picked the lock and slipped into the kitchen. He closed the door quietly and listened. It seemed no one had detected his entrance. He crept through the house, room by room, until he found Li Zhen in his study, sitting at his desk facing the door, listening to the local radio broadcast of news of the day with intermittent sayings from Chairman Mao.

Yu had to be patient. Li was too powerful. What he must do couldn't be deemed foul play.

Yu slipped back through the house until he found the door leading to the cellar. Then he found a closet door with a broom. Yu smiled as he pulled it out. He went back to the cellar door, opened it, and descended into the darkness. After stepping on the first step, Yu shut both eyes after pulling the door closed to let them adjust to the darkness. Standing completely still for a full minute, he opened his eyes. He could see like a cat.

He went into the area of the cellar he believed was under Li's study. He took the broom handle and tapped against the cellar's ceiling. He'd make several taps, then pause and listen. He did it again and paused, again and paused. Finally, he heard footsteps across the main floor. Yu moved quickly under the stairs. He closed one eye so if Li flicked the light on, then back off, he'd still have one eye good under any lighting condition.

The light came on in the basement, but at first Li didn't descend the stairs.

Yu tapped with the broom one more time.

186

With that, Li started down the steps.

Yu looked between the treads.

Li carried a Soviet Pistole Makarov handgun.

Yu maintained his position under the stairs until Li placed his foot down on the fourth one. Yu pushed his back against the wall. A spider dropped down in front of his face. Yu slapped it out of his way, reached from under the steps, and grabbed Li in the middle of his next step, sending him tumbling down the stairs to the hard dirt floor.

Li was dazed but still held his gun in his hand.

Yu moved silently but quickly. He grabbed Li around the neck from behind with his right arm while pushing his head forward with his left and began choking him.

Li dropped his gun and flailed his arms around, but Yu's grip was too tight. Li dug his hands and fingers into Yu's forearms. Yu had the man under his complete control. Yu felt him start to weaken and pushed him face down into the dirt floor. Yu delivered a hard punch to his left kidney. By that point, Li was coughing and gagging. Yu's weight kept his lungs from inflating as the man slowly quit struggling. Li gasped again and again for air. Then his body went limp. Yu flipped him over, then finished strangling him, breaking his windpipe.

Yu pulled the knife from his belt and cleaned out from under Li's fingernails to make sure there was no evidence of his presence left behind. When he finished, he ascended the stairs, relocked the back door on the way out, and returned to his car. He looked at his watch. He barely had enough time to get back to town and meet Dr. Wang.

CHAPTER TWENTY

April 3, 1973
Hong Kong

Tom Warren was seated at his desk going over the latest surveillance reports from his agents working the restaurants in Chinatown and those checking scientists and academics at the local colleges. There were several Chinese nationals on their watch list. His phone rang. "Special Agent Warren."

"Warren, this is Middleton. We just got a notice from the Taiwanese authorities that Dr. Paul Yu boarded a plane from Taipei to Hong Kong. It's in the air and will be here in less than two hours." Middleton gave him the flight and arrival time.

"You and Marty grab him when he lands. Let Marty bring him back to the U.S." Tom jumped up from his desk.

There was a long pause before Anthony replied. "Ah, well, you see, the British government is attempting to improve relations with Red China and, ah, well, they won't allow me to pick him up. In the conundrum I'm in, they won't allow him to enter the country, either. I've got strict orders to turn him away at the airport. I've already sent a team, and I'm headed there to supervise them."

"Damn it, Anthony, your bosses have a weird way of looking at things." Tom clinched his jaw trying to figure out what to do in just under two hours. If they were forcing him back to Taiwan, maybe the authorities there would be more cooperative.

"It seems logical that Dr. Yu's goal is get back to Red China."

"Of course." Tom sighed. He wondered how Dr. Yu had made it into Taipei without detection and wasn't flagged when he boarded the flight to Hong Kong. He got another idea. "Okay, Anthony, are you sure you won't let him off the plane there? You're absolutely positive you'll be sending him back to Taipei?"

"Yes, yes, of course. That's the plan. Can you work with that?"

"I've got to get my end coordinated. I assume Marty isn't in the office." Tom paced the length the telephone cord would allow.

"No, I just spoke to him at his apartment not twenty minutes before I called you, right."

"Got to go. Don't forget to call me, Anthony." Tom hung up the phone. He hoped Marty and Shou Li Cao were both at his apartment. He sat down and dialed Marty's place.

"Hello."

"Marty, Tom. Shou home from work?"

"No, she called a few minutes ago. Her boss wanted her to stay late and type up two big commercial loans. You know how those loan officers are at HSBC. She may be—"

"Dr. Paul Yu is in the air flying to Hong Kong."

"*What?* I'm on my way. We got the goods to question him."

"You can't pick him in Hong Kong. I already talked to Middleton. MI6 and London won't let him in. They are pushing him back to Taipei. I want you to get to the airport as fast as possible and get a plane ticket to Taipei. I'll arrange for you to work with the Taiwanese authorities to pick him up at the airport in Taipei."

"Got it. I'll see you. I'm—"

"Marty, don't hang up. I need to have Shou go to the airport, too. Call her and have her go straight to the airport. I want her on the same plane with Dr. Paul Yu when he's headed back to Taipei." Tom dropped into his desk chair.

"I want eyes on him all the way. Call her. Get her on it. Have her call me as soon as she gets to the airport. Does she know what Dr. Yu looks like?"

"Yes, when I was going over the file, she sat by me and looked at everything." Marty cleared his throat. "What are you going to do?"

"I'm going to get to Honolulu. If he can't answer your questions, arrest him and bring him there. One more thing, be careful. If Dr. Yu is trying to get back to Red China, there will be Chinese agents everywhere." Tom bit his lower lip.

"Don't worry about me. I got this."

Tom hung up the phone as he thought for a moment. How had Dr. Yu magically shown up in Taipei? It was likely that other countries' security hadn't paid much attention to Tom's request for notice. It was frustrating, but it was something he couldn't undo. He'd deal with that issue later, once Dr. Paul Yu was in custody. They had enough information to question him, based on his violations of the United States Federal Bankruptcy Act. But he wanted, no—needed—more. Yu had to mess up when he was being questioned.

Tom picked up his phone again and booked his reservation into Honolulu. Then he had to wait on Shou to call. The hands on the clock moved slowly. Finally, the phone rang. He grabbed it before the ring tone was complete. "Special Agent Warren."

"Tom, this is Shou. I'm at the airport. What do you want me to do?"

"I need you to purchase a ticket for Dr. Yu's flight returning to Taipei. It's Cathay Pacific Flight 182; departs 7:45 local. Everything is set. Marty said you know what he looks like, right?"

"Yes, Tom. I know. For sure."

"Okay, MI6 plans to stop the flight before it gets to the gate, but in case something fails, they will have agents stationed at all doors, baggage claim, and at Dr. Yu's gate."

"I got this, Tom. Thanks for trusting me. I'm going to call off work."

"This isn't going to blow your cover in any way, is it? We worked too hard to get you an excellent resumé to land at Hong Kong Shanghai Bank."

"Not at all. My bosses love me. It won't be a problem if you need me to do more."

"Good. Go get that ticket and get to that gate. The plane should be landing within an hour." Tom hung up the phone. In just under an hour, he'd pieced together a pretty good plan to take down his first arrest.

Middleton has to turn the doctor around and Marty has to beat him back to Taipei. It seems pretty simple. Now, to get Taiwan authorities to help Marty when that plane arrives.

Dr. Wang and his bodyguards entered the airport bar of the designated restaurant. Yu Qiangsheng was already seated there. Dr. Wang had been tipped this morning by Kang Sheng that Dr. Paul Yu, the Chinese agent who'd provided critical information to the Communist Party, was due to fly into Hong Kong at 6:25 p.m. local time on a Cathay Pacific Flight. Dr. Wang and his team had been in Hong Kong for three days, waiting. He returned to the bar table with his bodyguards, Wu and Chang, in tow. He waved them off as he sat down opposite Yu. "No change in plans," he said. "Dr. Paul Yu is at the airport and should be boarding his flight in the next couple of minutes."

Yu Qiangsheng nodded. "What's our plan?"

Dr. Wang leaned forward over the table and spoke in a low voice. "I waved my men off because I have some other news to share with you from Kang Sheng. He said all of the Communist Party is abuzz. The night before we left for Hong Kong, Li Zhen, the Minister of Public Security, was strangled to death in the cellar of his home." Dr. Wang kept focused on Yu to get his reaction to the news.

Yu sat there stoically, but Dr. Wang noticed his pupils dilate.

Dr. Wang squinted. "So far, there are no clues. Thus, no suspects. His death has put their offices into total chaos."

Yu just sat there, shaking his head as though in disbelief.

Dr. Wang waved his bodyguards back to the table. As soon as they sat down, Dr. Wang pulled out a picture of their agent, Dr. Paul Yu, then started to lay out the plan. "Okay, we are going to make sure we get to him the minute he enters the terminal. Yu, I want you at the gate. You let the doctor walk by. Someone will likely be waiting for him when he steps off. You assess who may be watching or following. We must assume MI6 likely will be everywhere."

Yu nodded.

Dr. Wang looked at Wu. "You go now and watch the front of this wing. You are watching for anyone coming into this terminal area."

Dr. Wang focused on Chang. "As soon as the plane has landed, you go get the car. I want you parked outside the front door so we can walk the good doctor straight off the plane to the car. No stops. We all walk out the door together. Except you." Dr. Wang pointed at Yu Qiangsheng. "Yu, you follow behind and observe who might be following us. You can take care of them anyway you see fit. It will be up to you to get to the Chinese border on your own. We will wait for you on our side of the border."

Dr. Wang stood up and straightened his gray suit, and then went to the window of the bar. Everyone else moved out.

CHAPTER TWENTY-ONE

April 3, 1973
Hong Kong

Marty Corley walked up to the Cathay Pacific check-in counter to book his reservation for Taipei and check his bag. This wing of the terminal was very crowded as he moved toward his gate against the flow of most of the foot traffic. Without obviously looking around, Marty tried to check the crowd for Chinese agents. Frankly, it looked like they were everywhere. He was paranoid. Yet, he believed even if they recognized him, they would let him walk straight through the terminal. After all, he was taking a flight out. But his concern was for his girlfriend, Shou. He saw several MI6 agents scattered discreetly in the crowd as he walked. At this point of the operation, there was nothing anyone could do. Just stick with Warren's plan.

Within a few minutes, Marty was on his flight bound for Taipei.

Wu watched FBI Special Agent Marty Corley walked into the Kai Tak Airport. The man was by himself and carried a suitcase. He hadn't seen the man since 1963, but he knew it was the American agent. While it was important, he didn't feel like it was important enough to leave his assigned station. He'd tell Dr. Wang later he'd seen the man.

He decided it was best to at least see where he was buying a ticket. After the FBI agent walked away, Wu went straight up to the counter, crowding in front of several women in line, and asked the agent where had that man purchased a ticket to.

She acted as though she didn't want to answer. Then Wu threatened her under his breath. She whispered, "He purchased a ticket to Taipei."

Shou Li Cao walked toward her gate for boarding the Cathay Pacific flight to Taipei. Since it was around dinner time, the number of flights coming in and departing had increased. People were running and bumping into each other. She managed to get in step with the flow of the passengers walking to that end of the terminal. In her mind, everyone seemed to be in a bigger hurry than normal for this busy airport. She was clearly paranoid.

As she walked up to the gate, she looked around and saw several Caucasian males. She wondered which ones might be the MI6 agents.

She sat down in the only remaining seat at the crowded gate, right next to a large Chinese man who discreetly glanced at her. Directly across from her was a handsome Chinese man who looked directly at her with a steely-eyed stare. She found the man masculine and attractive, yet intimidating at the same time. The man's gaze was fixated on her while she looked at him. She glanced down at the floor to try to relieve her stress.

Dr. Wang stood at the bar and watched flights come and go. He observed a Cathay Pacific jet bank over the city to line up with the runway. As he walked toward the arrival board to verify what he believed was Dr. Paul Yu's flight, he made a quick mental note of the gate, then walked in that direction.

San Francisco

Tom sat impatiently at his desk, waiting for the phone call from Middleton letting him know everything was in place. He pulled out a deck of cards and started to play solitaire. After about the fourth game, the phone rang. Tom snatched it from the switch hook. "Special Agent Warren."

"Middleton here. Everything is in place. According to the tower, Dr. Paul Yu's plane is in a waiting pattern over the airport, number four to land."

"Good. Then I'm calling a cab to get on the move myself. I'm going to meet Marty and Dr. Yu in Honolulu."

Special Agent Thomas Warren's cab let him off at the Pan Am departure terminal. He quickly paid the cabbie and headed for the front door. His jet for Honolulu was departing in forty-five minutes. He was excited, as it looked like all the FBI's hard work and collaboration with the British MI6 was coming to fruition. He was totally oblivious to the crowded airport. They were going to make their first big take down of a very important Chinese spy.

Hong Kong

After watching the Cathay Pacific jet approach the gate outside the large window, Yu Qiangsheng got up from his seat to lean against one of the pillars to get a better view of those deplaning enter the terminal. However, no one went over to open the doorway from the flight. The two agents at the doorway just stood there as though nothing was unusual. But something wasn't quite right.

After a couple of minutes, he walked over to the window and looked down at the jet, which was still sitting on the tarmac. He looked around at all those seated at the gate. No one else seemed concerned. His gaze remained fixed on the plane. Nothing was happening. Off to the left, two Jaguars pulled up alongside the commercial jet. Two Caucasian men dressed in suits got out of each of the cars just as a gangway was pushed up to the front door of the plane. The pilot opened the small window on the jet and frantically waved at those men.

This was not a good development. The door to the Cathay Pacific plane opened and the four men charged up the stairway. Things were moving too fast. The normally confident Yu was unsure of his next move. He was too far away from the jet to do anything. His anxiety climbed from his helplessness. Dr. Wang needed to find him.

He started to breathe easier as passengers started to deplane. Maybe he'd just overreacted. The ground Cathay Pacific agents opened the door for the deplaning passengers. Finally, it appeared everyone was off the jet—but not Dr. Paul Yu and the four presumed MI6 agents. The Cathay Pacific employees made an announcement that the plane was ready to board passengers.

Yu ran toward the front of the terminal and met Dr. Wang coming down the large hallway.

"Last boarding call for Cathay Pacific flight 182 for Taipei," the intercom announced.

When he got to Dr. Wang, Yu shouted, "Dr. Yu didn't deplane!" He pulled even with him. "Do we know for sure he even made the flight? Or are they preventing him from deplaning? What's our next move? Do I need to get on that jet and grab him? They just made the last call."

Dr. Wang jutted his jaw. "Go get a plane ticket to Taipei. Get on that flight if you can—or the next available. You stick to Dr. Paul Yu. You got it. Should they try to get him to the United States, see that he doesn't make it." Dr. Wang reached in his coat jacket pocket, produced a case, and handed it to Yu. "Inside this case is a tiny vial with two drops of VX. Let this be your last choice. You understand me? He doesn't get to the United States." Again, his hand returned to his pocket, producing a passport, and pushed it in Yu's hand.

Yu took the case, stuck it in the pocket of his Zhongshan coat, and quickly looked at the passport. His new false identity made him a citizen of Malaysia. He sprinted off toward the Cathay Pacific ticket area.

Dr. Wang fumed. He strutted around, attempting to compose himself. His plan had been foiled by MI6.

Wu jogged up to him. "Where's our man?"

Dr. Wang grabbed him by the shirt collar and pulled into his face. "*He was denied entry*. MI6 is sending him back to Taipei, into the hands of those dissidents." He let go of Wu.

Wu straightened his shirt. "I saw that one FBI agent—Martin Corley—come into the airport—"

Dr. Wang grabbed him again. "*What?*" He shook Wu hard, then threw him back. "FBI Agent Corley was here? Why didn't you tell me when you saw him? I should kill you right here."

"You wanted me to watch the front. The FBI agent came through more than an hour ago. He went to the Cathay Pacific counter and purchased a ticket to Taipei."

Dr. Wang still had a hold of Wu. "You better hope that FBI agent doesn't do anything to the doctor."

Shou boarded the flight. Her ticket placed her right in front of Dr. Paul Yu. There were MI6 agents on either side of the good doctor.

She wondered why she was asked to board the flight to Taipei. It didn't make sense, since the MI6 agents stayed on the plane.

Marty Corley and Taiwanese authorities sat on the tarmac waiting on the flight carrying Dr. Paul Yu to arrive back in Taipei. Air traffic control and ground personnel were under strict orders to hold the plane so that Corley and the Taiwanese could board it before it pushed up to the gate. One of the Taiwanese agents had a radio in the car to communicate with an agent in the tower. He tipped Marty that the flight with the doctor was approaching. As with the MI6 agents in Hong Kong, officially, Taiwan didn't want to get involved in the FBI operation, which would only create more unrest for them with mainland China. Unofficially, they were willing to go out of their way to assist the FBI. They were quick to let Marty Corley take the lead to takedown Dr. Paul Yu, as he was the expert on all his financial dealings. Within ten minutes, the plane was on the taxiway leading up to their designated gate.

Marty leaned up to inform the driver to get ground crew to stop the plane in front of their car. The Taiwanese agent with the radio replied that air traffic control had already informed the pilots that agents would be boarding the plane to take off their suspect.

"Once we are on board," Marty said, "Have them move the gangway to the back service door. I want to take him out the back of that plane, just in case there are Chinese agents on board."

As a gangway was brought up to the plane, Marty and the three Taiwanese agents swiftly ran the steps and banged hard on the door. Marty turned and faced them. "One of you go back on the ground and watch the service door. Two of you will follow me into the plane. You," he said, pointing to the closest one, "stay in the front. And you come to the middle of the plane, just like we planned. I want to emphasize, we don't know if the Red Chinese have slipped one of their agents on the plane or if there might be some sympathizers who might not care for our actions."

He stepped back as the door pushed opened. He bound into the cabin and raised his badge in the air. "Everybody please remain seated."

Then one of the Taiwanese agents repeated his message in the native language.

They moved through the cabin to the back of the jet to take Dr. Paul Yu in custody from the two MI6 agents on the plane.

Marty didn't so much as look at Shou sitting directly in front of the doctor, just in case anyone on the plane was watching his actions. He made sure he did nothing to jeopardize her deep cover role for the FBI.

He looked around to make sure all the Taiwanese agents were in place, then he flashed his FBI badge. "Dr. Paul Yu, will you please come with me? I would like to have a brief conversation with you."

The doctor gritted his jaw and moved it back and forth, but didn't look up at Corley. The MI6 agent sitting in the window seat nudged the doctor to move. Dr. Paul Yu looked up at Corley for the first time and nodded once.

By then, the Taiwanese agent at the service door helped the stewardess at the back of the jet open it.

They made it out the service door with no incident. Corley realized they may be vulnerable when they stepped out of the plane. A sniper or a Chinese agent disguised as a ground crew employee had free access to them. He took a deep breath and asked one of the Taiwanese agents to get in front and another trail them. They descended the gangway to the ground. Marty pushed Dr. Paul Yu into jogging toward the car.

Once everyone was in the car, Marty commanded the Taiwanese agent to take them to an arranged conference room at the airport terminal. The car lurched forward at a high rate of speed, throwing everyone back in their seats. Marty turned around to make sure the plane pulled up to the gate. He desperately wanted to know that Shou was okay. As soon as they were in the air and on their way to Honolulu, she was to fly back to Hong Kong and resume her secretarial position at HSBC.

Marty, Dr. Paul Yu, and two of the three Taiwanese agents entered the conference room, while the third agent went to pick up tickets for Marty and his suspected spy to go to Honolulu on the earliest flight possible. Marty didn't want to take his eyes off the doctor. He'd worked too hard, too long, to let anything happen now. He looked at one of the Taiwanese agents. "Frisk him. Make sure he has no weapons or any means to commit suicide."

The agents commanded the doctor to empty his pockets on the table. Then then closely searched his body before pushing him down in the chair.

Marty sat down opposite the doctor at the large conference table, while the other two Taiwanese agents stood on either side of the door. He decided he'd push a little to see if he could get him to break. "I'm the agent who was placed in charge of investigating your financial records dating back to 1964. The FBI has uncovered evidence that you have received funds you didn't declare on your taxes." Marty wasn't about to bring up the spying at this point. He believed that would make him less willing to talk than it already appeared.

Dr. Yu stared straight ahead without a response.

The third Taiwanese agent returned with two tickets for TWA Flight 742 departing in just over an hour for Honolulu.

Finally, Marty had no other choice, while the lack of answers didn't help his case. He rubbed his mouth with his left hand. "I'm placing you under arrest for committing bankruptcy fraud in the United States." Then he proceeded to read him his Miranda rights.

The doctor stared straight ahead, his facial expression not changing.

Marty leaned back in his chair. "Well, Dr. Yu, if you choose to cooperate with the FBI, we may be able to get a federal judge to lighten your sentence."

Taipei
Four hours later

Yu Qiangsheng stepped off the flight in Taipei. Now, his work was beginning. His mission was to find Dr. Paul Yu and either get him out of Taipei or make sure he didn't get into the hands of the FBI. He hoped that his relationship with Chiang Kai-shek through his mother would help, should he be caught. He entered the terminal and looked for signs of where they may have taken their Chinese spy. He'd gone over and over his plan as he flew to Taipei. What would he do with someone he'd captured and wanted to interrogate? He answered his own question—*get him on my home turf*. They would likely be going back to the United States as soon as possible.

Yu looked up at the departure board, checking for flights to Los Angeles, San Francisco, and Honolulu. He knew the main FBI office investigating Chinese spying was run by FBI Special Agent Thomas P. Warren out of San Francisco, likely his choice. But there was a flight to Honolulu within the next two hours—about the same time as one for San Francisco. He had to go to the ticket counter and figure out the layovers and arrival times.

As Yu Qiangsheng walked through the airport terminal, he checked all the side rooms and doors between gates on his way to the ticket desk. Could he be lucky enough to find his man on the premises? He was operating in the blind and desperately needed a break. There was one long shot he could try, but it was risky. He could contact members of the Taiwanese Independence Movement. While they hated the Red Chinese, they also hated Chiang Kai-shek's government, which had just taken over the island in 1949. There was a slight chance he could get someone from that underground movement to help him.

Yu had spies everywhere on the mainland, but none here—but his mentor Kang Sheng did, so he went to a pay phone and placed a call to Kang. He then stood anxiously by the phone for the next half hour waiting on a return call. Every time someone walked up to that pay phone, Yu intimidated them to move on. Finally, the pay phone rang. Yu picked it up, and Kang gave him the flight information—TWA flight 742 for Honolulu that Dr. Paul Yu was being taken on. Two tickets in the name of FBI Special Agent Martin Corley.

He got to the ticket counter for TWA flights and purchased his ticket. He was now on the same flight as his target. As he walked toward the gate, again he checked doors and looked in windows along the way. No sign of Dr. Paul Yu or the FBI agent. Once he took his seat at the gate, Yu Qiangsheng knew his mission had changed. He must now kill Dr. Paul Yu. Dr. Wang's orders were clear he couldn't fall into the hands of the FBI.

Three hours later
April 4, 1973

Yu Qiangsheng fidgeted to get comfortable in his seat waiting for his opportunity. He was one hour into his flight to the first stop at Honolulu. The

FBI agent and Dr. Paul Yu were seated behind him. He assumed that he was handcuffed or restrained in some way. He had just over eight hours to put together his plan. *Be patient. Be methodical. Seek your opportunity.*

After several hours in the air, one of the stewardesses at the front of the cabin announced that meals were about to be brought out. Which meant there would be a movie followed by a rest period when the cabin would be darkened. Yu thought that time might be his best opportunity to act, but all events would have to fall just right.

The stewardesses started through the cabin with two carts, one with meals, the second with drinks. Before either of the carts made it to his seat, he decided to try to get to the bathroom, in hopes that Dr. Paul Yu might be allowed to get up and go to the bathroom to wash his hands or something before eating his meal. He passed by the FBI agent and his prisoner slowly enough to hear the two speaking.

The agent told him fine, but he'd be accompanying him and stand at the door. Yu Qiangsheng had to rely on a little luck on his side here. When he got to the rear of the jet, there were four lavatories, and all were occupied. *Perfect.* As soon as one was available, he slipped in and opened the case containing the tiny vial of VX gas. He delicately held the tiny vial, peeking out the door and waiting to see Dr. Paul Yu get up. Several stewardesses moved in and out of the food station at the back of the jet.

Finally, Dr. Paul Yu walked in his direction with the FBI agent right behind. Yu Qiangsheng slipped a latex glove on one hand, delicately opened the vial, and let a single drop leak out on the latch to close the door to the lavatory. He reversed the glove over the tiny vial, then threw it in the toilet and hit the flush so as to make sure he wasn't exposed to the deadly poison. "Here you go, sir." Yu held the door until Dr. Paul Yu had slipped past him.

Yu Qiangsheng walked by the FBI agent, then watched the "unoccupied" sign shift to "occupied," and he smiled. Dr. Paul Yu wouldn't be emerging from the lavatory, and his death would look like a suicide. As he took the few steps to his seat, the FBI agent was still standing outside the door. *I must figure out a way to get off this plane without getting caught.*

After standing there for several minutes, Yu Qiangsheng heard the FBI agent pound on the door—several times, each more frantic than the previous. A stewardess hurried down the aisle.

After flashing a slight smile, he started to eat the meal of roast beef. His discipline allowed him to resist the temptation to glance back to watch the FBI agent and the stewardess work on the door. Within a few seconds, the stewardess gasped.

He'd been successful.

However, he was faced with a very big problem. If the FBI agent suspected murder, he had to find a way off the plane. *Or will I have to take my own life so I don't fall into the hands of the U.S. FBI? My life can't end on U.S. soil.*

April 4, 1973
Honolulu

FBI Special Agent Tom Warren stood at the gate waiting on the TWA flight to pull up and deplane. As the jet taxied up, he was paged to come to the closest courtesy phone in that terminal. *Corley must want me to board and discreetly help him escort Dr. Paul Yu off the plane, so as not to draw attention.* He found a courtesy phone and picked it up. "Special Agent Thomas Warren."

"Tom, this is Marty. We got big problems. Dr. Paul Yu is dead. I think it was a suicide, but I don't know how."

Tom leaned against the wall.

"Tom, are you still there?"

"Yes, of course. I'm thinking."

"I don't see how he committed suicide, but I don't know how he died either."

Tom pushed up off the wall. "No one gets off that plane until we figure this out. Get the flight crew to let me board." He looked around the hallway for a second. "Has the flight crew called for the coroner?"

"Yes, the stewardess just told me you can board with the coroner and the ambulance personnel. The ambulance is already here. The coroner is due at any minute. The captain called while we were still in the air."

Tom paused for a second. "Better tell them to hazmat up. We don't know how he died. If it wasn't a suicide—"

"You're right. Let me take care of that right now."

Tom slowly placed the receiver back on the hook. He rubbed his chin for a second, then slowly paced to the female TWA employee standing in front of the doorway and flashed his FBI badge. She looked at him, then opened the gate to the gangway. He walked down the long, covered walkway.

We were on the verge of making a big arrest of this likely Chinese spy, now he's dead. No resolution to the Kikue Nakamura murder, no resolution to the Jared Samuel murder, no resolution to the double murder, no resolution to the Chinese handler in San Francisco's suicide, and now this. This could get him removed from the case or give Adler the grounds he'd been looking for to fire him. While he and Marty had been creating real problems for the Chinese spy network, there had still been no arrests. The only leg he and Corley had to stand on was that temporary FBI Director Gray was under extreme scrutiny from the Senate and would likely not be confirmed. Therefore, it was unlikely he'd make any radical moves at this time. But this mistake was unforgivable—a high-level spy commits suicide under our watch.

Tom stood at the doorway to the plane watching the coroner and his team climb up the outside steps. He tapped on the door to the jet. An Asian stewardess pushed open the door, her eyes reddened as though she'd been crying.

As he started down the aisle, the pilot called out for him. "Agent Warren, I need to talk to you." Tom returned, and the two men walked into the cockpit area. "Is there any way possible to get everybody off this plane and continue with our schedule?"

Tom wanted to be respectful to the pilot, but if there was a death on the plane of someone in the FBI's custody, he couldn't agree with the request. "Sir, I'm conducting an investigation. Do you want to let a murderer get away scot-free?"

"*Murder?* No one told me anything about murder. I've been told this was a suicide." He looked around, obviously thinking, then continued. "Can we gather everyone in a room in the concourse, so that we can continue our flight?"

Tom jacked his jaw and stepped closer to the pilot. "Your plane may very well be a murder scene. It must be thoroughly combed for evidence. So, I can't do that. Sorry." He shook his head slightly. "No one in, no one out." He turned and rejoined the coroner and the ambulance crew as they continued down the aisle.

The passengers gawked at all the men walking down the aisle. When Tom got to Corley, he let the coroner slip by so he could overlook the body of Dr. Paul Yu, still slumped in the corner of the small lavatory.

Marty's voice cracked as he spoke. "I searched this man before he got on this flight. He didn't have anything on him to commit suicide. When he came back here to go to the lavatory, he was fine. Minutes later, dead."

Tom nodded. "I'm confident you did." He peeked in at the body of his lost prize arrest. "The pilot wants to continue their flight."

Just before the coroner reached down to examine Dr. Paul Yu, Tom commanded, "Don't touch the body!"

The coroner's head snapped back around to look at Tom. "*What do you mean?* How can I tell how the man died?"

Tom leaned over the coroner's shoulder. "If the man was okay before walking into the lavatory and was dead minutes later, there is no obvious evidence he committed suicide or was murdered—I don't see any evidence. It could be by deadly chemicals."

The coroner slowly nodded as he maintained his distance. "I don't have a clue what was the cause of this man's death." Then he turned and whispered some instructions to the two men who had accompanied him onto the jet. He looked back at Tom. "I didn't want them to put on hazmat suits just yet and spook the passengers. Hazmat suits tend to do that. Can we take the body out the service door here?"

Tom called the Asian stewardess who had ushered him on the jet from her station. "Can you let these men—" He pointed at the two men. "In through the service entrance at the back of the plane?"

She gave Tom a questioning look.

"They are coming back on board in hazmat suits. Do you want them walking down the aisle in front of all of these passengers?"

His comment upset her again for a brief second. She closed her eyes, squeezing out a tear. "I'll have to get permission from the captain."

Tom walked back to Marty. "If I believed it was a suicide, I'd let everyone off the plane. We can't just let almost three hundred suspects walk off this plane. These passengers are from all over the world." He paused and looked at the coroner. "Are the passengers at risk?"

The coroner replied, "Well, yes. If the cause of death was from exposure to an airborne chemical, then it's possible, but, frankly, they have been exposed for some time now—as have we. I don't know, but it might be better for their health to get everyone off."

Marty pulled Tom away from the coroner's team. "I went through the wastebasket in the lavatory, nothing. I don't think these passengers are in any danger." He ran his hand over his full head of hair, then gestured with both hands. "I mean, I feel fine. I was beside this guy all along. I feel fine. But maybe it would be best—"

Tom wanted to dress him down about letting this happen, but pushed it out of his mind. "I want you to go back to your seat and start writing up everything that happened from the time you boarded the flight in Taipei. Make your mind recall every single detail. This is what we are trained for. Walk up and down the aisle if you have to. See faces, remember things, see if anything jogs your memory."

Marty looked down at the body, then back at Tom. "I'm sorry I screwed this up. I just can't believe it." Then he returned to his seat and sat down.

Tom walked back to where the Asian stewardess stood. He hated to push her, but he had to. "Do you recall anything that could help us with our investigation? Did you see anyone act suspicious or who might have gone in the lavatory?"

She bit her lower lip. Finally, she replied, "I've replayed everything in my head. There was one man coming out of the restroom before this *poor man* went in."

Tom asked, "Can you identify him?"

She nodded.

Marty joined the two of them. Tom looked at him. "Did you come up with anything?"

Marty replied, "There was one man coming out of the lavatory as the doctor went in. That's about the only thing that sticks out in my mind. Hardly out of the ordinary."

Tom asked the stewardess, "Where is this passenger seated?"

The Asian stewardess briefly flashed a forced smile and went back to her assigned station, then immediately returned with the passenger manifest and offered it to Tom. "The airline just put together their citizenships." She poked her head through the curtain, then went and took the manifest back from Tom and pointed to the passenger from Malaysia.

Tom rubbed his jaw for a second. "Ask him to come back here and talk to me."

Within seconds, the man stepped through the curtain. He was slightly bigger than most Asian men. "Yes?"

Tom flashed his FBI badge and asked, "Do you speak English?"

He shook his head. "Only few words. Main language Malay." Then he switched to Malay and added. "Or some Mandarin."

One of the few Asian languages Tom was unfamiliar with was Malay, so he asked in Mandarin, "Do you feel okay?"

The Malaysian nodded.

Tom wanted to leave the stewardess out of it, so he continued, "According to my partner, FBI Special Agent Corley, you were the last person in the lavatory before the deceased."

The Malaysian shrugged and asked him to repeat the question more slowly, which Tom did.

This time the Malaysian replied, "If they say so. I wouldn't know." He glanced at Marty and the Asian stewardess.

"Why are you traveling, and what do you do for a living?" Tom inquired.

The Malaysian pursed his lips then replied in broken simple Mandarin. "I recently started a rare book business. I've been traveling to Hong Kong and Taipei from Kuala Lumpur to establish, expand my market. I was coming to Honolulu to see about opening up a new market in the United States, as well."

Tom asked, "May I see your passport, in case, we need to ask you some questions in the future."

The Malaysian nodded, then reached in the pocket of his Zhongshan coat and presented his passport to Tom, who immediately passed it to Marty. Corley made some notes, then passed it back to the Malaysian. Tom had maintained eye contact with the man the entire time to read his reactions to the ongoing investigation. "Do you have a business card?"

The Malaysian shook his head. "I was going to get some printed in English once I got to Honolulu."

Tom said, "No further questions at this time." As the Malaysian turned to walk away, Tom asked, "Could you provide us with a telephone contact number in Kuala Lumpur?"

The Malaysian nodded, gave him a telephone number, then went back through the curtain.

Marty looked at Tom. "What do you think about him?"

Tom put his hand over his mouth. "I didn't see anything to make me think anything at all. He seemed...okay, I guess. He had answers for all my other questions. I didn't like the business card answer, but I can't argue with his reason. But wouldn't he have had some printed in Malay?" He paused for a minute. "Also, seemed pretty cool for being questioned."

Marty looked at the stewardess. "No one else on this flight sticks out in my mind. What about you?"

The stewardess looked over the manifest again. "I just don't remember many people moving around at all, at least nothing out of the ordinary out of the last part of the flight. We had just served meals, then we darkened the cabin for the movie the last couple of hours just before we arrived."

Marty didn't make any eye contact with Tom. "Are you sure you want to hold all these passengers?"

Tom looked at the stewardess. "Special Agent Corley, organize all of the stewardesses to get the contact information from all of the passengers, including phone numbers, and let them go. Tell the pilot that if the airline company can provide another plane, you can continue your flight. We'll let the coroner do his job."

Marty started back toward his seat, but Tom waved him closer. "We just don't have the grounds to hold everybody. I wish we did, but we can't. I think we take the Malaysian into custody until the coroner has some idea how Dr. Paul Yu died."

The coroner stood up. "I can't tell you a thing until I've done a complete autopsy, including a toxicology investigation. This could take weeks, but I'm beginning to buy into your assumption that he was killed by an exotic chemical or something. I wouldn't touch his body, but honestly I can't tell if it is suicide or ...." Then he walked toward the front of the plane and the exit.

After the coroner walked away, Marty tapped Tom on the shoulder. "We can't hold the Malaysian that long. We're in America. The government and media will not allow us to infringe on his constitutional rights."

Tom frowned at Marty. "He isn't a U.S. citizen. Under the Constitution, he doesn't have those rights. We can hold him as long as we want."

"But we have no evidence that he is guilty of anything. Perhaps Dr. Yu really did figure out a way to commit suicide."

Tom shook his head. "He was going from Taipei to Hong Kong. He had no idea he was being watched, and once we had him, you said you checked. No one could have slipped him anything. The man doesn't just suddenly decide to commit suicide when he has nothing. This just doesn't fit a logical profile."

Marty looked down toward the ground.

Tom picked up the manifest. "I got it. We let Shou shadow the Malaysian once he steps off the plane in Hong Kong."

Marty turned toward Tom. "No, you can't do that. It's too dangerous."

"Let me finish. We don't have any choice. She's in Hong Kong anyway. She doesn't have to do anything else." Tom said as he put his hands on his hips. "You'll be on the next plane out of here. You should be there before the plane boards to Kuala Lumpur. If he boards that plane, you go on the same flight to Malaysia. He must be watched, at least until we know if he was involved. I'll check in with Middleton before we let him go—see if he's on the MI6 radar. I'm going to stay here with the coroner until we know something."

CHAPTER TWENTY-TWO

Late night, April 4, 1973
Honolulu

With the plan in place, Tom placed a call to Shou Li Cao for her to be back at the airport in Hong Kong at the gate when the Malaysian stepped off the plane. Marty would be on the next flight to Hong Kong. Tom knew he couldn't put him on the same flight, but if he was flying on to Kuala Lumpur, he'd likely be spending the rest of his time in the airport.

The Malaysian had told Tom in their interview that he was returning to his home after this misunderstanding in Honolulu. He was too shook up from this experience to continue building his business at this point.

FBI Special Agent Martin Corley was on the next flight just a few hours behind. Shou had strict instructions from Marty to just observe the Malaysian.

April 5, 1973
Hong Kong

Shou Li Cao had to call off sick again from her job at HSBC, but she believed it actually looked better if she stayed off the rest of the week. Shou went down to the street level to meet a courier, who was delivering a DHL photo of the Malaysian she was to watch. After she received the package, she hailed a cab to take her to Kai Tak Airport. As she settled into the backseat, she opened the package containing the picture and gasped. The man identified as the Malaysian had sat directly across from her at the airport yesterday. It was the man she'd been both attracted to and intimidated by. *Would he recognize me following him?*

When the cab pulled up in front of the terminal, she looked at it for several seconds before getting out. She walked slowly into the terminal, checked the board to see the gate assignment, then headed in the direction of the Cathay Pacific flight, waiting for the Malaysian to arrive. Her confidence in her ability to do her job had dropped significantly. She couldn't shut down her mind. If this Malaysian had killed Dr. Paul Yu and had made her, this assignment had just gotten *very* dangerous. As she over-thought everything, she even postulated that it all was tied to the situation at the Chinese restaurant in San Francisco.

As she traversed the terminal to the gate, she felt very alone. She looked around expecting, no hoping, to see MI6 agents, but she didn't see anyone. Surely, if Agent Warren called Middleton, they would be there looking for the Malaysian as well.

When she sat down at the gate, she was the only person sitting there. It was intimidating. Then she caught a glimpse of the clock across from her. She was about forty minutes early—if the flight was on time. *Focus, Shou, you must gain your focus.*

After a few minutes, she watched the Cathay Pacific ground agent step into the gate area and change the board to note that the flight was due on the ground within thirty minutes. Several more passengers came in and sat down as far away from her as possible. Soon the area was almost full of passengers. The ground agent called the names of several would-be passengers to come up and see her for some reason.

In minutes, the door was opened, and the same agent then picked up the microphone. "We would like to welcome the arrival of the...."

It was time to get in position. Shou decided the best thing to do was to move to the gate on the opposite side of the hallway to observe the passengers deplane. Her heart raced and a few beads of sweat appeared on her upper lip. The second to the last individual to step through the doorway was the man dressed in the same Zhongshan coat she'd seen him wearing only the day before. The man identified as the Malaysian seemed to keep his eyes straight forward as he stepped into the terminal and paced toward the main doorways. Shou fell in maybe ten feet behind. The man picked up the pace as he got closer to the main entrance. Shou was almost running to keep up with his long strides. The Malaysian man went out one set of doors, while Shou went out another set of doors, about fifteen feet away. As soon as he was outside, the Malaysian raised his hand to hail a cab. Shou had no choice but to do the same.

Shou jumped in the backseat and gave instructions to the driver to "follow that cab," as she leaned forward and pointed at the yellow vehicle the Malaysian had just taken. Her mind raced. Marty and Warren had both believed the Malaysian man would remain at the airport until time to board his connecting flight to Kuala Lumpur, but instead, here he was in a cab outside the airport. The two cabs raced across the city heading north. The farther they went, the more concerned Shou got. *She knew many Malaysians came from China, so his appearance meant little but getting in a cab caused her to conclude he was Red Chinese. Could he be a Communist Agent?*

Shou watched the cab meter as he continued through the city streets to the north. They were now outside the downtown business district, still moving north. The meter read twenty-five miles. The closer they got to the Red China border, the more Shou fidgeted. It now seemed likely this man was going to Shenzhen, China. Within another fifteen minutes, her suspicions were confirmed. The cab stopped at the Lo Wu Border Crossing.

Shou ordered her cabbie to pull over to the side so she could see what happened next.

The man stepped out of the cab, then walked toward the cab Shou was riding.

She begged the cabbie, "Turn around, *turn around. Let's get out of here.*" However, the traffic was too heavy coming and going along the road for him to pull out.

The man in the Zhongshan coat walked up to the cab and tapped on the glass beside Shou and made the gesture to roll down the window.

Shou reluctantly did so.

The man leaned over and put both hands on his knees. "Pretty lady, would you like to go into Mainland China with me?"

Shou lowered her head and shook it. She was terrified, yet somehow infatuated with the tall Chinese man.

He smiled. "Well, too bad. But know this—I took notice of you before I boarded the plane to Taipei, and then I saw you watch me get off the plane and follow me here." Then he turned and walked into the building to enter Red China.

Shou knew she had the difficult assignment of going back to Hong Kong to tell Marty and Tom that the man with the Malaysian passport was from Communist China. And if he had a Malaysian passport, he might well be a Chinese Agent.

CHAPTER TWENTY-THREE

December 12, 1979
Tokyo, Japan

Special Agent Thomas P. Warren sat in the far corner of baggage claim beside his small briefcase with a baseball cap pulled down low over his face. He'd purposely picked a busy area with a lot of people moving in and out, all focused on that luggage carousel. He was waiting for Hada Miyoko to pick him up. Thirty minutes after his flight was scheduled to land, she'd be sitting outside.

He kept looking at his watch, waiting for the designated time. Finally, at exactly 3:45 p.m., he stepped outside of the terminal. He stood on the cab line, looking up and down while cars rapidly moved in, some dropping off and others picking up passengers. The scene was total chaos. There she is. He swiftly walked toward her white Toyota Corolla and slipped into the front seat.

Miyoko didn't say a word. After a quick glance at Tom, she pressed down hard on the accelerator and pulled directly in front of a cab that had to slam on the brakes. Finally, Miyoko spoke in a Tokyo dialect, then quickly switched back over to English. "We are going to my aunt's home in Ashigarakami outside of Tokyo. That is where my father wants to meet with you."

"Wise move." Tom paused for a moment, then rubbed his chin. "Then you will bring me directly back here to wait for my flight back to Hong Kong."

Miyoko pushed down harder on the accelerator.

Tom watched the city pass by. "What made your father change his mind about talking to me?"

Miyoko shrugged. "I don't really know. He won't talk to me about it at all. I think he is just being protective—*overprotective*."

Tom's eyes were locked on the beautiful, spunky Japanese woman. He was becoming quite smitten with her, but she was a good bit younger than he. Had he messed up not pursuing the revival of his relationship with Judy, now almost fifteen years ago? For the first time in his life, he was contemplating what he might be missing, if his emptiness was due to his lack of a relationship with a female companion.

After a few minutes, Miyoko gave him a quick glance. "Why are you staring at me?"

Tom hadn't realized he'd been so obvious. He jerked his head away and looked back out at the passing downtown. Soon they were on the outskirts of Tokyo.

As they drove out of the large city, he checked behind as they traveled into the countryside. "Looks like we're in the clear. I don't detect anyone following us." Tom let out his breath.

As dusk was setting in, Miyoko leaned over toward Tom, then pointed with her head. "There is Mount Fuji. We are getting close to my aunt's home."

Tom glanced in that direction, but he was focused on talking to Miyoko's father.

Another fifteen minutes went by. She slowed the car and turned up a dirt road that seemed to head off into the woods. The view of Mount Fiji disappeared, shrouded by the trees. They bounced up the dirt road to a clearing on the hill and stopped in front of a tiny farmhouse. Miyoko smiled. "Come on, let me introduce you to my family."

Tom stepped out of the car, his briefcase in hand. He stretched his back. Clearly, her Toyota wasn't made for those kinds of roads. He hustled to catch up with the pretty Japanese woman. They both arrived at the front door at the same time. Miyoko pounded on the door. It was quickly opened, and she greeted her aunt with a bow and then a hug. She turned to Tom. "This is my Aunt Ai."

Tom bowed. Her name meant *love and affection*. She would be easy to get along with. "Good evening, I bring you greetings," he said in Japanese.

She motioned for Tom to step in. Miyoko grabbed his hand and led him directly to an older man sitting on a couch against the far wall. "Tom, this is my father, Hada Raden."

The man got up from the couch and reached for Tom's hand, offering an American handshake. Miyoko's father was taller than most Japanese and, despite his advanced age, he was thick and strong. It fit him, as his name meant *god of thunder*. He motioned for Tom to step outside. "I would like to speak to you in private."

Tom replied to him in perfect Tokyo dialect, "If you are comfortable speaking."

Miyoko interrupted, "I'd like to introduce you to my mother first, Agent Warren."

Tom nodded.

Miyoko opened her hand in the direction of her mother. "This is Hada Emica."

"It's a pleasure to meet you," Tom said.

"I'll prepare some tea, while you are outside talking." Emica spoke as she bowed.

The two men went outside into the dark, cool evening, walking quietly to the edge of the clearing, as far from the house as they could get. The old man looked up to the sky for several minutes, then stepped away from Tom. "I've never spoken to anyone about what happened in my assignment to Prince Takeda, as I had sworn my allegiance to him, Emperor Hirohito, and my country." He stepped back up to Tom. "Since I'm a Buddhist, as I grow old, I want to clear my soul. I think more and more about the terrible things I did when assigned to Takeda."

Tom raised his hand. "I don't need you to speak of anything you don't wish to speak of—atrocities or anything else. I'm only interested in what went on in NanJing. More particularly, what happened specifically at one individual's home."

Raden's hands started shaking as he took a few steps away, then turned his back.

The man was obviously struggling to speak of things he'd seen or done.

"I had just married when I was assigned to Takeda," he said. "I was young and had some indiscretions, but I didn't rape. I met a Chinese woman. I'll always believe she was a communist working for Mao in NanJing. She led us to some of the wealthier families in the beginning of our occupancy. She thought we would remove or kill them. I had an affair with her for a few days. That was one of the reasons I never wanted to speak of these things. I tried to keep it deeply suppressed. When she found out we were going to take their possessions back to Japan, she disappeared. I've always believed she went back and reported Takeda and me to Mao. Deep down, I've always believed due to my association with the Prince, I feared my family would be in danger from the Chinese communists and this man you are chasing."

"Your indiscretions are yours," Tom said softly. "I'm only interested in one house, one family." He stepped in front of the old man. "This man is one of the top spy handlers for Red China. If I can learn anything about him or his family in NanJing, perhaps, just perhaps, it will help me bring him and the spy ring down."

Raden nodded. "I will try to help you, but that was a long time ago. But as I've understood what you are trying to accomplish, I hope my actions will keep my daughter safe."

"I brought photographs of the man. This would've been a decade after he told me his wife and sister were raped and killed in front of him. So as a young man, he'd look a little different, but I'm hoping you might still remember, if you were there."

Raden started walking back toward the house. Tom followed. Once they re-entered the small home, he stopped at the kitchen table and motioned for his wife, sister Ai, and Miyoko to leave the room. Emica poured tea before leaving.

Tom had his briefcase in hand. He pulled out a picture of Dr. Wang from 1946 and a printout he'd given to Tom in 1963. He laid the picture in front of the old man. "Do you recognize this man?"

Raden picked up the picture and stared at it. Then laid it back down. "Not sure."

Tom picked up the large printout and flipped to the paper clip he had used to mark his place. It was a description of what the Japanese soldiers had looted from Dr. Wang's family.

Raden started reading over the list, then his finger stopped at the emerald bridal ring. He looked up at Tom. "I remember this item. Yes. But I wasn't in this house. I do remember this ring. The emerald was very large, and it was surrounded by diamond-encrusted gold curls. The ring was attached to an emerald wrist bracelet by a thin strand of diamonds set in gold."

Tom frowned. "Do you know what happened to the items from this house?"

Raden closed his eyes briefly. "Prince Takeda paid a lot of attention to the items coming from this residence. I never knew why. I always assumed it was because of the value of the items. There was a special list of things to go directly to the emperor. Besides this ring, there was a painting he was particularly interested in that is now in his home." His voice trailed off as he leaned back, appearing to be deep in thought. He placed both hands on the table, then pointed at the page. "Yes, yes, now I remember. That's what happened to these items, almost all of these were split down the middle between Hirohito and Takeda. In the beginning, Takeda's items went to Japan, but later, when we were losing the war, he moved some of them to the Philippines and put them in one of the bunkers."

Tom got up and looked over the old Japanese fellow's shoulder. "Do you know which ones?"

Raden looked up at him, then stated matter-of-factly, "You know that when Prince Takeda traveled, he used the name 'Kimsu,' not his real name."

That was a revelation to Tom, but he remained focused on the list, trying to clear his mind of what he'd just learned. "Go on."

Raden then whispered, "By the time, we—Takeda and I—went to the Philippines, I was isolated from most of the Golden Lily team. I was responsible for documentation, you know, like a bookkeeper. Therefore, I don't know all of the names of the Golden Lily team who served there, because I was isolated. Takeda and Chichibu worked really hard to compartmentalize everyone so no one would know the whole story. However, there were a few members that I worked with while traveling with Takeda. They were Kodama Yoshio—"

"Yes, I found out from my time in the Philippines that Yoshio was part of the Golden Lily and now is the head of one of the Japanese Yakuza."

"*You knew that already?*" Raden tipped his head to the side.

"I've been after this Chinese spy handler, Dr. Wang, since 1945." Tom put both hands on his hips. "But you haven't finished telling me what he took, or which bunker he put them in."

Raden picked up the pages and pointed. "Agent Warren, these are the items that I remember Takeda took with him to the Philippines. There may be more."

"Were there any pictures taken of these items or only the inventory sheets?" Tom inquired.

Raden closed his eyes. "I wasn't permitted, but I do believe Takeda took some. There were two sets, one for Takeda and one for the emperor."

Tom looked at the items the elderly Japanese man highlighted—it was jewelry and gold ingots. He thought back to his early days with the Bureau in the Philippines. The first Japanese woman Dr. Wang killed was wearing the emerald ring which he thought was from his family's estate in NanJing. It was highly unlikely she had access to any burial sites. But who did? The Japanese Yakuza. His thoughts flashed to his mole, Candy Man, who had taken him to a burial site near Montalban Gorge where he first encountered the Japanese Yakuza. It sure all seemed to tie together. He and his team ended up in a firefight. And Tom lost the first member of his team.

While Tom was thinking, Raden added one more thing. "Takeda was close to several cabin boys. They were Filipinos, but one of them spoke fluent Tokyo dialect. I later learned his father was Japanese and may have been former military."

Tom stepped to the side of Raden where he could look him in the eye. "Raden, thank you. You have been very helpful. You've given me answers I've been looking for, *for years*. I'm going to have your daughter take me back to the airport." He bowed toward the old man, then grabbed Dr. Wang's large report and stuffed it back in his briefcase.

As he finished, the old man grabbed his arm hard. "You have asked a lot of my daughter, who has taken many risks for you. You must look after her to see that nothing happens to her. We are all in danger. Some of our heightened danger is because of you and your investigation." The old man paused for a second. "But, ultimately, I suppose either Dr. Wang or someone else in China would have figured this out."

Tom stared at him. The old man's words were true. He decided to say nothing because, honestly, at this point, he could promise nothing. He started toward the door. "Miyoko, I'm ready to go back to the airport."

She walked over, kissed her father and whispered something in his ear, and then joined Tom going toward the front door.

As soon as they were in her Toyota, Tom licked his lips. "Your father was most helpful. I would still love to know if Prince Takeda has anything in his office. I would love to get pictures of the items or even the inventory list. They were bound to have pictures of a few of the items they inventoried."

Miyoko slammed on the brakes just as they reached the hard road. "I'm scared, Tom. This was a huge risk my father took, and I'm scared. Now you are continuing to ask me to take risks."

Tom caught his breath. She was young. "Of course, you are right. I'm sorry." He looked over at her. "Just take me to the airport. You can stop helping me. I appreciate what you've done, and I've gotten all that I need from your father."

Miyoko didn't say a word as they drove back toward the airport at a high rate of speed. After about a half hour, she finally spoke. "I just don't believe I can keep this up anymore. I'm scared for my family. Takeda has hidden everything or buried it so deep I can't find it." She wiped a tear off her face with the back of her hand. "And the Yakuza always seem to know what's going on. That is why my father wanted to meet you out in the countryside."

Tom didn't respond to her comments. *I have to make the right move here. She is right. Does the government have her home bugged?*

Miyoko turned into the airport. When she stopped at the departure gate, Tom pulled out two thousand yen and handed it to her. "Take this and go get yourself a motel room for a couple of days. Don't leave for at least two days. Call in sick at work. Let's make sure you are safe." Tom leaned over and kissed her on the cheek, wishing he could hold and kiss her. He grabbed his briefcase and exited the car.

December 16, 1979
Ulaanbaatar, Outer Mongolia

It was a bitter cold day as Yu Qiangsheng walked across the long, abandoned Sukhbaatar Square toward a bench on the west side for a meeting with Bernard Boursicot. Yu didn't like being in Outer Mongolia, nor did he like the low-level French diplomat, Boursicot, who was finishing his diplomatic assignment here, continuing to spy on his French government for two more years.

Boursicot waited in his designated spot. Yu sat on the bench beside him. "Good day, Monsieur Boursicot."

"*Bonne journée*, Kang." Boursicot continued staring at the bronze statue of Damdin Sukhbaatar in the middle of the square.

Yu reached inside of his Zhongshan coat, pulled up a fat envelope, and laid it on the bench. "Here is the envelope of information we want you to send to the FBI agent in the United States."

Boursicot reached for the envelope, but Yu slammed his hand down on top of the French man's hand. Boursicot winched as he struggled to pull his hand free, but it was no use.

"Let's make this quick," Yu snapped. "You are taking too many risks— you should be more careful. Going in and out of China from here is raising suspicions. We don't want you to get caught."

"Kang, this is my last package. My time here is over. I'll be leaving in a few weeks and going back to France, likely for good. I would like to take Shi and our son, Bertrand, with me." Boursicot nodded as he spoke. Then he detailed how easy spying had been, since the French Embassy consisted of a staff of only three individuals, and his role was that of a typist, archivist, accountant, and clerk. "I mean, the lock has been broken on the safe since I got here. So it has been easy picking up a few items for your government while I've carried the diplomatic pouch from here to Beijing every three weeks."

Yu pressed down harder on his hand on top of the envelope, causing Boursicot to flinch. "Not possible."

Boursicot nodded.

225

Yu lifted his hand from the envelope and stood.

"Kang, here is the information from the embassy that I brought today." Boursicot held out an envelope.

Yu snatched the envelope from his hand and walked off, leaving Boursicot sitting on the bench by himself.

December 18, 1979
Beijing

Yu Qiangsheng pulled up alongside Dr. Wang's parked car. Dr. Wang motioned for him to get out. The two men walked silently side by side through the cemetery, passing several generic tombstone markers. Finally, they arrived at the simple stone in the ground. Both men stopped and looked down. Yu said, "It is hard to believe it has been four years since Kang Sheng passed away."

Dr. Wang stared at the simple marker. "I felt it necessary to pay our respects to him." He stood there in silence for a moment, then continued. "He told me before we brought you over that someday you could easily be his replacement. You are ready now. Mao, Zhou, and Kang are now all gone. Kang, Zhou, and I brought China into the nuclear age. But we must advance our cause even more."

As Yu looked down at the simple tombstone, the words from his last meeting with Kang in April 1974 were still fresh in his mind. Yu had been called to come visit him one last time. Kang was so sick dying from cancer, he'd become a virtual prisoner in his own home. Yu had to help the ill man slowly walk into the area that Kang referred to as his Bamboo Garden. There, the two men just sat and enjoyed the peace for a short time. He was so ill he could barely speak. Finally, he leaned close and spoke barely above a whisper,

"The end of my life is close now. But yours is about to flourish. You must take full advantage of all that comes your way. I've watched over your growth since you were a youth."

Kang gasped for air and paused for a while, struggling to speak. Yu was patient with the man.

Kang trembled and leaned over in his chair. "Your future will be unlike anything I could possibly imagine in the old days. You must make an impact on the ways of China. Your star is rising." His head bobbed as he struggled to say more.

Yu had placed a hand on his shoulder to help him sit back up.

Dr. Wang waved his arms in the air, causing Yu to return to the present. "The ways of our world are changing fast. Ever since Deng Xiaoping began working with President Carter, we've become much too conciliatory to the United States."

"What do you mean?" Yu asked.

"President Carter and Chairman Deng have made a secret deal to build a listening station along the Soviet border. It's part of their SIGNIT system. Deng is allowing them not only to build it, but also equip and man it." Dr. Wang snorted.

Yu rubbed his chin as he processed Dr. Wang's words. Did Chairman Deng confide in him? Did his spy network in the United States provide that intel? It was imperative that he learn the real name of this man in his own quest for power.

Dr. Wang strolled back to their awaiting car. "These are the types of things I learn in advance from my man working for the CIA, but he wants to retire soon. I must start to look for a new replacement. He will have big shoes to fill."

Yu started to say something, but Dr. Wang raised his hand. "To keep up with Deng's objectives of changing China from an agrarian society to a manufacturing one, we must start stealing intellectual properties from the

Western World. We must find another Dr. Paul Yu—or come up with a similar scheme."

Construction on that SIGNIT project would be a golden opportunity to increase their spying efforts on Western manufacturers. Yu was now Bureau Chief within the Guoanbu. His network covered the entire country. Between he and Dr. Wang, they controlled all the spy activities inside and outside of China. Besides his role of handling spies, Dr. Wang was overseeing newly established Overseas Chinese Affairs in Hong Kong.

"Bernard Boursicot's assignment in Outer Mongolia is almost over, and he's returning to France." Yu cracked half a smile. "I've brought his last documents—about the Russian troops on the border. He wanted to stop and see Shi Pei Pu one last time before returning. Plus, I gave him your misinformation package for Warren, too. He asked that we help him with his petition of the Chinese government to allow Shi and Bertrand to come live with him in France. I told him you and I would discuss the matter. Frankly, I'm glad to be done dealing with him."

Dr. Wang took the package without saying a word.

Yu didn't tell Dr. Wang that he told Boursicot to stop spying, as he was putting himself at great risk. The two men strolled alongside in silence.

"You know, with my rising power in the Chinese Communist Party, if I could take down the leader of the U.S.'s effort to spy on us, someday perhaps I may even seek the Vice Presidency of China. Imagine—Vice President Liao." Dr. Wang straightened his red tie. Then he grabbed his chest.

Yu caught him before he almost fell to his knees. "You okay?"

Within a couple of seconds, he straightened himself back up. He tugged his gray suit back neatly in place. "I'm fine. Just a little shortness of breath from the cold."

Dr. Wang hurried into the backseat of his car, and his driver took off.

Yu watched him leave. It was very cold, but Dr. Wang had a health issue. His weight gain over the last few years could be part of his struggles. Yu slipped into his car and rubbed his hands together. The one thing he'd learned in his life was to trust few people. It was time to really push to learn about the name of Dr. Wang's top spy in the U.S. CIA. Also, whether or not Dr. Wang had gloated or trusted him enough to give him his real name, either way, his guarded secret was out. Liao. *Is he really in line to become the Vice President of China? Or is he delusional? Or just egotistical?*

CHAPTER TWENTY-FOUR

December 19, 1980
Hong Kong

Tom Warren had an appointment with MI6 Agent Anthony Middleton to exchange information on the Chinese spy ring. Tom took two steps at a time up the two flights of stairs to Middleton's office. He could barely control his own excitement to update the MI6 agent with what he'd learned in Tokyo.

No sooner had Tom sat down at Middleton's desk than Anthony blurted out, "The Communist Chinese have set up two new offices here in Hong Kong. One is the Affairs Office, and the other is Overseas Chinese Affairs Office. They may be doing the same thing in Macao. I'm betting it's a new office to use as their base to spy on everything going on here in Hong Kong. So you can guess who I think is in charge."

Tom pounded his desk. "Dr. Wang."

"Please, *please*, let me finish. Right." Middleton drummed his fingers.

Tom laughed. It was so easy to get under his old friend's skin. "Okay, but get to the point. FBI Director Webster is expecting me back in San Francisco the day after tomorrow."

"Look, we know that Dr. Wang has been coming in and out of Hong Kong to pick up his mail, but I can't imagine him staying here. He'd have to know we'd pick him up."

"Have you ever been able to put a name on the man who killed Dr. Paul Yu? He might get the assignment for the new office here."

"Why would you think that?" Anthony exclaimed, flattening both hands on the table.

"Mainly because I don't know anybody else." Tom flashed a quick smile. "Besides, that guy had to be pretty clever and well-trusted to carry out his assignment."

Middleton got up from his desk and went over to the file cabinet, pulled out a large file, and returned to his desk. "We have worked with your man Corley. We have your FBI photos and drawings of the man who killed Dr. Paul Yu, but our operatives in Red China haven't been able to get close enough to definitively identify who he is. But we do know he is certainly Chinese, not Malaysian, as he told you."

Tom picked up the file without a word and opened it. Middleton had just zinged him with that comment. Written on the inside of the manila file were several names with question marks after each one. Then he started flipping through the spare notes and pictures. There were pictures in the file of numerous Chinese individuals. There were several photos, but none included Dr. Wang. There were some photos of an unidentified old woman. Paperclipped to it was a note saying it could be this man's mother, but there were a series of question marks after that comment. He laid the file back down and closed it. "We know little about this man—or even if he is associated with Dr. Wang?"

"Actually, we think he's now the head of the Guoanbu." Middleton leaned back at his desk and folded his hands behind his head.

Tom repeatedly touched the file. "So, this man is now the head of the Counter Intelligence Division, and this is all we know about him?"

"Honestly, how much do we know about Dr. Wang? We ..." Anthony pointed at himself and Tom, then continued, "believe he's in charge of the Foreign Intelligence side, but do we really know? You and I both have been working on this since the 1940s and have failed miserably to unlock any of their mysteries, so don't try to put this all on MI6."

All Tom could do was rub his chin.

The door opened and Marty Corley walked in. "Hey, Tom, good to see you. What brings you to Hong Kong?"

Tom flashed a big smile. "I brought you guys news from Japan. I learned a lot about Dr. Wang—maybe as much as we will *ever* learn. However, after learning some things from Anthony here—" Tom pointed at Anthony. "I think we should try to set a trap for Dr. Wang here in Hong Kong and arrest him."

"How so?" Marty asked.

"I had something in mind when I left Japan, but with what Anthony told me, I may need to tweak it a bit. But I'm working on it." Tom frowned.

Anthony's phone rang and he grabbed it, turning his back so Tom and Marty couldn't hear his conversation.

Marty stepped over toward Tom. "So did you see Miyoko? You sly dog."

Tom smiled. "Of course. She's even prettier now."

January 7, 1980
San Francisco

Tom walked into his office and picked up the note left on his desk by another member of his team. He grinned as he read it. Back as early as 1972, their office had been receiving information from various sources, some good, most not so good. Tom was beginning to question the information Boursicot had sent from China. On top of that, CIA Larry Wu-tai Chin's translations of secret documents coming out of Red China had been accurately translated, but the man never seemed to have much insight into what was going on in the country. His excuse was that the CIA didn't have the best operatives inside Communist China. Tom scratched his cheek.

However, last year, the FBI was provided with a solid tip from inside Red China—a U.S. aeronautical engineer born in Taiwan and working in a high security area of the Lawrence Livermore Laboratory outside of town was giving Red Chinese scientists information on the U.S.'s nuclear developments and missile defense. The tip turned out to be credible enough that San Francisco's FBI received a special warrant from the secretive Foreign Intelligence Surveillance Court. They were able to bug the aeronautical engineer's phone and home. This led to conformation of this potential spy.

Tom looked at his watch. It was a good time to share the good news with his partner, Marty, who was in Hong Kong at the moment. He picked up the phone and dialed the MI6 headquarters. When Marty came on the phone, Tom blurted out, "Marty, we finally have some intel that is proving valuable. One of our team members here has uncovered a potential spy at Lawrence Livermore. Our team is really digging into the engineer's background—"

"Wow! This might be our first real break since Dr. Paul Yu. Do we know what information the scientist has stolen?"

Tom continued, "Our San Francisco team was able to document that just before this engineer would take a trip to Red China, he'd go to the Lawrence Livermore library and pull a bunch of research outside his job responsibility. They found some scientists over at Los Alamos to review all that he has taken so we can get an idea of what the Chinese can do with it. That might also help us figure out who he was taking it to in Red China."

"How do you propose to do that? Damn, the man is spying. What difference does it make who he's giving the information to?" Marty barked.

"Because it may lead us to Dr. Wang."

"I knew it. This is about revenge."

"No, Marty. It's about bringing down the number one spy network working out of Communist Red China," Tom retorted. "We have to capitalize on our first breakthrough in a number of years. I think we have to dissect it from every angle possible."

Then he noticed an envelope on his desk that had been lying under the note. It was from Miyoko. He quickly opened it.

There was a note:

> Sorry I was such a baby when you were here. When I realized I was safe, I got and copied this inventory list. I've talked to my father about pictures, but we figure Takeda has them under lock and key somewhere.

Tom rifled through them, making mental notes, then slipped them into his Dr. Wang file.

Hong Kong

Marty stopped by Shou Li Cao's apartment on his way home. Shou greeted him with a kiss. She was in her sweatsuit in the small apartment kitchen, fixing something to eat. "How was your day, honey?"

Shou replied, "This secretarial job at the HSBC is getting more and more tedious. I'm covered up with work. The two loan officers I'm assigned to are always wanting me to stay late to get the commercial agreements out. I just want to come home. Lately, there doesn't seem to be as much money coming out of mainland to keep me engaged in this job. I need something more exciting to do this spy work."

"Spy work isn't James Bond's movie stuff. It's the meticulous study of information that unlocks spying." Marty snorted. "Since Deng Xiaoping has come into power, we know they are spying more on Western manufacturing, which means they are watching these Hong Kong companies borrowing money to build stuff or buy stuff. You're in a great place to find us leads."

Shou opened her refrigerator and pulled out an egg carton and waved it around as she spoke. "Okay, okay. I'll pay more attention, but it is boring."

Marty smacked her on the butt and reached in for the iced tea pitcher. He grabbed a glass and some ice cubes. "As an example, Tom called this morning to tell me about an operation we've had running out of the San Francisco office for a couple of years. It has finally uncovered a spy working at a lab associated with California-Berkeley. But it took all that time to pull the pieces together, just like a jigsaw puzzle."

Shou pouted her lower lip. "Still, I'm bored. But I'll start paying closer attention to the documents I'm typing."

Marty sucked on an ice cube from the bottom of the iced tea he'd just chugged. "I have to get over to my place. I've got to get a report prepared for MI6 and send a copy to Tom back in San Francisco in the morning." He kissed her on the cheek, put the glass in the sink, and left.

After her boyfriend left, Shou sat down at her kitchen table and thought about what he'd told her. *Perhaps I should reach out to Tom and see if I can go into China to figure out who was getting this information.* The more she thought about that, the more it sounded like a dumb idea. Tom and Marty would never approve. Living this close to the Chinese border without doing anything was driving her crazy. Finding her father had always been in the back of her mind, but she hadn't acted. Why was she been so scared? In a country with a billion people, it should be easy to blend in.

Her head dropped. *Just go into China and try to find Father.* She hadn't seen nor heard from him since her mother and she escaped and came to the United States in 1964. Besides wanting to know about him, she had the unhappy task of telling him her mother was dead.

Maybe it would be better to ask for forgiveness rather than permission. Get into China, look for her father, and then reach out to Tom and Marty and see if they had learned any more information on the U.S. engineer they believed to be the Chinese spy.

And since she'd be in Red China, perhaps she could gather the needed information on this engineer to prove he was a spy.

When Shou got up the next morning, she started thinking about what Marty had told her the previous night, Marty and Tom were looking for information on a U.S. engineer being a spy. Plus, she still wished to see her father, who she believed remained in prison. She went to the kitchen, started the coffee pot, and then returned to the bathroom to get ready for work. As she was putting on her lipstick, she looked at herself in the bathroom mirror. She stopped.

Today was the day.

She walked back into her bedroom and packed her suitcase. Then she drew a deep breath and searched the back bottom of her underwear drawer. Finally, she pulled out an envelope. When she had come to Hong Kong almost nine years ago, she knew one day she'd need her Communist Chinese documents. As she was walking to the front door, she picked up the phone and called her boss at HSBC. "I won't be into work today. I think I have the flu."

She went to the parking lot, tossed her suitcase in the back of her car, and drove off toward the Lo Wu Border to enter Red China. She was going to find her father. Her first stop was to see her uncle, the man who told them to leave the country in 1964.

Thirty minutes later, Shou arrived at the border crossing. She presented her Communist Chinese documents. The Communist Border Security Agent glanced over the papers, then picked up his clipboard and wrote down the name Shou Li Cao, then handed back the documents. The Security Agent waved his arm for her to drive on.

Shou threw the papers on the seat, grabbed the steering wheel with both hands, and pressed down on the accelerator. She was headed toward Shenzhen, Red China.

CHAPTER TWENTY-FIVE

Thursday January 9, 1980
San Francisco

Tom had just walked into FBI headquarters. His phone was already ringing, so he picked it up. "Special Agent Tom Warren."

"Tom, Shou is missing!" Marty shouted.

"Missing? How long? When?" Tom replied, still standing beside his desk.

"I don't know for sure. After our conversation with her Monday evening, I left the apartment and went home. Yesterday, we didn't talk. I didn't think anything of it. So, this morning, I called her. No answer. I thought it was a little strange. I went to her apartment. Her suitcase was gone. I called her work, and she'd called off yesterday morning with the flu."

Tom quickly did a one-eighty glance around the room. "She wasn't kidnapped if she took her suitcase. Calling off with the flu implies she was planning to come back."

"Tom, I think she went into Red China," blurted Marty.

Tom tried to be calm, to keep Marty calm. "What makes you think or say that?"

"When I was telling her about our conversation, she told me she wanted more excitement rather than working at the bank."

Tom scratched his head. "Marty, I pray you are wrong."

"She has confided to me several times lately that she felt compelled to tell her father about her mother's death. You don't suppose—"

"I'll go talk to Adler—let him know I'm on my way to Hong Kong. Promise you won't do anything until I get there." Tom rubbed the back of his neck, then hung up the phone. He didn't want to hear Marty's answer. He got up from his desk and went to Special Agent in Charge Gerald Adler's office.

Adler sat at his desk. "Warren, come on in. What do you need?"

Tom sat down on the edge of the chair. "I'm going to talk to CIA Larry, pick up the immediate chatter, and then leave for Hong Kong. We have a situation there—I need to get there. We have a chance to grab Dr. Wang."

Adler stood up and walked around his desk. "I need more information."

Warren nodded. "Adler, as soon as I talk to CIA Larry, I'll get you that information."

Tom decided it was time to do more than just talk to CIA analyst Larry Wu-tai Chin. It was time to meet the man face to face. He went to the file cabinet and pulled out the Dr. Wang file and placed it in his briefcase.

January 10, 1980
Langley, VA

Tom drove up to the checkpoint at the CIA headquarters. The security guard walked up to his car. "May I have your reason for coming here?"

Tom looked in his rearview mirror and saw another security guard holding a high-powered rifle behind him. Tom held his FBI credentials out the window. "I have an appointment with CIA Analyst Larry Wu-tai Chin."

The security guard took his credentials, went into the small booth, and picked up the phone. Tom watched him speaking, but couldn't hear what he was saying. The security guard returned to the car, handed back his identification, and then waved to another security guard who went through Tom's rental car and held a mirror under the car. The security guard checking out Tom's car walked up to the other security guard and appeared to speak.

The first stepped back up to the car. "Mr. Chin will meet you just inside the main entrance."

Tom pulled ahead and parked at the main building. At the front door, he was met by a Chinese gentleman.

"FBI Special Agent Thomas Warren, it's a pleasure to see you again."

"Larry, we have aged a little since the late 1940s." Tom looked down at the CIA logo in the middle of the floor.

As the two men walked down the hallway, Larry said, "I looked it up. It was January 24, 1949, when you arrived at the U.S. Consulate in Shanghai. Seems like forever ago."

Interesting he remembered that date exactly. Tom glanced around, processing and reflecting back. He had a vivid memory of that day,—and Larry was right on the money.

The two men entered the elevator. Larry punched his floor button, then leaned against the wall. "How long have you been in the FBI?"

"Since 1945."

Larry watched the floors illuminate. "You've been in service of our country about as long as me. I'm thinking of retiring next year. Between Shanghai, the West Coast, and here, I'm ready to draw my retirement. You?"

"Larry, to tell you the truth, the thought has crossed my mind recently. But—"

The door to the elevator opened. Tom didn't finish his thought. The two men remained silent until they entered Larry's office.

Larry shut the door behind him. "Agent Warren, what can I do for you?"

"Larry, I have a desperate situation that I hope you can assist me with. We believe a girlfriend of one of my top agents has entered Red China in the last few days, and we haven't heard anything more from her. I was hoping you might have some scuttlebutt about her from inside the country."

Larry furrowed his brow. "I may not be able to provide you certain information without authorization from my superiors. But I need more information to help you."

"Yes, of course, I understand. Her name is Shou Li Cao. She's about five foot, four inches tall, long black hair, slender build. Very attractive, but no features standout. The only thing I know she has mentioned her father was placed in prison in 1964, and she has not seen him since. I know that's a long shot but it's all we got." Tom stared up at the ceiling. "It was right after that she and her mother fled the country."

Larry bit his lower lip. "None of that information helps. It just too vague."

Tom watched him move over to a file cabinet beside his desk. There were no tabs on the drawers. He pulled open the third drawer and rapidly flipped through the files. "While her name doesn't ring a bell with me, I thought I would check old, translated documents. But no file under that name has ever been created."

Tom put both hands on his knees and stood. "Larry, I know you have tried to be a big help to me over the years. It seems like I'm lacking adequate information. I wish I could stay and visit, but I have to stay after this situation. May I call you and check in with you? This situation is quite fluid."

Larry nodded. "Of course. I'm reviewing all sorts of correspondence coming out of Red China on an hourly basis. I'll be glad to help you. Let me see you out."

The two men quickly walked down the hallway to the elevator. Larry walked Tom to the front door. "Feel free to call for updates."

"Thank you." Tom turned and bolted out the door.

CHAPTER TWENTY-SIX

January 12, 1980
Hong Kong

Tom was met at luggage claim by his partner, Marty Corley. As Tom grabbed his suitcase, Marty grabbed his arm. "What took you so long to get here? Shou has now been missing for three days."

Tom stopped. "So we should just jump in a car and drive across the border without any information? Where do you look in a country of a billion people?"

Marty took a deep breath. "Okay, what's your plan then?"

Tom walked toward the door. "Let's go talk to Middleton. See what his sources have to say."

Marty grabbed Tom's arm again. "You don't think I haven't done that already? Come on, let's get into Red China."

"We need to make a call to CIA Larry to see if he can give us anything new since I've been in the air—maybe something that Middleton doesn't have—and, remember, we have to sneak into Red China. If we go through customs, everyone—including Dr. Wang and the man who killed Dr. Yu—will know we are there. We will be ducks on the pond, man."

Marty drove like a maniac through downtown Hong Kong to the MI6 headquarters. As soon as they arrived, both men ran as fast as they could up the stairs to Middleton's office.

Anthony waved them over to his desk.

"I need to borrow your desk phone to call a contact of mine at the CIA to see if he has heard anything about Marty's girlfriend." He picked up the phone and started dialing before Anthony could say a thing.

When the phone was answered on the other end, Tom said, "Larry, I'm in Hong Kong. Any information on Shou Li Cao?"

"Since you left two days ago, nothing."

"Okay, Larry, thanks. If you get any scuttlebutt, keep it at the top of the stack until I can check back in." Tom hung up the phone.

Anthony Middleton frowned at Tom and Marty. "So this girl is Marty's girlfriend? That's the first I've heard that. Is there anything more I need to know about her?"

Both men shook their heads at the same time.

Anthony leaned forward on his elbow at his desk. "Agent Warren, somehow I don't believe you. Remember, I've worked with you for years. My instincts tell me she is more to both of you than just Marty's girlfriend."

"That's just not true, *Anthony*. But I have a question for you," Tom retorted.

Anthony jutted his jaw. "I don't believe you, but go ahead and ask your question."

Tom looked at Marty and bit his lip. "How can I sneak into Red China without going through the border crossing?"

Anthony shrugged. "You know me better than that. I'm by the book. We don't sneak anyone, anywhere."

Tom got up and started toward the door. "I guess I'll have to find another way on my own, if you won't help me."

Marty stayed seated. "Anthony, come on. I've worked by your side for a number of years. This is my girlfriend. Don't hold out on us now with that bullshit."

About the time, Tom reached the door, Anthony slammed his hand down on the desk. His palm made a loud smack. "Come back, Tom. I'll help you. Come on."

Marty leaned back. "Thank you."

Tom walked back over and sat.

Anthony looked at Tom, then Marty. "Gentlemen, I have a very serious question for you. Please don't answer until you think about it."

Marty frowned as he glanced at Tom, who waved him off.

"Go ahead, Anthony, ask your question." Tom frowned as he put his hands on his hips. "Let's just get on with it."

Anthony folded his hands on top of his desk. "Where, exactly, are you going to go hunting in a country as big as China for a single girl? Why did she go there? Did she want to return home? Was she looking for something? I need answers to help you."

"I think she's looking for her father. This was why she fled China in the first place," Marty said in a low voice. "She wanted to tell him that her mother was dead."

The MI6 agent got up and went to a file cabinet, opened the drawer, pulled out a file, and tossed it on the desk. "In there is just a small list of the work camps that MI6 has identified in Red China. There are undoubtedly hundreds more. They move prisoners from place to place to do work detail. Cheap labor is how Deng is rebuilding their country."

Marty reached for the file and started thumbing through the pages.

Tom closed his eyes, processing what Anthony had told him. "We're so screwed."

Anthony raised both hands up over his shoulders. "Why do you think that? Let me give you a different scenario."

"Anthony, other than getting us into Communist China, what other scenario could there be?" Marty blurted out.

Tom frowned as he raised his right hand. "Let's hear him out."

Anthony stood up and started to pace. "What does Dr. Wang want more than anything?"

"*Me.*" Tom replied.

"Exactly. Why look for her, when you can exchange yourself for her? Let him bring her to you."

"What makes you think Dr. Wang will capture Shou?" Tom raised both hands palms up.

Simultaneously, Marty jumped up. "Are you crazy? First, how do we know he won't just kill her and bring us her head?"

Tom stood up and pressed Marty back into the chair. "Anthony may be at least partially right. We can't go galivanting off into China without a plan of where to look. Let's stay on top of CIA Larry. She never told you where her family is from? Odds are, that's where she is."

"No, if she did, I don't remember." Marty sat on the edge of the chair. "We can't just sit still."

Tom held his hand up as he continued. "We just have to get there before Dr. Wang does. We must assume she went through the Lo Wu Border Crossing. I wish we could just reach out to the Chinese authorities and see if they have her under surveillance." Tom pointed at Anthony. "MI6 is still monitoring Dr. Wang going to his mailbox here?"

"Righto," Anthony replied.

Tom sat back down. He looked at Marty, then at Anthony. "We have a very delicate situation. We can't do nothing." He paused, then continued, "I'll ask you one more time. Do you have a way to sneak us into China?"

"We have a couple of ways. First off, we have a small team of Royal Marine Commandos assigned to this office. Let me reach out to them about getting you into China."

Tom bit his lip. "*Let's go. Let's go.*"

Tom pulled out a deck of cards to attempt to pass the time waiting on information from CIA Larry. He dealt a hand of spades to Marty as they begin to play the phone waiting game. "Looks like you've lost some weight since traveling back and forth to Hong Kong."

"Between messed up sleep and the combination of Chinese and British food—yeah, two notches on my belt." Marty bit his lip then forced a brief smile. "No fried chicken here."

Tom opened his hand and checked his spades. Ace, queen. Good.

January 13, 1980
Beijing

Yu Qiangsheng furrowed his brow as he stuffed the piece of paper in his Zhongshan suit. It contained the name *Shou Li Cao*. It was almost time for his scheduled meeting with Dr. Wang. Four days had passed since the cute probably-FBI spy had crossed the border at Shenzhen. However, she'd disappeared after she passed through the Lo Wu Border Crossing and his agents hadn't been able to locate her. Why had she come back into China? She must be returning to the country to spy for the United States. But where was she working? His research into her background revealed her father was in prison. He believed she was too smart to go to the prison to find him. He wondered if Dr. Wang knew about her. If so, it could be a problem.

Yu entered Dr. Wang's office and stood opposite him. He was directed toward a seat on the opposite side of the metal desk. Dr. Wang slid open an office drawer, then laid a file on top of his desk.

"I called this meeting to brief you on several matters for the Communist Party," Dr. Wang said. "Of course, you are aware the United States put their

SIGNET here to spy on the Soviet Union. Since then, we've been able to reverse engineer much of their system."

"Isn't that the U.S. electronic spy network?" Yu continued before Dr. Wang could answer. "I still can't believe that Deng would allow them into our country—plus man that station."

Dr. Wang glared at Yu. "You don't understand the implications. Premier Deng out-negotiated Carter. Additionally, Deng convinced Carter to allow us to start buying U.S. manufactured products. We have already started reverse-engineering more items—thus, we will be able to manufacture them here. You see, we won't have to buy them from the Capitalists much longer. Deng wants to grow our economy."

Dr. Wang leaned forward and placed both hands on the desk. "However, all is not well."

Yu sat us straighter.

Dr. Wang continued. "I've mentioned this before, but now the time is getting close at hand that I'm about to lose my most valuable asset in the United States. My agent at the CIA is going to retire within the next year. I don't have anyone who can replace him."

Yu had tried to find out who this man was for years. Learning his name would be valuable.

Dr. Wang pressed his hand over his tie, pushing it against his starched white shirt. "Boursicot is coming in to see Shi today, correct?"

"Yes, I plan to meet him at the train station. This is his last trip here before returning to France. So, too it will be our last package from the French Embassy."

Dr. Wang pushed the file toward Yu.

He glanced at it as he picked it up. Documents for Warren.

Dr. Wang stared straight ahead.

Yu was relieved once again the young American spy wasn't on Dr. Wang's radar, but he needed to get out and find her.

As Yu started toward the door, Dr. Wang said, "I'm going to Hong Kong in the morning. I'll be back tomorrow night. I have to pick up a very important package. Fill me in on your meeting with Boursicot when I get back."

Yu had picked up the PLA officer Zhao before proceeding to the train station. As soon as he was parked, he looked at his watch. The train coming in from Ulaanbaatar, Outer Mongolia, was due within the next few minutes. He went into the station and found a secluded corner where he couldn't be observed. He looked at his watch again. The train was running late. Finally, after another fifteen minutes, he felt the rumble of the tracks. He had to be ready to pounce—he wanted to confront Boursicot as soon as he got off the train. He gave Zhao two instructions—make sure Boursicot didn't exit unless Yu was with him and to hold the train, just in case Yu had to put Boursicot back on the train to Mongolia.

When the train came to a full stop, Yu went between the front of the first car and the exit to the main terminal. After about half the passengers had stepped off the train, Bernard Boursicot exited from several cars back.

Yu walked back and fell in step beside him. Boursicot glanced over at him. The two men continued in silence out of the train station. When they got to the front door, Yu nodded at Zhao to return to the platform to hold the train. Once they stepped outside the terminal, Yu whispered, "Follow me to my car in the parking garage."

The two men walked to his car and slipped in. As Yu slammed the car door, he leaned over. "Where is my package from the French Embassy? If you want to see Shi and Shi Dudu, you better have brought some documents."

Boursicot reached inside his coat and pulled out a thick, legal size envelope and passed it to Yu. "Of course, Kang. Just as you asked. By the way, we call our son, Bertrand."

Yu grabbed the envelope, undid the clasp, shuffled through the papers, and then refastened the clasp. "Here is the information we want you to send to the FBI agent in the United States. You may go."

Boursicot took the package without another word and got out.

Yu stuffed the envelope between the seats, then went back to get Zhao.

January 14, 1980
Beijing

Dr. Wang was waiting on Yu Qiangsheng to show up at his office for their scheduled meeting. Ten o'clock sharp, there was a knock on his door. Dr. Wang had Wu open the door and let Yu in. Wu returned to his metal chair next to Chung. Dr. Wang motioned for Yu to take a seat. "How did everything go with Boursicot?"

Yu laid the legal envelope on the desk. "This is from the French Embassy. It's Boursicot's last drop. He was carrying a diplomatic pouch from Outer Mongolia to Beijing, and copied all the documents. Plus, he said he'd send your package to the agent in the U.S."

Dr. Wang opened his desk door, grabbed the overnight envelope he'd picked up in Hong Kong, and pushed it toward Yu. He trusted Yu, so for the first time, he shared the information he had about FBI Special Agent Warren. He wanted to watch the expression on Yu's face as he read it. It contained the latest information from Jin Wu-dai. "Open it and read it. This is from my top agent in the United States."

Yu picked up the package, looked at the cover, then pulled out the contents and began to read. He looked surprised as he read over it. "So a girl who may be attached to the FBI is somewhere in China? She has come looking for her father. Is he in prison here?"

Dr. Wang smiled, showing teeth that looked like corn on the cob. "Find the girl and bring her to me. Kang Sheng put him in prison, in a work camp, years ago. He is still alive."

"And Jin thinks Special Agent Warren is coming here after her?" Yu asked as he sat straight up in his chair.

"We don't know whether or not she has some to the FBI, but Warren and Corley are desperately trying to find her whereabouts." Dr. Wang pointed with his hand toward the ceiling. "Look for her in Zhangzhou. That is where her father's family is from. You are dismissed."

After Qiangsheng left, Dr. Wang looked at his two henchmen, Wu and Chung. "Go to the prison and get that girl's father, and bring him to our jail here. I have big plans. We are going to set the trap. I now have the cheese, the mouse, and the trap."

Shortly after Wu and Chung had left, there was another knock on Dr. Wang's office door. "Come in."

An elderly Chinaman slowly entered the room and limped over to his metal desk. Without saying a single word, the elderly Chinese dropped five chopsticks on Dr. Wang's desk. Then the old Chinaman bowed, turned, and slowly limped back out of the office.

When he was gone, Dr. Wang turned them over so he could read the words branded into the bamboo wood. "NanJing." He picked up one of them, held it up, and stared at it for a moment. Beside NanJing, it had "Thomas P. Warren" branded into the hardwood. As he clutched the chopstick, he leaned back in his chair and closed his eyes, letting his imagination run wild.

Early Tuesday morning, January 15, 1980
Beijing

Yu Qiangsheng stared out the window on his thousand-mile military flight to Zhengzhou. He was exhausted from the night of research into Shou Li Cao and her family. He'd put together as much information as he could gather from the central government files, but naturally the information was old, since she and her mother had fled fifteen years before. Yet, he was also anxious. He had to get to her before Dr. Wang's agents, who likely would be scouring the countryside in their search. They, too, would have the same information.

Yu was pissed off that Dr. Wang was still acting as his handler, yet in Yu's position of Bureau Chief of the Guoanbu, he was on the same power level inside the Chinese Communist government. Up until the last few days, he had accepted Dr. Wang's instruction, sometimes reluctantly, as aiding his professional growth. He'd wanted to follow the Chinese culture of respecting his elders, but he feared Dr. Wang's personal desires to capture, torture, and kill the U.S. FBI Agent Warren was causing him to step outside of his official position. He was certain, if he found the girl first, she'd be used as bait in some fashion. *I'm the man in charge of citizens inside China, and Shou Li Cao is still, after, all a Chinese citizen.*

Dr. Wang could have the FBI agent, Yu could care less about him, he'd even help torture the man. He still burned inside from the Dr. Paul Yu incident some eight years ago.

Finally, the hum of the plane's engines relaxed him in a strange way. He closed his eyes and leaned his head back in the jump seat of the military plane, full well knowing he'd get no rest until he found the girl. Plus, after all these

251

years, he finally had the name of Dr. Wang's best spy in the U.S.—Jin Wu-dai. This was very pleasing.

Soon, he dozed off.

Several hours later, Yu was awakened by a PLA sergeant advising him they were about to land.

He asked the sergeant, "Do you have any magazines or extra rounds for my handgun?" Yu held up his Czech CZ-52 handgun.

The sergeant looked at his gun. "Sir, wait a minute. Let me get you something better, if I may?"

Yu nodded and prepared to land.

The sergeant returned with two Czech CZ-75 handguns and four extra magazines and presented them to Yu. "If you don't mind me saying, sir, this is a superior gun to the one you carry. It doesn't have as much kick upon firing. I present these to you."

Yu smiled as he took both handguns and magazines, opened his small briefcase with the file information on Shou Li Cao, laid them on top, and closed it.

The sergeant hurried over to his jump seat as the plane started its descent into the airport. As soon as the plane was on the ground, Yu picked up his briefcase and headed down the stairs toward the waiting vehicle to begin his search.

CHAPTER TWENTY-SEVEN

January 15, 1980
Zhangzhou

Yu Qiangsheng pounded on the door of Shou Li Cao's aunt and uncle's residence. The second time he pounded on the door, a small Chinese woman cracked open the door. Yu pushed the door open, causing the woman to lose her balance. He stepped into their living area. Her presumed uncle was seated at a small kitchen table. "Where is Shou Li Cao?"

The aunt regained her balanced and bowed several times, each time stepping backwards.

Yu continued to move forward to the center of their small living area. This time, Yu pulled his credentials, held them up, and bellowed, "Answer my question or I'll have both of you hauled off to a work camp for the remainder of your god-forsaken lives."

The old man jumped up from the kitchen table and stepped around in front of his wife to protect her. "We haven't seen her for several days."

"Where was she headed?" Yu shouted.

"She wouldn't tell us. She said it was best we didn't know," the elderly man said.

Yu stepped toward them. "Tell me where she is. It will be better for her that I find her before the others looking for her."

The old man trembled, then dropped his hands palms out. "Honestly, I don't know."

Yu looked around the room. On the wall was a photo of four adults and a teenage girl. He stepped up and looked at the picture for a brief second, thinking how pretty the girl was. While he remembered every detail of her appearance, he pointed at the picture. "Do you have a more recent picture of Shou than this one?"

The two elderly people simultaneously shook their heads.

Yu walked back over and looked at the old picture of the girl. "If I find that you have given me bad information, I'll come back and kill both of you myself." He stared at them for a moment to further his intimidation before he left.

Once in his car, he drove to the central part of town looking for a business that had a phone. Finally, he observed a business he thought might be big enough that it would have a phone. He parked and jogged inside. He didn't say a word to the proprietor but only held up his CID badge. He picked up the phone and dialed his office. When one of the clerks answered, he barked, "See if there is a prisoner by the name of Lao-Tzu Cao at the prison outside of Jiangxi. If he isn't there, tell me where he has been transferred. I'll hold."

Five minutes later, the clerk replied. "Still there, Comrade Qiangsheng. He is scheduled to be transferred to Guangdong sometime next month. He is dying, and they have already made arrangements for organ harvesting."

Yu slammed down the phone and headed back to his car. Next stop—the airport for a flight to Jiangxi.

After the plane flight and commandeering another government vehicle, he was parked near the prison, anticipating that Shou Li Cao would attempt to see her father, if she hadn't already been there. It would be easy to find out. He walked into the prison. When a guard stepped forward, Yu demanded, "I want to speak to whoever is in charge of visitors from the outside."

The guard replied, "You must get permission from the warden."

Yu reached in his pocket and pushed his CID badge in the guard's face, then ordered, "Read it out loud."

The guard pulled his head back to focus. "Bureau Chief of the Guoanbu." After saying it, the guard cowered away from Yu. "Yes, sir. I'll take you to the supervisor immediately."

The guard escorted him to the small glassed-in office next to the large iron gate, then pointed at the man behind the tiny desk. "Yu Qiangsheng, Bureau Chief of the Guoanbu, is here to see you."

The man behind the desk bowed. "Yes, sir. What can I do for you?"

"I want to know who's been here to see the prisoner Lao-Tzu Cao, and when?"

The prison official pulled a book out of his desk. "Last night, two men representing the Overseas Chinese Affairs office came by and picked him up."

Yu closed his eyes. His face flushed. Dr. Wang had outmaneuvered him. He leaned over the desk. "Did an individual by the name of Shou Li Cao stop in to see him?"

"Yes, a very pretty girl. She only stopped a couple of hours ago. She seemed very frustrated and flustered she didn't get to see him."

"What was she wearing? What was she driving? And where she was going?" Yu folded his large arms across his chest.

"She was wearing an oversized blue silk outfit. I didn't see her car, nor did I ask where she was headed." The prison official shrugged.

Yu stormed out. *Where are you, Shou Li Cao?* Would she go to Beijing or give up and go back to Hong Kong? *I've made up several days—I'm within a couple of hours of her.* It was time to call on his network of spies throughout the country, which he'd built over the years since taking over Guoanbu. He'd created the largest in-country network since the bureau had been set up.

He went straight to the prison warden's office. He pounded on the door to his office. When he heard a voice from the other side tell him to enter, Yu stepped through the door. Without a word, he picked up the phone and called his office. His same trusted clerk picked up the phone. "Guoanbu."

"We have three agents working the area around Jiangxi. Get a notice out to be on the lookout for Shou Li Cao. If they see her, report back to you." He paused for a moment, then continued. "Put somebody to watch the uncle and aunt's residence back in Zhangzhou. She just might go back there. If anyone sees her, tell them to keep an eye on her, but don't try to apprehend her. Report back only to me. I will check back in within the next hour." Yu slammed down the phone and walked out without a word to the warden.

Shou Li Cao drove outside of the city of Jiangxi and pulled off the road. *Where would they have taken my father? Was he moved to another prison work camp? Or was he going to be released?* She was flustered and unsure of her next move. She was beginning to get scared that she'd made a huge mistake returning to China and should try to get back into Hong Kong. Yet, since she'd come this far and not been caught, she believed she was operating under the radar. Without knowing where they had taken her father, she decided her best move at the moment was to return to her aunt and uncle's home. First and foremost, to inform her uncle that his brother had been taken somewhere else. Plus, it would be a place of seclusion until she decided her next move.

She pulled back out in traffic. The gravity of her decision to come into China, find her father, and then attempt to find the scientists the American engineer had communicated with had become overwhelming. *What was I thinking when I crossed the border?*

One hour later, Yu Qiangsheng was back at the airport preparing to board the military plane. He stopped and called his office again to see what any of his field agents had to report. One of his agents had reported that Shou Li Cao was headed back toward Zhangzhou. That was all he needed to know. She was going back to her aunt and uncle's home. He could fly there and beat her to their home. He planned to be sitting there before she arrived. He jogged out and boarded the plane. "We're flying back to Zhangzhou."

Yu looked out the window as the plane approached Zhangzhou. A thick fog was rolling in off the coast. It was obvious a weather front was moving in, and the airport would be shrouded in the cloud. The copilot came back into the cabin. "We may have to land at another airport."

Yu pulled tight his belt on his jump seat and looked up. "Land here, *now*."

The plane started its bumpy descent into the airport. As soon as the plane landed, Yu headed toward his military-assigned vehicle. Unless the fog lifted, he'd have to drive out of this place.

When he was about to get into his vehicle, a PLA officer flagged him down as he jogged from the airport terminal. The officer handed him a note.

Yu opened it:

Yu Qiangsheng, as soon as you pick up Shou Li Cao, report in. Dr. Wang.

Yu wadded up the paper and threw it down. He had all that he could handle of taking orders from Dr. Wang. *I'm the head of one of the top bureaus in the country. I'm equal in power to Dr. Wang, and yet he continues to treat me as a subordinate.* He climbed into the military vehicle and drove off toward Shou Li Cao's relatives. *It's time for me to decide what I must do.*

Yu drove past Shou Li Cao's relative's home. There was no sign that she'd arrived. *So far his plan was working.* He parked on a side street so she wouldn't see his vehicle, then walked back up to her relative's home and pounded hard on the door. As before, Shou's aunt answered the door, and once

257

again, Yu pushed past her. He walked straight over to the family's kitchen table and pulled out a chair to sit. "I'm here to meet Shou when she arrives. Everybody take a seat in the room where I can see you. No surprises."

Her aunt and uncle clutched each other.

At one point, Shou's aunt asked, "May I go to the bathroom?"

While the woman was in the bathroom, Yu commanded the old man, "Get me a rope or some duct tape."

Yu nodded. He looked at the clock to make sure she wouldn't be in there too long, but he also noted that it had been almost a half hour since he'd arrived. If Shou was coming here, she should be showing at any moment. He wanted her aunt in the living area when she arrived.

About the time the aunt walked back in the living area, there was a light knock on the door. Yu put his finger to his lips and pointed the elderly lady to sit on the couch, next to her husband. There was another knock on the door, this time a little harder. Yu got up from the kitchen chair, took several long strides to the door, drew a deep breath, and flung the door open.

Shou Li Cao jumped as Yu leaped forward and grabbed her before she could react. Despite her struggle to free herself, Yu dragged her back into the small dwelling. He whispered in her ear. "You can calm down, or, after I tie you down, I'll hurt your family."

Shou stopped struggling against his strength.

"Go sit in the kitchen," he commanded. He pointed at her elderly aunt and uncle to join her there.

When everybody was in the kitchen seated around the table, Yu stepped closer. "I'm the Bureau Chief of the Guoanbu, which means I'm in charge of monitoring citizens and anyone trying to sneak out or sneak back into the country, particularly potentials spies from the United States, Ms. Cao. Now, you are going to do things my way, and I'll get you out of the mess you have created for yourself as safely as possible. Do you understand me?"

Each of them nodded while he focused on her alone.

"You will come with me."

He walked around the table and grabbed her up from the kitchen chair and pushed her toward the door.

Again, Shou attempted to resist, but under Yu's powerful hands, she was quickly brought under his control. He kept her moving toward the door, all the while trying not to hurt the woman. He was becoming more and more infatuated. "Please, just walk with me."

Once they were finally in the car, they started driving to the airport, but the fog had still not lifted. When they arrived, he parked at the military wing and ordered one of the nearby officers to stand guard on her while he made the phone call. When he stepped inside the PLA building on the property, he picked up the phone and dialed. "Dr. Wang, I have Shou Li Cao."

"How soon can you meet me in Shenzhen?"

"The fog is still bad here. I can't fly unless I wait." Yu looked out the window at the thick fog. "But I can be there this evening if I drive."

"I'll be there tomorrow afternoon. There is an old warehouse just south of the prison in Guangdong. Meet me there with the girl at two p.m. Do you understand me?"

Once again, Dr. Wang's condescending attitude toward him was pissing him off. He gritted his teeth. "What, exactly, is your plan?"

There was a long pause on the other end of the phone. Finally, Dr. Wang replied, "It is my intention to use the girl to set a trap for FBI Special Agent Thomas P. Warren."

Yu thought carefully how to respond. "Good, and let's get the other FBI agent, too. I think his name is Corley." He paused with clinched fists. "I don't want the girl hurt. She is innocent in all of this."

"The girl is of no concern to me one way or the other. I only am interested in killing Warren."

"I'll be there with the girl." Yu hung up the phone and walked back to the military vehicle, dismissed his appointed guard, slipped into the car, and then drove off.

"Where are we going?" Shou asked.

"We are going to Guangdong."

"Why?"

"You'll see. Get some rest. We have a long drive ahead of us." Yu spoke calmly as he pulled off the airport property onto the main road, then sped off along the foggy highway. He admiringly looked at the girl, his feelings were growing for her. Her spunkiness appealed to him. "If you are hungry, I'll get you some food."

She barely shook her head.

"Have it your way, then." Yu replied as he remained focused on the road.

CHAPTER TWENTY-EIGHT

Beijing

As soon as Dr. Wang hung up the phone, he closed his eyes and leaned back in his chair. It was time to formulate his plan to capture, torture, and kill FBI Special Agent Thomas Warren. Thirty years in the waiting, his time was at hand. With everyone meeting in the warehouse in Guangdong, they'd be close enough to Shenzhen and Hong Kong. He hoped he could draw Warren into Shenzhen, then on to Guangdong without him having to go into Hong Kong to lure him in. But he knew once he had Warren in China, it would all be over. Warren would be on his turf, his terms. With Yu Qiangsheng holding the girl, she'd be the bait.

He opened his eyes as he sat back up and pointed at Wu and Chung. "First thing in the morning, go get Lao-Tzu Cao and meet me at the airport. We're flying to Shenzhen. I want him shackled, and I want a black cloth bag over his head. Meet me at the airport at seven a.m. Understand?" Dr. Wang waved his hand at his two henchmen.

The two men nodded and left.

That evening

Shenzhen, Communist China

Just before dark, Yu Qiangsheng stopped his car just outside of Shenzhen. He looked over at Shou Li Cao. "If you promise to cooperate with me, we can check into a motel, get cleaned up, and be ready for tomorrow."

Shou looked over at him. "What is going to happen tomorrow?"

"You go back to Hong Kong. I assume you have a husband or a boyfriend or something to return to." He hoped she'd say nobody.

"A boyfriend or something," Shou replied with a slight nod.

Yu was disappointed with her answer, but it did give him some bargaining. If she had someone and she really believed she was going to be returned to Hong Kong tomorrow, she'd more than likely do what was asked of her to stay alive. "When I pull into the motel, you will go in with me to check in. Act as though we are together. Remember, if you make any mistakes, I will hurt or kill you, whether we are in public or private. You are in Communist China, and I have all the power. No one would dare question it. Do you understand?"

Shou looked down at the floor of the car and nodded.

With that, Yu pulled back into traffic, then drove toward the city. He wanted to find a place on the northside of the city toward Guangdong. If she ran, he wanted to make sure she was far from the border. He might be forced to reach out to local agents from the Guoanbu.

As he drove, he began to think about the next day and tried to speculate on what Dr. Wang was trying to pull off. If he could figure out his plan, it would give him a leg up to devise his own strategy to keep both him and the girl from being what Dr. Wang deemed collateral damage.

Yu was going to try to keep his promise and get the beautiful girl back into Hong Kong. And, he had more power than Dr. Wang realized. What did he want to gain out of this meeting?

Finally, he found a motel and parked. They walked into the motel.

After checking into the room, Yu said, "Shou, go get cleaned up, and then we'll get some food."

She nodded.

While she was in the bathroom, Yu looked up his list of agents, then made calls for two of them to come watch the front and back of the motel. Things were still unfolding in his mind. One thing was for certain—he needed the girl, and while she didn't know it, she desperately needed him if she were going to return to Hong Kong.

After about twenty minutes, she emerged from the bathroom fully dressed but with a towel around her head. She took the towel off and started drying her hair.

Yu sat on the bed opposite her. She truly was gorgeous. He needed to separate what he was required to do professionally versus his personal feelings. It was growing into an internal struggle, and he had to deal with it.

He looked at the floor. "I'd like to get cleaned up too. But I must trust that you won't try to run. I want to protect you." He paused. He wanted to tell her how he really felt about her, but he couldn't. "I will protect you tomorrow to make sure you get out of Communist China alive. But you must work with me. You must trust me—at least until you can get back across the border."

"I don't believe I have any other choice at this time. If I run, I'm sure I'd be caught again and…." Shou's lips twitched, and she used the towel to dot at the tears in the corners of her eyes.

Yu tried to decide if she was telling him the truth. But he had no choice. He got up and went to the bathroom. He hurried through the shower and was back in the room in five minutes.

Shou still lay on the bed with her back to the bathroom. *Boy, is she beautiful.*

Yu sat down in the chair, thinking about what he was going to do. While it was hard to figure out all of Dr. Wang's plan, he had to prepare for all possible scenarios. One thing was for sure—Dr. Wang wouldn't let anything stop him from capturing or killing the FBI agent.

He looked over at Shou, now asleep on the bed. He'd promised to get her safely back to Hong Kong—and he hoped that was indeed possible.

"I'll take you to get some food, but you must act like you are with me." Yu clinched his jaw as he spoke, loud enough to awaken her. He didn't want to sound threatening but he felt it had come out that way.

"Okay."

Yu reached at his hand to assist her up and off the bed.

She looked up at him as she accepted his gesture.

"Let's go." Yu nodded as he sensed at least a small level of trust.

CHAPTER TWENTY-NINE

Wednesday January 17, 1980
Hong Kong

It was still dark and cool outside when Tom and Marty walked into the MI6 office. Neither of them had been able to sleep. Between worrying and plotting how to find Shou, sleep came at short intervals. Agent Anthony Middleton was already sitting with his hands folded on top of the desk. Tom forced a humorless smile. "Anthony, did you sleep here last night?"

"No, Special Agent Warren, I just got into my office about an hour ago. I went home last night and slept in bed. Why do you ask?"

Tom laughed. "Why do you always look like you've slept in your suit?" He reached for Middleton's desk phone.

Before he could grab it, it rang. Tom pulled back as Anthony picked it up.

"Good morning, MI6 Agent Anthony Middleton here."

Tom looked at Middleton and watched his face flush and his upper lip curl.

"Okay." Middleton pushed the speaker button on his Vodaphone. "You are on speaker, Dr. Wang."

Tom gritted his teeth as he glanced first at Marty and then at Middleton.

"FBI Special Agent Thomas P. Warren, I assume you are able to hear my voice."

After breathing hard several times with his eyes closed attempting to control himself, Tom said, "I'm here."

"Good, good. Be in this office later this afternoon. I'll give you instructions on how you can get Shou Li Cao back."

Marty stepped toward the phone and tried to grab it. Tom quickly covered the receiver of the phone. Marty grabbed his arm, but Tom jerked away.

"I want to speak to her," Tom said, as he re-composed himself.

"Understand, I'm in complete control of this situation. You will talk to her when I allow you to talk to her." The phone went dead.

Marty stepped up into Tom's face. "Why wouldn't you let me talk to him? Shou is innocent."

Tom stared at Marty for a brief second. "I don't want him to know you're here. Dr. Wang knows nothing of your relationship with Shou. I want to use that to our advantage."

Marty ran his hand over his short, cropped hair and huffed away.

Tom turned his attention to Anthony. "Try to figure out a way to get us into Red China without going through the legal way. Plus, we will need a car and guns once on the other side."

Anthony ran his hands over his suit coat trying to make it more presentable. "Warren, let's see what Dr. Wang does first. But I have another method besides the Royal Marines to get you into Red China."

Tom dropped his shoulders. He just wanted Anthony to tell him how so he could formulate a plan.

Same Time
Shenzhen

Yu pushed back the curtain a crack, causing a stream of light to enter the motel room. This appeared to startle Shou awake, as she sat up in bed.

"Shou, we will check out of here in a couple of hours and head to Guangdong. I want to look over the area before going to our meeting." He watched for her reaction. The fearful look on her face made him question how cooperative she'd be today. To accomplish his task yet overcome his own feelings for her, he had to keep selling her on returning to Hong Kong.

Shou lay back down and rolled over in bed. "Who are we meeting today to get me home?"

Yu wasn't about to tell her anymore. He was afraid if he mentioned the name *Dr. Wang*, she might try to escape. "I'm not sure who will be there. But keep in mind, I'm in control of your situation completely. I'm trying to get you home."

He received no response. Yu pushed, "Now, let's go. Get a move on."

Same Time
Beijing

Dr. Wang looked out the tiny port window, watching Wu and Chung slowly walk another portion of his trap mechanism, Lao-Tzu Cao, toward the small private airplane. With his henchmen holding on to each arm, the old man shuffled his shackled feet, his head bobbing and weaving under the black hood. When they got him to the stairs, Dr. Wang looked back down at his watch. The timing of his plan was still perfect.

Within a few seconds, Shou Li Cao's father was seated on the opposite side of the plane. Dr. Wang gave the signal to the pilot to start the twin engine plane for their almost four-hour flight to an abandoned airfield outside of Guangdong.

He looked at his two henchmen. "The old man was unharmed?"

"Yes, Dr. Wang," Wu said. "We even had the prison get him cleaned up this morning."

As soon as the plane had leveled off, Dr. Wang went over and took the black hood off Lao-Tzu Cao. "Enjoy the plane ride."

The old man blinked repeatedly to adjust his eyes. He looked up at Dr. Wang for a brief second, then back down at the floor below his feet.

Dr. Wang sat back down, pressed his red tie in place, then refastened his seat belt.

Noon Wednesday January 16, 1980
Hong Kong

Tom and Marty still sat at the same vacant desk with a hand of spades dealt out on the desk, but no one seemed interested in playing.

Marty got up and paced around to stretch his legs.

Tom turned his attention to Middleton on the other side of the room working the telephones. He'd been on the phone since Dr. Wang's morning call to work out a way to get Tom and Marty into Communist China without going through the Lo Wu Border Crossing. Anthony hadn't been back over to tell Tom whether or not he was accomplishing anything. Tom believed that, in itself, was telling.

1 PM Wednesday January 16, 1980
Guangdong, Red China

Yu Qiangsheng drove up the dirt road that led to Guangdong Prison. After going about five miles up the road, he saw the abandoned warehouse he assumed was his meeting place with Dr. Wang. He parked his car next to the large loading dock set up to handle four or five large trucks. He got out of his car and motioned for Shou Li Cao to do the same. He walked into the cold, dank building. Immediately off from the side of the loading dock were two small offices, one upstairs and the other ground level. He continued on into the building and walked around.

"What are you doing?" Shou asked.

"Visualizing," Yu replied while he continued to walk and study the layout.

Shou frowned. "What?"

"The future." Yu slowly walked around until he had done a complete three-sixty view of the inside. "We are meeting here. I want to see how this is going to play out."

Shou froze in place, looked up and down, and then did a three-sixty. "Why are we meeting here? I have a very bad premonition."

He calmly stepped back over to her, put his hands on each shoulder, and looked her in the eye. "I'm figuring out how I'm going to protect you. I really care about you and will do all in my power to get you home." He smiled at her, then turned away, still traversing the large warehouse floor. He strolled over to the ground level office at the bottom of a flight of stairs at the back of the building. He peeked in, then went up the stairs to a large office area. When he entered, there was a dim bulb hanging in the middle of the room. Several windows were broken out. Some leaves were scattered about the floor. Yu closed his eyes and thought. He continued to envision what was about to happen here.

Shou grabbed his arm as she stepped over to him.

Yu opened his eyes, then looked at her. "Let's go. I know what I need to do. I don't want to be the first to arrive."

CHAPTER THIRTY

1 PM Wednesday January 17, 1980
Guangdong, Red China

After landing at the abandoned airport, Dr. Wang pointed at Wu. "Put the hood back over our friend, here. Drive to the prison."

The old man shifted around but didn't say a word. As soon as they pulled into the prison yard, Dr. Wang barked, "Wait on me."

He got out of the car and went inside the facility. At the guard gate, he flashed his CCP identification and commanded, "I need to use a phone."

The guard looked at his papers and pointed to a phone at the opposite side of the office. Dr. Wang slipped over, snatched it up, and then dialed Middleton's desk phone. The phone was answered quickly on the other end. He didn't wait for a voice. "MI6 Agent Middleton, put me on speaker phone, immediately."

"You're on speaker now."

"I'll make arrangements at the Lo Wu Border Crossing to provide FBI Special Agent Thomas P. Warren full diplomatic immunity to enter Red China." He paused and picked a thread from his suit coat. "You will cross the border alone into China, if you are interested in getting Shou Li Cao back. Let me tell you, I'm calling you from the Chinese prison outside Guangdong. This prison specializes in organ harvesting. The organs of a healthy young woman like Shou Li Cao would save many young men here in China. We could even arrange to do those surgeries while she is awake. Now, it's your choice. Those are your only options. Come alone or damn the girl to the prison doctor."

After a pause, Special Agent Thomas Warren's voice said, "I accept your terms. When do we meet?"

"I'll call now to make arrangements at the border. There is an abandoned warehouse before you get to the prison outside Guangdong. Be there at five o'clock sharp. Let me make one thing perfectly clear—any provocation or violation will undue your immunity deal. Do you understand?"

"I understand."

Dr. Wang hung up the phone. After a quick call to the Lo Wu Border Crossing, he returned to the backseat of his car. "Drive down the road about a mile. On the left is an abandoned warehouse. Pull in there and leave the car parked in front." His head grew light and a shooting pain raced up his left arm. He closed his eyes and leaned against the side of the interior.

Wu pulled the car out of the prison, then turned south on the dirt road leading toward Guangdong. After five minutes of driving, Dr. Wang leaned over the front seat and pointed. He gasped for air for a moment, then spoke in a very low voice, "There it is."

Same time
Hong Kong

Tom placed the phone back on the switch hook. "I'm going. Anthony, how can we sneak Marty into China without Dr. Wang knowing?"

Marty stood close to Tom. "I'm going with you."

Tom pushed him away. "How do you propose that? You don't think they'll check my car inside and out?"

"Now that we know Dr. Wang's plans, I have a way to get Marty into Red China." Anthony sat on the edge of his desk. He got up, went to the file cabinet, and pulled out a file. He offered a tight smile. "MI6 has ways of moving our undercover agents in and out of Communist China."

Tom and Marty gathered around Middleton as he flung the file open on the desk. Anthony pulled out a passport and Chinese Communist papers. "Here you Yanks go. Tom better get moving if you're to be there by five p.m."

"We have someone who works undercover for us. He drives in and out of Red China in our Chinese six-wheeler, panel truck. We can have it ready within the half hour. He can sneak Marty in." Anthony nodded as he turned toward Marty. "We'll handle this. If you stop at the intersection of Guangshan Highway and JingZhu Expressway, we'll have Marty in that truck to meet you there. Our spy will get out there, and Marty can take over and follow you up the road. You'll be close to your prison point where no one will pay attention to an English guy taking over the drive."

Marty pounded his fist on the table. "Let's do this."

Tom nodded. "Okay. It's risky, but probably the best we can do on short notice. We must make the impending coming of evening—the darkness—our advantage. Marty, we'll load what we need from the truck to my car. Anthony, have your people waiting on this side of the border. We're liable to be coming back at a high rate of speed. Literally, running across the border. Anthony, you got a car for me?"

Anthony nodded. "Yes, but there is no chance to run the border—too much security. No matter what, you'll be stopped, right?"

Both men nodded at Tom. "We aren't coming back without Shou," Marty added.

Tom started to say something, then just left. None of them may be coming back.

2PM Wednesday January 17, 1980
Lo Wu Border Crossing

Special Agent Thomas P. Warren held out his FBI Badge and his U.S. Passport, then said in Cantonese, "I was told there would be a diplomatic Visa here for me."

Tom looked at his watch. The PLA soldier carefully studied the passport, then waved at a fellow officer. After they frisked Tom, both officers thoroughly searched his car. Tom wiped his mouth with his hand as he checked his watch. He was on a very tight schedule to get through Shenzhen, then north toward Guangdong, and rendezvous with Marty before driving to the abandoned warehouse. If he didn't show at the designated time, he had no doubt Dr. Wang would torture or kill Shou.

Finally, both PLA soldiers walked directly up to him. One reached out a piece of paper for Tom to take then waved him on.

As he sped away into the heavy traffic of Shenzhen, he looked in his rearview mirror and saw the large panel truck that Middleton had provided pull up to the border crossing. He was tempted to stop and make sure they made it through, but he couldn't call attention to the truck.

Tom pulled into the rendezvous intersection and waited for Marty in his panel truck. As soon as he stopped, he checked his watch. His schedule was getting really tight. When the six-wheel panel truck pulled in behind him, the driver dropped down from behind the steering wheel and walked up to Tom, holding out a passport. "Special Agent Warren, here is an extra passport I always carry. Take it. It's a fake, but you never know if you might need it, should you capture Dr. Wang."

"Good idea. I hadn't thought of that." Tom accepted it. "You got a ride back?"

"Don't worry about me. MI6 has me covered. We do this occasionally."

Tom jogged to the back of the truck where Marty was riding, flipped the latch, and opened it. Before Marty could even get out, he barked, "I want you to show up about fifteen minutes behind me. Assume Dr. Wang will have me watched as I approach, if he hasn't had me watched already."

"No, you can't be there that long by yourself."

Tom laughed. "Every time I have ever been in his presence—" He opened his hands out to his side. "He always has a story to tell me. Plus, if he did grab me right off, he'll want to torture me. So, fifteen minutes or even a little longer. Me and Shou will be good. And watch your back. Now, what did you bring?"

Marty pulled out two Beretta 9mm handguns. "This was all I dared sneak. Plus, I'll have my nine-millimeter and a high-powered rifle."

Tom nodded. "Good enough." He grabbed the guns. "Wish me luck." Then he jumped out and took off.

CHAPTER THIRTY-ONE

4 p.m. Wednesday January 17, 1980
Guangdong, Red China

The afternoon had turned gray and a cold wind was blowing when Yu Qiangsheng and Shou Li Cao pulled up in front of the abandoned warehouse and parked at the loading dock next to the car already there. Yu looked over at Shou. "I assume that is Dr. Wang and his henchmen's car."

Shou closed her eyes tight. *Dr. Wang? I'm going to die.* Tears sprouted from her eyes, and she grabbed the door handle. "He'll rape, torture, and kill me."

She opened the car door and bolted.

He jumped from the car and caught her before she got more than twenty feet away from the car. "I told you, I'm going to make sure you get home."

"No. No, I'm not going in."

He pulled her back into the car, kicking and fighting him all the way as he pulled her across the bench seat. "You must trust me. Now more than ever."

She was crying uncontrollably. Yu reached over and gently wiped tears from her eyes. "I promise you, I'm getting you home. I truly care about you. I'll kill anyone who tries to hurt you in any way. You have my word on that."

When Shou heard his words, she looked over at him and laid her head on his shoulder. Yu put his arm around her. "You must be strong and focused. Follow my lead, and you'll get home unharmed. Now, let's go inside."

The two exited the car and walked toward the abandoned building. It started to drizzle rain. They walked inside. At first, Yu didn't see anyone. Then from the office underneath the metal staircase, Dr. Wang, dressed in his usual expensive gray suit and red tie, and his two henchmen emerged. He waved the two of them to approach.

Yu grabbed Shou by the arm and pulled her, faster than she wished to go, toward the man she feared. As soon as they stepped within fifteen feet of Dr. Wang, he pointed at Wu and Chung. "Take the girl back into that office and watch her. Don't hurt her. Understand?"

Both men nodded as they grabbed Shou and marched her into the downstairs office, almost dragging her. Before pushing her into the office, she turned and looked back at Yu, who gave her a nod of assurance.

As soon as the door was closed, Dr. Wang stepped up to Yu. "Warren will be here in about an hour. He believes I granted him diplomatic immunity to cross the border. I ordered two of your agents to follow him from the border crossing here." He gasped for air and held his breath for a moment, then swallowed hard.

Yu stuck out his chin. *He had no business ordering my men to do anything.*

Dr. Wang stepped closer to Yu. "I see from the expression on your face that me commanding your agents has surprised—maybe even angered—you. You must think I am overstepping what *you might deem* my authority. However, I will warn you to be very careful. You better get your anger under control. You see, over the last few months, Deng Xiao-Ping has been discussing my role in the Communist Party. They have seen that I've improved diplomatic relations with Hong Kong—" He raised both hands out in front of him, as he continued. "Plus, I've made diplomatic missions into Japan. There is talk within the Politburo that soon I may become the Vice President of the People's Republic of China."

Yu stood toe to toe with Dr. Wang, but chose to say nothing. His plan was in place. This man was not going to mess it up or distract him.

Dr. Wang folded his arms across his chest. "When Warren gets here to pick up the girl, I don't want her to be here."

Yu continued to focus on the man giving him orders. "Why?"

"You will go up the road toward the prison so he won't see you. Hide your car away from the road. Then I want you to come up behind him after he has entered the building to get the girl." Dr. Wang pointed out the door. "I want him to react to you coming up behind him. That way, when he turns to see who entered, I can attack him. I'll have set him up."

Yu cracked his knuckles. *Not walking out of here without her.* "I'm taking the girl with me. That will increase your safety. The FBI agent will not make any dumb moves without having the girl."

Dr. Wang started to speak, squinted, then only nodded. His face turned red as he coughed repeatedly. When his coughing fit was over, he straightened his coat.

Yu took long strides up to the lower office door to get Shou.

When Yu looked back, Dr. Wang was still bent over slightly with his eyes closed.

Yu opened the door. "Shou, come with me."

She stepped through the door with Wu and Chung behind her, each holding an arm.

Yu waved for her to come over to him.

"Let her go," Dr. Wang ordered his two henchmen.

As they made their way across the expanse of the warehouse floor, Dr. Wang looked down at his watch. "*Stop.* We have time for a little surprise for the young lady before our guest from Hong Kong arrives."

Yu bit his lower lip as he looked at the girl. *What was about to happen?* She latched onto his arm. When he'd walked into the building before, he

277

sensed a surprise would come, but he thought it would be when the FBI agent was here.

Dr. Wang pointed up the stairs, and Wu and Chung bounded up the steps. He walked to the edge of the staircase and waved for Yu and Shou to follow him.

They paused at the foot of the stairs, then followed. His henchmen entered the upstairs office first. At the top of the stairs, Dr. Wang straightened his gray suit coat and held the door open for Yu and Shou to enter. When they entered the room, Wu and Chung stood on either side of a man seated on a chair in the middle of the room with a black bag over his head and his feet and hands shackled.

Shou looked up at Yu, who jutted his jaw. He feared he knew who was under the black bag. Dr. Wang strolled over to the man on the chair and motioned for the girl to step closer. As she did, he removed the black bag.

Shou gasped. "Pa!"

Yu raised his eyebrows as he took a step forward. Shou's father meant an added element to returning Shou to the Free World.

"Yes, Shou, I've been told the reason you came back to China was to give your 'Pa' a message." Dr. Wang smiled, flashing his teeth. "So, I thought I would bring your 'Pa' to you."

Shou ran over, crying uncontrollably, and hugged her father. He fidgeted around, trying to get his hands free.

Yu's eyes darted around the room, trying to process this development. A sense of uneasiness—doom, even, overwhelmed him. *Nothing good was coming.*

Dr. Wang folded his arms across his chest. "Now, you may deliver your message."

Shou wiped the tears from her eyes and cheeks. "Pa, Ma was killed several years ago by Chinese agents." She turned her gaze toward Dr. Wang.

Lao-Tzu Cao lowered his head against the girl's shoulder.

Shou refocused on her father, tightening her grip, hugging her father.

Dr. Wang unfolded his arms. "Yes, Ms. Shou Li Cao, your mother was killed by my agents once we found out you were a plant for FBI Special Agent Thomas Payne Warren at our restaurant in San Francisco. However, it was you they were supposed to kill."

Yu took two rapid steps toward the young woman. "Dr. Wang, *you aren't* going to kill her. She is your bait for the trap for Warren." Yu now stood between Shou and Dr. Wang, all the while keeping his eyes on Wu and Chung.

Dr. Wang waved his hand in the air. "No, no. Yu, you are correct. While my agents missed their intended target, it all worked out for me and this day, which I've dreamed of for decades. I give you my word, Shou shall not be hurt in any way. My intention is to kill Special Agent Warren."

Yu bent down and grabbed Shou by the shoulder. "We must get out of here so Dr. Wang's plan can play out." Shou resisted his actions. Yu tugged at her, finally getting her to her feet.

Yu focused on Dr. Wang and continued to keep himself between Shou and Dr. Wang and his henchmen. As Yu got Shou to the door, Dr. Wang commanded, "*Stop.*"

Yu held Shou behind him.

"However, there are consequences for spying on the Chinese restaurant, Ms. Cao." Dr. Wang nodded at Wu, who stepped around, pulled his handgun, and shot Lao-Tzu Cao between the eyes.

"*No!*" Shou screamed and started to her father.

Yu grabbed her and jerked her out the door. He was infuriated Dr. Wang had done this in her presence. It was inexcusable, but he had no power at the moment to do anything about it.

Yu picked her up and carried her down the stairs leading to the ground floor. She punched him all the way. "You let that happen! You knew that was going to happen!"

He continued to carry her to the car and sat her down on the hood. "I had nothing to do with what you just saw. I find it totally disgusting and uncalled for. It has caused me to change my plans completely. But first and foremost, I have to get you back to Hong Kong safely. Then I will do what I must do."

Shou cried uncontrollably and wouldn't look at Yu.

Yu grabbed both of her shoulders. "That was pure evil. You must get yourself composed. I will not let anything happen to you. Now, get in the car. We have to get out of here before Warren arrives for my plan to work."

CHAPTER THIRTY-TWO

5 PM Wednesday January 17, 1980
Guangdong, Red China

As Tom slowly drove up the dirt road in the direction of the warehouse, the sky was already dark from the clouds and rain. The large, abandoned structure stood on the left hand side of the road with a car parked in front. As he pulled in, he noticed what looked like fresh tracks leading out of the parking area up the road. He breathed hard through his open mouth, slipped one gun under the front seat and put the other gun under his belt as he stepped out of the car. He believed he'd be frisked and the gun found, but Dr. Wang would expect him to be armed. The game of life was about to begin.

He surveyed the building, which was now nothing more than a giant gray shadow on the gray and brown ground ahead, slowly approached the entrance. He gradually opened the door, but didn't step through just yet.

When nothing happened from his action, he slipped to the opposite side of the doorway to get a quick look at the inside of the large warehouse. Still no response to his movements. Tom stepped through the open door, gun drawn and looking around. All he could see was a dim light in an office on the ground level and another above it. It was dark and musty in the building. Tom got against the wall and moved methodically in that direction. He held the gun in front and above his head. Within a few seconds, he was near enough to the downstairs' office door he could see in. There stood one of Dr. Wang's two goons. *So where is Dr. Wang? Where is his other goon? Where is Shou?*

No reason to approach that door. *What's my next move?* If he went up the stairway to the upper floor, he'd be trapped in one area. *My best move is to approach Dr. Wang's goon on the ground floor.* He slipped up to the door. Still no response to his action. He kicked it open, hard, and pointed his gun at the Chinese man. In Mandarin, he shouted. "Where is Shou Li Cao?"

The Chinese man stood there without flinching or saying a word.

Tom locked the door behind him, then walked up to him and pressed his gun against his forehead. He reached around and disarmed the man. "Where is Shou?"

The Chinese man calmly stated, "Dr. Wang will meet you out there."

This must be part of their plan. Otherwise, why hadn't the goon drawn on him? Tom got behind the man and pushed him toward the locked door. He unloaded the goon's gun and tossed it away from the door. "Unlock the door and step out." He pushed the gun into the back of his head, then he stepped through. There stood Dr. Wang in the middle of the warehouse.

He believed that Dr. Wang's other henchman would be close. He continued to push his gun at the back of his captive's head as he moved against the wall. The upstairs' door opened and closed.

It was the other henchman. Tom commanded in Mandarin, "Lay your gun down at the top of the stairs and come down, or I'll kill this man."

Dr. Wang nodded at his henchman to do it.

The man slowly laid down his gun, then descended the steps. Tom pushed the henchman he was holding with the gun at the back to his head. "Turn around back into that spot over there." Tom shoved him in the direction of the middle of the dirty, concrete floor about ten feet to the left of Dr. Wang, then focused his gun directly at the man in the gray suit.

As the other henchman made it to the ground floor, Tom ordered, "You go stand over there." He pointed with his free hand to a spot about ten feet on the right of Dr. Wang. The man slowly turned and backed into that spot.

"FBI Special Agent Thomas Payne Warren, you may put your gun away now. That is, of course, if you want the girl." Dr. Wang clapped.

Tom didn't flinch, he kept his gun focused on Dr. Wang, as he stepped closer.

Dr. Wang continued to clap until Tom was a mere ten feet away. "I'll repeat myself only one more time. Put your gun away if you want the girl."

Tom lowered the gun but didn't put it away. "Where is Shou?"

Dr. Wang straightened his red tie and cleared his throat. "You can see the girl is not here. But once we are done, I can have her here in a matter of seconds."

Tom assumed she was up the stairway behind him in the upstairs office.

Dr. Wang commanded the henchman to his left. "Wu, go get Warren's gun."

Tom responded by pointing his gun back at the henchman. "You may have my gun, but only after the girl is here. Frankly, I can kill all three of you and look for her myself. That's my deal."

The man in the gray suit motioned with both hands for his men to go toward Warren. "Rush Warren, *now*."

Tom glanced at each of the henchmen while keeping his gun pointed on Dr. Wang. "It wouldn't be a wise move if you like breathing." *Unless they have other guns or knives, they can't get me.*

Dr. Wang snarled. "I know your first shot would be at me, should you take it. But Shou Li Cao wouldn't make it home. Isn't that your mission?"

Tom continued to keep his gun pointed at Dr. Wang.

"The girl should be here at any minute."

Tom stepped closer to his adversary.

Yu Qiangsheng's mission of getting Shou home safely had been complicated by her father's execution. The girl was now in shock. She'd been through so much.

He looked at his watch. It was time. Yu pulled into the parking space at the abandoned warehouse. Another car was parked there. *The FBI Agent must have arrived. Perfect.* He looked at Shou. "When we enter the warehouse, you stay behind me, no matter what. Got it?" He slipped a handgun under his Zhongshan suit.

Shou was despondent. She mechanically stepped out of the car and walked toward the building. Yu jumped out and got in front of her. He heard a vehicle approaching, but he had to stay in front of Shou to protect her. He couldn't trust Dr. Wang not to shoot her to spite the FBI agent. The two of them walked into the warehouse.

Dr. Wang calmly pointed toward the entrance. "As I said, the girl would be here. There she is. Now, you must turn over your gun to me."

Warren quickly glanced at the entrance, then back at Dr. Wang. He took several more steps in the direction of his adversary.

"Yu, fix your target on the agent's head. Special Agent Thomas Payne Warren, I must tell you, you have no diplomatic immunity. I only gave the orders for the border guards to allow you to pass. In one command, the Chinese agent there will shoot you." Dr. Wang gasped for air, winched, then rubbed his chest. "You have no way to cross the border back into Hong Kong without my orders."

That son-of-a-bitch is less than ten feet away from me. His gun is still pointed directly at my head. I must change the odds, or I could die.

Dr. Wang glanced at Yu, who had pulled his gun but not pointed it at Warren. He screamed, in anger, spitting as he spoke. *"Yu, point your damn gun at Warren's head!"*

FBI Special Agent Marty Corley stepped through the entrance and focused his rifle at Dr. Wang. "Just thought I would stop by to even the odds. *Now, I'm walking out of here with Shou,"* Corley said. "It's your call. Your way or my way."

Tom continued to aim his gun toward Dr. Wang.

Marty shouted, *"Shou, come here. Now.* I have you covered."

Shou slowly turned and looked at Marty. She walked deliberately toward him. She glanced up at him with no facial expression. He pushed her behind him. "We are going to back out of here."

Simultaneously, the Chinese agent, who had been holding Shou, spun around, gun still at his side, and started walking toward Corley.

Dr. Wang shouted, *"Kill Corley!"*

Marty looked at the large Chinese man. "Tom, come on. Let's go. I have you covered. We have Shou." He took a step backward as he changed the focus of his rifle at the large Chinese man. "Shou, guide me out."

The large Chinese agent put his hands up in the air, including the one holding the gun, but continued walking toward Corley.

Marty continued to point his rifle toward the large Chinese man. "I can shoot you pretty easily from this distance. It's your choice."

"Don't shoot him," Shou whispered as she pointed at Yu.

The large Chinese agent stopped.

Tom kept his gun pointed at Dr. Wang's head. "Walk, Corley. Get Shou out of here."

"Tom, I'm not leaving without you!" Marty bellowed.

"I'm holding a gun at Dr. Wang's head. *Get out, damn it!*"

"I'm still in control of this. You're only creating more trouble for yourself." Dr. Wang smiled, then gritted his teeth. "Don't kill Warren yet. He is mine. Agent Warren, it is fitting we should die here together."

Tom maintained his gun at Dr. Wang's head and stepped closer still. He laughed, then smirked. "I don't quite see it your way, Dr. Wang."

Dr. Wang shouted at Yu. "Shoot Warren but don't kill him."

Tom shouted at Marty, "I'm in complete control in here. Get out of here now with Shou. That's an order."

Marty refocused his rifle at the large Chinese man standing directly in front of him. "Shou, keep backing me out of here."

Shou whispered into Marty's ear, "Don't shoot him."

"Get out of here. Get Shou out of here," Tom commanded. "That's what we came for."

Marty continued to push backwards out the door with Shou leading him. Once they were outside, Marty shouted, "Run to the panel truck and get it started."

Shou didn't run at first. She only continued walking mechanically before finally running a few steps.

Marty continued to back up all the way to the waiting vehicle, his rifle pointed toward the door. *Anybody but Tom stepping through that door is going to die.*

Tom was in control of Dr. Wang. "You are under arrest." He took two steps toward him and pushed his handgun into his forehead. "Now, turn around so I can put handcuffs on you."

Dr. Wang stood there defiantly. "How are you going to get back across the border? I didn't grant you immunity. I just order the border guards to allow you to pass."

Tom nodded. "Fine. They will let me cross. You'll be my ticket back into Hong Kong—or, I will shoot you in their presence at the border crossing. Either way, you are under arrest."

Dr. Wang was sweating heavily. He jutted his jaw. "Wu, Chung, on my command, charge Warren."

"Turn around so I can cuff you, or I'm going to knock you out and do it myself."

Dr. Wang shouted, "Yu, kill Warren, *now*."

Yu looked over his shoulder at Dr. Wang, then ran out of the building.

Tom glanced in the direction of the large Chinese man who was running out the door following Marty and Shou. He had to move fast. He stepped back and reached for his handcuffs. Dr. Wang swung his left hand to strike Tom's gun, pushing it out of the way, then lunged forward, throwing a right hand.

Tom recoiled his hand with the gun and struck Dr. Wang in the face, knocking him to the ground. He jumped back to avoid a leg sweep.

Dr. Wang quickly brushed his hand on the dirt laden floor and scooped up enough dust to throw in the direction of Tom's eyes. "*Get him*. Get Warren."

Both Wu and Chung rushed Tom.

Tom shook his head and blinked hard to clear his eyes, he thought he aimed at Chung's heart, but only hit him in the shoulder. He fired again and hit him in the stomach, doubling him over. Then he turned and shot at Wu, who was almost on top of him. He missed on his first shot. Wu struck him, knocking Tom off balance, but he managed to squeeze off another shot, hitting the henchman in the thigh. Dr. Wang struggled to get up. He was gasping for air.

Wu grabbed his leg as he bent down. Tom struck him in the face with his handgun, knocking him to the ground.

By now, Dr. Wang had rolled up on his knees and was going behind his back, presumably for a gun. He pulled a handgun.

Tom spun and kicked the handgun out of Dr. Wang's hand.

Chung was struggling to stand up straight, his left arm hanging by his side. Wu had regained his feet.

Tom turned in each direction, firing his handgun, striking both of them in the chest. "I'll kill you both where you stand if you take one more step." Both men were down.

Then he pointed the gun at Dr. Wang on his knees, still on the ground. There was a gash on the side of his head from the pistol whipping. "I'm going to cuff you now."

Dr. Wang held his hands in front as he slowly got up.

Tom glanced at the two henchmen as he reached behind his back for his handcuffs. Just then Dr. Wang charged at Tom again. Tom dropped the cuffs as he gripped both hands on his gun, then slammed Dr. Wang hard in the back with his clasped hands, driving him to the ground.

Dr. Wang rolled over. He started to reach up toward Tom, then suddenly grabbed his chest and started convulsing as he labored to get up again. But he fell back to the ground, turned red, then blue, and passed out.

Tom looked at his two henchmen on the ground, then reached to check his adversary's pulse. Nothing. He must've had a heart attack.

Just as he was about to finish off Dr. Wang's goons, gunshots sounded outside. Tom sprinted toward the door. He only had two shots left, and he had to make sure he could get to his other gun and to Marty and Shou.

When he stepped out the door, it was dark and raining. The panel truck flew down the road with the big Chinese man in pursuit in his car. Tom jumped in his car, reached under the seat, pulled out the other handgun, and laid it on the seat. He started the car, spun it around, and took off down the road in pursuit. Once down the road about a mile, the panel truck was off the road in the ditch with another car blocking the road.

The big Chinese man ran into the dark.

Tom assumed he was after Marty and Shou. He pulled over, parked, and picked up both guns and a flashlight from the glovebox. Quickly, he checked the panel truck to make sure Marty and Shou weren't inside, then took off running after the big Chinese man. The foliage grew thicker. He heard a scream and multiple gunshots fired from different guns.

Tom moved more methodically into the heavy undergrowth. Sounds of heavy breathing were close by. He stopped moving and slipped behind a small bush. Then he didn't hear a sound. As he got up to move out again, a click sounded behind him. He turned around to find the big Chinese man with his gun pointed at his head.

The big man said, "Put your gun away, now. I don't want to have to shoot you, too."

Tom swung his gun and pointed it at the Chinese man. "Where is my partner? Where is Shou Li Cao?"

The big Chinese man said, "She is tending to your agent. Now put your gun down. We need to talk, fast."

Tom continued to point his gun at the Chinese man. "How can I trust that you won't shoot me?"

"Because I could have killed you already." The Chinese man stuck his gun back under his Zhongshan suit. "We need to talk."

Tom put his gun in his belt, then walked over to the man. "Take me to my agent."

The man waved him to follow. Tom got in step.

"My name is Yu Qiangsheng. I'm in charge of the Guoanbu. I will help you escape, but we have to move fast. Your partner can't walk very well, as I shot him in the leg, but he'll be all right. Had they gone much farther, they would have been to the prison fence line."

Yu stopped. "But I have one condition for helping you escape, and I'll only trust you to assist me. No one else can know what I'm about to ask, including your partner and Shou. Understand?"

Tom winched. "Go ahead."

Yu stepped in front of Tom. "I want to get my mother out of China—if I can get her to go. Will you help me?"

Tom rubbed his chin repeatedly. "Yes, yes, of course. Now, where is my partner?"

Yu started moving again. "Good, we have a deal. Where is Dr. Wang?"

"I think he had a heart attack. He grabbed his chest and passed out."

Yu shrugged. "We got to get out of here before the prison guards working the perimeter come out to investigate my gunshots."

When he saw his partner, Tom started running. "Marty, are you all right?"

Marty was leaning against the tree and Shou was under one of his arms. "I'm all right, but I can't move very well. What are you doing with that murderer? Did you arrest him?"

Yu waved his hand. "*Come on, come on.* We have to move fast if we're going to get back across the border."

Marty slowly pushed himself up the tree then pointed. "That son-of-a-bitch was part of the plot to have Shou's father executed in front of her, Tom."

Tom tilted his head as he glanced at Marty then Yu.

"That's not true, Marty. That's not what I said," Shou spoke just above a whisper.

Tom went to Marty and supported him so he could walk back to the panel truck.

"Did Dr. Wang murder your father?" Tom asked Shou, then he looked at Marty. "Come on, we got to move. Yu, yes, please get us back to Hong Kong."

"One of his hench...." Shou stopped talking as she sobbed.

Yu grabbed Marty under the other arm.

Marty shoved him away. "I don't want your help."

"Let him get you," Tom commanded.

Marty snarled, "He's the one that shot me."

"Sounds like he kept you out of a Chinese prison. Is the panel truck still drivable?"

Marty grunted. "Yes, I got run off the road by an on-coming car. Two men got out of the car and pulled guns on us." He winced in pain, pausing for a minute. "They pursued us, and I killed them."

When they got to the road, Yu said, "I'll drive you across the border in this panel truck."

"How can we trust you?" Marty froze in place.

"We have to get all of these cars out of here. Let Shou drive the panel truck to the border." Yu pointed at her. "She can follow me in my car, then you follow me. When we get close to the border, we can all get in the panel truck. You can get in and ride up front with me and point a gun at me all the way across the border."

Tom nodded.

Marty grunted. "No, we can't trust him."

"By the way, you killed two of my agents. I could've killed you, but I only stopped you." Yu glared at Marty. "Think about it."

Yu didn't wait for their answer. He ran over to his agents' car and pulled it deeper into the foliage, then returned by his car. "I told Shou I would get her home. It's now or never. Your call."

"Go." Tom nodded, then looked at Marty. "We don't have any other choices. Let's go."

"I'll stop about a mile from the border crossing, and everyone can get into the panel truck." Yu pointed at Tom. "Like I said, you can point a gun at me all the way."

Tom and Yu helped Marty into the back of the truck. Tom got a medical kit from the back of his car. "Shou, bandage him up best you can."

Tom nodded at Yu, who ran up to the car.

She quickly finished bandaging Marty's leg, then jumped out and got in to drive the panel truck.

Just a little more than two hours later, Tom followed as Yu turned his car into a neighborhood. They were just a little under a mile from the Lo Wu Border Crossing. Yu parked and waved to Tom as he jogged to the panel truck. Tom joined him in the passenger seat while Shou climbed into the back with Marty.

Yu looked at Tom. "Ready?"

Tom nodded. They drove in silence until the border station came into view. Tom pulled out the passport that had been given to him in case he arrested Dr. Wang. He looked over at Yu. "Use this passport. That way, there is no record of you crossing the border and back. Keep it. You may need it in the future."

Yu glanced at it then stuck it in his Zhongshan suit.

Tom took in a big breath. He was taking a big risk, but Yu had helped him so far, and if he were telling the truth about getting his mother out of China, it would keep him from using his real passport. "Pull over and let me get in the back. It will bring less attention to us crossing."

Yu looked at him. "So you trust me?"

Tom didn't know how to answer, but he felt while risky, it would bring less attention to them crossing back into Hong Kong.

Yu stopped the truck.

Tom climbed in the back. Marty was asleep on Shou's shoulder.

"Is he all right?" Tom asked.

Shou nodded as the panel truck lurched forward. "I'm glad you trusted Yu. He could have killed us already. He's been on my side all along. Particularly, after Dr. Wang had my father executed in front of me." She shuddered. "I'm glad he's dead. I wish I could have killed him myself."

Tom nodded. "I understand. Trust me, I understand."

When the truck jolted to a stop, Marty woke up. "What are you doing back here?"

Tom looked at Shou, then at Marty. "Well, we'll find out in a minute if Yu is on our side."

In less than a minute, the panel truck lurched forward. They drove maybe ten minutes, then the road became bumpy and they came to a stop. Yu came around back and opened the door. "Agent Warren, will you drive me back up to the border crossing so that I might go home?"

Tom shook his head. "No, Shou should. It will draw less attention. Now go."

Shou bounded out of the back, splashing in a puddle of rain, then slipped behind the steering wheel.

Yu pointed at Tom. "Walk with me a moment."

Tom nodded.

Once they were away from Marty and Shou, Yu said, "A month from today, I'll check into a hotel in Hong Kong, and we can talk about my mother's situation. I'm dealing with you and you only. Understand?"

Tom squinted. "I understand."

Yu fixed his stare on Tom. "Again, neither your partner nor Shou should learn anything about this. It is too dangerous for me. I'm taking a huge risk. Agreed? I must keep my trusted circle small. This is a very dangerous time."

Tom tilted his head back and jutted his jaw.

"Oh, by the way. I had nothing to do with Wang and his henchmen killing Shou's father. I found it disgusting," Yu added.

Tom nodded and reached out his hand to shake. "I'll return to Hong Kong that week. Call MI6 headquarters. We'll arrange to meet." He shut his eyes and scratched his jaw. "Your code name from now on is 'The Planesman'."

Yu refused his hand. "Agreed. There is something else you must do."

"What?"

Yu pulled off his Zhongshan suit jacket and ripped the sleeve, then bent down and rubbed his jacket in the dirt and grass. He stood back up. "You must punch me as hard as you can in the face—hard enough to bruise me. I'll return to the warehouse, but I can't go back unscathed. I must look like I lost in a scuffle. I'll have to have a story for how you all escaped."

Tom nodded, then he pulled back and landed a hard punch.

Shou jumped out of the truck and rushed toward them, while Marty struggled to hobble that way.

Tom and Yu both held out their hands and in unison exclaimed, "Everything is all right."

Marty reached over to hug Shou, but she didn't respond to his gesture.

Shou slowly returned to the truck and Yu slipped in beside her, as Tom and Marty crawled in the back. Marty's leg had swollen, but the bleeding had seemed to stop. As the panel truck lurched forward, Tom grabbed Marty's shoulder. "We made it, partner. Great job."

Marty shook his head. "He's up to something. I just can't figure it out. He could have stopped me another way than shoot me, Tom."

"Yes, I thought the same thing. We'll figure that out in time. For the moment, here's what's important. We tell Middleton nothing about what went on other than Dr. Wang died, and we rescued Shou." Tom looked down at the wooden floor of the truck as they bumped down the road. "Plus, we got his panel truck back in one piece."

Marty frowned at Tom. "We couldn't have rescued Shou without him."

Tom nodded, then continued, "You're absolutely right. Look, Middleton is my friend. I just want as few details as possible out there. The more we tell him, the more we'll have to explain. Got it?"

Tom and Marty leaned back against the hard panel wall and closed their eyes. Both men were exhausted. Tom opened his eyes briefly to glance at Marty resting.

They rode in the back for about fifteen minutes, and then stopped. Tom assumed they were back to the Lo Wu Border Crossing. After about five minutes, they started moving again. Tom looked at Marty; he was sound asleep.

The panel truck stopped again. Within seconds, the door opened slowly and Shou whispered, "You gentlemen want to ride up front? Tom, will you drive?"

"Of course." Tom helped get Marty out, and then he bounded out.

Once everybody was on the bench seat, Tom ground the gears to get the panel truck moving. He wasn't a very good driver and had no experience driving anything this big, but he wanted to do it for Shou.

"Shou, will you accompany me to the hospital to get patched up?" Marty asked as he put his arm around his girlfriend.

She lifted his arm off and lowered her head. "No, I just want to go home and be by myself. Today has been too much for me."

Tom thought the same thing. Today *had* been too much. With Dr. Wang dead, was it time for him to retire?

CHAPTER THIRTY-THREE

January 20, 1980
Beijing

Yu Qiangsheng looked at his watch. Two a.m. He was dressed all in black, moving through the cover of darkness to a back door. He picked the lock to get into the building, knowing full well there were no alarms on the doors. There would be minimal security at this time of the night. He slipped through the door and quietly closed the metal door behind him. The hallway was dark as he slowly walked and listened for anyone coming. He peeked around the next corner—the door he sought was halfway down this hallway. He moved quietly, swiftly to the door. It was locked.

No problem. He easily picked the lock and was in. Once on the other side, he slipped around the desk and pulled a flashlight and camera from his pocket. Yu opened the side desk drawer and leafed through the files. Detective Bao Li? *Who is that?* Behind that file was a small black book. He pulled out both, while marking their place. First, he opened the file. Li was a San Francisco Police Detective. He snapped some pictures of the pages, then returned the file to its proper place. *What is this book?* He opened it. A lot of names in the front of the book with phone numbers. Again, this was an American book, mostly San Francisco numbers. In the back of the book were notes about comments from the man who ran the San Francisco bureau of the FBI. He snapped a picture of the notes. Then there were notes written in Japanese. Yu couldn't read Japanese.

He continued to flip through the small black book, photographing each page. Then he carefully stuffed it back into its respective place. He continued to go meticulously through the side desk drawer. *There it is. The Jin Wu-dai file.* He pulled it out, laid it on the desk, and flipped through it, taking pictures of every page, including the picture of the man. He heard steps in the hallway. He closed the file, returned it to its place, and turned off his flashlight. After he could no longer hear the steps, Yu turned on the flashlight one more time to make sure the file drawer and the desk didn't look out of place. He slipped back to the door, cracked it open, and listened again. Yu stuck out his head. Still nothing. He stepped out, locked the door, and then started back toward the same door he'd entered. In his camera he had everything he needed to work with the FBI agent.

On the drive across town toward his mother's residence, Yu tried to figure out what he was going to say to her. Another tough assignment. He parked in front of her housing complex and headed inside. The days of being followed to her residence or CCP officials watching who was coming and going to her apartment had ceased. He knocked on her door.

She cracked the door open to see who was there, then flung it open to hug him. "How are you, my son?"

Yu smiled as he gripped her tight.

She held him out and looked at his face. "Where did you get that terrible bruise? Looks like you've been in a fight."

Yu walked past her and sat down on her couch. "Ma, I want to talk to you about a very delicate situation."

"Go ahead."

"Are the government officials treating you better? I've noticed you're not being spied on anymore."

She sat down beside him and grabbed his hand. "Son, I like what Deng Xiaoping is attempting to do with our country."

Yu threw up his hands. "After all they have done to you? Seriously?"

Fan Jin patted his hand. "Yes, son. I didn't like Mao as he aged and got more paranoid, but I always remained close to Zhou En-lai. Deng is much more like Zhou."

Yu licked his lips. He was torn. His mother had thrown him completely off kilter. Should he ask or not?

Yu's Mother continued, "Actually, I'm thinking of seeking a political position in the city. Now, what did you want to talk about?"

He bit his lip. "Ma, are you happy living in China?"

His mother cocked her head as she looked at him. "Yes. Why do you ask?"

"With all that you've been through, I didn't know how you felt. I guess I have a good idea from your comments."

Fan got up from the couch and went to make tea.

Yu followed her as she grabbed the tea kettle, he kissed her on top of the head. "I've got one more stop to make. Don't make me any tea, Ma."

He went out her front door, dumbfounded. Everything he'd planned for his mother seemed to disappear in one fifteen-minute conversation. What was he going to do with the information he had secured to be sure the FBI agent would help him get his mother out?

As he went down the stairs to the ground floor, he thought about Shou Li Cao. He had to see her again.

January 21, 1980
San Francisco

Tom Warren sat across from Special Agent in Charge Gerald Adler's desk. So far, Adler was only occasionally looking up from the written report Tom had prepared regarding his recent trip to Hong Kong. After about ten minutes, he appeared to complete the reading. He got up from his desk and sat on its edge nearest Tom, then leaned forward. "You have a propensity for getting your partners shot, don't you?"

Tom stared straight ahead. He was expecting that remark, but he was prepared. "Gerald, we rescued Shou, and Dr. Wang died of a heart attack. We cut off the head of the snake. And everyone is alive. Marty will be fine."

Adler looked away. "MI6 London is very unhappy with the FBI because you won't provide a full report on what happened in Shenzhen. Frankly, so would the FBI. MI6 London feels very taken advantage of."

Tom knew it was best to keep his mouth shut. There was nothing he could say.

Adler's face grew red. He got up and walked back around his desk. "Well, while you were out galivanting around Asia, pissing off our friends, we have real agents here doing the hard work you were assigned. They're collecting a mountain of evidence against the potential spy in Lawrence Livermore Lab. What do you have to say about that?"

"We have great agents working here on the Chinese spies. Best ever. I'm very happy about any positive development."

Adler waved his right hand. "Then get out of my office. Go catch some real spies here in the United States. Remember? That was your assignment. For God's sakes, you're supposed to be in charge of this operation, but not anymore. Just get out of here until I can figure out what to do with you. And if you want a new partner, I'll assign you a temp until Marty is back. Who knows? He may not want to work with you anymore."

Tom got up, but at the edge of the door, he hesitated. It crossed his mind to bring up about returning to Hong Kong next month, but he thought better than to ask at this time.

After being dressed down by Adler, he went to the bathroom to cool off and take a piss. As he was washing his hands, he looked up at the mirror in front of him, replaying all the things Adler had said. He was right. Men in the bureau were doing a better job than him with chasing down the Chinese spies still working in the United States. Perhaps he needed to start focusing on the Chinese restaurants again. Adler had taken academia away from him several years ago so he could focus strictly on Dr. Wang's network.

Then he looked at himself in the mirror. This summer would be thirty-five years he'd been with the bureau. Once upon a time, he was told he looked like Cary Grant—which he did—but it seemed he was aging fast. He thought about Miyoko. Maybe when he went to Hong Kong, he could pass through Tokyo, going or coming.

He'd once been a great athlete, but now he was an old single man. Some of the words of his old friend Simon Brit came back. He was turning into the old secret service agent, alone, married to a career. His life-long adversary, Dr. Wang, was dead. For God's sakes, he died of a heart attack. Maybe it was time to retire.

The door opened to the restroom, and another agent entered. Tom dried his hands and walked out.

Beijing

Yu Qiangsheng walked into the hospital room to see how Dr. Wang was recovering from his devastating heart attack. Despite Wu and Chung being shot multiple times, they had been able to get him to the prison, where a doctor revived him. Because of his high position in the Chinese Communist Party, he was receiving the best care available in China. However, he still was in critical condition. Yu was sympathetic to Dr. Wang, but he knew how tough he was and believed he'd pull through. Plus, with the power that Dr. Wang could soon be wielding, if he survived, he didn't want to get on his bad side. Dr. Wang was hooked up to a several medical devices, including oxygen.

Dr. Wang opened his eyes when Yu walked into the room. He struggled to wave his hand to approach.

Yu stepped over and pulled up a wooden chair next to the bed.

Dr. Wang looked Yu over and pulled down his oxygen mask. In a weak voice, he said, "Did Warren escape?"

Yu nodded. "I struggled with him, but their other agent was on top of me. I couldn't beat both of them. They knocked me down then knocked me out. I came to about twenty minutes later, and they were gone with Shou Li Cao." He dipped his head. "I'm sorry, I failed."

Dr. Wang pulled the oxygen mask back up, took several breaths, and then continued. "We must learn how the other agent got across the border. And how did they get back across the border?" He pulled the oxygen mask for a few breaths, then took it back down. "I greatly miscalculated. That won't happen again, but I fear I missed my opportunity to kill Warren."

Yu noticed his vital signs were spiking as he struggled to speak.

"I fear it was the work of MI6 Agent Anthony Middleton," Dr. Wang said with his eyes closed. "He helped get Warren's partner across the border. We have to take care of that."

"You need to get some rest." Yu nodded. "I'll be back to see you soon."

Dr. Wang weakly waved his hand again. "We must check with the border crossing. We must stop this from ever happening again. I had Warren in my hands, and he got away. Never again. Never." He tried to sit up, but fell back as his vitals increased dramatically.

A nurse came into the room and looked at Yu. She immediately tended to Dr. Wang.

Yu frowned as he walked out of the room. Dr. Wang was somehow going to survive. *How is this going to impact my power in China? What should I do? Since Ma doesn't seem to want to leave, what do I do with this information to buy her escape? Do I even meet Agent Warren? I'll be taking a great risk.*

CHAPTER THIRTY-FOUR

February 14, 1980
San Francisco

FBI Special Agent Tom Warren was tired of staking out Chinese restaurants while other agents were working the academic side of the universities and colleges in the area. Tom had to board a plane the next day if he was still going to meet Yu Qiangsheng. He looked over at Marty, who had just returned to duty. "I've got to get back to Hong Kong tomorrow. Adler will blow a gasket if I ask his permission to go."

"What? Why are you going back?" Marty shook his head.

Tom raised his hand. "I can't tell anybody, you or him. I just have to go."

"You better watch your step," Marty said. "You going to try to stop in Japan and see Miyoko?"

He nodded.

After a few minutes, Marty said, "This shit assignment of watching Chinese restaurants is useless, and Adler knows it. He's just setting us up to get desk jobs or get us fired."

Marty was right. Director Webster would do whatever Adler recommended.

Tom sighed. Perhaps, he'd just call in sick.

Beijing

With Dr. Wang still recovering from his life-threatening heart attack, Yu Qiangsheng had the perfect excuse to go to Hong Kong. Yet, if he went across the border and Dr. Wang was having him watched, he could have some explaining to do. Initially, he thought he'd cross the border in his official capacity, but how could he explain traveling a day early but not showing up? This would be a red flag to Dr. Wang. No, he'd use the passport left to him by the FBI Agent. This would be his identity he'd use for all his moves in Hong Kong. He'd hidden that passport away with his camera and the film. He had yet to get it developed, fearing to do so anywhere in Communist China. It would have to wait for a one-hour shop in Hong Kong.

He carefully rewound and unloaded the film into the plastic canister. He took off in his car for the long drive to Shenzhen, then across the border into Hong Kong. He guessed it would take him about twenty hours to make the drive, get checked into his discreet hotel room, then sit and wait. On the drive down, he contemplated all he would and wouldn't tell the FBI agent. He needed to tell him enough to earn his trust, but he also had to hold many things back. His actions—past, present, and those he was contemplating—were creating a dilemma. Now he had twenty hours ahead of him to just think.

It would be good and bad—too much time on his hands.

Yu checked into his hotel under his new assumed name on the illegal passport and lay down immediately. Now, wait to see if the FBI agent showed. By agreement, he wasn't to call until tomorrow.

Hong Kong
February 16, 1980

FBI Special Agent Thomas Warren walked into MI6 headquarters and was escorted to Middleton's office. When Tom walked in, Middleton jumped from his chair. "Back here so soon, right? How did you pull that off?"

"I called off sick with the flu." Tom sheepishly smiled then faked a cough. "Who knows if they believe it, but it was the best I had to keep from getting fired. But if they find out I wasn't sick—"

"So why are you back?" Anthony inquired. "Or did you come to tell me face-to-face what really happened last month when you rescued Marty's girl?"

Tom sat down beside his desk. "You'll see some time in the next hour." He sat down at an empty desk, pulled out a deck of cards, and started playing solitaire.

Middleton looked over at what he was doing. "Do you know how to play bridge?"

Tom shook his head. "My mother and father played with their wealthy friends every Wednesday night when I was young, but I hated the game. At that time in life, my parents and I didn't get along, which is why I went to the West Coast to play football. I could have gone to any number of top Eastern colleges, but I wanted to get away from my family."

"Pity."

Tom didn't even look up or comment.

About that time, Middleton's desk phone rang. "MI6 Agent Anthony Middleton." He nodded as he listened, then frowned as he held the phone out to Warren. "It's for you. Someone, I think they said, *The Planesman*."

Tom leapt up, went to Anthony's desk, and snatched the phone out of his hand. "FBI Special Agent Warren here." Then he closed his eyes and nodded as he listened to the voice on the other end give him a phone number and an address. "I'm on my way." He hung up the phone and started toward the door.

Middleton stood up. "Hey, wait a minute. You come to Hong Kong to get a phone call, then leave without telling me a single thing? Right."

Tom spun around and looked at Anthony. "It's safer for you if you don't know." Then he continued out the door.

Yu Qiangsheng opened the door to his room and peeked out. When he saw it was the FBI agent, he opened the door. The agent slipped by him and into the room. He locked the door, then sat down on the edge of the bed and pointed Warren toward the chair in the corner. "Did the MI6 agent ask what was going on?"

"Of course, but I didn't tell him a thing."

Yu got up and looked out the second-story window. "Do you think you were followed?"

Tom shrugged. "Don't know, but it's unlikely. I had the cabbie drive me all over town before he brought me here. Cost me a pretty good fare, but I figured that would work."

Yu walked back over to the bed and sat down. "How is Shou?"

"She's fine. You know she's been dating my partner, Marty Corley, for a number of years?"

"Yes, of course." Yu sat back down and looked at the ground for a moment. "I've got a very serious matter to discuss."

"Isn't that why I'm here?" Tom picked up the pen from the desk and started playing with it.

"Everything has changed since last month." He leaned forward as he clasped his hands. "Dr. Wang survived."

Tom dropped the pen and closed his eyes. "How's that possible? He had no—"

Yu bit his lower lip. "His two bodyguards, Wu and Chung, took him to the prison. A doctor there revived him. He has been in the hospital in Beijing ever since, still in serious care—"

"Communist China has intensive care?"

"While we are a communist country, our top officials receive great care." Yu sat back and looked hard at Tom. "I didn't get a chance to tell you, but Dr. Wang has been told by Chairman Deng that he could be appointed Vice President by the Politburo. He has played a critical role in improving our country's relationship with Japan."

Tom raised his eyebrows. "Unbelievable."

"What do you mean *unbelievable*?"

He waved his hand. "Never mind."

Yu shrugged. "My mother doesn't seem to want to defect. I tried to talk to her about it, but never got around to asking her outright, as some of her remarks led me to believe I shouldn't pursue the topic at this time."

Tom got up from his chair and started toward the door. "I don't know why we're here, then. I didn't need to come to Hong Kong just to catch up."

Yu sprung up and stood in front of Tom. "Sit. Please, sit. Just because things have changed doesn't mean this meeting has no purpose."

The two men stood nose to nose.

Yu raised both hands out to his side. "Look, I believe my mother has been, as the communists call it, *rehabilitated*. She has been through a lot. I have to find the right time to discuss this with her, but...."

Tom stood his ground. "Go on."

Yu went into the bathroom, then emerged holding photographs. "Can you read Japanese?"

Tom half smiled. "I'm fluent in just about every major language spoken on the Pacific Rim."

"Dr. Wang told me you had a reputation as one of the top linguists in the world." Yu nodded.

Tom snarled. "Son-of-a-bitch. I should have shot him in the head while he was dying."

"These photos are from a black book I …was able to gain access to."

Tom stared at him for a second, then snatched the pictures from his hand. "You've got to be kidding me."

"In the front of this book was a bunch of San Francisco phone numbers, but in the back were these notes. I couldn't trust anyone in my country to translate them. Just you." Yu sat back down on the edge of the bed. He could read the FBI agent's face. He was genuinely excited to see this information.

"I don't understand. Why do you want to know what it says?"

Yu opened his hands palms out. "In Communist China, everything is about power. Both Dr. Wang and I have lots of power. I need to have one up on him. Particularly, if he's going to become Vice President. Chairman Deng has promised me several things, too, as he reshapes China. I must know things I'm not supposed to know."

"Okay. Here you go. This note is talking about spying on Dr. Wang's Chinese spy ring. The woman, er, the writer, goes on to say there was a Chinese cook who took a handoff. The writer says the Chinese spy was working at Los Alamos. Every two months on the second Tuesday of that month, the cook would hand the information off to the courier, someone in Dr. Wang's network, who would immediately leave for China that night." Tom stopped reading.

Yu pointed at the next photo. "What does this say?"

Tom shifted in his chair. "The writer was trying to find out what the United States was doing with gold brought into the country by H. H. Kung and T. V. Soong. Some of the gold was stored in Fort Knox, but others went to several large U.S. banks depositories."

Yu got up from the bed, went back over, and peeked out the window again. "A Japanese person was spying on both of us. Wonder who they were working for?"

"It doesn't say."

He frowned as he turned back around and snatched the photos from Tom. "Do you suppose Dr. Wang knew more than what is written here? Do you suppose this has anything to do with his diplomatic success in Japan?"

"Don't see how it could help him with diplomatic success. I would think just the opposite."

"What if Dr. Wang was blackmailing someone in the Japanese government?"

"I just don't see it." Tom eyed Yu. "Would you consider spying on Dr. Wang for me?"

"Not a chance. He'd have me killed." He shook his head. He didn't want to tell the FBI agent he'd already done some spying, but all for himself.

Tom shrugged as he started toward the door. "I assume we're done here. I sure would like to have a copy of the entire black book, including the phone numbers in the front."

"No." Yu wiped his mouth with his hand. "Give me your home phone number and address."

Tom stopped and turned back toward Yu. "My home address? Do you think I'm nuts? You could easily have me killed! If Dr. Wang found out, you know he'd have me killed." He scowled. "Okay, here is my home phone number. But go to a pay phone outside of Beijing when you call me. We can't trust either government at this point." He pulled out a business card and went back to the desk and wrote a number on the back. "I have an answering machine on my home phone. You call as 'The Planesman' and leave a message. Never be on the phone more than thirty seconds in case they have our phones bugged. Use as much code as possible. If you want to meet, just give me time to get here, but it better be worth my time. I'm taking great risks right now for absolutely nothing."

"You're not the only one taking risks." At the door, Yu gestured with both hands. "Help me gain power in China."

CHAPTER THIRTY-FIVE

March 3, 1980
San Francisco

FBI Special Agent in Charge Gerald Adler slowly hung up his desk phone. He had a real situation just handed to him by Director Webster. He was expected to get Warren out of town for a couple of weeks with an assignment outside of San Francisco. He thought for a second. No one had covered the universities or the colleges in Los Angeles—no, that was too close. He closed his eyes. *That's it!* He sat up straight and called out to Tom, "Warren, step into my office, please."

Within a couple of seconds, Warren stood in the doorway.

"Shut the door and take a seat."

"Do you want Marty in here, too?" Tom rounded his shoulders as he leaned forward slightly.

"Warren, I have something to tell you, since you're overseeing the Chinese spy operation. Our country's Department of Commerce has pushed President Carter to reclassify Red China in order to allow them to purchase U.S. manufacturing technology. Some of the new items on the list will undoubtedly be used to improve their military."

"You can't be serious! We're going to let them walk in the front door and buy the technology we've been fighting to keep from them for the last decade?"

Adler handed him a piece of paper. "Here's the partial list. The military brass haven't completed it."

Tom quickly scanned the list, then stuck out his chin and waved his arms. "This is unbelievable! We can't let them have any of this technology."

"I agree. As I understand it, neither Commerce nor Carter reached out to the military or us or your friends at the CIA to ask their opinions." Adler dropped his hands with a thud. "It's going to make all our jobs more difficult while our Military Industrial Complex makes more money."

"What's it going to do to our on-going investigations into our scientific and academic community?" Tom raised the list, scanned it again, then threw it on Adler's desk. "Because our country has so much freedom and good science programs, smart foreigners want to come here to study. Some stay, some leave, some leave with stolen materials. It looks like we just opened the front door. Letting it happen, legal-like."

Adler put his forehead in his hand. "Get off your soapbox, Warren. We're doin' what we're doin' until we're told to stop. Got it?"

Tom started to get up.

"Wait a moment. I'm not finished." Adler cleared his throat. "Sit back down for just a second."

Tom sat back down on the edge of his chair.

"Director Webster gave me a tip on something that came from the New York FBI office. We want you to go and check in on it. There are two restaurants in the Chinatown part of Manhattan they are zeroing in on. The New York office has requested your assistance. I said you could go out East and help them for a couple of weeks."

Tom shrugged. "Isn't the New York FBI one of our finest offices? Why do they need me?"

"Of course they are, but you've been the lead agent on the Chinese spy ring for fifteen years." Adler opened his hands out to his side. "You know more about the Chinese spy ring then anyone in the U.S. They were looking for you to assist them on the ground, get your keen insight. It's just temporary."

Tom nodded and left. The whole thing seemed strange. Just two months ago, Adler had busted his chops about his professional conduct and removed him as the lead agent. Their relationship had been contentious ever since. Now he was being told how good he was and being sent out of town. He walked over to his desk.

Marty hobbled over on one crutch. "What's up, partner?"

"I'm being sent to New York for a couple of weeks to help their office. Guess what doing? Staking out more restaurants in their Chinatown." Tom shook his head. He looked up to see Adler standing in his office door watching him. He scowled. "I'm going home to pack."

"I assume I'm still chained to my desk."

Tom nodded as he picked up a few items and went out the door.

Tom picked up his phone, then hit the play button to play back messages. The third message was in Mandarin. "Deng Xiaoping has requested the U.S. State Department give Dr. Wang diplomatic immunity, which was granted, so that he can come to the United States to have coronary artery surgery at Stanford University. The phone number on your FBI business card was one of the numbers in the black book. Were you aware of this?" The message ended. Tom slowly placed the phone back down on the switch hook. Why hadn't he been told? No, he knew why. Now the question was to determine whose decision it was to withhold this information. The first place to start was Special Agent in Charge Gerald Adler. Now, all he had to do is figure out when Dr. Wang was due to arrive. The question was, who could he trust to tell him? Surely, Adler would keep Marty in the dark.

Then it hit him. Michelle Galloway could get him the information he needed. His circle of trust was small but reliable. He checked his watch. It was early enough in the day to place the call to the D.C. office to try to find out his answers. He picked up the receiver and dialed Michelle's desk phone at the FBI headquarters in Washington D.C. "Hello. Galloway."

"Michelle, this is Tom Warren. How are you?"

"Special Agent Warren, I'm great. I've gotten married since we last spoke. How are you?"

"Hey, congratulations. But you are still using the name *Galloway*?" Tom retorted.

"Well, truth be told, only here at the FBI headquarters. I'm planning on retiring as soon as I have my twenty years in. It just seemed easier," Michelle replied.

"All fine here on the Western front. And, of course, when I call, I'm looking for a favor. I need some information."

"Of course, let me guess. Don't tell anyone you asked me to do this?" Michelle whispered.

"Michelle, you know me too well." Tom laughed. "I need to find out when a Communist Chinese citizen by the name of Dr. Wang was granted diplomatic immunity to be allowed to come to the States and when he is to arrive. If it helps, he's going to Stanford for surgery. It should be easy to find, as I suspect the FBI Director is responsible for signing off with the State Department."

"That should be easy. Do you want me to call you back in a few minutes at your office in San Francisco?"

Tom rubbed his chin. "No. Let me give you my home phone. Call me here as soon as you find it." He gave her the number, then hung up the receiver. He went to his bedroom to start packing. He had no more taken his suitcase out of the closet than his phone rang.

Tom hurried and picked up the phone. "Hello?"

"Special Agent Warren, Michelle here. Didn't find anything regarding a diplomatic passport for anyone named Wang, but did find one for another Chinese man, who, coincidently, is coming into the country tomorrow and going to Stanford. This guy is apparently some big shot in China."

"Hang on. Let me grab a new pen. The one by my phone won't write." Tom laid the receiver down for a second and picked up a new pen from his kitchen. "Okay, I'm ready to write."

Michelle gave him the name.

Tom wrote the name on the pad of paper and looked at it. One more piece of the puzzle to Dr. Wang's true identity, maybe. "Thanks, Michelle, I really appreciate it.

Tom went back to the bedroom to pack. He pondered the last part of The Planesman's message. Why would the FBI's San Francisco main number be in Kikue Nakamura black book? Time to rethink the murder of the Japanese spy.

6:20 AM PST
March 4, 1980
Stanford University Medical Center
Stanford, California

Tom walked into the Stanford Medical Center expecting to see Chinese security as he walked up to the information desk. A pretty young woman sat there. He thought he might have a chance of intimidating her into getting Dr. Wang's room number. He flashed his FBI badge at her. "May I see the list of the patients and room assignments?"

She looked at the badge, then handed him a clipboard.

Tom took her board in his hand and stood over her shoulder, flipping through the pages. There it was—last name *Liao*, with a diplomat flag on it, in the cardiac wing. He flipped the pages back and tossed the clipboard back down on the desk. "Thank you, ma'am."

"Yes, sir."

He headed toward the elevator. When the elevator doors opened, he entered and pushed the button for one floor below cardiac wing. He figured he'd be ahead to walk up the flight of stairs in case there was Chinese security.

On the ride up, he reached in his pocket and pulled out the list of Dr. Wang's assets that Miyoko had mailed to him. He smiled, as he had never taken the Dr. Wang file back to the office in the last two months. The elevator jerked to a stop and the doors opened. He stepped out and looked around before starting down the hallway. It was likely best not to go up the stairs nearest the main elevator. There had to be another set of stairs. He approached a nurse standing in the hallway looking at a chart. "Ma'am, I'm lost. Where is the cardiac unit?"

"You're on the wrong floor." She pointed at an exit sign ahead. "If you follow that exit sign, it will lead you to stairs that will take you right up to the entrance to the cardiac care unit. You'll have to check in with a nurse to enter that unit."

Tom turned down the hall, went around the corner, and saw the exit sign about halfway down. He hustled down the hall, opened the door, and then ran up the steps. Once on the landing, he peeked through the tiny glass window. No one. He cracked the door open and looked down the hallway. Still nothing. He stepped onto the floor and let the door close gently behind him as he looked in the opposite direction. He was about ten feet from the door with the sign "Cardiac Unit."

Quickly, he advanced to the door and twisted the knob. *Not locked. Good.* There was no window to see what was on the other side. He cracked the door. There were voices down the hall, but it didn't appear anybody was at the main desk. *I can't believe I have such good luck—early morning staff change, and patients being cared for.* He walked by one room before stepping up to the main desk, where a string of monitors beeped from behind the desk. He slipped over and glanced across the names. A little flag was on one of the monitors with the name tag Liao. Dr. Wang's room! He looked back behind him at the closed room. He knew the direction to go.

There was another hallway ahead. He moved to that corner quickly, then looked around. Nurses moved up and down the hallway, in and out of the various rooms, carrying charts and pulling IV poles. Plus, two men in suits. Hmmm. Were they State Department, FBI, or a private security company? The men were likely not FBI or he would know them. He started down the hallway toward Dr. Wang's room. The two men looked at him as he approached. He thought he'd try a bluff. He hoped Adler hadn't put his name on a list, thinking he was in New York. When they stepped in front of him, one of them said, "No one is allowed in."

Tom quickly flashed his badge at the two men. "I'm part of the local security. I was supposed to check in on our diplomat. Arrange for his future security when he returns to China. You know, diplomatic stuff." Before they could say anything or look too close at his badge, he was in Dr. Wang's room. He slipped up by the bed. The man was asleep, his face covered by an oxygen mask and an EKG machine hooked up to an IV in his arm. He stepped up and patted him on the arm. "Good morning, Dr. Wang."

Dr. Wang's eyes barely opened at first, then they grew large. He gasped for air. "You're forbidden to be here. Your name was supposed to be on the forbidden list. I have diplomatic immunity from the United States Department of State."

"Yes, I know." He looked back at the bedridden patient and continued to pat his arm. *The man was no longer the slim, lean figure he'd first met over thirty years ago.* "I'm probably not supposed to know you're here. No one told me yet...." Tom opened up both hands. "Here I am, none the less. I just wanted to stop in and make sure you're resting comfortably, since you somehow managed to survive our last meeting."

"You aren't going to kill me right here, are you?" Dr. Wang spoke barely above a whisper.

Tom shook his head. "Not me. I just came by to read to my old friend." He reached in his pocket and pulled out the list that Miyoko had sent him, then started to read. "These are the items that Prince Takeda had in his possession when he arrived in the Philippines in 1943." He read off several items. Then he looked up as he read, "Emerald ring, very large, surrounded by diamond-encrusted gold curls. Ring was attached to an emerald wrist bracelet by a thin strand of diamonds set in gold." He glimpsed at Dr. Wang, who was turning red, struggling to move, lying there snarling.

Detective Lee stepped into the room. "Warren, you aren't allowed in here. I left my two dumb ass detectives here to relieve me for thirty minutes, and they can't read the list. Now get out."

Tom ignored Detective Lee as he ran his finger down the page. "Oh, just one more thing before I go. There's a painting hanging in Prince Takeda's home in Japan, still today." Tom described the picture to Dr. Wang. Then Tom leaned forward. "I know your real name, Liao." The EKG readings became erratic while his blood pressure shot up.

Dr. Wang reached toward the paper Tom held just barely out of reach, then fell back on the bed. An alarm sounded on the EKG.

Just as Detective Lee grabbed for Tom, he couldn't resist just smiling at Dr. Wang. "See, I told you I wouldn't touch you."

Tom didn't resist Detective Lee rushing him toward the door. Once in the hallway, a nurse and a doctor ran toward Dr. Wang's room.

It was best to go in the opposite direction.

CHAPTER THIRTY-SIX

March 6, 1980
New York City

Tom trudged into the New York City FBI headquarters to meet up with their investigators. This was the last place he wanted to be. As a true Bostonian, he hated New York with a passion.

He introduced himself to the Special Agent in Charge, who walked him into the conference room where two young agents waited. They had a slide projector set up in front of them. Tom introduced himself, but the young agents didn't say a word.

Their boss replied, "Special Agent Warren has been chasing Chinese spies since the 1940s. You two could learn a thing or two from him."

Tom slumped down at the far end of the large table. The boss turned out the light and stood behind the agents. "Go ahead."

The agents flipped through the carousel of slides, pausing on each one no longer than ten seconds. When they finished the first carousel, they quickly changed it out for another, then continued. They still hadn't said a word. The room was icy. Tom sensed they didn't want him there anymore then he wanted to be there.

After the third slide was projected on the white pull down, a light knock sounded at the door. A woman stuck her head in and asked, "Is there a Special Agent Thomas Warren in here?"

He raised his hand like he was still in grade school.

She nodded. "You're wanted on the phone."

Tom waved at everyone. "If this is who I think it is, you won't have to worry about dealing with me. I won't be back."

The Special Agent in Charge frowned as he walked by.

Tom followed the woman to her desk. She hit the hold button and handed him the phone. "Special Agent Tom Warren."

"What the hell do you think you were doing yesterday? Trying to create a diplomatic crisis for the State Department, or start a war? What do you have to say for yourself?"

He'd expected this call, but didn't know when it would come. "Adler, we are already at war with China, but only a few of us realize it. Besides, I didn't do anything wrong."

"Warren, how do you figure you didn't do anything wrong? You entered the Chinese Diplomat's hospital room without authority!" Adler screamed.

"The State Department and President Carter are protecting Dr. Wang—the top Chinese Spy Handler—the man I've been chasing for years. That's right. That Chinese Diplomat was Dr. Wang. And don't tell me they didn't know or else they wouldn't have tried to keep me away. You better think about that for a second." Tom realized the woman was staring at him. He felt his face flush.

"The man had another cardiac event because of whatever you did. And the State Department is up my ass. I've defended you for years. Put up with some of your unorthodox activities, but you have stepped over the line. I can't defend you. You're fired. You can turn your badge and gun in there in New York. Don't even come back to our office. I'll have Corley bring the stuff from your desk to you."

Tom knew it was time to land his punch. "Why was your phone number in Kikue Nakamura's black book, Adler?"

"What did you say to me?"

"You heard me," Tom calmly stated. "Your phone number was in Kikue Nakamura's black book. Were you just having sex with her, or were you helping her spy on the United States?"

There was a long pause. Finally, Adler's scream landed on Tom's ear. "Warren, you better tread lightly! You are in very dangerous territory with that remark!"

"Come on, Adler, you can do better than that." Tom looked around the room, which by now was filled with people, all staring at him. Even the two young agents had stepped out of the conference room. "We'll see what Director Webster thinks about it."

"Damn it, Warren. Don't start a war between you and me. You can't win."

Tom smiled and handed the phone back to the secretary. He walked back over to the Agent in Charge, reached in his jacket pocket, pulled out his badge, removed his gun, and held them out. "I've been fired. Here you go."

The NYC Special Agent in Charge reached out with both hands and a dumbfounded look.

Tom walked out to the elevator. He hadn't been to his parents' home in a number of years. He was this close with nothing to do. It might be a good time to go to Boston.

March 7, 1980
Boston, MA

Tom sat in front of his parents' TV, watching the first round of the NCAA Basketball tournament, in which his old college rival, Arizona State, play against Loyola Marymount, his new favorite team. He'd always been too busy to follow basketball once he was out of college, so it was nice to sit and relax. It wasn't much of a game, as Arizona State was dominating them, but there

Chop Stix: Chinese Spies Among Us

was nothing else on TV to watch. Tom's brain was still on West Coast time, and his mother and father had long since gone to bed.

He was sitting right beside the phone when it rang. He grabbed it on the first ring. "Hello, Warren residence."

The voice on the other end replied, "Tom, glad you answered. Knew it was late there on the East Coast, but I had to call you. What the hell happened?"

Tom muted the TV. "Too much to tell, but why?"

"Adler came charging in this morning, yelling and screaming at me to clean out your desk and take all your personal stuff home until you come and get it, that he never wanted to see your ugly ass face again. And he hoped you hadn't started a war with China?"

Tom took a sip of his Coke and put his feet up on the footstool. "Well, here is the brief version. Dr. Wang was given diplomatic immunity and came to Stanford to have some kind of surgery. I went into his room and read a list of some of the items that were stolen from his home in 1937, and he had another cardiac event. That's all I did."

There was a long pause before Marty said, "Wow, what a story. Did Adler tell you, you weren't permitted around Dr. Wang?"

"Hell, no." Tom was already thinking of how to answer the next question that Marty would ask. How did he know? He tried to change the subject fast. "I'll be back in San Fran in a couple of days. I'll get my stuff then. This is not over between Adler and me. I've got some things on him. We both may end up fired before this is over."

"Both? Why me? I didn't do anything."

Tom got the reaction he'd hoped for. "Not you. Adler. Adler and me."

"Good. I was worried there for a minute."

"Adler may be under investigation soon, if I have my way. Hey, I'll see you in a couple of days. Goodbye."

Tom was taking a big gamble on a hunch. He remembered back when the investigation into the Kikue Nakamura murder case began, Adler was focused

322

on the black book. Tom's photographic memory kept a picture in his mind of Adler's face. He had some real concern. Tom hoped he wasn't overplaying his hunch, but what did he have to lose? He'd already been fired. Tomorrow, he was determined to reach out and attempt to get an appointment with Director Webster.

July 21, 1980
Beijing

Dr. Wang walked into his office for the first time since late December. He was glad to be able to return to work. He had many things to accomplish, but most of all he had to demonstrate his effectiveness so he could get the appointment as Vice President by the Politburo. Tops on his list was to shore up his spies working outside of mainland China. Plus, he needed to make a trip to Hong Kong to get his mail, but the risk at the moment was too great for him. His doctors here in China were communicating with the doctors at Stanford, and they wanted him to limit his workload and activity.

He desperately wanted to reach out to Jin Wu-dai. He needed some information badly. FBI Special Agent Thomas P. Warren had gotten the upper hand on him twice. The first time, he thought he had a fail-safe plan to kill Warren in Guangdong, but it had fallen apart because he hadn't anticipated the other FBI agent, Corley, getting into China. It was still a mystery how that happened. But he wouldn't make the same mistake again. He looked at his watch. He had a few minutes before Yu Qiangsheng was to show up for their meeting. Which gave him just enough time to find out how Warren learned he was in the United States.

He dialed the number. "Hello, Detective Lee."

"Bao Li, this is Dr. Wang. How did Warren find out I was in the hospital?" Dr. Wang asked.

"I spoke with FBI Special Agent in Charge Gerald Adler, Warren's immediate boss. He said when FBI Director Webster told him to keep Warren away from you, Adler decided on his own not to tell Warren, but just shipped him out of town immediately. He was afraid if he tipped Warren off you were at Stanford, he'd defy orders and come after you anyway."

Dr. Wang closed his eyes for a few seconds. "Do you believe him?"

"Yes, I think Adler has a good angle on Warren. But since Adler fired Warren, he has brought charges against Adler over dismissal. Something is going on, and I can't find out what's up. Its real hush-hush," Li added.

Li's comments only made Dr. Wang want to get his hands on the latest package from Jin Wu-dai. Perhaps there would be some insight into what was going on with Warren. "Do what you must with Adler. He screwed up, but wait to see the outcome of Warren's action, first."

"I'll carry out your orders, Comrade. Just let me know. It will take some coordination on my part to carry out such an operation."

Dr. Wang hung up the phone. He had to think. If Adler didn't tell Warren to stay away from the hospital, who tipped Warren off? He had a leak in his network, and that was unacceptable. It had never happened before.

He reached in the top drawer of his desk and pulled out a black velvet bag and dumped out five chopsticks. He looked at Wu and Chung. "As soon as I'm mobile again, we have much to accomplish."

Yu Qiangsheng knocked on Dr. Wang's office door. It swung open; Wu stepped to the side. Yu looked past him to Dr. Wang and bowed. "How is your recovery coming along?"

Dr. Wang pointed at a chair. "Let's catch up on the developments while I've been rehabbing. I must get up to speed as fast as possible. Have you been able to keep tabs on the Overseas Chinese Affairs Office?"

Yu pulled out some notes written on a pad and passed them to him to read.

Dr. Wang picked up the paper, then highlighted a few items.

When it appeared he got to the bottom of the page, Yu cleared his throat. "You'll note your agents have been monitoring both MI6 Agent Anthony Middleton and FBI Special Agent Martin Corley's every move," he said. "I particularly enjoy that last one. Corley's notes are minimal from just having returned to work after I shot him in January. He's only been back for a brief visit to Hong Kong."

After laying the paper back down, Dr. Wang looked up at Yu. "So Shou Li Cao has disappeared? No one can find her?" He gestured with his hands. "Do you think she returned to the United States?"

Yu had anticipated that he'd ask about her, but he had no good answer. "During the past month, I've ordered your agents to do a better job. Yet, we still have no evidence she went back to the United States. At the same time, no one has seen her in Hong Kong."

Dr. Wang folded his arms across his chest and closed his eyes. "I've had a considerable amount of time to think while rehabbing. I want your agents to shadow Western journalists in our country. Over the years, their reporting has done much to damage our image in the face of the world."

Yu licked his lips. "I think that's a good idea. I will assign new agents to the task—plus, I might pick out a few to watch myself."

"We are done here. I'll be going to Hong Kong soon to have our agents there pick up their skills—or be dealt with." Dr. Wang cracked his neck and then his knuckles while fixated on Yu.

Yu got up from the chair and left the meeting. As he walked down the hallway, he felt a sense of distrust from Dr. Wang. With Dr. Wang's power growing in the country, he had to do all that he could to offset it with his own. He must grow his stature in the mind of Deng Xiaoping.

San Francisco

Tom was riding with Marty to the FBI headquarters, mentally readying himself for his confrontation with Gerald Adler. He was figuratively going for the jugular vein on Adler. To make idle conversation, he asked. "What's going on with Shou?"

Marty tucked in his upper lip. "She has almost stopped talking to me. I don't get it. Things were going really well. Then . . . ."

"She's been through a lot. I can't imagine—she was kidnapped, confronted Dr. Wang, and watched her father get executed." Tom spoke while looking out the side window.

"I don't get it. I wanted to be there for her. She all but shut me out my last time in Hong Kong." Marty parked in the FBI parking lot.

Tom leaped from the car and headed for the door. He was going to go straight at Gerald Adler. He'd already filed a complaint with the resources department that he'd been wrongfully terminated. But that wasn't what he was going to challenge him about—it was over the black book. Because he'd lost his badge, he couldn't get past security, but with Marty he could come in as a guest. He was asking Marty to take a risk, but Tom felt confident all would be fine.

The minute Tom entered the office, Gerald Adler stood on the other side of the door. "Warren, I told you not to come back here. I'm going to have you arrested. And Corley, you knew better than to participate in this. I'm going to reprimand you as well."

Tom stood just inside the door, still holding the door open, while Marty remained in the hallway. He held both hands out in front of him. "Why don't you arrest me? Cuff me right here. It will only add to my complaint. I have been to Resources. And, I've talked to Director Webster about you being in the murdered Kikue Nakamura's black book. So bring it. Give it your best shot."

Adler gritted his teeth. "Warren, don't tempt me."

"No, actually, I am tempting you. Or call your friend Detective Lee to come arrest me. That'd make him happy, too." Tom calmly stated.

Adler stepped out of the doorway. "In my office, now."

"Is that an invitation?" Tom stood his ground. "Only if Corley comes in too. I want a witness to our conversation."

Adler waved his hand and walked toward his office.

Tom turned, nodded at Marty, and the two men followed Adler.

Marty closed the door behind him, then leaned against it, while Tom stared directly into Adler's eyes. He was about to play his best game of poker with no cards up his sleeve, hoping against hope that Adler wouldn't call him.

"You have created a shit storm everywhere," Adler said, his eyes narrow. "The State Department, Director Webster, the Chinese Foreign Minister—and you walk in here to challenge me? Pretty bold. Now, tell me why I shouldn't have you thrown out of here again?"

Tom leaned forward. "So your name was in Kikue Nakamura's black book just because you were having sex with her? No pillow talk? No way. The only one I haven't called is your wife, and that is my next call. Frankly, that is whether you re-instate me or not."

Adler sprung up from his desk. "You are starting a fight that I'm going to finish. You can't win, Warren."

"Can't win? *Can't win?* I've already won. You are the only one who doesn't know. Kikue Nakamura was spying on the Chinese *and* the United States, and you were having sex with her—and probably giving her information about FBI operations. When her murder investigation broke, you were more concerned about the black book than who did it. I couldn't understand why that was so important, but I do now."

Adler walked around his desk.

Tom stood up to meet him nose to nose.

"Warren, I'm going to throw you out of this office by myself."

"Go for it. But I'm walking out of here. And expect Internal Investigators in here any day to start taking you apart. Webster promised me they would be here soon."

Adler snarled. "Show me your evidence. Show me."

Tom shook his head. "You know I'm right. I'm not showing you anything. Now, you got me out of a job temporarily, but I'll have my job back soon, and you'll be gone. This will make a nice office for me." He shoved Adler out of his way, then nodded at Marty to open the door. The two of them left.

Tom slammed the door in Adler's face so hard that everyone in the large room looked up, even though they were already fixated in their direction. Tom laughed. He'd gotten the exact reaction he wanted out of Adler and everyone in the office. "Marty, I'm going to call a cab and head home."

"No, Tom, I'll take you home," Marty said. "That was quite a performance. Are you really going to call his wife?"

Tom winked at him and nodded, then picked up the phone to dial for a city cab.

Sunday August 3, 1980
Hong Kong

It was two o'clock in the morning when Wu pulled up in front of the post office. Dr. Wang got out and walked with a cane up to the building. Once inside, he slipped his key into the box, reached in, and grabbed the package. He slowly limped back to the car and slipped into the backseat.

The package was from Jin Wu-dai. In great anticipation, he tore through the package. As they pulled away from the curb, he flipped on the light in the back of the car, then sorted through the papers, looking for anything on Tom Warren. *Nothing.* But Jin had written a note, which Dr. Wang read silently:

> As you are aware, I am retiring next year. Let me know what
> you want me to wrap up. I'm in Vegas next week, August 12
> through August 17. I'll call you in your office.

Dr. Wang smiled. This couldn't come soon enough. He must learn about Warren's every move and try to find out where he'd gotten the information about his family's treasures. He had a diplomatic trip to Japan coming up as a follow up mission to his 1978 trip. On that diplomatic mission, he'd made tremendous headway with Japanese Prime Minister Takeo Fukuda, which had put him in the position of the Politburo to consider him for the vice presidency. He had an upcoming meeting with new Prime Minister Zenko Suzuki. Deng Xiaoping wanted Dr. Wang to continue to improve relations between the two Asian countries. One big obstacle was the Japanese planned revisions to their textbooks, downplaying their vicious aggression against the Chinese during World War II—a perfect opening for Dr. Wang to gain additional information regarding his family's treasures. Yet, if Jin could come through with where Warren got his information, it would be even better. If he had some names, he believed he could easily outmaneuver the Japanese Prime Minister to divulge many things.

San Francisco

Tom Warren had been out of work for six months. After interviewing several lawyers, he was just about to hire one to represent him in his case against the FBI. He'd started drinking again to pass the time. Marty was keeping him up to speed with the investigation into Adler. It was going well, but if Tom didn't come up with some hard evidence soon, he was afraid the tide would turn against him. He was blindly staring at the television when his phone rang.

"Hello," he answered.

The voice replied in Mandarin, "This is The Planesman. We need to meet. I'll be at our usual place on Saturday night August 30 through the next day."

Tom set down his Manhattan. "I need those photos you showed me at our last meeting. It's really important. There's no reason for us to meet if I can't get a copy."

"Okay, okay. I can do that. Get you a complete copy. It is of no use to me. But we have much to discuss."

The line went dead. Tom looked at his watch. Just under thirty seconds.

Tom picked up his drink. After taking another swig, he thought of his old friend Simon Britt, who had warned him back in 1963 that Tom would end up just like him. He seemed headed in that direction. Perhaps while he was in Hong Kong, he could talk Middleton into using him in some fashion. Marty hadn't been able to return to work there and was unhappy because he hadn't seen Shou since he was shot. Marty couldn't afford to retire. Somehow Tom had to sneak into Hong Kong without Marty or Middleton knowing he was there—unless of course, he decided to ask to work with MI6.

CHAPTER THIRTY-SEVEN

August 14, 1980
Beijing

Dr. Wang was focused on how to set up and kill Warren, all the while continuing his climb in the Communist Party. He'd been expecting a phone call from his top agent in the United States. Today was day three, and thus, far no call.

He looked at Wu and Chung. "You must make back up security arrangements for me in Japan. So far, the Japanese government is pushing back on letting either of you in the country. We can't find out why. You will need to find me an adequate security service there if I can't get the strings pulled to let you in. Surely, Suzuki doesn't know about our spy operation, but he and his family go back to the original Zabatsu families." Dr. Wang waved them out the door.

He was making notes for that upcoming trip when his phone rang. He grabbed up the receiver.

"Jin here. Sorry, I was winning at the tables. Hit a losing streak—and with the women, too—so I decided to call you."

Dr. Wang tolerated Jin's women and gambling issues, since he was still his best spy in the United States, so he had to accept it. "I need all the information I can get on Warren. I'm sure you know he came into my hospital room when I was in the U.S. and started telling me about my family treasures the Japanese stole in 1937. I've got to know how he got his hands on that information. Who gave it to him? I'm taking a diplomatic trip to Japan sometime this fall, and I want to know before I get there. He said Prince Takeda had one of my family's artworks in his home, and when he was in the Philippines during World War II, he took some of my family's gold and jewelry there. You must get me that information before you retire."

"I'll endeavor. By the way, I do know Warren still hasn't been reinstated by the FBI. He and Adler are the subject of a large investigation. Plus, the U.S. Department of State and CIA were still really mad about Warren coming into your hospital room."

"Not reinstated? Ha! *Good*. That will hurt his pride. I nearly died because of him coming into my room. He can burn in hell, for all I care." Dr. Wang leaned back. "The Chinese government did file a formal complaint. I can see where their State Department would take issue with him. With Carter trying to get along with Chairman Deng, Warren's FBI career may well be over."

"I'll try to get that information for you. It may not be easy, though," Jin replied. "Anything else you need? Remember, I'm still stepping down first of next year."

Dr. Wang rubbed his chin. "Just get me that information on Warren and the Japanese."

Sunday August 31, 1980
Hong Kong

Tom had the cabbie pull up a block away from the hotel, then walked around the block as an extra layer of security so as not to give away Yu Qiangsheng's location. He was at the point of trusting no one. He was now even worried that MI6 would have a tail on him. Surely, if they were monitoring the travel logs, they would know he'd flown into Hong Kong. He'd even become paranoid of Yu using the Chinese passport the British had supplied last year, and in Tom's current position, he couldn't put his hands on a replacement. He walked to the back entrance of the hotel, entered, and went straight to the elevator. When the elevator door opened, a couple waited to get on. Tom looked down so as no one could get a good look at his face, then went down to Yu's room and knocked on the door.

The door opened a crack. Yu peeked out, then opened the door. Once Tom entered, Yu immediately went to the chair in the corner of the small room.

"What's going on that I need to come here?"

Yu walked over to the bedstand and picked up an envelope. He held it out to Tom.

"What's this?" Tom asked.

"The copy you demanded from the black book."

"Thank you." Tom smiled and gently slapped the envelope on his thigh. "Why did you want to meet?"

"While I'm very secure in my role as one of the most powerful men in China. However, since Dr. Wang has returned to work, he has become even more powerful than before. Everybody in China respects the power he wields." He raised an eyebrow. "I need something to keep up with him."

"Power? How is he gaining so much power? What is he doing?" Tom rubbed his chin with the back of his hand.

"I don't know how he's doing it. But you should know Deng is sending him to Japan to meet with Suzuki sometime in the next couple of months." Yu leaned forward and opened both hands out to his side. "If he continues to improve relations with Japan, you know, opening more doors, he will become vice president of the CCP."

"How much do you know about his background?" Tom contemplated telling him about his past, but was a little hesitant.

"Probably not as much as you. Because of my own position, I've been through his files, but the government has done much to cover it up." Yu leaned forward. "Even when I was first introduced to him, I was never told his real name. It's as though there are actually two different people, as he has built this persona of 'Dr. Wang.' But one day not long ago, he was gloating about his power and let out his real name—Liao."

"Do you know his story about his hatred for the Japanese?"

Yu cocked his head. "You're lying to me. Why would our government have him doing diplomatic missions to Japan if he hates the Japanese?"

Tom frowned at Yu. "Believe what you will."

"I assume you have been reinstated at the FBI, so you can help me."

Tom stared at him for a minute. *How did he know I had been fired? Damn it, there* is *a spy in the FBI. Is it Adler?* "How did you know I was fired?"

"Dr. Wang told me."

Tom looked down at the ground. That confirmed it. Dr. Wang did have a spy on the inside.

"This is why I was willing to bring these papers to help you get back in. Since your FBI number was in the black book, I figured it would help you." Yu looked straight at Tom. "Now, what are you going to do for me?"

"Since you won't spy on Dr. Wang, I'm limited in what I can do. But don't worry, I'll be able to help you. If the FBI doesn't reinstate me, MI6 will use me. My connections haven't changed a bit." He gave him a nod as he picked up the phone and called for a cab to pick him up a block away from the hotel.

"Look, you are the only one I can turn to—and that's because of your ongoing fight with Dr. Wang. He could go to the government and have me put in a camp like my family—just on his word alone. Or he could have me killed and no one would question it." Yu walked over to the window and looked out.

Tom looked at his watch. With the random pickup spot for the cab, he had to be going soon.

Yu continued staring out the window. "The last time we met, I told you my mother was getting into politics, but I've never told you her background story. Bear in mind, before she was put into a rehabilitation camp, she was put in prison for protesting against Mao." Yu sat back down on the bed. "Now, my brother, who is an engineer of some renown, is thinking of getting into the political wing of the Communist Party. If my father were still alive, he wouldn't believe this. My father was killed by Mao's secret police. Now, even my own family denies it."

Tom leaned back in his chair. *If Yu's frustrations continue to build, I may have something here to work with.* "Sometimes family has your back and nurtures you. Sometimes they can be the motivation to get away. I know this personally to be true."

Yu crossed his arms over his chest. "You getting philosophical on me?"

Tom got up and started toward the door.

Yu asked, "How is Shou?"

Tom grabbed the door handle. "She is fine. Her life has returned to normal." He didn't know what else to say, as he hadn't had any contact with her since Adler dismissed him. He wished he could stop by to see her, but he couldn't let anyone know he was in Hong Kong.

Monday September 1, 1980
Tokyo

Tom sat at the small desk in his hotel room. He was waiting on Miyoko to stop by. He wanted to review the file with her, as she had become a real trooper in trying to ferret out information on Kikue Nakamura. Having the copies of Yu's photographs were his first real breakthrough, and he hoped this new information might assist Miyoko.

The front of Nakamura's black book contained only a few phone numbers—certainly not as many as he'd expected. However, one was the main number for the FBI San Francisco office. There were several local phone numbers that he wanted to test. They looked like local and state government numbers. So, not only did she have someone in the FBI in her book—likely Adler—but other government officials as well. Plus, there were two other numbers that caught his attention. The first, a 202 area code number, meaning the Washington, DC, area. The second number was a 212 area code—Manhattan downtown in New York City. Were these "johns" coming to visit the beautiful spy? Or were they contacts or business associates? Perhaps he'd never know. The numbers in the book created more questions than the answers he'd gained. He was beginning to believe she was a big-time spy who was willing to hop in bed with men to get information from pillow talk. Not exactly a prostitute—but maybe just a persuasive female spy.

A knock sounded at the door.

Tom opened it.

Miyoko bolted through, breathing hard. Before he could ask, she replied, "No, I wasn't followed. Came in the back door and ran up five flights of stairs."

Tom hadn't seen her in a couple of years. She had matured into a very beautiful Japanese woman. He wanted to grab her and kiss her, but he resisted. "Your timing is perfect. I'm just about to go through the back of Nakamura's black book. There was nothing in the front that would mean anything to you."

Miyoko sat down on the edge of the bed and flashed a big smile. "My father asked to be remembered to you."

Tom smiled, then started reading the back of the black book. "Here is something important. She was   frequenting the same Chinese restaurant where the courier from Los Alamos was making their drops. I bet that's the reason Dr. Wang killed her. But I don't see anything in her notes that make me think she'd it figured out—she only suspected something was going on there."

"What did she look like?" Miyoko asked.

"She was *very* beautiful—she was all foxed up the night she died. Anyway, long coal black hair. Heart-shaped face. Dark green eyes. She had a small mole on her left cheek. She was tall and slender."

Miyoko shuddered.

"I'm guessing she was just at the beginning stages of figuring things out. But her continuous stops for dinner made him suspicious." Tom shrugged. "Dr. Wang never misses an opportunity to kill a Japanese female."

Miyoko got up from the bed, walked over to the window, and peeked out. She appeared to wipe a tear from her face with her right hand.

"I'm sorry. I shouldn't have told you that," Tom said softly. "It says here in one of her last entries, she had the feeling she was being watched, but could never catch anyone. She planned to purchase a plane ticket home the next day, since she feared her cover had been blown."

Miyoko had composed herself enough to return to her place on the bed. "Tell me this Dr. Wang doesn't know anything about me?"

Tom spun around on the chair and grabbed both of her hands. "No, Miyoko. You're safe." Then he leaned over and kissed her on the forehead.

Miyoko flashed a forced smile. "Do you want me to try to get into Prince Takeda's files? I've been reluctant. My father tells me I absolutely shouldn't try—that Takeda is smart enough to have ways to figure out if I did anything suspicious."

"I believe your father. Takeda has never made any mistakes. It has taken me years to learn what little I have, and most of it comes from your father, who knows the man well. I think you should stop looking for anything. I'm on the verge of cracking this spy network wide open." Tom licked his lips then leaned back in the chair. "Instead, I'd like to focus on General Nakajima Kesago and General Matsui Iwama. Dr. Wang wrote about those two generals. See if they wrote anything about their mission in NanJing."

Miyoko leaned forward, grabbed Tom's hand and gave it a squeeze. "Okay."

"Knowing what I know now, this was the biggest reason I came here to tell you, face to face, to just sit tight. I believe the Yakuza hired Nakamura to spy—although I'm sure the Japanese government knew and likely blessed it. I can't tell for sure from her black book whether she was sent to spy on the U.S. or to work on the same Chinese spy network as me."

Tom reached for her other hand and returned the squeeze with both hands. "I wish I could take you out to dinner and spend some time with you."

Miyoko smiled, then leaned forward and hugged Tom. Tom returned the embrace.

Miyoko leaned toward him, her lips near his own. His heart pounding, Tom met her lips. They kissed passionately.

"I think I'm in love with you," Tom whispered.

Miyoko pulled him back into the embrace and kissed him again.

Wednesday September 3, 1980
San Francisco

Tom sat at the kitchen table in his apartment, still going over in his head the notes from Nakamura. The more he thought, the more he was convinced she was expecting Dr. Wang. She opened the door to her penthouse and let him and his henchmen in. No evidence of a struggle. So, she didn't know who Dr. Wang was? That hardly seemed right. If she were a good spy, wouldn't she know who he was? Or did he make his appointment under an alias? Or use his real name? But there was no note of his real name in the book. Had that page been removed?

The other information in the back of the book was more damning, as far as Tom was concerned. Miss Nakamura was attempting to gather information on what the United States was doing with the Japanese gold recovered in the Philippines during World War II. But why were the Japanese spying on the United States? Why had she set up her base in San Francisco if she was investigating the gold? He closed his eyes. All Tom could think of was the San Francisco Mint and the Federal Reserve Bank.

Both H. H. Kung and T. V. Soong had come into the United States—with their assets—through San Francisco. Were Asians with money and assets entering the country here?

He glanced again at the copied photograph. There was no mention of Jared Samuel, the doorman. It would seem that he certainly wasn't killed because of any relationship with Nakamura. So why was he taken out? Was he the doorman on duty when Dr. Wang entered the building? That would make sense, since Dr. Wang killed just about everyone he came in contact with when he was there in 1963. Still, who killed him? Dr. Wang was already out of the United States when the doorman was killed. Was it the Chinaman who committed suicide just before I questioned him? He was too old and too small. But did he order it? Tom was convinced this man was the point man for the Chinese spy network, but, that, too, was only a hunch.

He sat back up in his chair. His next move was to get this evidence to the FBI internal investigators investigating himself and Adler.

Next Morning

Tom picked up the phone and called the FBI internal investigator, George Rodriquez, to tell him what he had and wanted to put in his hands. The investigator agreed to grab the next available flight out of Los Angeles and meet at FBI headquarters downtown late in the afternoon, where he could sit down with Adler and go over all his information. Tom wasn't quite sure what to expect. The odds were against him. Not only was he opposed by the Washington, DC, FBI power, but the State Department and President Carter.

As Tom walked up to the FBI headquarters, he saw Detective Lee standing outside the main entrance. *How did he know?* He continued walking.

Lee stepped into his path, preventing him from entering. "Where did you get the photos of the black book, Warren?"

Tom tried to step around him to avoid a confrontation, but Lee stepped in front of him again. "This was an FBI investigation, Detective Lee. It is none of your business where I got it. The facts are, I did. The SFPD botched everything about that investigation. Remember, asshole, you were calling Nakamura a hooker, and she was anything but. Now, get out of my way before I put you out of my way."

Lee stepped in front of him one more time. "Are you going to assault an officer? I'd love to lock you up for assault."

Tom bit his lower lip and got himself under control. "Lee, you are impeding an FBI investigation. That's a federal offense. You want to get all legal with me? Let's go and see who wins. Now, get out of my way."

Lee purposely bumped Tom as he stepped aside and allowed him to enter the FBI headquarters. *How did Lee know I had a copy of the black book?*

Despite knowing he was no longer an employee of the Bureau, it didn't feel right having to sign in and put on a visitor's badge. Tom had made a copy of each of the photos and put them in his safety deposit box. He doubted he'd ever get the originals back, which would most likely be destroyed.

He walked into the office and winked at Marty, who gave him a thumbs up. Through it all, Marty had remained loyal.

Tom walked into the glassed-in conference room next to Adler's office. FBI Special Investigator George Rodriguez from Los Angeles sat beside Gerald Adler, speaking in low voices. He stopped when Tom walked in.

Tom sat down as far away from the two FBI agents as possible, then put the file under his hands. "The first thing I want to say, neither Adler nor Director Webster told me *not* to go to the Stanford hospital. So, I've been dismissed without any orders of what *not* to do."

Adler frowned at the Rodriquez. "Here we go. Warren has nothing."

Tom picked up the file and slung it across the conference table. "Read it and weep, Adler, you sell-out."

Rodriguez reached in front of Adler and picked up the file. He read each page out loud before passing each photo to Adler. Tom attempted to read the expressions on each man's face as the contents of the black book was read. This process went on for thirty minutes. Once it was finished, Rodriguez laid the folder down and looked at Tom. "How do you get out of this that Adler was giving away FBI secrets? I didn't read a single thing."

Tom had anticipated this question and was ready. "As I told Adler when I acquired this information, I distinctly remember the first day of the investigation. He was more concerned about the whereabouts of the black book than anything. If Kikue Nakamura was spying on the United States, she'd be in the position to learn much by pillow talk with Adler. You see, most everything hits the port of entry here in San Francisco before going to New York or Fort Knox. Besides cheating on his wife, he could have been providing key information regarding the FBI's role. Moreover, when T. V. Soong and H. H. Kung's assets were brought into the United States, they came in through here. Do you know who was responsible for assisting them? You guessed it. Adler. Check the files. If she were spying on the Chinese, keeping tabs on Soong and Kung would be part of her assignment. Plus, I'll state again, the U.S.—"

Adler jumped up. "That's just not true. Everything you say is conjecture and innuendo."

Pulling the file back in front of him, Tom calmly stated, "I'm not finished. If I'm getting railroaded here, I'm at least getting in my last say. There are two phone numbers in the back of the black book. One is for Citibank in New York City and the other the Department of Treasury in Washington DC. The woman had phone numbers for the places the gold and treasures were being taken once on U.S. soil. She'd only been in the country for two years when Dr. Wang killed her. Was she tipped off where to start looking? You have to decide. And, Adler, I'm not even saying you did it knowingly. You might not have been smart enough to know you were being played after being satisfied."

"You son-of-a-bitch! I'm goin' to kick your ass right here."

Tom didn't flinch.

Rodriguez got up and pushed Adler back into his seat. "No one is kicking anybody's ass on my watch."

Tom continued, "I believe Nakamura's first role was to spy on the U.S., not China. She was working for the Yakuza and indirectly with the Japanese government. They wanted to find from which sites the gold buried in the Philippines had recovered from. I believe the Yakuza knew about the Japanese treasure maps and wished to find out what had been recovered versus what had been claimed and not recovered. Having the maps would make their operations more successful. Why do I say that? Because during my time in the Philippines, I had a close encounter with Yoshio recovering gold at a burial site, and his men killed one of my partners. Yoshio is one of the top leaders of the Yakuza and a member of the original team that buried the gold. Also, it says right here." Tom pointed at a photo of the page from the black book. "While you were lying in bed with Nakamura, you mentioned I was being transferred to the San Fran Bureau. Then she started getting information about my research on the Chinese spy network, particularly, which Chinese restaurants the FBI was focused on. She started going into those restaurants, got exposed and that is what got her killed."

Tom leaned back in his chair. "One last thing. Let me remind both of you that the State Department and President Carter granted Liao, whose code name is Dr. Wang—the top Chinese spy handler—diplomatic immunity to be in this country. The Chinese government duped our government—and they bought it."

"Okay, you're finished. You have made your points." FBI Special Agent Rodriguez waved at Tom and looked at Adler. "Your turn."

"Everything he said about me was his wild imagination at work to get re-instated. That's all I got." Adler was still red-faced.

"But you did have sex with Ms. Nakamura multiple times?"

"Yes, that part is the only part that is true."

Rodriguez looked at Warren. "I'm going to recommend that you be re-instated. You and Adler will have to work out your differences. However, Adler, I'm not done with your investigation. I'm taking these photos from the black book back to LA and sending a copy to Director Webster for his review."

Tom stood up and stared at Adler. "Give me back my badge and gun."

Adler got up and slowly walked out of the room without a word.

"I sure as hell hope you know what you are doing. I don't care that you have put me in a tough position with Adler. It's going to be dicey around here. But the Japanese spy, Nakamura, certainly accumulated information awfully fast. Did Adler do it on purpose?"

Special Agent Rodriguez packed up his briefcase. He looked up at Tom and shrugged. "I'm just not sure he was smart enough to know he was being played."

Two days later
San Francisco

Tom sat at his desk working on catching back up with his workload.

Marty's desk phone rang. "Special Agent Martin Corley."

Marty wasn't saying anything—he was listening and nodding his head. Then Marty's jaw dropped, and he let out a "Holy cow!" He put his fingers up to his lips as he hung up the phone and waved for Tom to come over.

Tom slipped over by his desk.

Marty finally looked up. "You're not going to believe this. That was Detective Lee. Apparently, sometime last night, Gerald Adler drove his Ford Galaxy under the Golden Gate and committed suicide. He stuck his service revolver in his mouth and blew his brains out."

Tom slouched down in the chair beside Marty's desk.

"He left a suicide note saying he couldn't bring himself to tell his wife of his affair. He said up until the day before yesterday, he hadn't even told her he was under investigation, but since you were reinstated, he'd have to come clean with the whole story and couldn't bear to do that. His final line in the note was 'Warren, you won. See you in Hell'."

Tom just lowered his head. He'd been through many traumas in his life, but he had never had someone commit suicide because of him. What would it be like to have to face a wife about being unfaithful? He'd come to hate Adler and believed, willing or not, he was part of the leak in the FBI. But suicide?

October 1980
Beijing

Dr. Wang stepped back into his office. He was finally starting to feel better and had more energy after a long, trying week. His diplomatic trip to Tokyo to meet Prime Minister Suzuki had gone well, but had been taxing physically and mentally. Despite his personal quest and his malicious intent toward Japanese, it seemed obvious the Japanese government had no idea that Liao had an alter ego by the name of Dr. Wang. Yet, he was leading China and Japan cautiously toward better relations due in large part to his negotiations.

He sat back in his chair and closed his eyes. Besides the success of his diplomatic mission, he could now focus on what he'd learned off the record pertaining to his personal pursuit. He'd been going in and out of Japan since before World War II and had some knowledge of Prince Takeda. Thus, it was easy to bait Suzuki into providing a little more information about the Japanese Prince and his staff from his time in the Philippines. Dr. Wang knew Suzuki and his family were prominent members of the Zabatsu, the elite Japanese families who ran Japanese finances prior to and during World War II and who were very tight with the Japanese Royal Family.

He sat back in his chair and smiled as he relived in his mind his conversation with Suzuki about Takeda's role in the Olympics for nearly twenty years. He could slowly segue Suzuki to speak of World War II events in the Philippines, rather than bringing up either Japan or China. He correctly assumed Suzuki would speak more openly about the Prince's activities and personnel associated with him using that subject. As a result, he learned several names of individuals who worked around the Prince. Now, how was he going to do the research? He had to find some sources. He assumed that the Yakuza would be watching everyone associated with the Prince. He knew from Kikue Nakamura's black book that she had been working for the Yakuza—which was only acting as a front for the Japanese government; they had no official culpability. Unfortunately, Nakamura hadn't been able to uncover what the United States was doing with respect to the gold they had recovered in the Philippines.

He had good connections to the Chinese organized crime network Sun Yee On. Perhaps maybe Wu or Chang had some connections to the Sun Yee On or other Chinese Triads who may be working with the Yakuza? His plan was to find the people the Yakuza were watching around Takeda, which would lead him to who Warren got his information from. *Perhaps I can still recover my family's treasures.*

CHAPTER THIRTY-EIGHT

January 11, 1981
Hong Kong

Anthony Middleton was waiting at the airport for FBI Special Agent Martin Corley to land. The two men were going to take a tour of the city near the Overseas Chinese Affairs Office building. There had been reports of unusual activity, such as the illegal wiretapping of phone calls of some businesses. International businesses in the area claimed they believed their conversations had been recorded. MI6 had been brought in to investigate, and Middleton had requested that Corley re-join their team, since he was finally unchained from his desk.

"So you missed being around us blokes, eh, Corley?" Anthony said when he walked up to Marty at the luggage carousel.

"Yeah, in a strange sort of way," Marty said. "But this may very well be my last trip to Hong Kong. With the death of Adler, I've been temporarily placed in charge of the San Francisco Bureau. Soon, it should be permanent."

Anthony opened both hands as he stood beside him. "That is marvelous, right."

"Well, Lord knows, I've seen about everything hanging out with Warren. The orthodox and the unorthodox." Marty hoisted his bag from the carousel, then started toward the door.

"The first time I met Warren, several members of his team were wearing Hawaiian shirts." The MI6 agent chuckled as they walked.

Marty smiled as he continued through the door to the waiting car.

As soon as they were in the car, Anthony grew serious. "We are going to head over by the Overseas Chinese Affairs building. We believe they are jamming or illegally tapping phone signals. Are you aware of any technology they may have stolen from the U.S. that would allow them to carry out such activity?"

Marty shrugged.

"Pity. They have been harassing Hong Kong businesses—and some Chinese citizens around their building, as well. We've had a couple come into our office and tell us the Communists have asked them to spy on their workplace." Anthony hesitated briefly. "They have definitely upped their quest for spies in Hong Kong."

"Do you all have a stake-out set up where your phones can be affected? That would be a great test to collect the data," Marty suggested.

"As soon as I drop you off at your girlfriend's apartment, that's where I was headed, right."

"No, take me to my apartment. Besides, things haven't been that good with Shou and me since we rescued her," Marty mumbled as he looked out the side window. "Something changed. Maybe I was laid up in the States for too long. Get me the address where I can find you. As soon as I freshen up, I'll be over."

"Righto."

"If you wait for me at the stake out, we can talk further. Tomorrow, I want to go over to the phone company. They must have someone working on the inside. We need to check it out." Marty lightly pounded the dash of Anthony's Jaguar.

Beijing

Dr. Wang opened the most anticipated envelope he'd received from Jin Wu-dai, who had promised him all his research into FBI Agent Tom Warren. He pulled his knife out of his pants pocket and carefully, meticulously, cut the top of the package, then delicately pulled out the contents. He laid it on his desk, picked up his glasses, leaned back, and started reading the report:

> I'm sorry it took me so long to get you this research before I retired, so let me explain. While researching FBI Special Agent Warren, I was unable to find any communication with anyone in Japan. Next, I went into old CIA records looking for anything I could find on Prince Takeda. Again, this turned up very little. I found a few names from his Golden Lily team. Yes, the CIA spies on Japan, just like Nakamura spied on the U.S.

Dr. Wang snarled. *Edward Lansdale or that Priest must've destroyed all the CIA records from the Philippines. I knew what I saw and heard from the Huks while I was there. I know Kodama Yoshio, who has always been tight with the Yamaguchi-gumi, the biggest Yakuza organization in Japan, was recovering gold for someone there in the 1940s when I was there.*

He continued reading:

> Then I went into Japanese employment records for people working with Prince Takeda at the Olympic Committee. I found only one name that also showed up on the Golden Lily team of Takeda. It was a female by the name of Hada Miyoko, who'd been with him since 1964, but no other information could be found.

So a female who works in Prince Takeda's office has the same name as a soldier who served Prince Takeda in the Philippines during World War II. Hada was a common Japanese name, but this seemed to be more than a coincidence.

It was time to set another trap—and this time he wouldn't fail. His problem was all his sources in the Sun Yee On had come up empty on who the Yakuza was watching around Takeda. But now at least he had a name.

Virginia

Tom entered the CIA headquarters. He wanted to meet Larry Wu-tai Chin face to face one last time before he retired. He and Larry had developed a rapport over the years, despite Tom's hatred for the CIA—mostly due to Edward Lansdale, God rest his soul—and his time in the Philippines. Tom had relied on Larry to provide him with stolen Chinese documents that the CIA had intercepted regarding his on-going pursuit of Dr. Wang. Sadly, it was rare this information had ever paid any large dividends. His Chinese adversary was still running the most successful spy ring out of China, causing havoc in the United States.

Larry came into the reception area to meet Tom, who stood near the large CIA logo in the floor looking at the stars on the wall representing CIA operatives who had died in service to the country. No names—just stars to protect their identity. Fitting. Tom spun around to greet Larry. "I wanted to catch up with you before you retired."

"I'm not done. The Agency has asked me to stay on as a consultant. After they decided to give me the Distinguished Service Medal, I decided it might be too good of an offer to turn down. But I can still go to Vegas and play." Larry laughed.

"Boy, that sure is good news." Tom stuck his chin out. "I feel I'm finally closing in on my adversary, Dr. Wang, and may need your help. Now that I know his real name."

"I'm due into another meeting here—" Larry looked down at his watch. "In another fifteen minutes. Can you just give me the name, and I'll get back to you?"

Tom nodded as he passed him the piece of paper with Dr. Wang's real name on it.

On the drive back to the airport for his next leg of his trip—to visit his parents in Boston—Tom thought about all the success the San Francisco Bureau was now having taking down the Chinese spy ring. In the last few months, they had closed in on three big Chinese operators—one was a rocket scientist, another worked at Lawrence Livermore, and the last was a Chinese woman who was supposedly an informant for the FBI who now seemed anything but. Tom was proud to be a part of the success of this operation. Despite his on-going fighting with his deceased boss, Adler, his death ruled a suicide, something didn't feel right, but he couldn't put his finger on it. Just a hunch. While he hadn't spent any time studying his case, there was just something in the back of his mind that hauntingly reminded him of the Jared Samuel suicide.

October 1981
Beijing

Yu Qiangsheng waited patiently on a bench inside the train station. He was staking out journalist Tiziano Terzani, who had been assigned to the Guoanbu. It felt similar to his initial operation against Bernard Boursicot. Two agents were assisting him. The first was to watch Terzani when he was in Tibet. The second agent was to follow the journalist once he boarded the train, all the way back to Beijing. Yu had given this agent strict orders to make sure he didn't get off the train in any other town or area. He was not to approach—just make sure he went straight back to Beijing.

Yu had agents under him before assigned to the journalist, but when he returned to China, Yu took over as lead agent due to his concern that Terzani returned to write more articles for *Der Spiegel*, which would bring more attention to the internal strife going on in China at the moment.

Since Deng Xiaoping had taken over for Mao, he was trying to change the country while still keeping the people under tight communist control.

While he waited for the train, Yu sat on the bench reviewing Terzani's file. Then Yu realized his conundrum—Terzani was writing things Yu thought himself. But China had to change from within, without foreign assistance.

Previously, when Terzani was in the country in the spring, he'd tried to mingle among the people, seeking interviews, pushing the limitations allowed foreign journalists. When he returned to *Der Spiegel* headquarters in Germany, he'd written an editorial on the Gang of Four trial, still fresh in the minds of the Chinese. While the article was withheld from the Chinese people, it circulated to the Western World and generated negative publicity, which was not good for his country. Due to his article on that trial, just completed at the end of last year, he'd become the top journalist to watch. His article highlighted the persisting divisions that remained in the country.

Terzani had committed a grievous error of judgment in his editorial of the trial. He pronounced the role of the PRC as a reign of terror over the last decade, which included the time during which Deng had come to power. Also, he proclaimed that Mao Zedong was the one really on trial.

Shortly after he'd first arrived, Terzani had even taken a Chinese name, Deng Tiannuo, a most troubling development. Why would an Italian journalist choose a Chinese name—with the same surname as the chairman? A little more than a year ago, Dr. Wang's team of spies working in Europe had discovered editorials from the previous ten years of his commentary and criticism of Mao and the Chinese government. Deng Xiaoping's new open policies needed foreign investment; thus, he was willing to allow a little more latitude to foreign journalists so their governments might consider assisting the "new" China. Part and parcel to Chairman Deng and the People's Republic State Council, new regulations for foreign journalists seemed to reduce restrictions, provided the journalists only focused on Chinese society and not the government. However, no foreign journalist could question Chairman Deng's reforms to Mao's society. In reality, the Communist Party still controlled what foreign journalists and their Chinese counterparts could and couldn't write.

Yu wanted to make sure the foreign journalist maintained proper distance from Chinese citizens. It was a mistake giving this foreigner permission to travel about Beijing and the countryside. Rarely did a journalist change his approach for reporting, and Yu was determined he'd adhere to the government's restrictions.

Yu reviewed the latest authorization given to Terzani. The government now permitted him to go to the Tibetan region of China along the border. This was why he'd assigned agents throughout his trip to watch his every move. Adhere to the law—or be expelled or imprisoned.

Yu needed to score some points with the Chinese Communist Party, and cracking down on journalists was just the situation he believed would give him that opportunity. Deng was very supportive and pleased, as was Dr. Wang, of his role in watching the *Der Spiegel* journalist.

Terzani stepped off the train, carrying his suitcase and his typewriter. Yu waved at his subordinate agent to join him as he followed the foreign journalist. His agent got in step with Yu as they followed Terzani out of the train station straight toward the rickshaw line.

As they walked, his agent gave him a verbal report of Terzani's conduct in Tibet; daily he'd hop on a bicycle, then seek out interviews with the citizenry of the area. According to the first agent, Terzani was seeking information beyond his allowed scope, questioning some about the political climate. At one point as Yu and the agent walked behind Terzani, he turned and looked directly at the two of them.

Yu's subordinate agent questioned Yu. "Do you care that the journalist sees us?"

"I definitely want that journalist to know I'm watching his every move. We will see how he responds." Yu kept his steely-eyed stare focused on the journalist.

CHAPTER THIRTY-NINE

January 25, 1982
Hong Kong

Just before Dr. Wang stepped on board the private jet to take him from Hong Kong to the small airport at Fukui, Japan, he opened his briefcase to make sure he had the five engraved chopsticks. It was a sixteen-hundred-mile flight, and he was traveling under a fake passport so as to keep his identity a secret. Since he knew his every move was watched inside China, he devised a plan. He informed the Chinese Communist Party that he was going to Hong Kong to celebrate the Chinese New Year and would be gone for a couple of weeks. He'd been working hard since returning to work from his serious heart issues and wished to "recharge his battery" before resuming his official role in the government. He had to be careful not to do anything to hurt his chance of gaining more power—that was, his potential to become Vice President of Communist China.

As the plane lifted off the runway, he smiled. He had everything set up just right in the old warehouse in Guangdong—the mirrors, the lights. Now all he needed was the bait to attract the prey into his trap. Timing was everything. Tom Warren would soon be dead—after significant torture, of course.

Once in Japan, Wu and Chung were to meet him in Yamanashi, just an hour outside of Tokyo. This would be his operational base for the next two weeks. This was his last and best chance to get the answers to his family's treasures.

As soon as the plane landed, he made arrangements for a rental car, which he'd drive to Yamanashi. Before exiting, he leaned over the pilot's shoulder and spoke into his left ear. "Meet me at 12:01 on February 8 at the Toyama Airport. Wait only long enough to refuel plus one hour. If I don't show, leave with the assumption that I'm dead."

Two hours later, Dr. Wang pulled up to a small cabin on the outskirts of Yamanashi. Upon entering the small structure, he was greeted by Wu and Chung, who had been in Japan for two weeks. "Have you found the Hada family and Miyoko?"

"Yes. We have located them," Wu answered. "As you requested, we have plotted out their routines over the past two weeks, including Miyoko's."

Dr. Wang smiled as he clasped his hands behind his back and closed his eyes. "This is good."

"But the Yakuza are always close by, watching."

"It's a chance we must take. Perhaps I made a mistake seeking information from the Sun Yee On. Perhaps the Chinese gangs and the Japanese gangs are closer than I anticipated." He rubbed his chin, then began to pace.

"We can move on your command," Chung said.

Dr. Wang sat down on the couch, then drummed his fingers. "Hand me your notes. Let me study them."

Wu passed him several pieces of paper, which he immediately reviewed.

Wu and Chung sat down on the floor on opposite sides of the small room.

Dr. Wang looked up as he held one of his fingers at a place on one of the sheets. "Here is the plan. Continue to follow the Hada family for another week. Make sure they do stay mostly in their home. Then next Thursday, when Miyoko leaves to go to the grocery store, we will make our move." He closed his eyes and thought for a moment. "By Thursday, I'll tell you how we proceed from there. Too many variables now to decide."

Beijing

Yu Qiangsheng leaned against a wall on the street opposite a small restaurant. This was one of the more popular restaurants for locals celebrating the Chinese New Year. He'd stopped to watch Tiziano Terzani lock his bicycle to a tree. The journalist soon was seated at a table in the glass front window. The journalist was difficult to follow as he slowly peddled his bicycle around the town, attempting to interview people. Yu believed Terzani did so on purpose, to make tracking difficult by car without being obvious. Some of Yu's subordinates were assigned to keep tabs on the man's activities. Conversely, Yu believed the journalist knew he was never far away, yet he continued to interview locals. Almost taunting him.

Today, Terzani seemed to want to have his every move watched.

Yu continued watching the people entering and leaving the popular restaurant.

A young Chinese couple glanced in his direction as they walked into the restaurant. Within a few seconds, they were seated at the same table as Terzani. *Did they know who he was? Doubt it.* No one looked out the window at Yu as Terzani placed a tape recorder in front of them. Was Terzani openly goading him? Or was he attempting to be forthright and not hide his actions? Perhaps it was time to turn up the heat on the Italian journalist.

January 26, 1982
San Francisco

Tom hung up the phone. Retired CIA officer Larry Wu-tai Chin had called to tell him there was very little documentation floating around in China under Dr. Wang's real name—which was odd if he were being considered for the vice presidency of Communist China.

Tom went into New Special Agent-in-Charge Martin Corley's office and sat down with his old partner. "Just got off the phone chatting with CIA Larry about Dr. Wang."

"What have you been able to learn? Has CIA Larry been able to pick up any new chatter?" Marty asked.

"Since I first encountered Dr. Wang in the Philippines in the 1940s, plus in his eighty-page manifesto, he has always spoken of watching his mother and sister raped in front of him by Japanese soldiers during the Rape of NanJing. I haven't been able to determine if that is true. When I first learned his real name and went through the few records I could find, guess what I discovered?"

Marty shrugged.

"Dr. Wang, Liao, was actually born outside of Tokyo, but raised in Guangdong. So then I started to think his whole story had been made up." Tom leaned back in the chair and clasped his hands behind his head. "But the list of information Miyoko sent me from her father included some of the deaths of members from wealthy families in NanJing and the inventory of their stolen items. What I theorize, his mother had brought him and his sister to NanJing to visit their family. They happened to be in the wrong place at the wrong time. Dr. Wang's mother and father were very poor, but his relatives in NanJing were quite wealthy. So I still sorta get his frustration, being in the wrong place at the wrong time. Kinda adds to his anger issues, if I'm right."

Marty raised his eyebrows. "*Anything* you tell me about Dr. Wang, I have to believe. You know more about him than he likely does himself. What's your next move?"

"That's a good question, but let me finish the rest of the story. Dr. Wang has been going in and out of Japan under his real name, serving as a diplomat to improve relations with China—and he has been extremely successful."

"The Japanese have no idea about his alter ego?"

"Not that I can tell. But that's about to change. I'm going to see if I can get Director Webster to notify the State Department to send a formal message to the Japanese government." Tom grinned.

"Great idea." Marty stroked his chin.

"I believe he took this alter ego to be able to search for his family assets without impacting his political career. Here is the cherry on the sundae; he is being considered for vice presidency of China." Tom sat back up and pounded Corley's desk. "I believe only a few at the top of the communist party know that he's the top spy handler for China. They only know of him as a diplomat. That way, his true identity can't leak out."

Marty got up from his desk. "When are you going back to Hong Kong?"

Tom stood at the same time. "Soon, my friend. I've fallen in love with Miyoko. I'm thinking of retiring, going to meet her parents again, announce my intentions, and ask for her hand in marriage."

Marty stared at Tom. "Marriage? You're a whole lot older than she is."

Tom shrugged.

"You won't retire," Mary continued. "You bring it up, but something always happens to reel you back in."

He nodded. "I know, but this time might be different. Dr. Wang seems to be staying in China. He has a bad heart and political aspirations. I don't see him doing anything foolish to jeopardize his political career." Then he opened both hands palms up. "And culturally, the Japanese don't object to older men marrying younger women."

"So, when are you going back to Hong Kong—or Tokyo?"

Tom started walking towards his desk. "Maybe in the next couple of weeks, if the boss lets me go. I'd like to go over my findings with Middleton, face-to-face. I hear he's thinking of retiring, too."

Marty folded his arms across his chest. "He isn't, but MI6 is forcing him out. He's been in for over thirty-five years and he's in his sixties. They don't like field agents to be on the job that long. But he knows everything going on in Hong Kong, so he'll be tough to replace."

Tom picked up his football from his desk and threw a pass to Corley. "Some time you just have to know when to go."

CHAPTER FORTY

January 31, 1982
Beijing

Another boring day with too much time on his hands. Yu was trying to figure out a way to go to Hong Kong. The day had been spent shadowing Terzani until he returned to his hotel. Deng feared that these foreign journalists would cause another Tiananmen Square incident like in 1976, and the Italian journalist, who worked for German magazine, was one of those high on the list that Deng and Yu feared the most for inciting the population. Additionally, his status with Chairman Deng Xiaoping was still on the rise due to his efficient running of the Guoanbu, including tracking of one of the foreigners most concerning to his country for his reporting and writings.

On his way home, he checked in with the agent assigned to shadow the second-most troublesome journalist on their watch list, John Fraser of *The Globe and Mail*. Yu was disgruntled with the goings on inside his country, yet preventing foreigners from having an influence gave him a sense of purpose. Change must come from within China, not led by outsiders.

Despite his feelings, he found himself in constant conflict with the Ministry of Public Security, considering them nothing more than common policemen interfering in his investigations—more specifically, that of Terzani. Also, since he'd distanced himself from Dr. Wang, he could no longer consider him a confidant or an ally. Because of Dr. Wang's health issues, it seemed he was more focused on his political desires. Therefore, Dr. Wang was becoming more and more loyal only to Deng to serve those political aspirations.

The disgruntled Yu looked at his watch. He stopped at a payphone and dialed FBI Special Agent Tom Warren. He hoped that Warren would be home to pick up the phone. He paused for a second before he dialed. He was seeking help from a man he'd been complicit in providing misinformation to every time he passed the envelope between Dr. Wang and Bernard Boursicot. Nevertheless, he needed Warren. That was all that mattered at this particular moment.

He punched in Warren's home phone number. No answer. He left a message, "I'll be in Hong Kong on February 7 at the end of the Chinese New Year. It's urgent. Come and meet me. It's imperative we meet now. It will be worth your time."

After hanging up the phone, Yu realized how lonely and unhappy he'd become. He started back toward his empty residence. He couldn't even go visit with his family, as all they wanted to talk about was politics and their own careers. *Perhaps I should go into Hong Kong early and try to find Shou.*

Ashigarakami outside Tokyo
Saturday evening, February 6, 1982

Dr. Wang's car pulled to a stop half a block up the street and parked. He observed Hada Miyoko pull into the driveway of her family residence. Her mother and father were in the backseat. It was a cold winter night in Tokyo—maybe cold enough that once back in their residence, they—including their daughter—wouldn't come back out for the evening. He leaned forward over the front seat. "Perhaps this is an opportunity to strike tonight. Let us sit and watch for a time. So as not to be so obvious, Chung, you get out and watch. We'll be back about an hour after dark."

As soon as Chung was out of the car, Dr. Wang pointed ahead for Wu to drive off. "Take me back to our hideout so we can get our devices. Today may be the day I get answers."

It was a little past six-thirty local time when Dr. Wang's car pulled up to the same place they had dropped off Chung several hours before and parked. He sat quietly, attempting to control his excitement while focusing his mind.

Within fifteen minutes, Chung shivered as he re-joined them in the car. "No activity in the house. No one in or out, boss."

Dr. Wang nodded, then leaned back and forth looking at the Hada residence. "Pull ahead. I want to see something."

As Wu pulled forward, an alley behind the house became visible. Dr. Wang tapped on the side window glass. "Let's see if we can get in that alley."

Wu nodded and drove down the block and turned, then crept down the next street until he saw the little lane, which went behind two houses, including the Hada residence.

Dr. Wang barked, "Back down the lane. Chung, get out and direct him. We want to be able to drive straight out. I don't want any problem with the Yakuza, but if it comes, we must be prepared."

Chung jumped out and, without a word, used hand signals to guide him down the alley. When they stopped moving, Dr. Wang sprung from the backseat, his briefcase in hand. He waved at his two henchmen, who knew exactly what to do. They quietly opened the trunk and took out the items needed. Each of them glanced around, then walked toward the back of the house.

Once at the back door, they stopped and peered in. It was dark. Dr. Wang put his ear up to the wooden door and listened. *No sounds.* Then he nodded at

Chung, who laid down the battery and the cables. He grabbed the doorknob and turned it slowly, but the door didn't open.

Chung pulled out two slender pieces of metal and started to work on the lock. After ten seconds, he wiggled the doorknob again, and the door opened. Dr. Wang pointed down at the items on the ground, then shook his head. Wu put down the big duffle bag he was carrying.

The three men slipped inside the door, then quietly closed it behind them. Again, Dr. Wang put his left index finger up to his mouth. Each man paused and listened. He motioned the men to move into the house, but in different directions. He sat his briefcase in the center of the kitchen table.

They crept silently through the downstairs, room by room. Wu went down a narrow hallway, while Chung entered the living room. Wu stepped back and motioned them down the short, narrow hallway. Dr. Wang pointed at two different doors. Wu put his ear up to one, then held up a hand, thumb up. He looked at Chung, who did the same thing at the second door.

Dr. Wang held up three fingers, then two, then one. Wu and Chung broke through the doors.

In the bedroom Chung entered, there was a large commotion, while in the one Wu entered, there was none.

Within thirty seconds, Chung emerged with a gun held to an old man's head while carrying the old woman. From the other bedroom, Wu pushed Miyoko from the room while holding her right hand behind her back in an arm bar while pressing her other arm into her side. Dr. Wang pointed at Wu, who pulled back her hair so she'd have to look at Dr. Wang. He then pointed at Chung, who carried the mother over his shoulder with the gun pointed at her father.

"Miyoko, you will stop struggling, now?" Dr. Wang asked quietly.

"Who are you?" Miyoko asked.

"I . . . am . . . Dr. Wang." He tilted his head slightly. "I'm sure you know who I am."

She closed her eyes and nodded as a tear dripped from the corner of her eye.

"Take them to the kitchen." Dr. Wang pointed at Chung. After they were all secured, he stepped outside, picked up the duffle bag, and returned. He handed a rope to Wu to tie up Miyoko. Once he finished, Wu picked up two more ropes, and he and Chung tied Miyoko's parents to kitchen chairs.

Chung turned. "What's next, boss?"

"Get the battery and the cables." He turned to Wu. "Stand guard out front, but make sure you can't be seen from the street. Watch for any signs of the Yakuza."

As the two henchmen hustled to complete their orders, Dr. Wang calmly walked around the small kitchen, pausing for a few seconds behind each of the restrained individuals. Finally, he stopped behind Hada Raden, leaned over, and whispered in his left ear, "Let's have a discussion about my family's treasures from NanJing that you and Prince Takeda are aware of."

Raden closed his eyes tight. "I'll tell you what you want, but please just let my wife and daughter go. We'll not say a word."

"I've been searching for years for information regarding my family's stolen treasures. When I was in the Philippines looking for my family's stolen treasure, I didn't have the name Prince Takeda. I only knew of a Japanese diplomat by the name of Kimsu—but then I learned they were one and the same." Dr. Wang paced back and forth in the small kitchen with his hands folded behind his back. ""Then my . . . associate . . . in the U.S. discovered a list of those assigned to Prince Takeda, there was the name Hada, in NanJing, in the Philippines."

Raden squirmed in the chair, but it only made the ropes tighter around his neck.

Dr. Wang stepped over and grabbed Miyoko's chin. "Then I was able to discover that your daughter here, this beautiful young lady, has worked for

Prince Takeda at the Japanese Olympic Committee since she was in her late teens. Therefore, you must be the Hada that served under Prince Takeda."

Raden squirmed harder in his chair.

Dr. Wang pointed at Chung, who stepped over and punched him hard in the stomach, causing Raden to bend over as far as the ropes allowed.

"So my research *is correct*?" Dr. Wang started to pace again. "What was taken from the Liao residence in NanJing in 1937?"

Raden spoke through drool. "I wasn't at that home. I was a supply clerk at the time. I don't remember, I—"

"We have ways to assist you with your memory." Dr. Wang nodded at Chung.

Chung walked over to the bag that Dr. Wang had brought and pulled out a pair of pliers. He walked over to Raden and placed them on the end of his right index fingernail and jerked it out.

Raden screamed in agony as his head fell forward and drool dripped from his lower lip. By now, both Emica and Miyoko were sobbing.

Dr. Wang stepped behind the old man, whose hand dripped blood on the linoleum floor. He leaned down to his right ear. "Now, let's try again."

Raden slowly raised his head. "I only remember a few items from a list I've recently seen. I wasn't at that residence. I wasn't at that residence. I was in the military then, not assigned to Prince Takeda. Honestly, I was a supply clerk working far from there."

Dr. Wang moved slowly around the old man, then leaned down in his face. "Then you were there serving under General Nakajima Kesago and General Matsui Iwama."

Raden nodded, struggling to hold up his head. "Please do what you will to me, but please let my wife and daughter go."

With that comment, Dr. Wang nodded at Chung, who walked over to Emica and kissed her on the lips.

Miyoko closed her eyes. "*Leave my mother alone*," she pleaded quietly.

Dr. Wang stepped in front of Miyoko and grasped his hands behind his back. "My dear, I'll not harm a hair on your head—just yet, that is. You will be leaving with me, though, as we have a date with a certain FBI Special Agent. Thomas Payne Warren. But unless you get your father to answer my questions. Well—"

"No. I'll not go anywhere with you."

He pointed at Chung. "Gag her. We don't want the neighbors to hear her screams."

Emica rocked back and forth.

Dr. Wang stepped behind Raden. "What can you tell me about General Nakajima Kesago and General Matsui Iwama? What were their orders to the soldiers?"

"I don't know. I was assigned to inventory the items taken by the Japanese soldiers before they were taken back to Shanghai. The only orders I was aware came after the soldiers started showing up with valuables. We were told not to enter certain houses and businesses—doing so was only for Prince Takeda's team. We were never told where items came from, but once the gold, art works, and other treasures came in, Prince Takeda arrived with his team to separate them and decide where they were to be sent. I remember a ring—it had a very large emerald and was surrounded by diamond-encrusted gold curls. The ring was attached to an emerald wrist bracelet by a thin strand of diamonds set in gold. The items were set aside, and Prince Takeda came in and divided them—what was to go to Emperor Hirohito and what was to go to him."

Dr. Wang pointed at Chung again. This time, Chung ripped Emica's robe open and ran his hands inside it.

Raden shook his head adamantly. "That's all I know. That's all I know. No, wait. There was a picture that is in Prince Takeda's residence here in Japan. But most of the items from that list went to the Philippines with the

Prince. I wasn't assigned to Prince Takeda until he went to the Philippines. Honestly, that is all I remember."

Dr. Wang went over to the stove and pulled off a large pot, then stepped over to the sink and started to fill it with water. Chung opened the kitchen door and brought in the battery and the jumper cables and set them down in front of Raden. Dr. Wang smiled at Raden, then dumped the water on his chest. He pointed to Chung.

Wu charged through the back door. "Boss, a car has circled past twice in the last hour. I think we need to watch the alley. Both times, they turned down the street to go past the alley. I couldn't get back here in time to see if they looked up the alley."

Dr. Wang glanced at his two henchmen. "*Damn it.* I'm not done here." He looked up in the air for a second. "Grab the girl and our tools. We'll be out-gunned if we have to take on the Yakuza. Let's move. Let's move!"

Chung undid enough of Miyoko's ropes to release her from the chair, and then retied her hands behind her back. He shoved her out the door. She kicked at him repeatedly but was unable to free herself.

Wu pointed with his head at the two old people. "What do we do with them?"

Dr. Wang closed his briefcase and started out the door. "Leave them. We don't have any more time."

They quickly gathered around the car. Dr. Wang whispered, "Wu, get the car started. *Let's go. Let's go.* Chung, put the girl in the backseat with me, then put the tools back in the trunk."

When Chung closed the trunk, the car bounced. Dr. Wang was still leaning over the car. He looked around and listened, then paused for a minute. He leaned back in the car, then turned toward Chung. "Torch the house. No witnesses."

When he got back in the car, Miyoko was gagged and tied up on the floor of the backseat.

Soon, Chung sprinted back to the car and slipped into the passenger seat. He turned to Dr. Wang. "It's done, boss."

Dr. Wang waved at Wu. "Back to the hideout. *Let's go.*"

The car jolted forward, spinning gravel behind it. A loud explosion sounded behind them.

Miyoko squirmed and tried to scream, then started crying.

Dr. Wang smiled as the car hit the pavement, then the tires squealed as they turned hard to the right and sped off. He glanced back to see flames coming out the kitchen window. *No witnesses.*

A little more than five minutes down the road, Dr. Wang noticed a car that had pulled in behind them a few miles back was still following. It was a situation that was making him a little nervous. "Wu, pick it up. Look at the car following us. Is that the one you kept seeing?"

The car lurched forward as Wu turned his head toward the rearview mirror and nodded.

Dr. Wang straightened his tie. "See if you can lose them. Or there will be more."

The car sped up again. Dr. Wang glanced at the speedometer. Over one-hundred-twenty kilometers per hour. He looked over his shoulder out the back window. *We must lose them. Our plane isn't coming until February 8. Can we hide out this long without detection? Were the Yakuza tipped off?*

After driving at high speeds north toward Kawagoe, Japan, the tail disappeared. Dr. Wang wasn't certain if they'd run out of gas or entered into another Yakuza gang's territory, but either way, they were free of their tail. He leaned up. "Wu, take the back roads to Yamanshi to our hideout. Then we must lay low until our flight out of this hellhole."

CHAPTER FORTY-ONE

Sunday February 7, 1982
Yamanshi, Japan

Dr. Wang looked at his watch. "Wu, drive me out to a pay phone about an hour away from here. Chung, make sure nothing happens to Miyoko while we are gone. No one outside. Got it?"

Wu started toward the door with the car keys in hand.

Chung nodded.

Dr. Wang followed Wu out the door.

He'd spent the last day questioning Miyoko regarding Prince Takeda, but he couldn't interrogate her as he normally would. She was the bait for killing Warren. Once done with the Japanese girl, he sat and revised his escape plan. While he contemplated the Yakuza discovering him, he hadn't anticipated having to run and hide from them until he headed to the airport. He'd mistakenly believed they wouldn't discover him at the Hada residence. He spent the hour thinking and planning as they drove out Japanese Route 141. When he spotted a phone booth in front of a little market along the route, he pointed. "Pull over here. Pull the car around to the side of the building."

He checked his watched, closed his eyes, and calculated. Two a.m. Tokyo time should be nine a.m. Saturday morning, San Francisco time. He opened his eyes, stepped out of the car, entered the booth, and dialed the number "0."

In Japanese, an operator answered. "May I help you?"

"Yes, I would like to make an international call to San Francisco in the United States."

"I'll connect you to an international operator."

When the international operator came on the line, Dr. Wang spoke in eloquent Japanese, "I would like to make a call to the United States for a Special Agent Corley. Here is the phone number...." He gave her the number of the FBI Bureau in San Francisco.

"FBI San Francisco, Special Agent in Charge Martin Corley."

"Ah, FBI Special Agent Martin Corley. I would like to speak with FBI Special Agent Thomas Payne Warren."

"Dr. Wang, Warren isn't here."

"Where is Warren? I want to speak to him directly. I have something of his."

"Wang, he isn't here. That's all I know. Now, you can give me the message and I'll relay it to him as soon as I talk to or see him."

"Very well, Special Agent Corley. You tell him I have his girlfriend, Hada Miyoko." Dr. Wang slammed down the receiver as hard as he could, then looked up and down the empty roadway and contemplated his next move. Again, he looked at his watch. Just twenty-two hours before he needed to be in Toyama. It was a good time to get on the road and get to or near the airport. He exited the phone booth and double-timed it back toward the car.

9:00 AM Saturday February 6, 1982
San Francisco

Martin Corley looked at the phone receiver. *Did Dr. Wang really have Miyoko? Where was Tom? Even on Saturdays, he was normally in the office before anyone—when he was in town.* He pressed down on the button on the switch hook, then dialed Tom's home phone. No answer. On the third ring, it went to his answering machine. *Strange, he didn't mention he wouldn't be in today. He's going to flip out when he hears Dr. Wang has his girlfriend.*

Then he pushed down on the switch hook again, and called the switchboard operator. "This is Corley. Where did that last phone call come from?"

"Just a moment, Agent Corley." After a few moments, the operator replied, "It came from Japan."

Without a word to the operator, he tapped the switch hook. He picked up his address book, from his time in Hong Kong working with MI6, he had Anthony Middleton's home phone. It was very early in the morning there, but this was an emergency. He dialed the number.

After the sixth ring, a groggy voice answered. "Hello."

"Anthony, this is FBI Special Agent Martin Corley calling from San Francisco."

"I recognized your voice. There must be a big problem for you to call me at this hour."

"Yes, yes, we need your help. Dr. Wang just placed a call from somewhere in Japan. He says he has kidnapped Warren's girlfriend and I can't find him. Do you—"

"Whoa, whoa, slow down. Catch your breath."

Marty paused briefly to gather himself. "Do you have a way to find out where Dr. Wang is or track him in anyway? We both know he can't stay in Japan for very long."

"I'm short on staff for a Sunday morning. Let me round up some blokes, but our only shot is if he is flying—you know, if his pilot files a flight plan. Otherwise, we have nothing." Middleton clicked his tongue. "Give me some time to pull this together, but I'm on it."

Marty hung up the phone and sat at his desk. "Tom, where the hell are you?"

Marty had tried to keep his mind busy as time passed. No word from Tom, no word from Middleton. He thought about picking up the phone to call Shou. They hadn't talked much since he'd taken his new assignment as the head of the San Francisco Bureau. Just as he was about to grab the phone and dial her number, his desk phone rang. "Special Agent in Charge Corley."

"Middleton, here. There have been lots of private flights going into Japan from Hong Kong, so we tried to match them with return flights over the next couple of days. This cut the numbers down, but still nothing conclusive. I'll send you the list." There was a pause on the line. "But one of our agents found this. Tom Warren is due to fly in here tomorrow evening and to Tokyo tomorrow."

"What?" Marty pounded his fist on the desk.

"Did you—he couldn't possibly know what was going down?" Anthony asked.

"Hell, no. I knew nothing. What the hell is going on? Can you find him?" Marty bit his lower lip.

"Wait a minute. Got something else. One of my agents just handed me a note." Anthony paused. "Give me a sec to read it."

"Go ahead." Marty studied the floor. He was still trying to process why Tom had gone to Hong Kong without telling him. Did he already know what Dr. Wang was up to? *Impossible.* He was going there for another reason. But what? *He'd mentioned he was going to ask Miyoko to marry him.*

"This might be something, might not," Middleton said. "A private flight went into Fukui, Japan, on 25 January. Guess when he's scheduled out of Hong Kong to Japan—specifically, Toyama, Japan, then back here?"

"Tonight?"

"Bly me, you guessed it," Anthony replied. "I'll have my team at the Hong Kong airport when they're due back early in the morning."

"Thanks, Anthony. I appreciate it," Marty replied. "I'm booking a flight out as soon as I hang up. Wang's got Miyoko—and we know what he thinks of young Japanese women. Warren may have found out about this somehow." Marty hung up the phone. *I've got to let Shou in on this. As soon as I book my flight.*

CHAPTER FORTY-TWO

February 7, 1982
Yamanashi, Japan

Dr. Wang and Wu walked into the hideout. Again, he checked his watch. Three-thirty a.m. "Let's move out. I want to be on the road. We need to cover as much ground as possible before daylight. That way, if anyone's following us, we can see headlights. Wu, I want to take back roads all the way to Toyama. Be ready to go in thirty minutes. Everything packed up," he barked. "Wu, Chung, wipe the place down thoroughly."

In about fifteen minutes, they started loading the car.

As Chung carried the bags out to the car, Dr. Wang commanded, "Get our guns out of the trunk and put them under the front seats."

Chung smiled as he headed out the door.

Dr. Wang stepped over to Wu. "Before you grab the girl, make sure to put the black bag in the backseat and bind her tight. When we get close of Toyama, I'll give you the signal to pull off on a side road, where we'll wait until it's dark again to finish the drive to the airport. Got it?"

Wu bowed.

Within ten minutes, they were on the road. Throughout the trip on the backroads toward Toyama, Dr. Wang continued to glance behind them at cars passing in the opposite direction on the narrow two-lane road. They continued to clip along, staying within the speed limit so as not to draw the attention of law enforcement.

When their car was just about thirty minutes outside of Toyama, Dr. Wang leaned forward and tapped Wu on the shoulder.

Wu immediately slowed down. He glanced from the map to either side of the road. Within five minutes, he turned off on a dirt road and drove far enough down it that they couldn't been seen from the hard road.

Dr. Wang looked at Miyoko. "If you promise not to try anything, I'll loosen your ropes. But if you try to escape, I'll have you bound to the point you will be miserable. I do not plan to hurt you. You are the flame for the moth."

He looked at his watch. Seven a.m. Fifteen hours until their escape flight arrived to take them back to China.

"Where are you taking me?" Miyoko asked.

Dr. Wang just stared at her.

It was pitch dark and cold outside, and eerily silent. Just a little less than two hours before their flight arrived. "Time to move out," Dr. Wang said. "Drive the speed limit and go straight to the airport."

Miyoko asked again, "Where are you taking me?"

Wu started the car, pulled back down the dirt road, and turned up the hard road leading directly to Toyama Airport on the edge of town.

Dr. Wang looked out the side window.

Traffic started picking up about twenty kilometers outside of Toyama.

Chung glanced in his side mirror.

Dr. Wang assumed he was watching to see if they were being followed. He had more concerns about the Yakuza than the police.

Once on the outskirts of the small city, Chung turned around to Dr. Wang, "Two cars have been following us for the last couple of clicks. What do you want to do?"

"Keep driving. Don't stop. When we get into town, if you run into any traffic lights, time them. Don't stop."

Chung continued to intently watch his side mirror.

Wu and Chung said almost simultaneously, "Boss, the car right behind us just flashed their headlights." Then Wu continued as he watched the road ahead. "Two cars pulled in front of us."

Dr. Wang barked, "Let's be prepared."

With that command, Chung grabbed his Czech VZ58 Automatic Assault Rifle, checked it, then picked up both his and Wu's Czech CZ75 pistols and checked them. "We're ready, boss."

"Hand me the map and a flashlight," Dr. Wang commanded.

Chung passed the two items over the seat. Dr. Wang flicked on the flashlight, holding it low over the map, then checked a few signs along the Etchu Higashi highway. One advised *airport ten km*. "Keep driving at the same pace until I tell you otherwise."

The two cars in front started to slow down as the ones following closed in. Dr. Wang stroked his chin, then cracked his neck before checking his watch. "Don't let them intimidate you. We still don't know this is Yakuza. They have made no moves yet, so neither should we. But try to maintain some space behind the car in front—give us room to go around if necessary."

Within a minute, Dr. Wang saw the sign for the turn to the airport. He checked his watch again. Just over an hour before his private plane would set down. He watched the two cars in front turn toward the airport.

"The cars behind are accelerating toward us, boss," Chung said.

Dr. Wang replied, "Wu, don't turn off. Pick up speed. Head straight into downtown. Don't stop, not even for traffic lights, but try to time them." *We'll see if they really are Yakuza.*

Once they were downtown, they approached a series of traffic lights. Dr. Wang glanced over his shoulder. "Chung, get ready to fire your automatic weapon. Wu, just before the next traffic light, slow down, get them slowed down behind us, then accelerate into a one-eighty and pass by them. Let's get a good look at them. If they know we have Miyoko, they won't fire. They will want to protect her. But we will fire on them."

They passed through the first light. The two cars behind closed in. Just before the second light, he said, "Get ready. Just before this light, execute the plan. Wu, put your window down, we want clean shots."

Just as they entered the intersection, Wu slammed on the brakes. He simultaneously threw the car into a hard left turn and spun around, smoking the tires, and started back down the same street in the opposite direction. Dr. Wang held Miyoko's shoulder so she was stuck in the side window, then said, "Wu, duck down so Chung can shoot around you."

As they passed the other car, guns were pointed at them. "Chung, hit them, hit them."

Chung let loose with his automatic weapon, peppering the first car with a hail of bullets, then the same at the second. The Yakuza returned gunfire, but Chung's Czech VZ58 Automatic weapon was too effective. It was impossible to tell what damage they had done, but the second car ran into the back of the first car. No one followed.

Dr. Wang calmly said, "Stop at the entrance to the airport."

"Yes, boss."

Within fifteen minutes, Wu slammed on the brakes just as they turned up the street leading to the airport. Dr. Wang instinctively believed there would be more Yakuza waiting up the street, blocking access to the airport.

Dr. Wang ordered, "Wu, walk up the left side of the road. Chung, walk up the right side. Secure the Jap girl's ropes. I'll drive the car. As I approach the two Yakuza cars, first, I'll slow down, then accelerate at them, which they may expect, then lastly flip the high beams. I suspect they will be ready to fire on me. You two must catch them in a crossfire. Take them all out. No witnesses."

The two henchmen jumped out of the car, each carrying their weapons, then disappeared into the darkness of the moonless night.

Dr. Wang pushed Miyoko down in the backseat, then used the front seat adjustments to wedge her in so she couldn't move. He slipped behind the steering wheel and started up the long road leading to the airport. Just as he had suspected, two Yakuza cars blocked the road.

He sat for a moment, giving his henchmen time to get up the road. Pain shot through his chest. Dr. Wang rubbed it. His repaired heart was working at its limit from the stress. He had to ignore it. With his left hand on the steering wheel and right hand on his Czech CZ75 pistol, he pushed down harder on the gas, picking up speed. *Wu and Chung better be in place—or this is the end for me.*

As he approached, eight Yakuza emerged from the cars, both in front and behind the vehicles, and fired on Dr. Wang's accelerating vehicle. He leaned down as low in the car as he could while holding the steering wheel straight and pushed the accelerator to the floor. More bullets rained down from both sides of the road—Wu and Chung had finally opened fire on the Yakuza.

In ten seconds, it was over.

Dr. Wang sat up and slammed on the brakes, sending the car sideways.

Miyoko thumped around behind the passenger seat. He hopped out of the car and shouted, "Check their tattoos and pins. *Quickly, quickly.* I want to know what faction of the Yakuza they are from."

Wu and Chung jerked jackets and shirts off the dead men. Finally, Wu shouted, "Boss, this must be their boss. He's in a suit with a Rhombus pin. They must be Yamaguchi-gumi."

Dr. Wang pointed at the two men. "Get these cars out of the way and drag the bodies into the ditches. Hurry, hurry. We must get to the airport where we can secure ourselves until our flight arrives." As he went back to his car, he noticed antifreeze leaking from the radiator. "Wu, get one of their cars. This one is shot."

His mind processed all that had happened. He opened the front door to the car and raised the seat that had imprisoned Miyoko in the backseat, and then opened the back door. "Get up."

As cars drove past them, Dr. Wang worried about another wave of attack. "Come on, come on. Let's go." He dragged Miyoko faster than her bound legs would allow her to move.

They drove up to the private section of the airport, then out onto the tarmac, waiting for their plane to get them out of Japan. He looked at his watch again. *My plane should be here within the half hour, if he's still on schedule.* "Find as dark a spot as possible to park. We must become invisible."

Dr. Wang sat in the backseat. On the exterior he was cool, but on the inside he was nervous and his chest hurt. His men had few bullets left, and there was a lot of time.

Finally, a plane coasted in on the runway. He looked at his watch—just a little behind schedule. As the plane taxied, Dr. Wang ordered, "Flash your headlights."

The plane taxied over close to the car.

Dr. Wang commanded. "Let's go, let's go!"

The pilot came down the ladder to the ground. Dr. Wang stepped up to him. "Get back in."

"I need to refuel and go to the restroom."

Dr. Wang pulled his gun and pointed it at the pilot's head. "Fly now or die here."

"But we need fuel."

Dr. Wang replied, "We'll find another airport. Now fly. Get in the air, immediately."

The pilot turned and trudged back up the steps. As the others boarded, he cranked up the engines. Dr. Wang remained behind him the whole time.

Chung closed the door, the pilot started the plane back out to the runway. Dr. Wang leaned over and looked out both sides of the plane. A car approached from the entrance. He leaned into the pilot's left ear. "Go, go! Get in the air."

As soon as he hit the far edge of the runway, the pilot pushed down on the button for the radio. He gave his tail numbers and asked for permission to take off.

Dr. Wang looked out the side windows again. The car drew near the plane. He pushed his gun to the pilot's head. "Now fly or die."

The pilot pushed the throttles forward, and the plane picked up speed down the runway with the car in pursuit. Just as the front tires lifted off the ground, a hail of bullets streamed past the plane, but nothing seemed to be hit.

"What was that all about?" the pilot asked.

"Yakuza."

Once they had leveled off at cruising altitude, Dr. Wang said, "Refuel in Fukui."

The pilot nodded but didn't say a word.

Dr. Wang spent the first hour of the flight pondering all that had happened in Japan. *Had the Yakuza been tipped off? He was aware the Hada family was always watched. Perhaps it was just that simple. But now he was questioning if he should fly back into Hong Kong. For his political career, he knew full well the Communist Party would expect him, Liao, to pass back through the Shenzhen border crossing. He knew it was what he must do, but there could be MI6 or gang members or even the FBI waiting for him at the airport.*

After taking off from the Fukui airport, Dr. Wang asked, "What is our ETA to Hong Kong?"

The pilot raised his hand, signaling five hours.

Dr. Wang closed his eyes. *I almost have to fly into Hong Kong for my political future. If I can get in before daylight, perhaps making my moves under the cover of darkness, this could still work.*

CHAPTER FORTY-THREE

7:30 p m February 7, 1982
Hong Kong

Tom's travel plans to Hong Kong via Tokyo first had been delayed by nearly continuous questioning by Director Webster, who was weighing his options regarding contacting the State Department over the allegations that Dr. Wang, the spy handler, was Liao, the Chinese diplomat. The FBI Director continued to state that Warren's assertions would clearly create a diplomatic nightmare for Communist China—but if wrong, he'd be creating a nightmare for the Free World.

Tom had to go straight to Hong Kong for his appointment with The Planesman. He booked his flight back to San Francisco through Tokyo.

Finally, after weighing his own options, Tom gave up and left for Hong Kong. He couldn't miss meeting with The Planesman, despite the fact it would get him in trouble with the Bureau—yet again.

It was just after dark and raining when the cab dropped him off on the street more than a block away, as per his usual routine to meet with The Planesman. Tom pulled his fedora down, opened his umbrella, and walked in the streets several blocks in different directions before entering the back of the hotel. He slowly trudged up the stairway. *Something had to be of the utmost importance for Yu to want to meet on such short notice. I've put my career in jeopardy for this meeting. Webster will be pissed when he finds out that I just left.* He knocked on the door.

Yu opened it and let him slip past. "You weren't followed, were you?"

"No, my usual routine. Today, I walked around in different directions covering a couple of blocks away from the hotel before coming here. Got soaked in the process. Plus, I went two floors up until my shoes were dry so that if I were followed, they would think I went in several floors above yours."

Yu pointed him toward the small desk in the room.

He maneuvered around the hotel room to the desk.

"How is Shou? I've looked up her address at the apartment complex, but I couldn't let my feelings get in the way of being caught, tortured, and killed by my government." Yu stared at the floor.

"Please tell me that's not why you brought me here." Tom decided not to tell him that Marty and Shou were no longer dating.

"No, Agent Warren. I just wanted you to know I'm feeling isolated in my own country. I've got great power, but it's becoming more and more meaningless. I'm losing faith in my country, my family and...." He reached inside his Zhongshan suit and pulled out a small envelope. "I brought you something."

Tom's shoulders dropped as he slumped over in the chair. *Why is he being so hesitant?* "Please tell me this is why you brought me here. I don't need a lecture on yours or the communists' problems."

Yu raised his hand. "No, but you must hear me out first."

Tom shook water off his fedora. "Okay, but—"

"I've got things I need to accomplish. While it benefits Communist China, it's part of my DNA to complete assignments I consider of great importance. But there's another Chinese agency, which Chairman Deng himself has created, that's interfering in my final mission in China."

Tom focused on Yu's words, *my final mission*, as he cocked his head.

He looked straight at Tom. "I want to defect. I want out, but I want out on my terms."

"Terms? What do you mean terms? Either you come out or you don't."

"I can't leave until Dr. Wang is dead. If I defect while he's still alive and his network is fully functioning, his agents will hunt me down and kill me."

"All you have to do is get me in front of Dr. Wang, and I promise you, he'll be dead."

"Let me remind you it didn't happen the last time." Yu waved the envelope in front of Tom. "What I'm about to give you will demonstrate that I want to defect, but I want to live once I'm free. Not eat a bullet. My gift will show you how powerful he is—and he is gaining more power. I'm going to help you bring down his network—if you agree to do this *my way.*"

Tom shrugged. He was trying to be cool, but he was anxious for whatever Yu had brought him. "Depends. If you want my help, this better be good."

Yu smiled as he waved the envelope. "Check this out. It is your gift."

Tom snatched the envelope from Yu's outstretched hand and began going through it. On the front page was the name *Bao Li*. It meant nothing to Tom. Then he flipped over to the next page. His face burned. There was the picture of the man he'd known for the last twenty years—Detective Deshi Lee. He looked at Yu. "*This man* is a spy for Dr. Wang?"

Yu nodded as Tom continued through the envelope, slamming pictures of the notes from the conversation between Dr. Wang and Detective Lee on the small hotel desk. The man was born in San Francisco, his father was white, and his mother was Chinese—but born in Shanghai before the fall of Nationalist China. Then two things stood out in the file—he staged the death of Jared Samuel to look like a suicide. Lee had killed Samuel before he could leave town—only because he'd seen Dr. Wang enter the building the night they murdered Kikue Nakamura. *Damn.* Then there were instructions on how to handle the two men who'd assisted the Los Alamos runner's escape. Lee was the one who killed both men with guns he planted on them. *Holy Shit.* There were more instructions, but the last entry in the file notes was 1980. Everything before Dr. Wang had come to Stanford hospital.

Tom wondered what else might have happened due to Detective Lee, but it really didn't matter. *Did he have something to do with Alder's suicide?* He had enough information on Bao Li, alias Detective Deshi Lee, to put him away for espionage.

"This envelope is mine, right?" Tom picked it up and stuffed it into the inside of his black jacket, then zipped it up before Yu answered.

Yu nodded. "I have the negatives stashed away in a secure space."

"When I get back to San Francisco, I'm going to go pick him up myself."

"No need for an investigation by your law-abiding authorities?"

Tom got the sarcasm of his remark. "Of course, there will be an investigation. You know it as well as I do—in the United States you are innocent until proven guilty. But with this, Detective Lee or Bao Li is a damn guilty spy—besides being a murderer."

Yu smiled. "Oh, of course your laws are better, your ways of handling criminals are better than ours. I'll give you a big test. Prepare yourself for this one."

Tom frowned as he sat back on the wooden desk chair.

"You claim to be such a good investigator, here is a clue—there is an Asian employee of the U.S. Government who's spying for China. And you know the man. One more clue—he once delayed a planned government flight to Hong Kong to meet his control agent." Yu crossed his arms over his chest. "You think you are so good, figure that out."

Tom closed his eyes and thought as he lowered his head, then looked back up, totally puzzled. The only thing in that clue was Dr. Wang had a P. O. Box—Box 88, in Hong Kong—where he'd pick up correspondence. But MI6 had never been able to get approval to examine the mail before it hit the box. Middleton had tried.

Yu raised his shoulders. "If you are any kind of an FBI Special Agent, you should be able to do this. Do you want me to hand you everything?"

"You make that accusation, but give me no evidence?"

Yu pointed at Tom. "Oh, that one's right under your CIA's nose. This man—"

Tom rubbed his chin. He took offense to Yu's comment. There were so many CIA operatives operating all over the world, this was going to be impossible.

Yu laughed, then continued. "Jin Wu-dai."

"*Jin Wu-dai?* Who the hell is that?" Tom shrugged at the challenge.

Yu leaned forward. "Since you obviously don't know, I'll give you his undercover name—Larry Wu-tai Chin."

Tom felt blood rush to his face. CIA Larry? "You're lying." He pounded the small desk with his fist. "The CIA just gave the man a commendation, and you expect me, just on your word, to start an investigation? You don't have any information you can share with me?"

"Do your damn job." Yu sat back on the bed and grabbed one knee.

As it all sunk in, Tom stood. "That son of a bitch! That no good—God, I've been played like a fiddle."

"You want to take down Dr. Wang? Start by taking down his network. You must weaken him—or this man is going to be Vice President. If that happens, you'll never touch him."

Tom leaned forward. "Come on, defect now. Help me take Dr. Wang and his network down."

Yu shook his head. "No, absolutely not. He has to die first. He'd hunt me down to the four corners of the world to have me killed and bring my head back as a trophy to display in Beijing."

Tom slowly composed himself. "Okay, okay, I'm fine. I'll get you out safely when you're ready. You have my word. You work with me and, if need be, I'll be your personal bodyguard."

"You'll have to do better than that. I've seen you in action." Yu half-smiled again. "But I understand what you're saying. Go start taking Dr. Wang down, start taking his network down. Everything else will crumble."

"Done." Tom got up from the small chair and stormed toward the door.

"I'll be a great asset to the West when I come out. Whenever that will be."

He opened the door, then stood outside Yu's door. He heard the door lock and the chain slide from the other side. He hurried down the hallway and stairs, but he wasn't ready to call a cab. He'd just been at the ceremony where CIA Larry received a distinguished service award. A thirty-four-year Chinese spy got a distinguished service award!

How do I even initiate this? I already have a bad reputation with the CIA.

Tom walked for almost an hour in the rainy, cool evening trying to absorb and process all that he'd been told.

3:30 a. m. February 8, 1982
Hong Kong

Anthony Middleton and his team were deployed around the private jetway at the Hong Kong airport. It was time for the waiting game. Dr. Wang, his two henchmen, and his hostage should have to enter this area once their plane was on the ground. He spoke into the small microphone on his suit coat pocket. "Team one, check in."

"This is team one. We are in position opposite each other on the taxiway."

"Team two, check in."

This is team two. We're on the walkway to the parking lot. One of us is stationed near the gate, while I'm seated on a bench on the walkway to the parking lot."

"The target should be on the ground in just over two hours."

CHAPTER FORTY-FOUR

1:25 AM February 8, 1982
Tokyo, Japan

Tom took the red-eye flight between Hong Kong and Tokyo. Before leaving San Francisco, he'd asked if Miyoko would pick him up at the airport. She'd happily agreed and said she'd pick him up before going to work. But there was no Miyoko. *Surely, she didn't think I was coming into one of the other airports. Since I was flying in from Hong Kong, she had to know it was Haneda Airport.*

As he picked up his single piece of luggage at baggage claim, he found it odd she hadn't showed. He went over to the closest pay phone and dialed her residence number. No answer. *Her parents weren't home to answer at seven a.m.? Very strange. Had they all come to the airport to greet him and were stuck in traffic?*

He walked over and sat down in the closest chair.

After waiting almost thirty minutes, he dialed the residence again. Again, nothing. He went to the airline check-in area just in case they had stopped her due to a misunderstanding. Didn't seem likely. What should he do? He decided the best thing was to take a cab to the Hada residence.

He picked up his luggage and headed down to the cab line outside the baggage claim area. The Japanese man in charge of the cab line waved Tom to step up. When Tom gave his destination, the man ceremoniously pointed at the third cab in the line, then spun around and pointed with both hands for the next cab to pull up by him. Tom was briefly entertained by his gyrations and gestures.

Tom gave the cabbie the address of the Hada residence, and the driver merged quickly into the line of cars departing the airport. It was about an hour's drive to their residence. As they turned down the street and the house came in view, he could see it had been burned. *No, no, it can't be.* Before the cab had even stopped, he leapt from the car with the command, "Wait on me!" He ran toward the firemen line investigating the burnt structure. *That son-of-a-bitch! No, no.*

He was stopped by one of the forensic scientists working for the fire department. Tom flashed his FBI badge, which didn't impress the scientist. Then Tom pushed his role hard. "I'm assigned and in charge of the FBI investigation into a Chinese spy ring. I have every reason to believe this fire was not accidental but intentional. Now, let me speak to whoever is in charge of the crime scene."

The scientist shrugged, still not impressed, but he did reply. "Wait here. I'll get him." The scientist looked back twice as he walked over to a man wearing a white hard hat and pointed at Tom. The man in the white hard hat waved him over.

He repeated his spiel about his assignment, then asked. "I have every reason to believe this was arson. How many bodies were discovered in the fire?"

The man in the white hard hat put his hands on both hips. "What makes you think there were bodies when you just showed up here a few seconds ago?"

"The house is burnt up. That is tip one. You have forensic scientists here on the scene, and the fire is cold. That is tip two. And tip three, when a house is burnt as bad as this one, an accelerant was probably used." Tom stepped closer to the man in the white hard hat. "Now, this place was either torched by the Yakuza or my Chinese spy, who's MO is *no witnesses.*" He struck a wide stance and thrust his chest out. "By the way, this Chinese man hates and kills Japanese women. Now, are you going to answer my question? *How many bodies were discovered?*"

The man in the white hard hat held up two fingers. He turned to walk away.

"Where were the bodies found?"

The man in the white hard hat turned back until he was nose-to-nose with Tom. "You can look around. I'll allow you fifteen minutes, but don't touch anything. And don't ask me anymore questions. I'm not answering anything." The man in the hard hat stormed off.

Tom moved over to the burnt structure and snooped around. *Is this Japanese investigator afraid of the Yakuza?* The remnants of two kitchen chairs sat askew. *This may be where the two individuals were murdered.* Tom squinted. *Miyoko's mother and father?* He wondered if they were shot first or just burnt alive. He methodically stepped through the burnt structure. The man in the white hard hat seemed to be keeping his eye on him. He went through the rooms—no signs of any other disturbance. He paused and attempted to visualize, but nothing was coming to him. He went back to the kitchen area. If Dr. Wang were involved, would he take Miyoko? There was no evidence regarding a third person. Perhaps she hadn't even been there.

Too many questions and not a single answer or even a wild guess.

As he got back in the cab, he realized how lost he was. He had no idea where Miyoko was, but odds were Dr. Wang wouldn't stay on Japanese soil any longer than necessary. Better reach out to MI6 in Hong Kong—and hope Middleton knew something.

On the drive back, he passed a pay phone and shouted for the cabbie to stop so he could make a call. He looked at his watch—a little before four o'clock in Hong Kong. He dialed the number.

"MI6 Hong Kong. Chapman speaking."

"Can I speak with Anthony? This is FBI Special Agent Tom Warren."

"MI6 Agent Middleton is out on location at the Hong Kong airport."

"Does this have to do with Dr. Wang?"

"Yes, as a matter of fact it does. Special Agent Warren, everybody is looking for you. Special Agent Corley spoke with Middleton yesterday morning. They couldn't find you."

"As soon as I can get a plane, I'll be there. Let everyone know."

On the remainder of the drive to Haneda International Airport, his mind raced. Too many things to process.

No sooner did the cab stop, Tom tossed some yen on the front seat, grabbed his bag, and sprinted inside toward the airline counters.

CHAPTER FORTY-FIVE

5:30 a. m. February 8, 1982
Hong Kong

The plane carrying Dr. Wang, his henchmen, and Miyoko slowly dropped out of the sky to the runway. He had a little more than an hour before daylight to get on the road and go through the Lo Wu Border Crossing at Shenzhen. As the plane taxied to the end of the runway, Dr. Wang stepped up by the pilot and waved his gun next to his right ear, then pointed with it. "See that hangar over there? That is where I want you to taxi. Is that understood?"

The pilot nodded as he tried to lean away from the gun.

Dr. Wang grabbed both seats as he walked back. "Wu and Chung, black bag Miyoko off the plane. Make sure her ropes are tight on her wrists, but give her a little room to walk, but make sure she can't get loose. Look sharp. Who knows what kind of greeting party we may find?"

As the plane taxied toward the hangar, Dr. Wang, Wu, and Chung looked out the windows, searching for MI6 agents, whether on the roof or ground. He waved his henchmen to lean in. "MI6 agents will likely close in on us sitting here, believing we are sitting ducks, but we are in control, not them. Wu and Chung, when you exit the plane, there's an agent on the rooftop on both hangars, right and left. Open fire on them to keep them down. Wu, you stay focused on the building directly in front of you. Chung, once you get off a few shots, you must turn and fire on the agent at the hangar behind us. He is likely their most dangerous. I'll put Miyoko in front of me. No one will fire near her. I'll hustle her toward the terminal. You two have to be ahead of me and take out anybody in front of us. As soon as the plane stops, be ready to follow the pilot out the door. Let him be your shields as best as you can."

The plane bumped its way to the designated parking space. The pilot shut down the engines, proclaimed they had arrived. He dropped the stairs and exited quickly. Wu and Chung had their guns and extra magazines ready as they followed close behind.

Dr. Wang watched Chung exit first, then he laid down a spray of bullets from his VZ58 assault rifle. The MI6 agent on the hangar roof disappeared. Was he hit? Then Wu went out the door as Chung leapt to the ground and fired at the opposite hangar roof. Wu pointed his gun back at the roof in front of him, then looked toward the gate. He saw the fire from an agent's handgun. He returned fire in that direction, but couldn't see the results. *Time to move.*

He grabbed his bag containing his chopsticks, stuck his gun in his pants, then jerked Miyoko up from her seat and started pushing her toward the exit. Miyoko stumbled forward, but Dr. Wang had a hold of one of her ropes to keep her from going down. He leaned over her shoulder at the steps and commanded her down each step, but stayed behind her the best that he could. It was at this moment he was reminded he was no longer as slender or fleet of foot as he once was.

When they stepped on the pavement, it was eerily quiet. Turning toward the private terminal, Dr. Wang continued to clutch Miyoko. Off to his left, he saw one of the MI6 agents on the ground. Wu had his back against the terminal, while Chung continued to peer around looking for other MI6 agents, but none appeared.

Wu entered the building, clutching his stomach. Wet stains darkened his suit.

As Dr. Wang and his hostage made it to the outside of the terminal, he believed his men had either killed the two agents on the hangar roofs or they had repositioned themselves for another attack. Chung got directly in front of them. Dr. Wang barked, "I want Middleton alive. Kill everybody else. *Go, go, go.*"

Chung nodded as he grabbed the doorhandle to the terminal. With Wu on the opposite side of the door, they charged through the door. Dr. Wang pushed Miyoko up to the exterior wall of the terminal. The gunfire inside seemed continuous. Miyoko sobbed under the black hood covering her head. Then everything went quiet. Dr. Wang dragged her behind him as he entered the private terminal. Two MI6 agents were dead, as was the employee at the desk.

Anthony Middleton was seated in a chair. Chung held his assault rifle at his head. Middleton looked old and defeated, bleeding from his wounded right shoulder during the assault on the terminal.

Dr. Wang set his bag down in front of the MI6 Agent. "Wu, get our car and bring it up to the door. Move! The Hong Kong police will be here any minute." He checked his watch. Less than five minutes had passed. The Hong Kong police response time should be about eight minutes.

"Chung, hold Miyoko and watch the door." Dr. Wang pushed Miyoko toward Chung, who lowered his assault rifle as he caught the girl. Chung was bleeding from a shot in his shoulder and one in his leg.

Then Dr. Wang pulled his gun and walked around Middleton. "MI6 Agent Anthony Middleton? Unfortunately, I don't have time for pleasantries. Where is Warren?"

"We don't know." Middleton's head was down. Blood from his shoulder dripped down the sleeve of his suit jacket.

Dr. Wang struck him across the face with his gun. "Wrong answer." He scowled. "Now, I know better than that. You do know where he is. I will give you one more chance. Where is Warren?"

"I don't know. We have tried to find him, right."

Dr. Wang pointed at Chung, who pulled his handgun and shot Middleton in the kneecap.

Miyoko jumped from the gunshot. "Chung, keep a grip on the girl."

Middleton slumped over further in the chair, now bleeding from two places. He made grunting sounds.

"Okay, where is FBI Special Agent Corley?"

"I talked to him a couple of hours ago in San Francisco."

"Wrong answer." Dr. Wang pointed at Wu, who pulled his gun and shot Middleton between the eyes, killing him instantly.

Miyoko screamed.

Chung and Wu grabbed her by either arm, then pushed her toward the car.

Dr. Wang went over to his bag and grabbed a chopstick and stuck it in Middleton's mouth. Then he jutted his lower jaw. "I know you aren't Japanese. I'm breaking tradition here, but over the decades you have caused me such trouble. You deserve this." Then he turned, picked up his bag, and started out the door toward his waiting car.

As their car drove away from the private terminal, they passed four Hong Kong police cars going in the opposite direction. Dr. Wang smiled. They had escaped his two biggest adversaries, the Yakuza and MI6 Agent Anthony Middleton. *Soon, I'll be on my turf, and I'll have Warren in my grips.*

Daylight was just breaking as they pulled up to the Lo Wu Boarder Crossing to return to Red Chinese soil.

CHAPTER FORTY-SIX

6:40 PM February 8, 1982
Hong Kong

The commercial plane taxied up to the terminal. Tom was on the side of the plane overlooking the private section of the airport. Numerous blue and red lights flashed in the vicinity of the hangars and the private terminal building. Once off the plane, he grabbed his suitcase, then hailed a cab to that side of the airport. He was met at the gate by a Hong Kong police officer. "This is a crime scene and a restricted area."

Tom flashed his FBI badge, but the police officer resisted.

A Jaguar with several MI6 officers pulled up. Tom slipped over to the car while the policeman checked their badges. Once they identified Tom, they let him in the car. He crowded into the backseat with two other men. "When Dr. Wang came in here, was there a girl with him?"

No one answered his question at first. Finally, the MI6 agent in the passenger seat turned around. "Your friend Middleton is dead, along with about five other agents and a couple of bystanders."

"Dr. Wang? That son of a bitch, Dr. Wang? Was there a Japanese girl with him?" Tom blurted out.

"We're not sure. Probably, from the evidence. Everyone at the terminal was dead. No witnesses, that we can find. We're almost certain it was him." The same agent gulped hard. "One of our agents who worked with Middleton for years said to tell you there was a chopstick with *NanJing* branded on it in his mouth."

Tom looked out the window. *God, please let Miyoko be okay.* He didn't even know if there were a god or not, but he was out of options. He needed all the help he could get. Was she alive? Was she with Dr. Wang? His stomach flipflopped. Damn you, Dr. Wang! And Middleton! Middleton was one of the good guys. He tapped his fist against his leg. As the car stopped, Tom tried to compose himself. His hands shook as he spoke. "Where's the plane they arrived on?"

"Please refrain from touching anything, but you can walk through carefully, if you wish. The crime scene is spread out all over, from the plane here to the terminal. It's a bloody mess." The MI6 agent who was driving pointed straight ahead. "Middleton was due to retire in a month. Just before he turned sixty-five."

"How long ago did this happen?" Tom gritted his teeth as he spoke in a low voice, trying to control his rage.

They got out of the car and walked toward the private terminal building. "Just before daylight, according to the tower. Their plane landed at 5:38 a.m."

Tom looked at his watch and calculated how much of a lead Dr. Wang had on him with Miyoko. *Dr. Wang has almost an hour lead on me.* He stepped cautiously around the crime scene.

Lots of blood—and some seemed to be out of the area of the marked points where the dead were found. He followed a couple of trails that went out the back door to the tarmac. One trail went into the plane. He shouted over the background noise of the tarmac to one of the MI6 investigators at the site. "Where were your officers located when the plane landed?"

The MI6 investigator walked over, presumably where he could talk. Then he pointed in opposite directions. "On the roof of each hangar."

Tom looked at the plane, the roof, and the blood trail. Somebody—or somebodies—in Dr. Wang's entourage had been hit and were wounded. He let out a deep breath. Hopefully not Miyoko.

Tom already was going to kill Dr. Wang, but this potential development only fueled his inner rage. He stomped back inside and stood behind the chair where his friend Anthony Middleton had been killed. There were drops of blood there and at the front door. This seemed to confirm at least someone Dr. Wang or the people with him had been shot. That would slow them down. They may have stopped at a hospital in Shenzhen to get patched up if they were wounded badly.

Tom walked over to one of the MI6 agents who'd given him a ride to the crime scene. "Can I get someone to take me back to your headquarters? I have to make plans to go after Dr. Wang. I need to get to your office—he'll call for me there."

The agent didn't respond. Instead, he walked over and spoke in a low voice to fairly large man, then pointed at Tom.

The man walked over and introduced himself. "MI6 Agent Pembrooke, at your service. I've been assigned to you, whatever you need."

"Please take me back to your headquarters, immediately."

Beijing

Yu Qiangsheng's phone was ringing as he walked into his office at Guoanbu to get caught up on his work. He picked it up. "Qiangsheng here."

"I need your help immediately." It was Dr. Wang. "FBI Special Agent Warren is getting ready to cross the border. He's chasing me, and both Wu and Chung are badly wounded. I need back up, and this is in your jurisdiction—foreigners on Chinese soil."

"You're in Shenzhen? How did Warren come upon you? Where were you?"

"No, Guangdong—at the prison. They are in the hospital here. How soon can you get me assistance? I came to Hong Kong to celebrate Chinese New Year. Warren was here, believe it or not."

Yu had been aware Warren was in Hong Kong. The impossible seemed possible. One thing was certain—he wasn't going to tell Dr. Wang, he'd just returned to his office. He didn't believe Dr. Wang had provided the whole story. "Let me make some calls to my agents in Shenzhen. Call me back in fifteen minutes."

Yu tapped the button, then dialed another number and ordered a team of agents to go to the Guangdong prison to assist Dr. Wang's escape. He also ordered his team to arrange for a helicopter.

In exactly fifteen minutes, the phone rang. "What have you accomplished?"

"I've arranged for a team and possibly a helicopter to evacuate you, Wu, and Chung."

"Are you coming?" Dr. Wang inquired.

"No, I can't get there in time, even if I left now." Yu wanted no part of this rescue mission.

"Your team better come through. If they do, I'll get you a major citation from the Communist Party. You'll be spoken highly of—as soon as I become Vice President. But if they don't show, you'll be held accountable."

"Understood, Dr. Wang." He hung up the phone. His life situation was very complicated. While working to complete his last mission before he defected, he had to put up a front—including helping people he no longer respected.

Tom walked into the MI6 headquarters in downtown Hong Kong. He wanted to see the body of his friend, but he had to stay focused on making sure Miyoko got back safely. After all these years, he'd finally found someone to love and someone who would love him back. His job was to try to save the living—he could pay his respects later. He believed she was safe at the moment only because of his knowledge of Dr. Wang. If he was going to kill her, it would be in Tom's presence for impact. *That wasn't going to happen.*

As soon as Tom entered M16 headquarters, he demanded to see whoever was temporarily in charge of MI6 Hong Kong with Middleton dead. A small man stepped away from his desk. "I suppose I am, since I have senior status. London is still making some decisions, as they were only notified hours ago of Middleton's passing. He was due to retire, so they said all they had to do was accelerate their plan."

"Let's step into your office."

The Englishman scowled. "Hey, Yankee, you know you're at the MI6 headquarters, right?"

"I don't have time for formalities. We have to rescue Miyoko from Dr. Wang before he ceremoniously murders her. Do you want her blood on your hands?"

"At the moment, we have a lot of blood on our hands. Just so you know who you're ordering around, I'm MI6 Agent Alston Chapman."

"Sorry," Tom said. "I'm just focused on taking down that bastard."

"We're very engaged in taking down Dr. Wang. He's brought about the death of six of our friends here, all top agents. And another is in serious condition in the hospital."

"I'm sorry for your losses. When I get back to the States, I'm going to tear up his network."

"Okay, Yank, what do you want us to provide? We can give you just about anything you want but human assets. We are too thin on agents here. Can't afford any more losses."

Just as Tom was about to speak, the desk phone rang. Chapman snatched it off the switch hook. "MI6 Hong Kong."

Chapman nodded as he listened.

"Do you want to give him the message yourself?" Chapman held out the receiver to Tom.

Tom snatched the phone, speaking before he even had the receiver up to his head. Fully expecting to be talking to Dr. Wang, he snapped, "FBI Special Agent Tom Warren, you bastard."

"Tom, it's Marty. I just picked up my bag. I'm at the Hong Kong airport. Come get me. Let's go get Miyoko back."

"Sorry, Marty, I was expecting Dr. Wang. I'll be there shortly, just working out the details with MI6."

"Who the hell answered the phone? It wasn't Anthony."

"Anthony is dead. Dr. Wang killed him." Tom elected not to tell him about the chopstick, as only he understood the true significance of that gesture.

Corley didn't speak for a moment. "I can't believe my friend—your friend—is gone. Come get me. Let's go."

"Sit tight, I'll be there." Tom hung up and looked at the Englishman.

"Okay, your former partner is in Hong Kong. So, what can we do to help you?" Chapman asked.

Tom hadn't finished formulating his plan. He needed to know what MI6 would do.

The phone rang again, but neither of them reached for the phone. Within seconds, another MI6 Agent stuck his head in the door. "Phone call for you, Chief."

"Hello, MI6 Hong Kong."

Chapman nodded as he listened.

"Mate, you want to give the message to him yourself?" Without hearing the answer, he handed the phone to Tom.

"FBI Special Agent Warren, here."

"Ah, FBI Special Agent Thomas Payne Warren, I have something you want."

"You better not hurt Miyoko. Let me speak to her." Tom's face burned. He put his hand over the receiver speaker and whispered, "Can you trace this if I keep him on the line?"

The MI6 Agent nodded and stepped out of the room.

"Sure. As a good faith gesture, you may speak with her," Dr. Wang replied.

"Tom, I'm so scared," Miyoko said in a low voice.

"Miyoko, I'm coming for you. I promise I'll rescue you. You know I love you. I'll not let anything happen to you."

MI6 Agent Alston Chapman stepped back in the room and held up four fingers. Tom interpreted that to mean if he could keep Dr. Wang on the phone for a few more minutes, they could trace the call.

Dr. Wang came back on the phone. "Special Agent Warren, come rescue your damsel in distress. Good luck finding me. I must go so you won't be able to trace my call."

Tom slammed the phone down. Chapman shook his head.

The agent stuck his head in the office. "What we got can't be right. We couldn't get an exact location, but he's somewhere outside Guangdong. It doesn't make sense."

"I know where he is." Tom's eye was twitching as he gritted his teeth. He looked at the assumed head of MI6 in Hong Kong. "Give me a team. We will stop and pick up my partner, then go into China, rescue Miyoko, and kill Dr. Wang."

Chapman stared at the FBI agent for a few seconds. "I'll remind you that I just said we don't have any agents to spare now."

Tom squared his shoulders. "Come on, Chapman. The least you can do then is get us across the border, just like two years ago. You have to act now or

Miyoko will die and have a chopstick driven in her head like Middleton. Come on, I can get Dr. Wang."

"Okay, okay. I'm thinking, I'm thinking."

"You've got to sneak us into China through the Lo Wu Border Crossing."

"*Pembroke*, get Warren out of my hair so I can think." Chapman pointed out the door.

Tom stepped into the open area and fell into a chair where he had a view of Chapman's office.

Chapman grabbed up the phone and dialed.

Tom had to figure out how he was going to handle Dr. Wang.

Within in a few minutes, Chapman emerged from his office, rubbing his chin with his left hand. "We're going to send both of you Yanks in the panel truck, just like a couple of years ago. That way, you can smuggle whatever weapons you want to take. Plus, this time, unlike last time, we have several Chinese spies who go in and out of Shenzhen regularly. Been going on for a couple of years. They will meet you at the intersection of Guangshan Highway and JingZhu Expressway and give you a car. But, as before, you will need the panel truck and our driver to get back across the border. Good luck."

Tom slipped over to their gun cabinet and pulled out four Beretta 9mm handguns and two AR 15 semi-automatic rifles. "Pembroke, you wouldn't happen to have any walkie-talkies?"

He nodded, then went to another cabinet, where he pulled out three, and then handed them to Warren.

Tom nudged Pembroke out the door, then down to the back parking lot to get to the panel truck. The same six-wheeled panel truck was waiting for them behind the MI6 headquarters—driven by the same Chinese driver as two years ago. Tom slipped into the passenger seat, and off they went. "We need to go to the airport."

They pulled up to the baggage claim area, and Tom waved at Marty, who slipped in, leaving Tom in the middle. "What the hell happened to Anthony?"

"I don't know for sure. I was at the crime scene earlier. He was sitting in a chair when he was executed. I assume Dr. Wang captured him. Damn it. I was told he was found with a chopstick in his mouth. This is the first I know of a non-Japanese getting a chopstick. But I also think that at least one of Dr. Wang's henchmen has been wounded, maybe both."

Marty replied. "What's your plan?"

"I think Dr. Wang went to the hospital at the Guangdong prison to get them patched up. My guess is he'll be waiting for us at the abandoned warehouse." Tom drummed the dashboard with his fingers.

"Up ahead we'll get in the back and Kim here will smuggle us across the border with our weapons. Then we're going to the intersection of Guangshan Highway and JingZhu Expressway, where we will meet some MI6 operatives who will take us by car the rest of the way. Kim will wait for us. Once we grab Miyoko, we'll have to make a run to get back across the border. Simple, hey?"

"Yeah, simple as hell," Marty replied.

After a few minutes of driving, Kim pulled the panel truck over and the two FBI agents got in the secret compartment. Stepping over the weapons they had placed in there, they both sat down on the floor. The truck lurched forward. Tom looked in Marty's direction. "Here we go."

"So you went to ask Miyoko to marry you?" Marty asked.

Tom jutted his jaw. "That was my intention, but Dr. Wang burned her parents up in their house after capturing Miyoko."

"Damn, this son-of-a-bitch is ruthless."

Tom just looked down at the floor of the panel truck.

After the stop and go through Hong Kong, he presumed they were on the road to the Lo Wu Boarder Crossing. Thirty minutes later, the truck slowed. Hopefully, that meant they were at the border crossing. Finally, there was a long pause. Tom leaned over toward Marty and whispered, "This seems to be taking longer than normal. Hope everything is okay."

"Mm-hmm," Marty mumbled.

"Will you be my best man in our wedding?" Tom whispered.

Marty put his finger to his lips. "Of course. Now stop talking or we'll get caught."

Finally, the truck lurched forward, and they were on their way again.

"Okay, Marty, I didn't want to say anything else, even in front of Kim. When we get to the road leading up to the warehouse and the prison, I want you to go up the road to the prison. Remember, that's how Wang escaped the last time. We want to trap him between us. No way out."

"You're planning on going in after Dr. Wang alone?"

"I'm going in the door by myself. My girl. My fight. He won't try to do anything to Miyoko until I'm there. She's the bait. Remember, this is all about him killing me. You'll enter from the loading dock. But count on one thing—I'm walking out of there with Miyoko, and his body will be dead cold on the ground. Now let me update you on some things I have learned." Tom proceeded to tell Marty about what he had learned about Detective Lee and CIA Larry.

"Where did you learn all of this?" Marty inquired.

"My source is good—it's from Nakamura's black book. I got copies."

"Where did you get it?"

Tom ignored him. "You talked to Shou?"

"You're not going to tell me, huh? Okay, I called to tell her I was coming. She doesn't want anything to do with me since I agreed to take over the San Francisco Bureau. Honestly, after her episode with Dr. Wang, things were never the same. I get it, I guess. I just feel like I wasted fifteen years of my life."

Tom looked down at his feet, not knowing what to say. *I wonder if Yu Qiangsheng has anything to do with this?*

CHAPTER FORTY-SEVEN

Guangdong

Dr. Wang charged into the room where the doctor was stitching up Wu. Chung leaned against the wall on the opposite side of the dingy room with his big fat hand on Miyoko's shoulder. "Hurry up, doctor. We need to go immediately."

The doctor gave him a quick glance. "I'm about finished, but these men are in no condition to do anything but get some rest."

Dr. Wang leaned over the doctor's right ear. "They are my bodyguards. They are sworn to protect me to their death. Now, you have your orders. Do you understand?"

"Yes, Dr. Wang. I'm just trying to tell you they have both lost a lot of blood and may not be capable of guarding you. This one here could start bleeding again with any movement. Who knows what's going on internally?"

"That's my and their decision, not yours," Dr. Wang snarled into his right ear as he leaned over the smaller doctor, pressing against him. Then he went over and jerked the despondent Miyoko off the small bench and dragged her into the hallway.

Within a few minutes, Wu and Chung came out of the doctor's office.

"Let's go, boss," Wu said. "We'll be fine."

After the short drive to the abandoned warehouse, Dr. Wang barked, "Hand me a flashlight. Follow me in with the girl."

He grabbed the extended flashlight, jumped out of the car, and ran into the large, dark building.

He slung the door open, then moved as fast as possible toward the first large mirror leaning against the far wall. He grabbed it, then took it over and stood it up. Then he ran to a second mirror and set it slightly off center but opposite the first. Finally, he moved quickly, picked up the third large mirror and set it in a third direction from the other two. He stopped only long enough to grab several deep breaths, then went over to where several large floodlights sat.

Wu came over and put his hands on the floodlight. "Boss, let us help you."

Dr. Wang sat down on the wooden chair. "Okay, yes. Set it opposite the first mirror."

Chung came over and picked up the second floodlight. "Boss, where do you want this one?"

Dr. Wang pointed opposite the second mirror.

Wu grabbed the third one and put it opposite the third mirror. "Now what, boss?"

Dr. Wang placed the chair strategically in front of the first mirror, then dragged Miyoko over and sat her down hard on that chair. "Wu, go grab those extension cords and plug in all of the floodlights." He pointed at the far corner as he checked his watch. "Hurry, Warren, will be showing up soon."

Miyoko squirmed in the chair. Dr. Wang commanded, "Chung, get over here and hold the young lady in the chair. Her position is very important."

As soon as Wu plugged in all the floodlights, Dr. Wang shouted, "Turn on the one in front of the Jap girl."

Wu did. The mirror intensified the light.

Dr. Wang started walking around the space, adjusting the mirrors and the floodlights so the image of Miyoko showed in each of the mirrors. But the lights also intensified the illumination of the area. He was proud of himself. He'd gotten the concept from a martial arts movie starring Bruce Lee.

Wu followed behind, looking at the various refractions of the light.

Dr. Wang walked to the entrance to the warehouse and looked back. "Wu, move that mirror you are standing by slightly to the left. Good."

Wu stepped over to the third mirror.

Dr. Wang slipped over to the loading dock and looked again at the refraction on the image of Miyoko. "Turn that mirror a little bit to the left…good."

Wu slowly rotated it.

Dr. Wang moved back and forth between the door and the loading dock, simulating where Tom may enter, to make sure he was creating the visual affect he sought. Then Dr. Wang stepped in front of the closest mirror, adjusted his tie, and tugged his suit coat down as he smiled. But no one could see how satisfied he was with himself. "Wu, Chung, turn off the lights. Chung, bind the girl to the chair and put the black hood on her," Dr. Wang commanded. "Then both of you meet me over there."

Chung tightened the ropes around Miyoko so she couldn't move, then walked over to Dr. Wang.

Both of his men were bleeding again. Dr. Wang pointed at the two mirrors the farthest away from the Japanese girl. "Each of you get your weapons and sit by the switch of the lights. When Warren enters the building, we will turn the lights on simultaneously. Hopefully, this will confuse and blind him at the same time. I want him shot in each knee and each shoulder so his limbs are useless. Got it? No kill shots. That is for me." He walked toward his station. "I'll be standing by the Jap girl. She is not to be hurt. Now, we listen and wait."

Each man went to his designated place.

Shenzhen

A chill ran down Tom's spine, which surely had nothing to do with his upcoming confrontation with Dr. Wang.

Cars whizzed by in both directions in and out of the intersection. No one seemed to pay attention to the two Caucasian men. *Odd.* He kept his head down as he walked up to the car the panel truck was parked behind and tapped on the glass.

It was disappointing that MI6 only provided them one car and two spies. Still, Tom worried he and Corley would stick out, being Caucasians in Red China, so he motioned the four men, including the driver of the panel truck, over to the opposite side away from the highway.

The two spies approached Tom. The taller one grinned as though they were on a field trip. "I'm Yang and he's Yin." He chuckled. "MI6 assigned us those names."

Tom scowled, then reviewed his plan with the men and the driver of the panel truck. Kim, driving the panel truck, was to leave for two hours, then return and wait for them until dawn. If they weren't back, he was to leave—no matter what.

After they loaded the weapons into the car, Tom and Marty got in the backseat and were on their way to the abandoned warehouse. The one identified as Yang drove.

They turned up the dirt road leading to the abandoned warehouse. Tom leaned into the front seat. "Let's finalize my plan. Let me out about a quarter of a mile from the old structure. Then I want one of you to get out just below the prison with one of the AR15s and a walkie-talkie. No one escapes via the prison route. Then, whichever one of you wants to stay with the car, get a handgun, drive back down to the hard road, and block it off. No one comes up that road, got it? Do you have a flashlight in this car?"

Yang replied, "I'll stay with the car."

Yen jutted his chin with a nod. Then he reached in the glovebox, pulled out a flashlight, and passed it to Tom.

Tom pounded the car door with his fist. "Marty, you take a walkie-talkie and one of the ARs. You're with me."

"Good. I'm ready."

"Let's synchronize our watches—it's two-thirty on the mark." The car stopped.

Tom glanced around at his team. "I'll be initiating my attack at exactly oh-three-oh-oh. Got it? Everyone must be in place." He grabbed the handgun and a walkie talkie, then stepped out of the car. Before he closed the door, he leaned back over and gave them a thumbs up.

Marty stepped out on the other side with a walkie talkie slung over his shoulder while holding the AR15 in the air.

The car drove off. He and Marty walked along the side of the road toward the old warehouse. "Remember two of them may be badly wounded."

When the warehouse came in sight, Tom stopped. "I'll open the front door but not enter. You'll be ready on the loading dock. I'll tell you when to enter. Got it?"

Marty nodded. "On your orders."

"In all likelihood, Dr. Wang's henchmen will be aiming at me. Take them out if you can get a clean shot. Don't hurt Miyoko, but if you can get a clean shot at Dr. Wang, take him out."

Marty nodded, then moved swiftly to the loading dock.

Tom leaned against the outside wall. He watched the second hand on his watch move around.

The walkie-talkie buzzed. "I'm in place on the loading dock."

When it was three o'clock sharp, Tom drew a deep breath and pushed open the door. It made a horrible scraping sound as the metal door dragged across the concrete floor and stuck there. He didn't enter, but stood just outside the door. Immediately, the inside lit up with blinding light. Bullets rained down on the open doorway and ricocheted off the floor. Metal door fragments hit Tom in a few different places, but nothing serious. The gunfire stopped.

"Tom, Tom, you okay?" Marty asked over the walkie-talkie.

"Good. Just a few fragments from ricocheting bullets."

"It's so bright in there, I can barely see anything," Marty came back.

"Just get inside while they are firing at me. You won't be detected. Be ready on my mark."

Tom paused, then clicked the mic again on the walkie-talkie. "Fire at the two henchmen. You got to protect me. The odds are they'll try to shoot me the minute I go through the door." Tom drew a couple of breaths. "I'll get to Dr. Wang. Ready. On my mark. Try to hit the flashes. I'm going to try to get through the door. On three—one, two, *three*."

Tom put his handgun in his pants, held his breath, then sprinted through the door. He immediately hit the ground and rolled.

Both Wu and Chung stepped around the mirrors and fired multiple rounds at him. Bullets ricocheted off the floor all around Tom as he continued to roll ahead of their firing.

Marty unloaded five rounds at the henchmen. They both dropped to the ground.

Again, the shooting stopped. It grew quiet.

"FBI Special Agent Thomas Payne Warren, step forward. I'm holding a gun at your girlfriend's head. You must show yourself or she'll die."

Tom was in a game of high stakes poker. He had to try to bluff, praying the blinding lights also affected their vision. He shouted, "I'll try. I've been hit in the leg and can barely stand on it."

"No excuses, Warren, or your girl dies."

Tom quickly assessed Dr. Wang's elaborate setup and got his bearings. He saw three images of Dr. Wang with his gun held at Miyoko's head. Tom hopped up, pulled his handgun, and fired at the three mirrors. He hit each of them.

Dr. Wang tried to grab Miyoko off the chair, but she'd been tied down so tight she came up with the chair. Tom had to fire at Dr. Wang or he'd likely kill Miyoko at any second.

Marty fired several rounds over the top of Dr. Wang, who turned and dropped the chair. It fell over with Miyoko still tied to it.

Dr. Wang fired twice in Marty's direction, then once in Tom's direction as he ran off in the opposite direction from two of FBI agents.

Several of Marty's bullets shattered one of the mirrors. Tom realized with Miyoko out of the way, he should fire at the floodlights—except for the one pointed in the direction that Dr. Wang had run. He immediately shot out two of them as he sprinted toward Miyoko.

Tom yelled, "Dr. Wang has let go of Miyoko. Shoot him! Shoot him!"

Marty fired in the direction, that Dr. Wang was running.

Tom reached Miyoko. "Cover me, cover me." He started to untie Miyoko.

Wu, still lying on the floor, opened fire at both Tom and Marty. He hit Tom in the closest arm and leg. Tom fell over and fired his handgun, hitting Wu between the eyes. Dead, finally.

Marty grabbed the remaining floodlight and adjusted it to see better in the direction Dr. Wang. "Tom, you okay?"

"I'm good. Keep searching for Dr. Wang. He can't get away."

"*I see him, I see him.*"

"Go, go." Tom finished untying Miyoko, took off her black hood, and pointed. "Run and hide in that corner. Lie flat on the ground."

She struggled at first to run, then picked up speed.

Tom stood. The pain in his arm and leg was excruciating, but he was going to kill Dr. Wang. He shot Chung in the head as he walked by his likely already-dead body, just to be sure.

Gunfire erupted again, but this time it included both the sound of the AR and of a handgun. Dr. Wang must be cornered.

Again, the handgun fired. Tom took off. *Where was the return fire from the automatic weapon?* He ran the best he could in the direction of the gunfire, toward the back door to the large building. He heard screaming—sounded like Marty—and then he heard a sound of a metal door across concrete ahead of him. He ran in the direction of the door, which opened. Someone—he could just see the silhouette—jumped out the door.

A body lay on the ground. Tom limped over to it. His former partner was down. And a chopstick was stuck in his mouth. Tom's heart raced. He felt for his pulse and put his head down on his chest. Marty was still alive, but barely. Three bullets had entered his body near his heart, another in his head, and one in his leg. "Marty, Marty."

Marty's eyes barely opened.

Tom put the AR on his shoulder, but struggled to put his arm around Marty's shoulder to get him up. He'd decided long ago he'd never lose a partner again, no matter what.

Marty's legs wouldn't hold him. "Leave me," he whispered. "I'm not going to make it. Go get Dr. Wang."

"No, damn it, *you ARE going to* make it. I'm not leaving you. Dr. Wang can't get far." Tom dragged him toward Miyoko. She was now his first priority. Dr. Wang could be circling back around to get her.

Outside, he heard exchanges of automatic gunfire. *Shit.*

When he finally got to Miyoko, she jumped up and kissed him. Tom grabbed her hand. "Come on. We've got to move. Stay behind me. We aren't out of danger just yet."

"No, let me help you with your partner." Miyoko grabbed Marty's other arm. They slowly dragged Marty outside, who was now unconscious. Tom found a bunch of shrubs and sheltered them there. "Miyoko, stay in there with Marty and hide. I'll be back for you."

Miyoko grabbed a hold of his hand. "No, you aren't leaving me again. I'm scared."

"Miyoko, you've got to keep Marty alive. I'm going to go finish off Dr. Wang. No one is safe as long as he's alive." The AR15 fell off his shoulder as he laid Marty down. Tom picked it back up and moved as fast as he could around to the back of the old warehouse in the direction of the back door. At the moment, adrenaline was overcoming his pain.

There was more gunfire in the direction of the prison. Yin must have engaged someone.

Tom moved as fast as his injured leg would let him. As he rounded the corner to the back of the warehouse, he heard more gunfire off in the distance. *I hope that's my MI6 friends—or else we are in big trouble.* When he got to the open steel door, he clicked on the flashlight to examine the floor. There was a trail of blood. He turned off the light so as not to make himself a target.

Marty must have wounded Dr. Wang, who was likely headed back to the prison. *If I can get to the road, I can move faster than Dr. Wang can through the woods. Beat him there, and I have another chance to finish him off.*

He no longer desired to capture him, as his diplomatic status would cause the FBI or MI6 just to release him back to the Communist Chinese government.

Tom stumbled, tripping over a downed tree and landing on his injured leg and arm. *Augh.* "Damn it."

He stumbled back to his feet. He took off again toward the prison. Again, gunfire sounded from the direction of the prison. After fifteen minutes, Tom approached a stopped car.

Gunfire was still being exchanged between two men behind the car with their backs to Tom and someone ahead. Yin was holding his own.

Tom focused on the backs of the two men and fired off a burst of six shots from the AR15. Both men dropped to the ground. "I've got to get to Dr. Wang before he gets to the prison," Tom said aloud.

As he ran the best he could, a shadow of a running figure appeared through the trees and brush. Tom tried to move faster. For a brief second, his mind flashed back to that day in the Philippines watching Dr. Wang run for a boat while his partners lay dead around him. He stopped and fired in the direction of the moving silhouette. It still moved. He shot until he'd emptied the AR15.

Dr. Wang dropped to the ground.

Tom pulled his handgun, then methodically, cautiously moved in that direction. *Did I hit him? Did I kill him?* He continued his cautious approach as he held his handgun ready to fire. He got within about thirty feet of where he thought Dr. Wang had been shot when he heard gunfire behind him, and two bullets barely missed him. He dropped and looked to see where the gunshots had come from, but he couldn't see anything.

Yin fired in the direction of a hill across the road overlooking the prison.

As Tom remained in the crouched position, he faced a real dilemma. Go make sure he'd killed or wounded Dr. Wang, or go help Yin. Again, several rounds passed over his head. He looked around again. Still no movement in the direction of Dr. Wang. He struggled to get as low as he could, increasing the pain in his leg. He moved toward Dr. Wang. Again, bullets landed all around him.

Yin fired repeatedly in the direction of those firing at him.

Tom stopped. Yin was not firing as frequently, so Tom assumed he was saving his ammo. He had to go help him. He turned and ran from tree to tree. The two men Yin had been firing at started down the hill, but there was no more firing from Yin's direction. *He must be out of ammo.* As the two men reached the road, Tom stopped and raised his gun. *Forty-foot shots.* He fired three times. He hit each man once, but they were still coming.

Tom was about out of ammunition, too. He advanced to the next tree and sheltered behind just as the two men were about to step into the road. He spun around the tree and squeezed off two more shots. They were down.

A car came up the road. It was Yang, who slammed on the brakes as the car came to a sliding stop. Tom barked and pointed. "Yin is over there. He hasn't returned fire for a while. I'm going over to see if Dr. Wang is dead or wounded."

Yang shouted, "Hurry, they'll have reinforcements here any minute."

Tom's arm didn't hurt too badly, but his leg was still bleeding as he moved judiciously toward the last position he'd seen Dr. Wang. The sky was starting to lighten. Sunrise was a little more than a half-hour away.

Dr. Wang was gone. Tom could see where he'd laid. There was a lot of blood on the ground, but he was gone. *Damn it.*

Yang dragged Yin. "Come on, *come on!* We have got to get out of here."

Tom moved back through the brush and trees. He moved more and more slowly. He lost his balance several times, then fell over.

Gathering himself back up, he finally got to Yin. He looked dead. Tom swallowed hard and struggled to help Yang drag Yin into the backseat. Yin had been hit with several rounds in the chest.

As soon as they were in, Yang backed down the road, increasing speed as he drove.

Just before the warehouse, Tom commanded. "We have to stop and get my girlfriend and my partner."

Yang snarled. "Hurry, Hurry. Daylight is coming. We could be attacked by the air, or forces from the prison, or anyone coming up the road. Then none of us will make it."

The two men ran as fast as Tom could go to get Marty and Miyoko from the brush cover. "What the hell happened here?" Yang cried out.

Tom didn't say a word, only struggled to maintain consciousness himself.

They got Marty up, who was going in and out of consciousness, then dragged him over to the car. Miyoko got in the front seat and Tom held Marty in the back beside Yen's lifeless body.

As a glint of sunlight hit Tom in the face, he looked at the sky and his watch. "We're not going to make it back to the panel truck."

"I'll try, but I don't see how." Yang shook his head as he stepped down on the accelerator, throwing everybody back in their seats.

Their car pitched and rolled as they sped along the empty highway as fast as possible. It still took thirty minutes to get to the rendezvous point. He slammed on the brakes as he pulled up behind the panel truck, lurching everyone forward. A quick look revealed the driver was gone.

"Let's get my partner into the hidden compartment first," Yang said. "I'll drive you back across the border."

"Won't that blow your cover?"

Yang shook his head. "Got to get you guys back to Hong Kong. Plus, I need to get my partner buried properly. That's all that matters."

"Do you have anything we can bandage Marty with?" Tom leaned over, exhausted.

Tom and Yang put Marty into the hidden compartment, then Miyoko and Yang helped Tom slip into the back. Once in there, Miyoko laid her head on Tom's shoulder and trembled.

The panel truck bumped down the road. Tom turned and faced Miyoko. "This isn't how I imagined this happening, but will you marry me?"

Tears streamed down Miyoko's face. "Yes, *yes*. Of course, I will."

Tom smiled. "Then you'll be going back to the States with me. I'll not let you out of my sight ever again."

Miyoko leaned back over on his shoulder and fell asleep.

Tom cuddled her for a minute, then leaned forward to look at his partner, who was unconscious. "Come on, Marty. You gotta make it. You're going to be my best man."

The conflicted Yu Qiangsheng dragged Dr. Wang the last few steps into the prison hospital infirmary. He looked at the doctor. "You've got to save him."

The doctor walked over. "Get me a gurney, hurry, hurry. Get him into the operating room, immediately."

As Yu helped lift him on the gurney, a black velvet bag fell on the floor. With everyone focused on Dr. Wang, Yu scooped it up and slipped it inside his Zhongshan suit.

CHAPTER FORTY-EIGHT

February 10, 1982
Hong Kong

Tom was startled awake by a nurse leaning over his bed. He had no idea where he was as he looked around the drab room. He blinked several times, trying to focus. Then he saw Miyoko in an awkward position, asleep in the chair.

He remembered coming into the hospital with his partner Marty, but that was all he could remember.

As the nurse was leaving the room, a doctor walked through the door.

They talked loud enough to wake up Miyoko. She jumped up and stood beside Tom's bed. "How do you feel, honey?"

Tom smiled for a second until his face hurt from the bullet fragment, which had been dug out and patched up. When he rolled over to hug her, a pain shot through his leg from the bullet hole in his upper calf and another in his right arm and shoulder. "I feel like I've been shot. How is Marty?"

"He's in ICU, very serious condition. That's all I know."

The doctor came over to Tom. "We're planning to discharge you this afternoon. You'll need to take it easy for a couple of weeks."

"Do you know anything about my partner, who came in with me last night?"

The doctor shook his head. "No. You'll need to re-dress those bandages on your leg tomorrow, then every other day until the wounds are healed. Watch for infections."

Before Tom could ask another question, the doctor was out of the room.

Tom lay back on the bed and beckoned Miyoko closer. "Look in the hallway and see if there's any security outside the door."

Miyoko peeked out, turned back around, and shook her head.

Tom waved her back, but before she could get to his bed or the chair, he ordered, "Grab my black jacket out of the closet."

Miyoko went to the closet and pulled out the jacket. "Are we leaving now?"

Tom snatched it out of her hand, then flipped it on the bed, and reached inside to unzip the inner pocket. He pulled out the envelope he'd received from Yu, opened it, and discreetly glanced at each page without pulling them out. Everything was still there. Then, methodically, carefully, Tom put the envelope back in his jacket pocket and zipped it back up. He still hadn't answered Miyoko. He looked at her. "Let's go up and check on Marty. He was really in bad shape when we got here."

Miyoko helped him out of bed.

Tom winched as his injured leg hit the floor.

"Are you sure you can make it?"

Without a word, Tom continued.

They arrived at the ICU desk. Tom asked, "May I see Martin Corley?"

The nurse looked at Miyoko, then at Tom, then back down and started writing again. "Family only."

"Okay, can you tell me how he is doing?"

"Family only."

CHAPTER FORTY-NINE

March 1, 1982
Beijing

Yu Qiangsheng was seated around the large conference table next to Dr. Wang. Chinese Vice Minister Hui Ping conducted the high-level meeting of all the leaders of the top Chinese Intelligence services. Yu was conflicted. He hoped because of his life-long performance in the intelligence area inside China, he'd be named as the head of the newly formed Chinese Secret Service, the Ministry of State Security. This new organization was a consolidation of several intelligence bureaus. However, his personal struggles with how his own mother and the general population had been mistreated caused his dissatisfaction to grow each day.

To prove his point, the first speaker was Wang Renzhong, the Head of the Propaganda Department. In his speech, the one comment that stood out to Yu was "There will always be espionage intrigues directed against us...." He surmised the job of the head of propaganda was to make sure the Chinese population was always told nothing but good things about the Chinese leaders, while nothing good could be said about foreign countries or their leaders. Yu respected the power that Wang Renzhong wielded in the Communist Party. He'd served in some capacity or another in Communist Propaganda since 1938. To state the obvious, the man was always extremely paranoid. For a brief time, he'd fallen out of power, but when Deng rose, he was reinstated and became the vice premier of the State Council. His friendship with Deng was strong, and his role keeping Deng in power was great. Once again, nepotism was alive and well in China.

After several other speakers, Hui Ping took to the podium. This caused Yu to refocus. The Vice Minister remarked he wanted more pressure applied to Chinese dissidents and other elements inside China, which he believed were attempting to destabilize Deng Xiaoping's regime. He made a couple of indirect references to the 1976 Tiananmen Square event that started as a celebration of Zhou En-lai's life but quickly turned into a large protest.

Yu remembered the event very well—but Hui's "facts" were different from his remembrance. The celebration of Zhou's life had been peaceful until the military and police were sent in to break it up. That was when it turned violent.

Hui Ping insisted there was still an underlying element in the Chinese population that wished for a more open government. He viewed it as his role to flush out and remove that element at all costs. Finally, he got around to his concluding remark. "So, tonight, I'm naming the man to assume—"

Yu sat up straighter in his chair, fully expecting his name to be called.

"The top position at the newly formed Ministry of State Security, starting next year, will be Ling Yun. All of the Chinese Communist Party intelligence departments will coalesce under his authority."

All in attendance clapped.

Yu tightened his fists under the table, but since he had to put on a good show, he clapped too. But he felt betrayed, for a second time, by Dr. Wang. Previously, when Dr. Wang stepped away from the Guojia Anquan Bu, he'd appointed Min Bu-ying instead of consolidating his old department with the Guoanbu, giving Yu more power. Yu was determined he was not going to let Dr. Wang deceive him again with lies and promises.

As soon as the meeting let out, Yu bolted from the conference room. He didn't want to have a conversation with anyone in attendance. He was off to take out his frustrations on Tiziano Terzani or "Deng Tiannuo," as he liked to refer to himself. The dumb son-of-a-bitch looked Italian, but he gave himself a Chinese name—while writing unfavorable articles about China.

Just as he was about to get into his vehicle, Min Bu-ying called out to him. "Yu Qiangsheng, may I speak with you for a moment?"

Yu stopped but didn't immediately turn around. "What do you want?" he snarled.

"I have a plan for taking down Tiziano Terzani that I would like to discuss with you," Min said with a brief smile.

"Terzani is of no concern to you."

"Dr. Wang told me to assist you in keeping the journalist under our surveillance. I would like for us to share notes," Min replied.

Yu didn't respond. Min was nothing more than a glorified cop with no talent for intelligence or surveillance. Yu already had his own plan to get the Italian thrown out of the country, and he didn't need anyone else interfering in his work. With Terzani, it had become personal. "I'll reach out to you. I'm late for an appointment."

March 14, 1982
San Francisco

Tom shook his head as he followed Marty into his office. From previous conversations, he knew most of Marty's pain was gone, but he'd likely have a slight limp for the rest of his life from his gunshot wound.

Immediately, Marty started shuffling papers as though looking for something. "I hate it when someone else has sat at my desk."

Tom laughed. His old partner was starting to get better.

"What does Miyoko think of San Francisco?" Marty asked as he continued to shuffle papers from the top of the desk.

"She's pretty homesick. I've had her down to Japantown a couple of times. It's helped a little." Then Tom frowned. "Late at night is when she has the toughest time. Still hasn't gotten over what happened to her parents. You know, no closure. Parents dead and can't go home. She found out from a friend that Prime Minister Suzuki was told that Miyoko had spied on Prince Takeda."

"How did she find that out? How did that happen?" Marty pulled the pencil resting on his ear and tossed it on his desk.

"She still has friends in that office. She called one of them one night when she was particularly lonely—you know, missing home and stuff. They told her. She got scared and upset."

"How do you think that story got started?" Marty leaned back in his chair.

"We can't figure it out ourselves. Yakuza? Liao? Liao's relationship with Prime Minister Suzuki? Who the hell knows?" Tom folded his arms as he stood in front of Marty's desk.

"Dr. Wang is such a bastard." Marty licked his lips. "It's still good she didn't see her parents get burnt up."

Tom nodded. "She really wants to go back to Tokyo and bury her parents, but I keep telling her, between Prince Takeda and the Yakuza, we can't take that chance. Plus, she still frets over Dr. Wang's spies."

"You know, since we took over the operation of bringing down the Chinese spies, it's taken a while, but we are finally making a dent." Marty drummed the pencil on his desk. He pushed an FBI memo toward Tom. "Here is one New York is about to wrap up. Has a familiar ring to it."

Tom grabbed it:

FBI agent out of the New York office trapped Kuang Shin Lin
attempting to steal advanced radar and electronic surveillance

technology for Red China. They also arrested his accomplice, Da Chuan Zheng.

Tom pushed it back over. "Did they get enough evidence to prosecute?"

Marty nodded. "The New York Federal Prosecutor believes so."

"It sorta reminds me of our case against Dr. Paul Yu." Tom paused as he rubbed his chin. "Well, besides the Chinese stealing the blueprints of equipment, they've upped their game by actually stealing our equipment, since they can't exactly duplicate ours."

"Da—a big-time businessman in Hong Kong—was someone Middleton always had his eye on. God, I miss Middleton. What a great guy."

All Tom could do was look down. It was hard to think about his old friend.

Marty slowly shook his head. "Director Webster believes we are finally making real progress taking down their network."

Tom refocused. "Did he give me the green light to take down Detective Lee?"

"Well, if you hadn't interrupted me, that was where I was going," Marty shot back. "Yes, you can bring Lee in to interrogate him with your evidence."

Tom got up and closed the office door. "What did he say about CIA Larry?"

Marty raised his eyebrow. "That one is touchy. Webster wants to tread lightly here. Before you start your investigation, he wants to speak to the CIA Director first. He believes Casey will be on board with it, but it must be done following proper protocol."

William Casey. Lansdale's buddy. Tom sighed deeply. He expected Casey to resist him every step of the way.

Tom went over to the closed door, grabbed the handle, then turned back to Marty. "Get the interrogation room set up. I want to administer a lie detector test on Lee. Can you set it up?"

"Do you want to take anyone with you? I'll assign you a junior agent to accompany you."

"No need. I got this." Then Tom thought about it. "Perhaps you should assign the newest agent. Someone who can drive me over there. You know how I hate to drive."

Marty limped to the door. "Agent Mendoza, you're assigned to Warren. Go get the car, meet him downstairs."

Mendoza jumped up, held up and shook some keys, then headed for the door.

Ten minutes later, Tom and Mendoza were on their way to the San Francisco Police Department. After a few minutes driving in the stop-and-go traffic, Mendoza finally asked, "What's our assignment, Special Agent Warren?"

"We're going to arrest a Chinese spy. Someone who has been operating for a long time, controlling many things in San Francisco." Tom looked out the side window trying to be calm so he wouldn't go crazy when he went into the police headquarters.

"Can you enlighten me, since I'm new here?"

"Mendoza, tell me your first name. Sorry, I don't know."

"Hector."

As they pulled up to the San Francisco Police headquarters, Tom focused on how to conduct his arrest of Detective Lee in front of his peers. He was torn. Did he want to make an example of the man? Or be very low key in his handling of the obviously delicate matter.

"What's my assignment, Special Agent Warren?"

"Watch my back. You don't need to watch me—watch everybody else in the room, if we're in the bullpen." Tom squared up his shoulders. The two FBI agents walked into police headquarters and stopped by the desk sergeant.

"Special Agent Warren, haven't seen you in a while. Assume you're here to see Detective Lee?"

Tom nodded.

"Back at his desk. You know the way."

Tom and Mendoza walked through the bullpen to Detective Lee's corner office. He rapped on the open door. He glanced back to make sure Mendoza stood directly behind him, watching the room.

"Special Agent Warren, come in. To what do I owe this pleasure?"

"Get up. I need you to come with me."

"What? Where are we going? I'm in the middle of wrapping up an investigation here."

Tom had decided to try not to create a scene, so he had one more play. "I've uncovered some evidence that pertains to several of your investigations. I'd like you to come with us to discuss it."

"Sure. How about if I follow you? That way you won't have to bring me back here." Detective Lee pursed his lips.

"No, you need to come with us, *Bao Li*," Tom insisted. "This evidence pertains to you. I don't want to make a scene, so don't force me. I think you know what I'm talking about."

Li started to open a drawer.

Tom pulled his sport coat open, exposing his gun. "Please don't reach for anything. I want to see your hands at all times."

Li twisted his shoulders but placed his hands on his desk. He slowly got up and stepped toward the door.

"Bao Li, I'm arresting you for espionage. You are an asset of Dr. Wang's spy network," Tom whispered as he leaned close to the detective.

Li stuck his chin out. "You can't prove anything."

Tom stood nose to nose with Li. "I'm only going to ask you to turn around one more time."

Li licked his lips, then slowly pivoted.

Tom put the handcuffs on him. The click of the locking of each handcuff brought a bigger satisfaction to him. He turned to see all the detectives, police officers, and secretaries in the bullpen standing up and gawking in his direction.

"You have the right to remain silent," Tom said. "Anything you say can and will be used against you in a court of law. You have a right to an attorney. If you cannot afford an attorney, one will be appointed for you."

Mendoza's face was pale, but his eyes moved from side to side, watching the room.

"Bao Li, you and I are going to walk right out of here. The Federal Bureau of Investigation wants to thank all of you for your cooperation in this matter. This man is going to be questioned for espionage." Tom announced as he pushed the detective through the room with Mendoza moving in front of them, clearing the path of the detectives and officers who had stepped around their desks.

At the FBI vehicle, Tom asked, "Mendoza, open the back door so I can put him in."

Mendoza did as told, still continuing to look around.

Once Tom shoved Lee in the backseat and closed the door, he slipped around to the other side, then got in beside him.

Mendoza started the car and they headed toward FBI headquarters. The ride was silent except for Li's request for attorney representation.

Upon returning to the FBI headquarters, Tom took Bao Li to the interrogation room and sat him down. Then he went to the file cabinet and pulled out the envelope from Yu Qiangsheng. Tom waved at Marty that he was ready to start the interrogation.

Marty walked over to Tom's desk and picked up his football. "Do you want me to go in with you?"

Tom rubbed his chin, then took his football back and slammed it on the desk. "No. Just make sure the video is running. I want your opinion. But I don't expect him to say anything. He already asked for his lawyer. If he's smart, he knows he's had."

Marty turned and walked off toward the observation area.

Tom opened the door, sat down on the opposite side of Bao Li, aka Detective Deshi Lee. "You have been arrested for espionage. You are a member of a Chinese spy network working in San Francisco. Do you wish to make a statement?"

"I want to call my lawyer and have him present for your questioning. I want my phone call *now*."

Tom smiled as he got up from the table. "I'll get an agent to take you to make your call. I got the goods on you, Lee. Your lawyer better be better than F. Lee Bailey, 'cause you are going to need it."

Lee folded his arms across his chest and stared straight ahead.

Tom left the room. He was going to get back on building a case against CIA Larry with no evidence at all from The Planesman. Tom had known all along the Chinese had infiltrated U.S. intelligence, but this was going to be a rough, complex one.

March 16, 1982
Beijing

Dr. Wang hung up the desk phone at his residence. It had been a disturbing phone call. Bao Li—Detective Deshi Lee—had been arrested by the San Francisco FBI. And that meant Special Agent Thomas P. Warren. He clenched his jaw, then curled his upper lip. He was trying to focus strictly on his political career, but his spy handling kept sucking him back into a bad mental place.

Dr. Wang was due for a meeting with members of the Chinese Communist Party. The agenda covered several things, including his vision for continuing to improve relationships with Japan and how to start a similar plan with

Taiwan. He thought about writing a letter to Chiang Ching-kao, the new president of Taiwan. He picked up the letter lying on his desk regarding his alma mater planning to give him an honorary doctorate. *I've fooled them all.* All these things were good optics for him to be appointed Vice President and working with Chairman Deng. But he had to deal with this potential problem before leaving for his meeting. Otherwise, it could damage his chances to become the Vice President.

He was going to break protocol, but it was necessary. He picked up his phone and dialed. When the voice on the other end answered, he said. "Is this the airport?"

"No, old number."

Dr. Wang had given the code to go to a pay phone and call. He sat for fifteen minutes waiting on the return call. Finally, his phone rang.

"This is Jin Wu-dai. What is the situation?"

"Bao Li has been arrested. I can't figure out how this has happened. But I wanted to put you on notice," Dr. Wang replied.

"Boss, I'm fine. Nothing unusual is going on around me. I've been keeping a very low profile—and you know how careful I am."

"Jin, you should consider going to Toronto to get out soon." Dr. Wang jutted his jaw. He was uncomfortable with Jin's *laissez-faire* attitude. He had a bad feeling. Warren had more than just information on Li—and he didn't need anyone messing up his chance to become vice president.

"Boss, I'm telling you, I'm fine. The CIA continues to send me documents to translate. Plus, I haven't heard from Warren in some time. Don't worry."

"Be aware of what is going on around you, Jin. You can't fall into the hands of the government. It would be bad for both countries. You must listen to me." Then Dr. Wang hung up the phone.

Two hours later, Liao, alias Dr. Wang, walked into the high-level Communist Party meeting. When it was his turn to speak, he stood at the podium. "If we are going to try to ultimately unify Taiwan, we must try diplomacy first. I plan to write a letter to Taiwanese President Chiang Ching-kao and propose the two countries seek common ground that could lead to reunification before we take military action. Also, I may seek the assists of one of our colleagues, Yu Qiangsheng, who also has ties to the Chiang family. I believe I can have the same success in Taiwan I've had in Japan."

As he finished the brief synopsis of his plans, all those in attendance broke into a loud boisterous response—except for Yu Qiangsheng, who clapped but didn't appear as enthusiastic. Once again, Dr. Wang had scored points with the Communist Party at his expense. All those in attendance would know he had ties to Mao and Zhou En-lai through his mother, but few if any would know of his ties to the hated Chiang Kai-chek, Chiang Ching-kao's father.

CHAPTER FIFTY

September 8, 1982
San Francisco

Tom was sitting at his desk when the FBI mailman brought in a large package and laid it on his desk. It contained seven years of Larry Wu-tai Chin's bank records. Tom had been having considerable difficulty trying to initiate an investigation into Jin Wu-dai, alias Larry Wu-tai Chin, whom he had affectionately called CIA Larry for years. After begging a judge to give him a warrant to access his bank records and getting help from the IRS, he finally had the information. He was hoping something would show up to give him some direction.

Tom picked up the package and looked at it. There was a least a week's worth of work just to organize it. He decided not to draw attention to his clandestine investigation. He walked into Marty's office. "I'm out of here for the rest of the week. Just got CIA Larry's bank records. I'm going to do what you showed me to do when we worked on the Dr. Paul Yu case. Hopefully, we won't need a forensic accountant on this one."

Marty looked up from his desk. "If you need any help, call me. I'm sick of all the administrative stuff."

"I'm good for right now."

Marty looked back down at the file on his desk and waved him off.

Tom figured he'd earned that respect from his former partner.

As he walked into his home, Tom called out to Miyoko. "Aikata, will you help me with something?"

Miyoko strolled into Tom's office, a converted bedroom with a small desk and a single, two-drawer file cabinet. "What do you need, my love?"

Tom pointed to a stack of statements. "Help me sort these by year. Oldest on the left, newest to the right. They should be in decent order."

After about an hour, all the stacks were neatly laid out on top of Tom's desk. He started through the stacks, beginning with the oldest year to the newest. For the rest of the day, he painstakingly went over all the deposit records. The government payment was easy to track, but there was a considerable amount of other income flowing into his account, but it was irregular. A little more than one hundred thousand dollars was unexplained. This might be the first clue, but not enough to bring him in.

Tom paused and looked at the piles of bank copies of statements, deposit tickets and checks. He jutted his jaw and squinted. For all the years the CIA handed Larry Wu-tai Chin top-secret documents to translate, he never seemed to have anything revolutionary. It was starting to make sense. Not only was he fed bad information from Boursicot, but also by CIA Larry—all likely through Dr. Wang.

More dull, painstaking investigating was required.

CHAPTER FIFTY-ONE

June 5, 1983
San Francisco

Tom and Miyoko sat in their living room with a Bing Crosby album playing in the background, putting the final touches to their wedding plans. They were going to fly to Boston and get married in the Park Street Church that Warren's family had attended for five generations. Tom's parents were excited their son was finally retiring and getting married.

Just as Tom sat down with his reading glasses in hand, his phone rang.

"This is The Planesman."

Tom waved at Miyoko to mute the music. "What is your purpose of this call?"

"I must talk fast. We need to meet. You must move fast. Really fast."

"You're bringing out the file I need?"

"Not now, something else has come up. Someone just was taken to the hospital with some old health issues. It occurred at their home. The government is trying to keep it quiet. Let's talk about this. See you on June 8."

"I'll be there." He looked at the receiver as the line went dead.

Miyoko tilted her head and stared at him as though waiting for an explanation.

Tom sat for a minute.

"Talk to me, honey."

Tom sighed. "I've got to go to Hong Kong."

"What are you talking about? We're supposed to be finishing our wedding plans and—and you have to go to Hong Kong?"

June 8, 1983
Hong Kong

As per his usual routine for meeting with Yu Qiangsheng, Tom had the cabbie drop him off several blocks from his hotel. Due to the lateness of the night, the sidewalks were deserted while the traffic moved at a steady pace. It was a warm summer evening in Hong Kong. He believed he could walk straight to his hotel, yet he pulled his fedora down in an attempt to shield his face.

He entered the back door and climbed the stairway up to Yu's floor. He rapped lightly on the door and was immediately greeted by Yu. "Where is Larry Wu-tai Chin's file?" Tom inquired. "I need it desperately. My investigation thus far is getting blocked by the CIA, and I've only been able to turn up circumstantial evidence."

"I told you not now. We have more important matters to discuss."

"The status of Dr. Wang?"

"He is getting better. The Communist Party is pulling out all the stops to get him well. They are desperate to name him the Vice President, mostly because of his work in improving our relationship with Japan. And now they have him working on Taiwan."

Tom frowned. "Are you going to murder him?"

"No, you are." Yu smiled, then started to say more.

Tom's jaw dropped. "How do you figure?"

"If he gets Taiwan to even talk about unification, who knows how much power he'll gain? And he continues to work against my growth. Ultimately, I'll fall out of power completely. Besides, you always bragged if I got you in front of him you would kill him. You have failed twice so far. Are you all just big talk?"

Tom bit his lower lip. "I can't just walk into the hospital." He sat down on the small chair next to the desk.

Yu reached inside his Zhongshan suit and handed him two pictures, one of a doctor, another of a nurse. "These two fit the physical body description of you and Shou. Your various agencies have ways to make disguises?"

"I can't tell you that. You are a foreign agent. I could be brought up for treason, if I told you. Besides, I'm not getting Shou involved in this mess."

"Wang's doctor always travels with this nurse. If you were to show up by yourself, it would raise questions. This doctor is supposed to be on vacation this week," Yu said.

"Won't this get the doctor in trouble with the Communist Party?"

Yu laughed. "Of course, but certainly the West has ways to kill someone that isn't tracible, don't they? Certainly, it's not only us and the Soviets that have methods of eliminating someone."

Tom walked over to the window and cracked the curtain open for a brief second.

Yu fidgeted on the bed, then snarled, "Are you sending someone a message by peeking out the curtain? Setting me up?"

"Hell, no. I'm thinking."

Yu got up from the bed. "You have four hours to decide. If you aren't interested, I'm leaving to get back across the border. If I'm out of sight too long, the CCP gets nervous. Dr. Wang's comments have only turned up the heat and observation on me."

Tom got up, stuck the pictures in his coat pocket, and walked toward the door. "I'll be back, I need to think."

"Four hours."

Tom was tired of Yu setting the ground rules on everything. "After this, I'm done. This is my last trip here until you decide to come out. When you finally figure out you want to defect, I want you to give me the code 'The pie is baked.' Got it? That means you'll be in position and ready in four days."

Tom looked at him briefly to see if he was going to respond, then turned and left Yu's room in a hurry. He ran down the stairway to the ground floor and exited the way he'd come. He searched for a pay phone. After several blocks, he found one and dialed.

"Hello?"

"Shou, this is Tom. I need to stop by and talk to you. May I come by?"

"Sure, what's it about?"

"Not over the phone. See you shortly." Tom hung up, then called for a cab. Soon, Tom knocked on the door of Shou's apartment.

When she opened the door, she gave him a one-armed hug. "Good to see you again."

"Do you want to accompany me on a mission into Red China to take out Dr. Wang?" Tom asked after sitting down on her couch.

There was a long pause. Finally, she replied, "Count me in. After all the grief he has caused me, yes. I'm in."

"Okay, we are going into a hospital, and you'll be my nurse." Tom pointed at her first then at himself. "And I'll be his doctor. We have to be ready within a few hours. We'll get more details on the way to Beijing."

"Is The Planesman involved?"

Tom stared at her. How did she know that code name? Only Yu and himself knew the code name—or so he thought. "Obviously, you've had contact with Yu Qiangsheng. I thought only he and I knew the code name The Planesman."

Shou leaned over and whispered to Tom, "I will always have a special place in my heart for Marty. After my father's execution, I was a mess and didn't want to be around anyone. So we started drifting apart. Then when he took over the head of the San Francisco bureau, I knew I wouldn't be seeing him as much. Long distance romance doesn't work. Also, I found myself falling for Yu. I didn't realize how much until a couple of years ago. He started calling me, then we met a couple of times in Shenzhen. He confided in me that he was working with you, told me his code name, but I've kept his secret. I know he wants to defect. I know it will be us getting him out—"

Tom wanted to press her more but he wanted to stay focused on the task at hand. "Okay. I'm good with that...for now. We've got to leave now." He picked up her phone and called a cab to take them to MI6.

When he hung up the phone, she grabbed Tom's arm, then continued, "It will take both of us to get him out. Trust me. He'll be in big trouble when he comes out. It will be a big deal. He won't just walk across the border. He's always watched."

Tom pointed his head toward the door.

As Shou grabbed her purse, she said, "I've waited for this opportunity since Dr. Wang killed my father."

Tom and Shou walked into the MI6 headquarters. Tom continued straight to MI6 Agent Alston Chapman's office. "Wait here," he said to Shou, and he entered the office.

Chapman looked up from his desk. "Well, FBI Special Agent Tom Warren, I see you still have your Yankee manners."

"Listen, Chapman, I don't have time for pleasantries. I need your help and I need it immediately."

Chapman took off his glasses, placed them on the desk, and then folded his hands on top. "Well, one thing is for sure—you might be the most pushy Yank I've ever met."

Tom ignored the remark. He was too focused on the task before him. He reached in his pocket and laid the two photos in front of Chapman.

Chapman leaned forward, glanced at them, and raised his bushy eyebrows. "Yes?"

"I need your people to make a mask so I look like him, then do the make up so Shou looks like her. And I can't tell you any more than that. Plus, I need a syringe filled with as much potassium as possible."

"So without telling me anything, you think I'm capable of that kind of magic? Who the hell do you think you are?"

Tom stood up and put both hands on the desk. "I'm protecting you by not telling you what I'm up to. If I'm successful, you can guess. If I don't return, you can assume I'm dead. I'll tell you it is about revenge—our revenge."

Chapman looked unconvinced.

"Come on, you lost six of your agents—including one of my best friends and your boss, Anthony Middleton."

Chapman got up from his desk and stood directly in front of Tom. "I'm also supposed to provide you with that drug? You're out of your mind. Get the hell out of my office."

"Look, I've got to do this. This is a rare opportunity. And you're going to help me because you owe that much to Middleton."

Chapman picked up the phone and punched in four numbers. "Quinn, I'm sending a man and a woman down to you. Do whatever he asks and don't speak a word to anybody. I'm authorizing you. Got it?"

Tom sat back down. "Chapman, I should just come around there and give you a big ol' slobbery kiss. But I'm in too big a hurry."

Chapman raised his eyebrows and sighed. "Basement level, door four on the right. There is no identification on the door. Just knock."

Tom contemplated calling Corley and discussing his mission. However, in the end, as with Chapman, he believed it was best to keep the circle close for this delicate mission.

Tom and Shou went to the basement level. Before knocking on the door, he grabbed her by the shoulders and held her out. "You know this is a very dangerous mission."

Shou nodded.

"Dr. Wang, aka Liao, will have tight security. So if we're caught, we will be in labor camps for the rest of our lives—if they don't kill us on the spot."

"If Yu is assisting us, we'll be fine." Shou smiled.

Tom knocked on the door, then winked at her.

The door opened, and they walked into the large MI6 lab.

Quinn pointed them to chairs opposite each other in front of the largest makeup mirror Tom had ever seen. He handed the pictures to Quinn.

After a few seconds of looking at the pictures, Quinn handed the picture of the nurse to one of his assistants, who immediately started to work on Shou's disguise. Quinn hustled Tom out of the room to make a mold of Tom's face, then left the room.

An hour passed, then Quinn stepped back into the room with a mask. He grabbed Tom by the shoulder, had Tom rejoin Shou in front of the mirror, and watched them do the make up on Shou.

Tom sat down on a chair beside Shou. "Let's talk about the mission. We're going into a hospital where Dr. Wang or Liao is, disguised as a doctor and his nurse, then administer the drug to give him a heart attack."

She looked just like the nurse. *Amazing.*

Quinn slipped Tom's full mask on, then went to work, touched up the last bit of makeup. When the scientist finished Tom, he picked up the phone and called for a cab.

Quinn handed Tom a small case. "Here is your syringe of potassium. It will act very fast." Then he turned and handed Shou a smaller case. "This is a sedative. You may want to administer it to your target. It will slow down the potassium a few minutes. Perhaps giving you the escape time you may need. Good luck to the both of you."

They held up their pictures and looked in the large mirror. Tom nodded at her. "I think we can pull this off."

Yu opened the door and pulled them in. He hugged Shou.

Tom pushed past them.

When Yu released her, she went to the chair and sat.

Tom followed over to the edge of the bed. "You should have told me you two have been in contact."

Yu looked at Shou as he sat down away from Tom. "You told him?"

"I'm sorry, I let it slip," Shou replied, refusing to make eye contact.

Tom grimaced. "You two can figure out your personal lives later. Yu, in a couple of hours, we are prepared to go over the border with you. Let's go over the mission. You have to be sneaking in and out of Red China. Are you prepared to take us with you when you go back? And how are you going to get us into the hospital? And just as important, how are you going to get us back into Hong Kong?"

Yu scowled. "I have several passports and papers for your use. Here are your passports to travel with me over the border. Then these papers are replications of the doctor and nurse to get you in the hospital and room, if you're asked. This doctor is a heart specialist, and Dr. Wang has been his patient, his most important patient. As to the hospital, I've learned the routine of this doctor and nurse, how they go to the hospital. You will do everything the same way he always has. You enter the hospital with the night shift." Yu reached for Shou's hand. "If questioned, you are leaving tomorrow morning early, which is why you are checking in on Dr. Wang tonight. It is unlikely that any of his family will be there, as he's been getting better. They've been with him around the clock over the last few days. As to the security, they are familiar with the doctor and the nurse. I brought a tape of the doctor's voice so that you can imitate his voice the best you can. Lastly, here is your plane tickets, passports, and papers for your flight back to Hong Kong on the morning of June tenth. Oh, one last thing—you may be asked to sign in and out of the hospital room. Here is how you write their names."

Tom looked at the paper and then at Yu. "Why are you really doing this?"

"Because Dr. Wang has undermined me over the past few years. I believe he got jealous of my climb and my relationship with Chairman Deng. He realized he couldn't control me anymore. He has always had people around him he could control. Now his new people have started working against me instead of with me."

Tom looked at Shou. "Any questions?"

Shou stood and shook her head.

Yu looked at them. "I want to cross the border during the night. Let's go."

Yu pulled up to the checkpoint, and everyone handed over their passports. Tom noticed Yu was still using the passport he'd given him in 1980. In a matter of seconds, they were waved on. No problems. Now, they were on their way—the long drive to Beijing. The plan called for each of them to take turns so they could drive as long as they could find fuel to stop along the way. Between driving all night and limited gasoline available in China, the twenty-two-plus-hour drive turned into twenty-six hours.

Throughout the night and the next day, there was little conversation. One would sleep in the back and one would stay awake with the driver.

A little after nightfall, they pulled over on the outskirts of Beijing. Yu took back over driving. His plan called for them to go to the doctor's residence, get his car from his garage, then Tom and Shou would drive to the hospital. Just before Tom pulled the car from the garage, Yu went over their plan one more time. "I'll be in the area of the hospital at midnight, and I'll be in the parking lot to watch both of you enter the hospital. But once you are in the hospital, you're on your own until you come out. Then I'll lead you to the airport."

CHAPTER FIFTY-TWO

June 10, 1983
Beijing

Tom sat in the car. He looked at himself in the rearview mirror. It was at that moment, seeing his disguise, he realized he had to get into character. Then he looked over at Shou. Despite riding with her in the car for the past twenty-eight hours, Shou looked like the nurse in the photo. While he'd never taken any acting classes or appeared in a play, he was about to have to do something he'd never done before. He reached in his white coat pocket—just to verify he had everything he needed—and then he looked at Shou. "Ever taken any acting lessons or appeared in a play?"

"Of course," she replied. "Back when I was in seventh grade."

"Well, since you have the experience, you do most of the talking once we get inside." As they exited the stolen car, they walked toward the employee entrance to the hospital. There were no PLA soldiers or other security to monitor who was going in. This was good.

Shou punched the up button on the elevator, which immediately opened. They both stepped in. Tom looked at his watch—12:07 a. m. So far, everything was running close to schedule. On the first floor, two more staff members, two PLA soldiers, and several haggard visitors got on board. The two PLA soldiers gave everyone a once over before they turned around. The elevator was packed with Tom and Shou in the very back pushed up against the wall. Tom stared straight ahead. Shou touched the back of Tom's hand with the back of hers. Tom could feel his pulse increase, but he didn't flinch.

The elevator seemed to stop on every single floor, with staff and visitors getting on and off. *I thought hospitals didn't allow visitation after 8 p.m. But maybe that's only in the U.S.* When they got to Dr. Wang's floor, not only did Tom and Shou get off, but so did the PLA soldiers. *Game time.* The last time he'd had this adrenaline rush was going on the football field in 1942 to play an away game against Arizona's rival, Arizona State.

Shou looked up at Tom as they followed the soldiers down the hallway.

If we time this just right, we might get caught up in the changing of the guards on Dr. Wang's room.

As he'd suspected, the two soldiers stopped right in front of Dr. Wang's room and relieved two other soldiers who were on duty. Just as Tom and Shou were about to slip by, one of the soldiers leaving his duty assignment said, "Doctor, show me your credentials. You too, nurse."

Tom calmly reached in his pocket, careful to avoid the case carrying the syringe of adrenalin. Then he confidently spoke in Cantonese, "Yes, sergeant. At my favorite patient Liao's request, he asked that I come in to check on him one last time. I'm leaving on holiday early in the morning."

The soldier waved the two on. They both moved expeditiously into the hospital room so nothing else could be asked of them.

Once inside the room, Tom looked at Dr. Wang, who was sound asleep. Then he leaned over and whispered to Shou, "Check the medicine on his IV bag."

Shou slipped up and read it out loud. Tom knew little about medicine but the MI6 doctor he'd spoken with told him to make sure they were giving Dr. Wang something that wouldn't interfere with the adrenaline. They were giving him a diuretic drug to keep him from having congestive heart failure. Tom slipped over to the IV bag, pulled the case out of his coat pocket, popped it open, removed the syringe, stuck it in the top of the bag and quickly plunged out the potassium. He bumped the bed by accident.

Dr. Wang groggily opened his eyes and looked straight up at Tom, but didn't react, since he was disguised as his doctor.

Tom couldn't resist. He pulled off his mask as he put his hand over Dr. Wang's mouth to muffle any attempt to scream or shout.

As he did, Shou stepped up beside him. "What are you doing? Don't take that off. We won't be able to get out of here."

He leaned over. "Marty didn't die, but you are going to, you rotten bastard."

Dr. Wang's eyes grew large as he seemed to realize it was Warren talking to him.

Shou quickly pulled out a syringe from her pocket and stuck it in Dr. Wang's arm and plunged it.

"It's methohexital, a quick acting sedative. *Damn it.* Get your mask back on and let's get out of here." Shou leaned over Dr. Wang and held him down until the sedative knocked him out.

Tom hustled into the bathroom.

Just then the door opened, one of the soldiers stepped in and inquired. "Everything okay? You all have been in here a long time."

Shou smiled as she nodded. "Yes, we are finished. The doctor just stepped into the bathroom for a minute."

The sound of the toilet flushing could be heard as the soldier went over to the door and threw it open just as Tom stepped to the door with his disguise back in place. He took the back of his hand and wiped his mouth. "Upset stomach. I had to throw up."

The soldier looked past him at the toilet, then turned around and went over to Liao. He looked at him peacefully sleeping. Then the soldier stepped back up but closely examined them before he left the room.

Shou leaned forward as she rubbed her temples with her fingers. *"Oh my God, that was close.* Let's go. Let's go. I don't want to go to prison."

When the two of them stepped outside the room, the other soldier held out a clipboard. "Sign out, doctor."

Tom took the clipboard, then paused. He gathered himself hoping he could make the characters of the doctor's name correctly. His photographic memory pictured the characters, but he'd never practiced it. He made the two characters, then handed it back to the soldier.

The soldier asked, "Off to vacation now?"

"What? Oh, yes, of course."

He looked at it then handed the clipboard to Shou.

Tom's heart raced. *Did Shou remember the nurse's name?* Particularly with the soldier standing over her, the slightest mistake would tip the soldiers. He tried not to hold his breath, but he couldn't help it. She stroked through the two characters like nothing. *Perfect.* They turned toward the elevators and paced with a purpose.

Shou punched the down button, repeatedly, as though it would speed up the arrival of the car. Finally, the doors opened. Shou looked up at Tom as the elevator dropped toward the main floor, but he kept his gaze straight forward. He couldn't turn his head. When he'd taken off the mask, he hadn't got it exactly sealed back up to his face. He was afraid any move would cause it to fall off.

When they got to the ground floor, they walked out the back door toward the doctor's car at an exaggerated pace. Once through the glass doors to the employee parking lot, Shou looked up at Tom. "We did it. We made it."

He continued his brisk walk. "Not so fast. We got to get on the plane and be out of their air space before we can celebrate."

They slipped into the car. Tom adjusted his mask and pushed it back in place as Shou started the car and they drove off.

"What the hell were you doing in there? That stunt of pulling your mask was pretty stupid." Shou cast a side glance at Tom.

Tom didn't say a word. She was right, but he had to show Dr. Wang that in the end, he had won.

Yu pulled out in front of them to lead them to the airport. Despite the hour, the early morning traffic was heavy, making the drive nerve-wracking. As they pulled up to the traffic light leading to the airport, Yu pointed, then turned off in the opposite direction. Shou pulled the car into the long-term parking lot.

Tom handed Shou a rag. "Let's wipe down everything we've touched."

They quickly did so, then walked up to the shuttle pick-up. Tom asked, "Got a match or cigarette lighter?"

Shou shrugged, dug in her purse, and pulled out a nightclub pack of matches. "Didn't know you smoked."

"I don't. We have to destroy those papers. If we get stopped and searched, we'd be in deep you-know-what." They verified they'd kept the proper documents to get on the flight. Then Tom lit the doctor and nurse papers.

They seemed to wait an inordinate amount of time. This time of night, Tom reasoned the shuttles didn't run as often. They stayed in the dark, just in case authorities came by looking for them. If Dr. Wang had already died, they would be the first suspects. Finally, the lights of the shuttle indicated it was approaching. Tom and Shou stepped from the dark into the lighted waiting area. The shuttle took a good twenty minutes to make it to the terminal.

They went straight to their gate, but elected not to sit there—again, out of an abundance of caution. Their tickets were in different, separated seats on the plane, so if there were issues, they wouldn't be identified being side by side. Finally, they called for boarding the flight to Hong Kong. Tom and Shou got up and walked toward the gate.

There were four PLA soldiers at the gate. One observed the ticket agent reviewing the tickets, passports, and visas. Tom slightly elbowed Shou. "I'll go first to test these documents. Don't be right behind me in line. If there's any issue, find a reason to get out of line and try to disappear." Tom looked at his watch—it was 3:35 a. m. Dr. Wang could still be alive, although his heart should be beating out of his chest. Maybe his heart monitors would have sounded the alarm. *He didn't know if was happy about that or not.* He had expected the potassium to work faster on someone with a bad heart, but had the sedative counteracted it? *Damn, I wish I had more medical training.*

Finally, he stepped up to the ticket agent and handed her his papers. He made a concerted effort not to make eye contact with any of the soldiers, particularly the one overseeing the agent.

She stamped everything. "Have a pleasant flight."

Tom moved slowly down the ramp, just in case there was an issue over Shou's fake documents as she went through the check-in process. He didn't know what he'd do, but he knew he couldn't abandon her. She entered the tunnel to the plane. Then they proceeded down the ramp. He leaned close as he was about to duck into the plane. "Now, in the air is next."

After taxiing out, the captain finally made the announcement over the speaker, "Stewardesses to your stations, we are number one to lift off."

Tom looked out the window. Within thirty seconds, the captain came back on the intercom. "We have been ordered to return to the gate. Please be patient, we'll be in the air shortly."

Shou jerked around to look at Tom, who knew it was best to be unresponsive.

The two-hundred seat jet turned and taxied back to the gate. When they returned to the gate, the captain came back on the intercom, "Everyone please remain in your seats. We are about to be boarded by several soldiers."

Within a couple of minutes, four heavily armed PLA soldiers walked through the plane checking IDs and passports. Tom wished he could be sitting with Shou to keep her calm. When the soldier reached his row, the soldier stood over them with an outstretched hand waiting for the papers to be handed to him. He calmly looked up, smiled, and passed his documents. The soldier looked at them for two seconds, then handed them back. Tom strained the best he could to see how Shou reacted when it was her turn four rows in front of him. Shou passed her documents. The soldier looked at hers much longer than his documents had been examined. The soldier appeared to ask her a question. Tom strained to hear, but there was too much cabin noise to hear either the question or the answer.

The four soldiers went through the jet in less than twenty minutes.

Thirty minutes later, the plane rolled down the runway, lifting off for Hong Kong.

Six hours later, Tom finished showering at Shou's. They sat opposite each other in her apartment living room, waiting for fresh coffee to finish brewing. They were dog-tired, but the adrenaline in their veins still flowed from what they perceived as a successful mission.

Tom lowered his head—not from fatigue, but due to regret. His hatred for Dr. Wang had driven him to enter the man's hospital room and make sure he didn't leave. After all, Liao—alias Dr. Wang—was a helpless hospital patient, not his thirty-year adversary. He felt his chest tighten. Was he having a heart attack? Or was it the deed? He tried to reason with himself. The man would have been appointed Vice President of Communist China. His reward was not only because of his public diplomacy, but also for running a tight and extremely effective spy ring. Still, none of this was helping Tom at the moment. He had murdered a helpless man.

The coffee pot dinged, letting Shou know it was ready. She got up and poured each of them a cup. They sat there silently, sipping coffee and waiting and wondering about the success of their mission.

Another twenty minutes passed, and, finally, the phone rang. Shou sprung up and answered it.

She nodded as she listened. By then, Tom was standing by her. She rolled the receiver in her hand so Tom could hear. "Liao passed away at 5:22 a.m.

from a heart attack, surrounded by his family. They were called in at 4:05 after his heart started racing. His death is part of an on-going investigation. One of the doctor's neighbors, who was asked to watch the house, reported the doctor's car was stolen. All intelligence agencies were alerted, including mine, to initiate an investigation immediately. The soldiers on duty at the hospital were arrested. When they discovered the doctor's car at the airport, all departing planes were recalled back to the gates to check identifications. That is all that has been reported."

Tom returned to the couch to drink his coffee, still contemplating what he had done.

After a couple of minutes, Shou hung up the phone and sat back down. "That son-of-a-bitch is dead. He killed my father in cold blood. May his soul rot in hell."

Her comments were harsh, but they did cause Tom to think about his fellow agents and the number of innocent Japanese who died at the hands of Liao's alter ego, Dr. Wang. Still, the death of Dr. Wang wasn't how he'd envisioned. It was something he'd likely have to reconcile the rest of his life.

Despite the strength of the Asian coffee blend, Tom suddenly was exhausted.

"You going to tell Marty?" Shou asked.

Tom closed his eyes. At first, he thought he'd ignore her question, but that wouldn't be fair. He opened his eyes. "Ultimately, I may have to. Someday, but for now, no. You see, he's in charge of the San Francisco office. He'd be obligated to tell Webster, who would be obligated to tell Reagan. It's best not to create that mess." He tried to suppress a big yawn.

"I get it." Shou's eyes were also getting very heavy.

He looked at Shou. "I'm going to try to get some sleep before going to the airport to fly back to the States."

Shou nodded, as she'd already called off work at the bank. "I may lay down, too. This coffee isn't working anymore. You can stretch out on the couch."

Tom was already leaning over with one foot up. He nodded and closed his eyes.

CHAPTER FIFTY-THREE

June 30, 1983
San Francisco

Tom leaned back in his chair at his desk, flipping his football over his head, thinking that in just under two weeks, he'd be married to the love of his life and about to retire from the previous love of his life. He'd never been so at peace.

His desk phone rang, and he picked it up. "FBI Special Agent Tom Warren."

"This is the international operator. I have a person-to-person phone call from an Inspector LeBlount for FBI Special Agent Thomas Warren.

"This is Special Agent Warren."

"Go ahead, Inspector LeBlount."

"Special Agent Warren, I'm Inspector LeBlount of the French Direction de la Surveillance du Territoire. I'm conducting an investigation here in France. May I ask you some questions?"

Tom held the receiver away from his ear. He couldn't imagine being questioned regarding an investigation in France. "Sure, what can the FBI do for you?"

"We are launching an investigation into a French diplomat, a Bernard Boursicot, for possible espionage. Your name was discovered in his rolodex. Could you explain this, Special Agent Warren?"

Tom scratched his chin. "Absolutely, but I think I'd like to have the FBI's attorney on the phone with me when we discuss this matter. That's standard procedure with the U.S. Federal Bureau of Investigation."

"But of course. Can we do this today or first thing in the morning, accounting for the time difference?"

"If you give me your desk number, I'll have the attorney contact you to work out a mutually convenient time." After writing down the number, Tom pushed down on the switch hook, then dialed the attorney's number.

July 7, 1983
San Francisco

Tom and the FBI attorney Terrance Bullock sat in the FBI conference room waiting on Inspector LeBlount of the French Direction de la Surveillance du Territoire to call. Tom showed him the complete file of the correspondence received from Bernard Boursicot. The first batches came between 1970 and 1972, and the second batches started in 1978 into late 1979.

After Bullock reviewed all the correspondence, he took off his glasses, then tossed them on the file. "Warren, I don't see anything that implements you into any spying on the French. Everything in these files pertain to Chinese business."

"I might add, nothing he sent me was ever correct. It was all misinformation planted by Dr. Wang."

"Okay, then here is what I want you to do. Only answer the question from the French as briefly as possible—'yes' or 'no,' is preferred. The fact that Boursicot didn't send you anything regarding French policies or documents, keeps you out of it. However, you have some liabilities in that a French diplomat did provide you information." Bullock rubbed his eyes with his thumb and index finger.

Tom shrugged. "But he offered to do this for us. Hoover approved it."

"As long as no money was sent to him—at least tracible—and you didn't correspond back with him, I think we can slide by."

Fifteen minutes later, the phone rang. Bullock picked it up and introduced himself to the French investigator. After an exchange of pleasantries and an acknowledgement that each party had someone in the room who was fluent in both French and English, Inspector LeBlount questioned Warren how the two met, under what circumstances, and what was shared. The conversation continued for almost an hour. Bullock never once told Warren not to answer any question. Warren divulged to LeBlount that everything received was misinformation, passed to Boursicot by Dr. Wang.

Upon hearing that, LeBlount replied, "I've never heard of a Dr. Wang nor seen his name in any of the correspondence. Boursicot told us that he worked with a Chinese citizen Shi Pei Pu, a man who claimed to be a woman. For the record, we are also interrogating Shi, who claims his Chinese contact's name was "Kang.""

This comment startled Tom. He knew of Kang Shang, but it didn't seem to fit.

The investigator asked Tom to provide a brief profile on Dr. Wang to add depth to their investigation into Boursicot's espionage case, which he did so in about two minutes.

"Has Boursicot given you a description of this Kang?" Tom asked.

"No, is it important?"

"Just curious." Tom couldn't let on anything about his operation with The Planesman, but he was certainly curious. From his research, he knew Yu had worked under Kang Sheng early in his career. Was the cover name a coincidence, probably not.

As their conversation was wrapping up, LeBlount asked, "May we have copies of all of the correspondence Boursicot sent to Special Agent Warren?"

Bullock put his finger to his lips as he looked at Tom, then replied, "Inspector LeBlount, we must get clearance from Director Webster to release any documents. I'll endeavor to make this happen. FBI protocols. I'm certain you understand. Here is my contact information here in San Francisco." Bullock gave him his address and office phone number.

"You say Boursicot is being investigated for espionage? May I ask what records you discovered?" Tom asked.

"I suppose that wouldn't be a problem. He supplied the Chinese with over one-hundred-fifty documents between 1970 and 1972 while he was stationed in Beijing. We are accumulating the total from 1977 to 1979, but this is at least another fifty while he was stationed in Mongolia. He is going to be sentenced for espionage against the French government shortly, and his accomplice, Shi, will serve time also," Inspector LeBlount replied.

"I was just curious," Tom replied.

"I believe we are done here," Bullock stated.

"Yes, thank you for your cooperation," LeBlount said.

After they hung up, Tom looked at Bullock. "So, whoever was giving Boursicot information for me, this Kang, was getting information for Dr. Wang and the Chinese."

Bullock shrugged. "So, does that mean something to you?"

"It makes something I've been working on for years delicate, very delicate. I'm afraid if my hunch is right, I may not like the answer." Tom rubbed his chin. "How did I do with the French Inspector's questions?"

"Only a couple of areas that kind of got you into the weeds. Nothing serious."

"Are you going to talk to Webster about this?" Tom asked.

"If they push for it, I'll talk to them. Right now, let's just let it die. They got their man, and they can tell you are outside their investigation."

Tom got up and left the room. This inquiry by the French government had only complicated his own situation with The Planesman. His hunch was The Planesman had been part of Dr. Wang's role to deceive him. He felt like he was being played. When the time came to defect, was it going to be a trap for him or was The Planesman truly coming out? He seemed to be pretty focused on his own power all the time, and that was dangerous for all parties involved. *The Planesman capturing me for the Communist Chinese would be a real feather in his cap, for a man always struggling for power. Particularly, since he knew I was the one who killed Liao or Dr. Wang, things could get really dicey.*

July 9, 1983
Park Street Church
Downtown Boston

Tom was finishing trying to get his bow tie tied correctly so he'd look just right in his tuxedo when Marty walked around the corner in his tux. They both stood back and admired each other. Tom put his arm around his best friend. "We sure are a couple of handsome men."

"I've got to tell you, I'm a little jealous. I always wanted to find someone and settle down. You, you didn't seem to be lookin', and here we are." Marty spoke in a pronounced Southern drawl. He looked down at the ground, then back up and laughed. "You're really going to do this—marry a Japanese girl twenty years younger than you?"

Tom raised his eyebrows as he finished adjusting his bow tie, then combed his hair one more time. "Let's get downstairs."

The two men skipped down the stairs. Tom stayed in pace with Marty, whose shot up leg would never be the same. When they got to the ground floor behind the chancery, Tom peeked into the sanctuary. There were many people, but as he scanned those seated in the pews, he realized he didn't know many of them. They were mostly his elderly parents' friends. There were a couple of Arizona football buddies, including his old college roommate Pete Maston, and a couple of FBI agents. Since Miyoko didn't know anybody in the United States, Tom's family flew her two best friends from Japan over to be her maid-of-honor and bridesmaid, plus Tom asked her to include Michelle Galloway, his old FBI analyst from Washington DC.

The two men stood in silence for a short period of time. Then Marty, being a good best man, said, "You seem pretty calm for getting married for the first time at the age of sixty-three."

"For the first time that I can remember, I'm really at peace. But I also just realized, I don't have many friends. My work has always been my friend." He looked up at Marty. "Not saying that is a bad thing, just makes me different from most people. Talk about being married to your job."

"I understand. Believe me, I understand."

"Miyoko doesn't know anyone here. She can never go home. It's time I pay attention to her." Tom bit his lower lip. "My parents bought us a worldwide cruise, to start whenever we want. I think that will be fun." Tom peeked back out into the sanctuary. "Marty, I can't tell you when the last time I used *fun* in a sentence or thought the word. That's what this woman has done to me."

In their combination Christian and Japanese wedding ceremony, they did the procession Japanese style. The organist broke into the song before the procession was to begin. "Marty, let's go. Let's get in position." Tom grabbed Marty's arm to move him along as fast as he could go. They had just three minutes to get in position.

The two men hustled to the back of Park Church. The ushers and the best man were dressed in tuxedos, while the women wore traditional red Japanese kimonos. The contrast was stunning.

With everyone in position, the organist played the first notes of *Canon in D* on the large pipe organ, the congregation stood, and the procession began. When the song ended, everyone faced the back of the church.

Tom in his tuxedo, and Miyoko, dressed in an elaborate all-white shiromuku and white zoris, and Tom's family remained standing at the back of the church. Then a traditional Japanese song, *Kunihico Hashimoto, The Heavenly Maiden's Dance,* was played on the organ, accompanied by a violinist. This was when Miyoko opened her white parasol. As they started their march to the front of the church, Miyoko leaned over to Tom. "My heart is racing, as is my love for you."

After the wedding ceremony, they rode over to his parents' home for the reception. On the ride over in the limousine, Marty, Michelle, and the two women from Japan rode with Tom and Miyoko. Tom poured each a glass of champagne, and they clicked glasses.

"Tom, where are you and Miyoko going for your honeymoon?" Michelle asked as she quickly downed her glass.

Tom hugged and kissed Miyoko. "Go ahead and tell them, Mrs. Warren."

"We're going to spend four weeks in London, touring England." Miyoko took a tiny sip.

Marty raised his free hand and laughed as though faking surprise. "A month?"

"Of course. As I told you, I'm retiring. I don't believe I've had a vacation in my almost forty years at the Bureau."

Marty's jaw dropped, faking surprise, then he sarcastically replied, "All the places you've been around the world on business assignments? You've always been on vacation."

"When I get back, there will be a letter on your desk, effective at the end of the year or sooner. Think you can replace me?" Tom laughed. "Besides, I'm going to be busy. Miyoko's friends have agreed to come and stay with us as long as they wish. I want to show them around the United States. Then, Marty, we are moving back to Boston."

As the limo came to a stop, everyone jumped out into the midst of the wedding guests. Tom and Miyoko walked into the reception at Tom's parents holding hands. The music playing in the background was *Wonderful Tonight* by Eric Clapton. Tom had never evolved to modern music, yet he thought the song was appropriate for his total love of Miyoko. He'd reluctantly agreed to let Miyoko work with his sister to pick out the music to be played, as long as he got to pick a couple of Sinatra songs, including *The Way You Look Tonight*.

The couple was escorted to the head table by the entire wedding party. All the other guests had already been seated. Waiters moved quickly through the fifty guests, pouring a Chardonnay from the Napa Valley.

Before they sat down. Tom's father remained standing and tapped his wine glass with his spoon. "A toast. Those of you who know me and my son know we had a tough relationship when he was young. So tough, he ran off to Arizona to go to college and became the quarterback of the team. Then, when I thought he'd come home and take over the family business, he joined the FBI and went to the Philippines. It wasn't the plans I had. But in the end, I'm proud of your career and achievements, and I, we, love your new bride and welcome her not just as daughter-in-law, but as a daughter into our family." With that, he raised his glass.

Everyone replied, "Here, here." They all drank.

The DJ kicked off the next segment of the music with *Another One Bites the Dust* by Queen. By the time that song finished playing, most of the room was clapping with the beat of the song.

Dinner was served, along with another round of Chardonnay.

When dinner was over, Marty got up to give his toast. "To my best friend, who tried to get me killed not once but twice." This brought a huge laugh from the crowd. "While he may be the most unorthodox FBI agent of all time, he also has to be one of the most effective. We are going to miss him when he retires, which he keeps telling me is soon. Also, Miyoko, I hope you know what you just signed up for with your new husband." Again, this drew a big laugh. "But I'll tell you this. I've never seen a man so madly in love with a woman at any time in my life. May you all have a long, blessed life together."

CHAPTER FIFTY-FOUR

On February 6, 1984
Beijing

Yu Qiangsheng begrudgingly sat down opposite Min Bu-ying to review the surveillance that Yu's Guoanbu and Min's Guojia Anquan Bu had obtained on Italian journalist Tiziano Terzani. Yu's initial boredom watching the Italian journalist had changed recently, as it had developed into an opportunity to score points with the Chinese Communist Party—and perhaps even earn him more power. The journalist even seemed to enjoy taunting him. It was time to put him in his place. He was ready to move.

The two leaders of the intelligence community decided it was in the best interest of China to set the journalist up to be perceived as a spy for the West. This way, they could arrest him. Once he was in jail, they believed the Chinese Communist Party could exchange him for dissident Chinese communists held in the Italian or German jails.

Some of the elites in Europe viewed the Italian, Terzani, as an expert on the Far East, which was why he'd initially been hired as the correspondent in China for the German magazine *Der Spiegel*. However, despite his standing in Europe, Chinese intelligence services continued to build their respective cases against the journalist.

Yu and Min each believed they had almost completed their task of accumulating and generating enough evidence to make him the scapegoat they desired.

As Yu walked away from the meeting, he realized he was in a race to get the upper hand over Min's investigation. It was up to him and his group of agents to find enough evidence to move and make the arrest first.

February 8, 1984
Beijing

Yu reached in his lower desk drawer and lifted the false bottom. He pulled out the black velvet bag, opened it, and dumped out the chopsticks on his desktop. One of the NanJing engraved chopsticks included an additional engraving—Thomas P. Warren. He picked it up and examined it, then smiled as he quickly put them all back in the bag and back into the concealed drawer. With Dr. Wang dead, there was still unfinished business.

On the top of his desk was his extensive file on Terzani. He reviewed it and made notes. He needed to move first to get the upper hand on Min Bu-ying and the Guojia Anquan Bu. One of his agents working at the Lo Wu Border Crossing tipped Yu off that Terzani had just crossed the border back into Shenzhen. While in Hong Kong, he'd purchased an offensive figure of Mao Zedong and several national relics. This gave Yu the opportunity he'd been seeking. He headed off to Terzani's residence and knocked on the door.

The door opened. "*Ciao*."

Yu stared at him. "I know you speak our language. Now, speak to me in Cantonese."

Terzani raised an eyebrow. "What do you want, Yu? Have you come to harass me more?"

"You are under arrest," Yu replied as he showed the handcuffs. "You have finally crossed the line."

Terzani's body stiffened, caught completely off guard. "For what? I have done nothing wrong but try to blend into your society and write about your wonderful culture."

Yu smiled. "You are under arrest for taking national relics and, more importantly, having an offensive figure of Mao. Turn around so I can cuff you, Terzani."

February 9, 1984
Beijing

Yu Qiangsheng was seated across from several officials from the Ministry of State Security, including the powerful Ling Yun. Also seated at his table was Min Bu-ying, who had been invited to bring investigative materials. As the meeting began, Ling Yun congratulated Yu on his arrest of Terzani.

In his opening remarks, Ling Yun concluded that the CCP had determined Terzani was attempting to create insurrection within China by stirring up the Chinese population against the Communist Party. He continued, "This should bring to an end Terzani's effort to try to infiltrate China and ultimately poison the people against our government. Further, it gives us the potential opportunity to trade Terzani for jailed Chinese dissidents in Germany and Italy. Perhaps if we can create a big propaganda campaign, build up the story of Terzani, and create an international incident, we can get some good mileage out of his arrest. In closing, Yu Qiangsheng, Bureau Chief within the Guoanbu, we owe you a huge debt of gratitude for your efforts for the Peoples Republic of China."

Yu was pleased with the accolades he was receiving. However, it was of equal importance to him that he'd removed someone attempting to undermine China, and he'd won his personal conflict with the journalist. Terzani underestimated Yu's power in the country and was paying the price.

Lastly, when the accolades were passed out for taking down Terzani, Min Bu-ying received none. The man who had tried to capitalize on Yu's investigation wasn't even mentioned. It was another moral victory for Yu. While it clearly was a win in his quest for more power, his victory still somehow seemed hollow, as he was soured on China and how the Communist Party had treated him and his family.

As he was walking out of the building, someone called out, "Yu, wait up."

He turned to see Ling Yun approaching. "We didn't get a chance to hear your opinion on what we should do with Terzani."

"No one asked. But if they had, I wouldn't trade him just yet for anyone being held somewhere in Europe. Their prisons are soft. I would put Terzani in a work camp for a while. He wanted to be Chinese with that Deng Tiannuo crap. Let him see what it's like to be a Chinese citizen who taunts our government."

Ling Yun pouted his lips. "That is not what the Communist Party wants. Remember, Deng wants to improve our standing in the world. He has won over several European countries and, more importantly, the U.S.—at least, under Carter. We still don't know about Reagan."

Yu turned and started to walk away. Deng was no different than Mao as to how he treated Chinese citizens.

Ling Yun spoke louder, "One more thing."

Yu turned back and stepped toward Ling.

"I wanted to advise the French Intelligence service has gone through diplomatic channels to learn who is 'Kang' in the espionage case against Boursicot. The way you handled Shi and Boursicot was masterful. Boursicot told them he gave French documents to Kang, but Shi said that Kang—you—

only met with Boursicot to discuss Maoist teachings. The French investigators have conflicting stories and can't sort it out." Ling Yun smiled as he finished. "You should train other handlers."

"Shi knows that if he returns to China, he will be put in a work camp because he's a homosexual. I told him that years ago. He'll say anything to stay in France. Same goes for Boursicot. If he hadn't provided the documents he did, I would've put him in prison because he was homosexual, too." Yu smiled snidely, then turned and walked off.

Dr. Wang and Kang Sheng were right. Yu would achieve power, more than even they had imagined. But the acknowledgement of his abilities and achievements were too late. It was time to put the finishing touches on overall plan. *The Chinese Communist Party are soon going to learn just how valuable I am and what I really know.*

July 9, 1984
San Francisco

Tom walked into the FBI headquarters. He picked up his football sitting in the center of his desk and moved it aside. Time to sit down and review the mail and the inner-office memos. In the mail was something he'd never expected to see. MI6 Hong Kong had finally received the international mail that had been delivered to Dr. Wang's post office box in Hong Kong. Upon opening the envelope, there were numerous mailings, but Tom was focused on the ones coming out of Virginia, Maryland, Delaware, North Carolina, West Virginia, or even Washington, D.C. Those were the routings he expected CIA Larry to use. Never from the same place to look as random as possible.

He got up from his desk and headed directly to Marty's office. "I got a package from MI6. This may contain the final information I need to tie the random deposits to mailings from CIA Larry." Tom held up the thick envelope. "I'm headed home to try to tie it all together with the banking information."

Marty held up his hand. "Close the door."

Tom stepped in and closed the door behind him, but remained standing.

Marty put his hand over his mouth then rubbed his chin. "I know you know the laws, but remember chain of custody of evidence, since CIA Larry is a U.S. citizen. You take this information out of the office, you won't be able to use it against him. You know you'll already be on thin ice going after a decorated, retired CIA employee."

"You're right. But we will have to submit a whole new round of warrant requests to judges to really get this guy." Tom raised the package up from his side.

"That won't fly with any judge, so you're on your own on this. I just wanted to remind you of what you already know so well."

Tom started to leave the office. As he put his hand on the doorknob, Marty added, "Hey, something coincidental and strange. My mom sent me an article from a magazine she always reads, *Der Spiegel*. It's published somewhere in Europe—"

Tom interrupted. "Germany, it's a German magazine. My mother used to read it, a long time ago."

"Anyway, before you interrupted—" Marty opened his briefcase and handed a magazine to Tom. "Read this. It's about a journalist in China hassled by Yu Qiangsheng."

Tom snatched it from Marty's hand, opened the office door, and left. He knew Marty didn't care for Yu. *Wait till he finds out what I'm up to.* He walked straight past his desk, then stopped and went back to pick up his football. If he was going to be studying these mailings, he wanted his football to help him think. It worked. He looked at the stack of papers. This evidence was too critical to the case he was building. He called over one of the clerical staff, "Log these in as evidence. Then please make me clear, clean copies of these pages. Finally, put the originals in the file cabinet and give me the copies."

After fifteen minutes, with his arms now full, he went out the door. He'd take these home and put them with his stack of bank statements. See if the mailing would line up with any deposits.

When he got home, he pulled out his notes from the bank statements, then made sticky notes of the dates and amounts of the random deposits. Then he went through the mailings. If CIA Larry were a spy, then there would be a correlation between the date of the mailing and when he received the money.

Dr. Wang hadn't received as much mail as Tom had originally anticipated. That was a good thing and a bad thing. While it made his job going after CIA Larry via this mailbox easier, it also made him leery of another mailbox or means of communication. Did CIA Larry have a courier inside the United States or Canada? A different problem for a different day.

After spending four hours going over the mailing dates, a pattern started to emerge. Between five and six weeks after something arrived in P. O. Box 88, Hong Kong, a deposit was made into CIA Larry's account. What really surprised Tom was that it was not a large amount of money, compared to the amount some spies working for foreign governments would receive.

He sat back and closed his eyes to process this. Do the Chinese who believe in what the Communist country is doing believe in the cause so much they didn't ask for much money? When people in the U.S. spied for countries or on businesses, it was usually for financial gain or revenge or power. But the Chinese might do their spying for a cause.

Now that Tom had a pattern, he tagged each of the sticky notes with the location the international stamp was cancelled. CIA Larry received about forty percent of his random deposits from these mailings. Therefore, he continued to hypothesize that he had to have a courier carrying information back to China.

Did he have enough information to go before a judge to get another warrant to dig deeper into CIA Larry's activity?

Tom picked up the phone and called Marty. "We got a pattern on CIA Larry. That son-of-a-bitch is definitely a spy. Now, I just need a few more things to nail him to the wall."

CHAPTER FIFTY-FIVE

October 4, 1985
Beijing

Yu was driving over to his mother's for dinner. This would be the last time he'd be with his family. When he knocked on the door, his brother, Yu Zhengsheng, answered the door.

"Good evening."

"You're late. Mother was expecting you a long time ago."

Yu walked past his brother and grabbed a plate of his mother's Chinese noodles, then went for the spicy sauce, her own secret recipe.

As he sat down at the table and wolfed down his plate of food, his mother, Fan Jin, and brother joined him.

"Have you ever considered a role in politics?" his mother asked.

"Mother, I'm a criminologist. I see enough bad guys without getting into politics," Yu said with a laugh. While he said it in jest, he believed power and money was the game for Deng Xiaoping's chosen few.

"Very funny. You should be a comedian," his brother said. "It's all about connections, not being among the chosen few. I have been asked by Deng's son, Deng Pu-fang, to move to the Shandong province to serve as Deputy Party Secretary of Yantai."

"You're making my point about nepotism," Yu replied. "I've seen too much of it in my job."

"Where would you be without Kang Sheng's influence?" his brother retorted. "With the clout you have and our family relationship to Deng's family, you could easily get a high-level political appointment."

"Like I said, I'm happy being a criminologist." He wanted to add, *I don't see much of a difference between Mao and Deng*, but kept his mouth shut. He didn't want to tip even his family, who now seemed to be getting eaten up with their new-found power. His brother, the hot shot electrical engineer, had always been enamored with power and always pursued power, but not his mother. She'd changed considerably now, even holding a seat on the Beijing Municipal Committee. It was like she'd forgotten she'd been jailed for trying to bring some power to the people. Apparently, she was so brainwashed, she believed Deng was better than Mao; really disappointing. But he knew better. He'd seen personally that Deng was just as ruthless to the Chinese people as Mao. The only difference was that he hadn't murdered as many Chinese citizens—yet.

After sipping tea for a brief time after dinner, they moved to the living room for light conversation.

Finally, it was time to go. He got up and lightly punched his brother in the arm, then hugged his mother—a little longer than normal. It would be his last time. Then he headed out the door.

On his way home, he stopped at a pay phone and called Shou. "Meet me in our usual spot in Shenzhen. I've scheduled a trip in the morning to the Overseas Chinese Affairs Office. I've haven't been there for a while, so no one will question my leaving. But I'm not going to show up. Come and get me at six a.m." Then he hung up the phone. The die was cast.

October 30, 1985
San Francisco

Tom and Miyoko were sitting in bed watching and laughing at the television show, *Night Court*, when their home phone rang. He picked it up. "Hello."

The voice on the other end replied, "This is The Planesman. The pie is baked." Then the line went dead.

Miyoko mumbled, "Wrong number?"

Tom rolled over and hugged her. "No. I'll have to leave in the morning. One last mission."

Miyoko cuddled up with Tom. "Can I remind you that you are retired from the Bureau? And where are you going? Hong Kong?"

Tom didn't say a word. Miyoko already knew his answer.

The next morning at breakfast, Miyoko set toast and coffee in front of Tom while he read the morning newspaper. She leaned over and gave him a big kiss. "So tell me about your mission. Again, I thought you were retired so we could spend more time together?"

Tom calmly laid the paper down and looked up at her with a big smile. "This should be my easiest mission. It's something I've been working on for years. It's my final blow to Dr. Wang's spy network." He paused for a minute. "No, make that my largest accomplishment in taking down the Chinese spy network."

Miyoko came over and rubbed her hand over the top of Tom's already messed up morning hair. "Go get 'em, Tiger. Anything you can do to make his soul burn hotter in hell is fine with me."

Tom flexed his right arm while sitting there in his robe.

First, Miyoko laughed, then asked, "Are you going to tell Marty?"

"I don't think I'm going to at this time." Tom frowned, then sipped his coffee. "It will only complicate my plan."

CHAPTER FIFTY-SIX

November 3, 1985
Hong Kong

Tom watched the pilot glide path lights as the jet set down on the runway. He'd mentally wrestled with himself on the flight to Hong Kong. He was upset with Yu, but he knew what a final blow it would be if he could get him out of Red China. He'd left his wife behind again on short notice, which he didn't like, and then there was his own issues with Yu. First, it seemed likely that he was the liaison between Dr. Wang and French diplomat Bernard Boursicot, feeding Tom misinformation, and second, Yu had always told Tom he had one last mission inside China, which turned out to be a set-up to remove Tiziano Terzani, the journalist, who only reported the truth behind what was going on inside Communist China. According to Terzani's article, he was set up and Yu was directly involved. Lastly, Yu had continued to withhold the file on Larry Wu-tai Chin/Jin Wu-dai, which would solidify Tom's investigation to take down the most damaging spy in U.S. history. The San Francisco FBI team had done marvelous work building a case through their secret investigation of CIA Larry, but they desperately needed that file to finish it off.

This trip to Hong Kong was different because this was the first time Tom traveled as a private citizen. No FBI to back him up. Furthermore, he hadn't notified MI6 of his potential actions. Tom had deep-seated fears. If Yu, in fact, was going to come out, his notification to both agencies would have to be done

474

at the last minute to prevent leaks. If Yu actually did defect and he came out with CIA Larry's file and maybe more, it would be the biggest win ever against Communist China.

The more he thought about the developing situation, the more he realized he was also putting his relationship with his best friend on the line. But deep down, he knew if he'd told Marty, he'd be obligated to pass this information up the ladder, which would then go to other cabinet level departments—a damn daisy chain, including the CIA and President Reagan. The potential leaks were too great. But Marty would never forgive him—not to mention Marty's former girlfriend Shou was going to be an integral part of Tom's privately planned operation.

On the cab ride over to Shou's apartment, he wondered when he'd be seeing The Planesman. He watched a seemingly endless number of skyscrapers go by along the way. It began to dawn on him how crowded downtown Hong Kong was. Why, after all these years, had he just now paid attention to such detail? The city hadn't really changed that much since he first came here in the 1940s—the buildings were only newer, taller.

He timed how long it took to drive from the airport to Shou's apartment. They were barely halfway there, and they'd already been in the car forty-five minutes. He leaned up to ask the cabbie, "Is traffic consistently this heavy between downtown and the airport?"

The cabbie nodded. "Friend, we're hopping twenty-four hours per day. Seems to be more crowded every day."

After another thirty minutes, he pulled up in front of Shou's apartment building.

Tom exited the taxi and entered the building, then climbed in the elevator and punched the button. When the doors opened on her floor, he admired the carpet and décor lining the hallway to her new apartment. It was a really nice place. He knocked on the door. Shou opened it and let him in. Once he was inside, he set his suitcase down. "I just wanted to check in with you before I went to my hotel."

Yu stepped out of the bedroom.

Simultaneously, Tom flipped his coat and instinctively went for his gun. "What are you doing here already?"

"I've been here two days," Yu replied. "I've been in hiding for almost a month. I left China October 12. Shou smuggled me across the border, took me to the hotel. She was bringing me food for a while. But I got nervous about being there. Nervous for Shou."

Shou interrupted, "We decided it would be safer if he just came here to hide out. We don't believe he was followed, but he just didn't have anywhere else to go."

Tom went over to the kitchen table and dropped down. He was followed by both Shou and Yu. "*Damn*, this is not what I expected at all. You or Shou should have told me when you got here. I've still got to make arrangements to get you out of Hong Kong."

Yu raised both hands palms up as he stepped toward Tom. "I had to think, just be by myself. You can't begin to understand what's going through my mind. I've been thinking about this even longer than you know. But to actually do it—well, that is overwhelming."

Tom hadn't realized the gravity of the move Yu had made. It would be like Director William Webster running to China. Despite his personal conflict with the Boursicot and Terzani situations, Yu had made an extremely dangerous, bold move. He could see it in Yu's face—he was paler and more haggard looking than before, likely due to his internal conflict.

"You can bet that the Ministry of State Security has already sent a hit team for me." Yu rubbed his hands together.

Tom raised his right hand. "*Are you nuts? A hit team?* This town must be crawling with agents looking for you."

Yu nodded as he looked down. "I've tried not to even think about it. They can't let me defect, and they won't bring me back alive. They have to take care of me outside of China—this would never be a news event there."

"I don't think anyone is following me," Shou chimed in. "I've been extra careful, just stopping for groceries when I come and go to work."

"That's good, real good. But if they are watching you, they pay attention to you buying more groceries than normal. But for now, you'll keep doing the same things until we are ready to move out." Tom faced Yu. "Yu, I want some answers before we go forward. Why did you railroad Terzani, which benefitted the Chinese Communist Party you claim to hate?"

"Because he was constantly taunting me. He was conducting interviews in my face after me telling him to stop. Then that Italian tried to take a Chinese name to act Chinese. That really pissed me off. Is that good enough for you?"

Tom didn't like the answer, but he believed that at least Yu was being honest with him. That was important. "Okay, here's the tough one. The French government called me about Bernard Boursicot. I studied their information. I believe you were 'Kang.' Am I correct?"

"Maybe you're a better detective or investigator than I've always thought," Yu replied with a sneer.

Tom ignored the insult because it now confirmed his suspicion. "You were the courier of misinformation for me between Dr. Wang and Boursicot, right?"

Yu stared directly at Tom. "Yes. This started before I knew you and before I thought of defecting. To tell you the whole truth, I was the one who arranged Shi Pei Pu to get close to Boursicot, because I knew he was a homosexual. Later, to keep the French man spying, I found a boy to look like he came from a Caucasian/Chinese relationship. Boursicot was crazy."

"But, Yu, we were working together at that time. Right?"

"No. His last activity for Dr. Wang was in 1979. In the end, I couldn't change out handlers, as Dr. Wang and Boursicot would both have suspected something." Yu's face flushed.

"Fair enough." Tom had to keep his focus on the here and now. The prize he had at hand. "Now, Yu, what did you take beside CIA Larry's file that the Ministry of State Security wants to kill you? Has to be something more?"

"I brought your damn photos out." Yu got up and left the kitchen. Within a minute, he returned and threw an envelope on the table. Then Yu pointed at his head. "Most of what I brought is right up here. I have a few items for the CIA. Now, what's your plan to get me out of here alive?"

"I've got it, but as I just said, I have one last detail I need to work out before we go."

"You better get your shit together on this, or they'll be taking me out of here in a body bag." Yu got down in Tom's face.

Tom leaned back and calmly replied, "Do you think you're the first person I've snuck out of the country? I was doing this while you were still in grade school. Like I said, I've got a plan. Let me handle the last detail, and then we go. Got it?"

Yu turned and huffed out of the room.

"Don't worry, he's just uptight and worried. He's tough. He'll do whatever you plan and do it well. Remember this—as tough as the guys the Chinese have sent after him, none of them are as tough as you two." Shou leaned over and whispered, "I'm going to check on him."

Tom tried to show confidence with a forced smile.

Shou left the room.

Tom sat back up in his chair. It was time to figure out how to do the airplane. His plan was the same as June 10, 1949, when he smuggled T. V. Soong out of Shanghai to escape the communists—the only thing missing was the airplane. Not to mention a trustworthy pilot. Who to trust? Who would perform? While he tried to act cool with Yu and Shou, circumstances of Yu being out for almost a month had turned this into a life-or-death mission.

After sitting there staring at the knick-knacks, he came to the only logical conclusion—get Marty to cooperate with him somehow. It was going to be a tough sell. Then he realized Shou was walking around in the kitchen. He'd been so deep in thought he'd barely noticed.

Shou laughed. "Welcome back."

"I'm going to go check into my hotel so I can use the phone." Tom got up from the table and picked up the envelope containing the photos that was so important to his investigation into CIA Larry. "Call me a cab. I'm going downstairs to wait and think."

"Okay, good luck. We both know you're going to call Marty," Shou said as she kissed Tom on the cheek. "I'll keep Yu occupied."

Tom went to the elevator and punched the button.

Tom told the cabbie to take him to the hotel closest to Shou's apartment complex. He worried that Shou's phone could be tapped if she were being watched. They drove just a few blocks away. As they rode around, he realized he needed to get a very accurate map of downtown Hong Kong to lay everything out. His plan needed accurate detail.

As soon as he checked into his room, he dialed Marty's home number. When Marty answered, Tom said, "Hey, Best Man."

"Uh-oh. Something is coming."

Tom put his forehead in his hand as he leaned over the tiny hotel room desk and paused for a minute. "I need a private jet sitting at the private section of the Kai Tak International Airport, ASAP."

"Do you *care* to provide me any more details, or should I just blink and make it happen?" Marty replied.

"Marty, I know you are—were—my boss, so the less I tell you, the happier you'll be. You're the only human being I can trust. Pull some strings. I don't care how."

"That's the damn problem with you—you don't care how. What do I tell whoever in God's name I ask? Hey, just take your jet, fly to Hong Kong, and sit there and wait? Yeah, that's going to work. Think about it. *Damn*, you've got to give me something."

"If what I got going on works," Tom said quietly, "it may be the biggest breakthrough we've had in years. Maybe ever."

"*Great,* wonderful. Stop placating me. I got to know something, anything. My ass is the one hanging out here. You're retired. I'm the one taking career risks here."

"I have a package that has to be delivered with a fast-approaching expiration date." Tom lowered his voice even more to offset Marty's pitch.

"Damn it, Tom. Damn *you.*" Marty grunted, then sighed. "Okay, let me see what I can do. I'll call you back as soon as I have something," he said, his voice much calmer. "I'll reach out to SAT Pacific. I'll come through, somehow. Just don't hang me out to dry here."

Tom gave him his hotel phone and room number, then hung up the phone. Now the waiting game began. To pass the time, he pulled out the photos Yu had taken from Dr. Wang's Jin Wu-dai—or Larry Wu-tai Chin's—file. He started through the pictures.

The first thing in the file was about his recruitment by Liao, in 1948, to work for the Chinese and spy on the U.S. It was his success in recruiting Jin Wu-dai that made Liao decide to switch to his alter ego, Dr. Wang, from then on. Dr. Wang gave him his new identity, Larry Wu-tai Chin. Tom assumed that Dr. Wang had recruited lesser spies, but CIA Larry was likely his best and brightest. His first assignment was translator and interpreter for the U.S. Army.

Tom sat back, closed his eyes, and relived CIA Larry helping to patch up him and his team members, Ricky and Sal, after Dr. Wang had worked them over in Shanghai. Was that just to gain his trust?

Oh, damn, look at this. During the Korean Conflict, he was assigned to the State Department, interviewing Chinese prisoners of war. He revealed their identities and what they said in their interrogations, then sent the information back to the Chinese Intelligence Service—or Dr. Wang.

There were several pictures from 1952, detailing Chin's move to the CIA Broadcast side in Okinawa, where in he'd hand-carried information in and out of Hong Kong meeting his handler, sometimes Dr. Wang.

The next set of pictures were from 1961. *Strange—a gap in time with no records.* Chin was moved to California, and Dr. Wang set him up with a courier in Canada.

There it is. My answer to the payments and mailing gaps.

Next was a picture showing he'd become a citizen in 1964.

There were notes from the Vietnam Conflict, where North Vietnamese and Chinese soldiers were taken prisoners and whether they talked or not. Chin had a sense of humor. He sent Dr. Wang a picture of the note he'd passed the FBI polygraph test in 1970.

Tom remembered that. He and Marty had joked about it, since they were already using CIA Larry.

It was after that things really picked up. Chin was sending reports from U.S. CIA agents in the field in China and their documents to his handler.

No damn wonder Dr. Wang always seemed to be a step or two ahead. Tom closed his eyes as he wondered how many CIA undercover agents were imprisoned or killed because of this.

Chin had access to Nixon's desire to open relations with Communist China, allowing Zhou En-lai to know in advance what Kissinger was going to say and ask. The consummate diplomat that Zhou was, this information would have given him the upper hand.

Tom turned over the last round of pictures. He was physically ill with what CIA Larry had done to the United States.

When he was finished, he carefully put the photos back in the envelope and stuck them in a pocket in his suitcase as though handling gold.

November 4, 1985
Hong Kong

Tom woke up after less than four hours sleep and brewed some coffee in his room before going down for breakfast. He decided to take a trip around Hong Kong, not as a tourist but to get a feel where, exactly, to initiate his escape route. Before going back to the hotel that evening, he went by the old hotel where Yu usually stayed when they met in the past. Nothing out of the ordinary. His last object of the afternoon was to go by Shou's bank and tail her back to her apartment to see who was watching her. He identified maybe two different teams of men.

He waited a little more than a half hour after the suspected teams left to go into Shou's apartment building to eat dinner with the two of them. When he was let in, the first thing he did was ask Yu, "Did you bring your handguns out?"

"Of course. Why do you ask?"

"Shou may have a couple of shadow teams watching her. I'm not positive, but we need to err on the side of caution."

"Agreed. When are we getting *out of here*?"

"Soon. I've been out today working on the plan. That's how I discovered those two teams."

Shou stepped back into the living room from the kitchen. "Should I be worried?"

"Worried? No. Cautious? Yes. Observe everything going on around you. Every detail. Ask Yu—he'll tell you the same thing."

"They won't do anything to you as long as I'm not around you." Yu placed his hands on both knees and gripped them. "But all bets are off when we're together."

Tom looked at him, then back to Shou. "Here is what I want you to do. Tomorrow, you call MI6 and ask for Agent Alston Chapman. Ask him if he'll give you a handgun and a backup. But tell him to get an agent to deliver it to you at work. Don't you go there or have him come here. Have him bring them to you at the bank."

Shou returned to the kitchen, and Yu went back to the bedroom. Tom shrugged and sat down on the couch, then let out a big sigh of relief. As he'd hoped, Yu and Shou were as prepared as they could be. Neither of them panicked at his news, and that was a good thing.

CHAPTER FIFTY-SEVEN

November 17, 1985
Hong Kong

Tom was sound asleep when his room phone rang and awakened him from a deep sleep. His first thought was that it might be Miyoko calling. No such luck. He immediately recognized Marty's voice.

"Wake up and grab your note pad, old man. No time to sleep."

"Give me a sec to turn on the light, grab pen and paper—okay, go."

"Tomorrow evening, a Southern Air Transport Pacific division plane will be on the ground at seventeen hundred local."

"Hmmm. CIA. What kind of jet is it?"

"How the hell should I know? *Damn.* You'd be lucky if I could get you a crop duster. I get you a plane with no information at all. I'm surprised you're not asking me about the meal to be served."

Tom chuckled. "No, but I would have asked about the wine."

"The pilot has agreed to be sitting at the private terminal at Kai Tak International Airport for exactly two hours. If you don't make it, he's wheels up. Here's the tail number. I know you have a photographic memory, but write this down. Who knows? Something could happen to you."

Tom did as he was instructed. "Got it, Marty. Thanks. When I get back on U.S. soil, I'll fill you in."

"Hey, the people at the CIA I spoke with said there is a lot of chatter coming out of China. Four teams in Hong Kong are looking for a high-level official. Three teams of agents and a four-man PLA sniper team. Be careful."

"Damn. I've identified two teams, but that's all," Tom huffed.

"Keep your head on a swivel, buddy," Marty said.

"One more thing. Could you let Miyoko know I'll be home in three days?"

"You got it. Good luck, my friend. With that many on the lookout, you're gonna need it." Marty paused, then lowered his voice. "Take care of Shou."

Marty was pretty preceptive knowing Shou was involved. Tom rolled back over and tried to go back to sleep. After a half hour, it was impossible.

That evening, after spending another day riding around in a cab going from Yu's old hotel to Shou's bank through the downtown business section, Tom finally had the cabbie let him off three blocks from Shou's apartment building just so he could walk the area and see who was still watching her. He needed to do a better job recognizing the PLA teams. He finally went up to her floor for the nightly dinner.

The conversation was light around the kitchen table. After dinner, Tom got up from the table. He felt like he was going to hyperventilate. "Do you have any whiskey or wine?"

"Sure, why?" Shou picked up the dishes from the dinner table.

"Tomorrow is the day. I want to go over the plan. Everything top to bottom. And I want to enjoy a drink. You know, relax." Tom placed his hands on his hips, trying to show confidence despite what he felt inside.

"Whiskey," Yu chimed in.

Shou walked into the living room with a bottle of whiskey and three glasses. She sat them down and pour three fingers in each, then set the bottle in the middle of the coffee table.

Tom held up his glass, and everyone clinked together. "The next time we toast, we'll be somewhere else."

Yu downed his, then calmly set the glass down. "Let's go over the plan." He was focused.

Tom was pleased. He'd hoped that would be the case.

Shou tried to down the whole glass, but was unable. Her faced turned red as she coughed several times.

Tom took a deep breath. "Shou, Yu and I are leaving tomorrow. What are you planning to do? And before you answer, understand something. If you go with us, we're going somewhere else in the world. You'd be given a new identity and your past would be completely erased."

Shou reached over and grabbed Yu's hand. "My past was wiped out by Dr. Wang. My family is gone. Yu is my future—that's where I want to be."

Tom smiled. That was what he expected to hear. "Okay, you're not going to work tomorrow, but don't call off sick. Don't answer the phone. You'll do exactly what I say and exactly at the time I tell you. When I show up, be ready to go. Leave everything behind as though you are coming back—but you never will."

Shou started to protest.

Tom put his right index finger up to his lips. "You must do exactly what I'm telling you so we have a chance to make it."

Yu nodded as Tom spoke.

Tom smiled. "So, we're all in? Good. That makes my plan even better. When I leave here this evening, I'm going to the airport to rent a car. I'm going to leave it on the Chung Ying Street overnight parking lot."

Shou tilted her head and looked at Tom. "What? I don't get it."

"Let me finish. Shou, you will act like you're going to work. Leave at the normal time, but don't go there, drive around for a bit, go shopping, but everywhere you go, be around a lot of people. Just before you come back to your apartment, call for a cab to be at your apartment building at one o'clock. Park your car, but don't go upstairs. Just wait for the cab there. Then, you'll get in the cab, then tell the cabbie, wait a minute, I'm looking for something in my purse."

Tom looked at Yu. "You need to be downstairs but not in sight at one o'clock, waiting to get in the cab. As soon as she gets in the cab, look around and see if you see anything irregular. If nothing, hustle to the cab. Once in, keep down low in the seat, so only Shou will be seen. Be sure to have your gun on you. This is the time you'll be the most vulnerable—in the cab. I'll be in a cab behind you and will follow you out to the shopping area on Chung Ying Street. I want to see who might be following you. You should be in the shopping area about two o'clock. Both of you go shopping. Make sure you're always in big crowds. Yu, you'll have to keep a keen eye out for the men who may try to grab you."

Yu smiled, then frowned. "That seems dangerous. I'll really be exposed."

"Maybe, but I'm relying on the crowds to keep you safe, observed or not. I'll also be following you all around, watching who might be watching you. Marty has confirmed from his sources there are at least three teams of Ministry of State Security teams in the area looking for you, plus four snipers ready to be dropped on a rooftop or whatever to take you out." Tom rubbed his mouth with the back of his hand.

Shou wiped tears from her eyes, then finished her whiskey. "Tom, are you sure this is the right plan? I'm scared."

"It's going to be dangerous as hell. But the way I see it, if we try to make a straight run for the airport from here, we'll be sitting ducks. We've got to be in an area where there are a lot of stores to move in and out—so they'll have to find us or follow us." Tom reached for the bottle of whiskey and poured another double shot. Then held it out toward the other two.

Yu held his glass up to be refilled. Shou didn't.

Yu took a sip, then said. "I like your thinking, and I agree. When do we take off?"

"At exactly four o'clock. I'll be in the rental car, and I'll pull up at the corner of Chung Ying Street and Shun Lung Street. You both jump in, and we make a run for the airport, the private section. I'm going to take us on roads skirting the Hong Kong business district—Fanling Highway all the way to

Tates Cairn Highway. It should take us about an hour to get there. The plane will be on the ground at five o'clock waiting for us. Then away we go. Piece of cake. Any questions?" Tom took another drink.

Shou's face was flushed red and tears rolled down her cheeks. "Are you sure this will work?"

"Just like June 10, 1949, when I snuck T. V. Soong out of China the same way, right from under Dr. Wang's nose. With Dr. Wang dead, no one will remember how I did it. It worked then, it will work now."

Yu got up and paced around the couch for a minute, then turned around. "Yes, I believe it will work. Unless they kidnap us off the street, the assassins can't afford to shoot into a crowd of Hong Kong citizens. It would start a national incident with the British."

Shou got up and hugged Yu. He held her and smiled at her.

"I need to know why you're doing this. Why defect now, when you have all the power you have?" Tom asked.

"My father was killed by Mao's secret police when I was very young. My mother always denied it, but I had the security clearance to see the file. My mother was a spy for Zhou En-lai early on while Mao was forming his government. But she turned against Mao during the Cultural Revolution. She was arrested and put in prison for several years. I swear she was brainwashed while she was there. Now she's in local government—and she believes Deng is better than Mao at dealing with the Chinese people, but he is not. Not at all. Then there is my brother—he's always been pro-communist." He hugged Shou again. "Lastly, I fell in love with Shou. From the first time I saw her. Early on, as we talked, she was emphatic she wouldn't come back to China—not that I wanted to stay. Despite my climb in the Guoanbu and my success, when they could have put me over the Ministry of State Security, they passed over me for someone more political. The more I saw of the freedom of the West, the more I longed to be free."

Shou smiled. "He is giving up so much for me. That's why I'm willing to go wherever necessary so he can go into hiding. The Chinese Communist Party will never give up trying to kill him. I understand that."

Tom looked down at the bottle—Jameson Irish Whiskey. He remembered a toast his old friend Maston gave him one night as they were finishing off a bottle of Irish whiskey. He poured more whiskey in each glass, then held up his. Yu and Shou picked theirs up. "A toast, to our success. 'May the road rise to meet you. May the wind be always at your back. May the sunshine warm upon your face, the rain fall soft upon your fields, and until we meet again, may God hold you in the palm of his hand'."

They all downed their whiskey—this time, even Shou. With that, Tom looked at Shou. "Get me the gun that MI6 gave to you. You keep the backup gun."

While Shou was out of the room, Tom looked at Yu. "Tomorrow, when she leaves, get your gun and sit there focused on the door. Anybody messes with that door—well, you know what to do."

Yu cracked his knuckles.

Shou returned and handed the handgun to Tom.

He stood. "Let's be at the top of our game in the morning." He called a cab for himself, then went downstairs.

November 18, 1985
Hong Kong

Despite the three whiskeys, Tom struggled to get a good night's sleep. A lot was on the line—a lot of pressure on Tom to be successful. His final mission, even though he'd been retired for more than a year. And it was the first time he'd been really nervous.

At the designated time, a strange calm came over him. He went down, started his rental car, and drove over near Shou's apartment and parked. Time to watch her drive off. He'd decided during his restless night not to take the car out to the drop spot. While it had its own set of risks, he believed he'd be less conspicuous in the rental—and he wouldn't have to take a chance on a cabbie reporting his fare.

Fifteen minutes later, Shou drove off in her Volkswagen Beetle, heading in the opposite direction from where Tom was parked. No one seemed to follow her. Tom decided to sit tight and see if anybody who might be Chinese assassins went into the apartment building. The rest of the morning dragged on. Several times, he got out of the car and walked around, looking up as best as he could toward the roof tops. Nothing. Good.

As one o'clock approached, Tom sat in his car watching the door. Shou pulled around behind her apartment building. A few minutes after one o'clock, a yellow cab pulled up in front of her door. Just as planned, she got in the cab. Within thirty seconds, Yu hustled into the yellow vehicle. Then it pulled away from the curb. Again, Tom looked around. No one seemed to be following. That was good. Where the hell were these teams? *They must be out here, and I'm just not reading them.*

As he followed the cab through the city, he never did see Yu's head. He laughed as he wondered what the cabbie thought about all of this. About ten minutes after two o'clock, Shou and Yu's cab stopped on Chung Ying Street to let them out in the shopping district. Tom began to second guess himself on the plan. They were fairly close to Shenzhen and the Red Chinese border. Tom backed into a parking place on the adjacent street, facing forward so they could get in and go at four o'clock. He hustled around front where he could watch Shou and Yu from a distance and check the crowd and roof tops as he moved around the shopping area. Finally, he was able to see Shou and Yu going in and out of stores. He tried to find a discreet spot to stand and spot anyone watching Yu.

Yu and Shou moved in and out of the various shops. Tom continued to scan the rooftops, looking for snipers. This was getting easy. He looked down at his watch. Only thirty minutes had passed. That made Tom nervous. He was getting overconfident, which was never a good thing. He decided to start following them into the shops, then exiting the building before Yu. Tom continued this process for several stores. When he stepped outside the corner store, he saw two men across the street catty-corner standing among several large trees, looking in their direction. To act like he'd forgotten something, he stopped, padded the pockets of his slacks with both hands, then turned and went back inside. He walked over to Shou and Yu. "We have to go out through the back of this store. Then follow me straight to the car."

Just as they were about to open the back door, the clerk at the counter shouted, "Hey! You can't go out that way."

They slowed down long enough for Tom to get in front of them before going out the back of the store. Tom put his hand on his concealed gun but didn't pull it, as he stepped through the back door. He looked straight ahead at another group of suspicious individuals near several large trees. He returned back inside. "Okay, change of plans. Both of you stay here, stay in the middle of the store. I'm going to go get the car and park it right up in front, then come in and get you. Then we'll head for the airport."

Yu inquired, "What do these men look like?"

Tom rubbed his face with his left hand. "Like they could be Hong Kong plainclothes police. They were wearing sunglasses, short-cropped hair. I couldn't see any weapons, but that doesn't mean anything—they could be spotters for snipers. They certainly weren't shoppers looking to pick up dinner or something. They just seemed out of place."

Yu started to go toward the backdoor, but Tom grabbed his arm. "No, you're not going anywhere but out the front door with me. We don't know whether they have seen you, but let's not let them."

Yu wiggled his jaw but stopped.

Tom turned and calmly walked out the front door of the shop and headed toward his car. As he walked, he tried to look out of the corner of his eyes at the two men standing catty-corner to Chung Ying Street. Neither man was among those he previously believed were watching Shou. They may have been the other two teams that Marty had referred to.

As he walked, the two men across the street seemed to pay no attention to him—or they were trying not to be obvious. Within two minutes, Tom was at his rental car. He walked around it, looked underneath, then got in it. He put the key in the ignition and turned it. Nothing happened. Had someone messed with his car? Or was he just being paranoid? He turned the key again, and this time it started. He pulled it into gear, drove around the corner, and parked in a no parking zone. He thought for a second. He had to turn it off and take the key with him.

He jumped out, but he didn't look in the direction of the two men. He went into the store and found Yu and Shou on the aisle closest to the wall. "Let's go. Yu, if you want to get a look at the two men, they haven't moved."

Yu and Tom walked in front of Shou toward the door. Yu slipped to the side and peeked around as Tom moved a little slower.

Yu said, "Hey, I see them, but I can't tell whether they are State Security agents or not. They certainly aren't any of the men who were around me."

Tom stopped and looked back at Shou just as a young man and woman entered the store. The three of them stood near the front of the store but out of the sight line of the two men. Tom said, "When another group of people go out, we go out with them. Got it?"

While they waited, Yu continued to peek out at the two men across from them, and Tom looked at his illegally parked car, almost hoping law enforcement would show up. He checked his watch—three forty-five. He bit his lower lip. Things were starting to get tight on time. Finally, two families, which included a tall teenager, stopped at the doorway ready to walk out of the shop.

Tom turned to Shou and said, "Look as sweet and helpless as you can, which should be pretty easy under these circumstances, and play along."

Shou frowned but nodded.

Tom stopped the families just in front of the doorway. "Can I get you all to help me?" Before they answered, he pointed across the street. "See those two men standing over there? They have been planning to kidnap this woman here. They sell women into the slave trade down in Malaysia. Her brother and I are trying to get her away. Will you all just walk out of here and walk straight toward them but shield us from my car parked over there, giving us enough time to get away?"

The older woman looked at Tom really hard, then went over to the door and looked across the street. "I've heard of men doing evil things like that. Sure we will. Are you ready to go now?"

Shou looked down at the ground and nodded.

Tom, Yu, and Shou slipped in the middle of the two families as they walked straight to his rental. Tom got in on the passenger side, slipped across the bench seat, and started the car. This time it started first try and took off. They caught the two men off guard. When Tom looked in the rearview mirror, he could see Yu looking back at them, watching the men run off, likely toward their car.

Tom continued to drive toward downtown Hong Kong on Sha Tau Kok Road.

Yu shouted from the backseat. "We're going the wrong way! You missed the turn off! You missed the turn off!"

"No, I wanted them to see me driving off in that direction before cutting back over to Sha Tau Kok Road. If they really are a hit team, I want to throw them off." Tom calmly turned, then discreetly looked down at his watch. Four-fifteen.

Yu shook his head in disbelief, but said no more.

Shou looked at him, then back toward Tom. "*Hurry. Please hurry.*"

Tom drove slightly over the speed limit on Sha Tau Kok Road. It would take about an hour of driving through heavy traffic.

After about fifteen minutes, Tom looked in the rearview mirror and saw two cars approaching at high-speed, weaving in and out of traffic about a quarter mile back. This was his worst nightmare—not only did he not like to drive, but he wasn't particularly good at it. He stomped down on the accelerator, causing both Shou and Yu to look behind them.

Tom continued to look straight ahead now, driving twenty miles an hour over the speed limit. "Could that be those two groups of PLA officers chasing us? Or plainclothes Hong Kong police?"

Yu slowly shook his head. "Just drive faster, *drive faster.*"

Tom was going as fast as he dared. He watched Yu slip a black velvet bag from his Zhongshan suit. Traffic had thinned out, and now he was going close to a hundred miles an hour. He was weaving on the highway, occasionally running off on the berm.

Shou shouted from the backseat. "Can't you drive?"

"No, I hate to drive. I'm not good at it, but we'll make it." Tom shook his head as his knuckles turned white from gripping the steering wheel and trying to reassure himself as well as his passengers.

He looked back in the rearview as he turned on to Tates Cairn Highway and drove a few minutes. Had he lost them? Tom turned around. "I think it'll be another thirty minutes or so, if the traffic lets up a little.

Yu moved around in his seat, trying to look out the window. "It's not going to let up on the way to the airport. If anything, the traffic will get heavier."

Tom continually checked the rearview mirror. *Nothing.* As they approached the airport, the traffic became stop and go, adding to the tension. If there were assassin teams close by, they were sitting ducks. It was frustrating to see big planes land and take off, while they still seemed so far away. Finally, forty minutes later, they could see the terminal.

494

Traffic started to let up. Shou shouted from the backseat, "Oh, shit! They're back."

Tom checked the rearview again. She was right. He weaved in and out, changing lanes back and forth. He saw Yu pick up his gun and roll down the window.

Tom leaned back and tilted his head as he pushed down on the accelerator, simultaneously swerving to the left. "What the hell are you doing? Don't shoot at anybody in this traffic. You're just wasting ammo you may need."

"I'm not going back. I made that decision two months ago," Yu gasped. "It's either them or me. I'm not going back."

A loud explosion sounded behind them. One of their tails had run into a fuel truck going in the opposite direction on the Tates Cairn Highway. Tom couldn't see the other car. What happened to it? Where did they go?

Within five minutes, Tom pulled into the private terminal at Kai Tak International airport. He looked at his watch. Five-fifteen. He parked as close as he could to the building, and they ran until they were inside, fearing rooftop snipers. Tom went straight to the window and looked for the SAT Pacific jet. He didn't see one.

Then he looked at the middle of the floor. The last time he was in this terminal, it was right after his old friend Anthony Middleton had been murdered. Tom went to the desk, where a large Chinese man on duty was writing on ledger paper.

"My name is Tom Warren. Have you heard anything about my scheduled flight?"

Without even looking up, the Chinaman raised his pen from the paper and pointed toward a man sitting in the shadows of the building, wearing sunglasses and a baseball cap pulled down.

Tom walked over. "I'm Tom Warren, I—"

Before he could say anything else, the man in the sunglasses put his fingers to his lips. "I heard you when you came in. Are you and your cargo ready?"

"Yes. Let's get in the air as fast as possible."

The man in the sunglasses got up and walked at a fast pace.

Tom waved for Yu and Shou to follow. Once outside, they all ran toward the jet as Tom checked the tail number, just to make sure. Tom noticed Yu still carried the black velvet bag.

They bounced up the steps of the Challenger Jet. Before Tom, Yu, and Shou were in their seats, the plane was taxiing out toward the runway. When the pilot announced they were next to take off, Tom went back up to the pilot and leaned over. "Just in case, the PLA has scrambled jets. Fly below radar as far out as possible. I want to go directly to Clark Air Force Base in Manila."

The pilot didn't turn around, but he gave a thumbs up.

As the jet thrust forward and accelerated down the runway, Tom slipped into his seat and buckled up. Yu and Shou were glancing at each other rather than looking out the small window.

Within seconds, they were off the runway, and within minutes, they were flying over the ocean. Tom looked at Yu, who made eye contact with him. Yu opened the black velvet bag and quickly pulled out a chopstick.

Then the pilot pushed down so the jet dove toward the water.

Yu was thrown forward and off balance. He resettled his large body in the seat. "I brought you a souvenir. Look at the engraving. It was intended for you a different way, I guess."

Tom leaned forward and grabbed it. It read "Thomas P. Warren" and "NanJing." He smiled and looked out the window. They now flew less than a hundred feet over the ocean below, going as fast as Tom had ever experienced in a jet.

He reached inside his jacket pocket and felt the file. Larry Wu-tai Chin could be arrested almost immediately—plus, he had the highest-ranking intelligence officer to ever defect from Communist China safely stashed away. The adventure that began twenty-three years prior almost to the day had finally yielded huge success. Yu Qiangsheng, alias The Planesman, hadn't only defected with the file on the most effective Chinese spy in U.S. history, but also with years of insider knowledge and microfilm on the Communist Chinese operation.

Tom had his crown jewel. But what really mattered was that he was on his way home to his beautiful bride.

Tom watched the black ocean only feet beneath them as the jet raced into the darkness of the night.

THE END